PRAISE FOR *IN THE EYE OF HEAVEN*

"The world and its cultures that Keck unveils in *In the Eye of Heaven* are brutal and raw, and through it all the reader senses a fierce authenticity, a depth of knowledge in the author assuring that every detail, every nuance, is precisely as it should be. This novel marks the debut of an exceptional series, revealing the mythical depth and resonance possible within the genre of fantasy—a rare feat these days." —Steven Erikson

"In David Keck's new fantasy, the gritty reality of medieval warfare is all the more believable against the backdrop of an Otherworld whose magic is rooted in folklore. Caught between them, the hero wins our sympathy." —Diana L. Paxson

"A very intelligent book, with a hero who starts out as raw and physical as the world in which he finds himself but who proves able to use his mind to get out of the situations his body's gotten him into." —David Drake

"Is it too early to label a writer visionary based only on a debut novel? Not when that novel's as impressive as *In the Eye of Heaven* . . . This novel marks the arrival of a genuine new talent in the field." —*Quill & Quire*

"A work of laudable ambition and a promising debut." —*Locus*

IN THE EYE OF
HEAVEN

David Keck

A TOM DOHERTY ASSOCIATES BOOK
NEW YORK

This is a work of fiction. All of the characters, organizations, and events portrayed in this novel are either products of the author's imagination or are used fictitiously.

IN THE EYE OF HEAVEN

Copyright © 2006 by David Keck

Edited by Patrick Nielsen Hayden

Map by David Cain

A Tor Book
Published by Tom Doherty Associates, LLC
175 Fifth Avenue
New York, NY 10010

www.tor.com

Tor® is a registered trademark of Tom Doherty Associates, LLC.

ISBN-13: 978-0-765-35169-2
ISBN-10: 0-765-35169-2

First Edition: April 2006
First Mass Market Edition: March 2007

Printed in the United States of America

0 9 8 7 6 5 4 3 2 1

To my parents, Eileen and Tony, and my wife, Anne,
for their faith and support. I have been very lucky.

Acknowledgments

First, I must acknowledge the support of friends in education like Carol Braun, Carmen Friesen, Chris Friesen, Leanne Braun, and many others over the years. As a student and as a teacher, I've met some of the best people I've ever known in schools. I also owe a great deal to writers and friends like Steve Lundin, Dennis Valdron, Ian Ross, and Darren Lodge who have shown quiet faith in my work over the years. On the professional side, my agent, Howard Morhaim, and editor, Patrick Nielsen Hayden, deserve credit for taking a chance on a new voice. Last, I offer my gratitude to every poor fool I ever dragged up a castle or around a ring of old stones. To all of you, and many more, I am grateful.

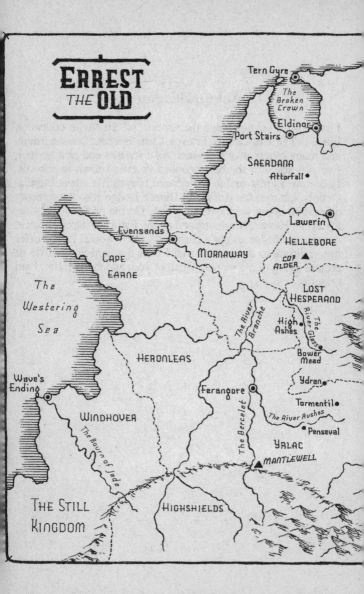

The Winter Sea

GERMANDER   BEORAN

The Red Winding

FARONA

Red Winding

THE HALLS
OF SILENCE   HALLOW
Down

Silvermere

The Handglass

THE
WARRENS   Yestreen

MERCHION   ▲ GLEN OF THE IDOLS
GIRETH   Rush Landing
Burrstone Walls

FETCH
HOLLOW   Acconel

SALLOW
HYTHE

The River Maidenshier

▲ Towerknoll
Wrothsilver
Swanskin Down
Balian   THE
HONEFELLS   GARELYN

The Bandera
The Plaitwater

Gravenholm
The Col   BEDRIN GATE   The
Deep

THE PENDURAN
MARCHES

THE BLACKROOTS

PENNONS
GATE

↙ THE FELLWOOD MARCHES

Map by David Cain

In the fifth year of Ragnal's reign on the Hazelwood Throne.

In the Year of the Sundering of the Heithan March.

In the two hundred and fifty-ninth year after the Fall of the Burning City.

IN THE EYE OF HEAVEN

🪢 1. The Path of Knots

Traveler's Night was coming on, and the horses were uneasy. It was almost as if they knew the numbering of days.

Durand scratched the back of his neck, peering through drizzle and branches.

He was meant to be riding home, guiding his lord up familiar tracks, but now he couldn't see for trees, and every breath of wind had the old forest alive with a sound like whispers. In an hour, it would be dark, and they would be caught on the road.

On Traveler's Night, no one slept outdoors.

Sir Kieren joked, "If I had known your father lived so far up in these wilds, I would have said, 'No reason to climb the forests of Gireth for your father's handouts, we'll have you knighted in the clothes you're wearing.' It isn't fine linen that makes a knight, after all. Now, I begin to wonder. In these wilds, a baron will have a house? Walls? Will he have a roof? Lad, if it's a bear's den, I won't think any worse of you—so long as I know."

Durand glanced back. They called old Kieren "the Fox" and he looked the part: A small-boned man, he sported silver-tipped red mustaches that made him look as if a pair of the creatures had just jumped up his nostrils. It had been Sir Kieren's idea to make the journey, and, from the glint in the man's eye, Durand judged that the Fox knew how lost they were.

"He's not *quite* a bear, Sir Kieren," Durand said.

"And this village? Your inheritance? I would like to see little Gravenholm, I think. And meet this poor old Osseric whose grief gets you your fiefdom. The man whose son was lost upon the waves. Who lives alone in his forest hall knowing that his lord's obdurate youngest boy will have every stone of it one day."

"Not this time, Sir Kieren." Durand meant to give Gravenholm a wide berth and head straight for his father's stronghold. The tracks he'd chosen would lead them leagues from Gravenholm.

"I knew you had come down from the wilds," Kieren was saying, "but now I wonder what sort of—Host of Heaven!"

As his master swore, Durand's head crashed into the branches. Brag, his big bay hunter, screamed and pawed the air so that only a wrestler's grip kept Durand in the saddle. He fought the maddened animal for a look at what had spooked it and caught a glimpse of a pair of yellow eyes flashing up from the track. Then Brag was rearing, and it was all Durand could do to hang on.

After a moment, he found a better grip and took a look. Something had appeared between Brag's hooves: a pup, mottled leaf red and iron gray, and he could see the little fellow looking up with those yellow eyes, shrinking against the earth as hooves chopped down around it.

"Come on, Brag," Durand said. "Come on. Calm now." And, though Brag was no warhorse, the steady pressure of Durand's voice calmed the hunter enough that he could step back.

The pup shivered against the clammy track and looked up as Durand smeared bark and grit from his face. Suddenly he was not so sure the beast was a dog after all. He turned to say: "You know—"

And the monster must have stepped out just then, for Durand found the Fox's face stiff and pale, his blue eyes fixed on something.

Slowly, Durand turned back.

Gray and more massive than a man, a wolf flowed into the track only a few paces away. Never had Durand seen such a beast at close quarters. In the wastelands, a wolf was a sob on the wind and a winter thief of children, not a thing a man blundered across. Now, the brute's corpse-candle eyes caught Durand. Lost, and leagues from any village, he could not look away—lost things were what this monster hunted. Beyond the glowing eyes rose a rumble deeper than dungeon chains.

While Durand and his master—both armed men—sat frozen, the wolf cub rolled to its outsized paws and nuzzled at the monster. The tiny creature paid no heed to the long spines of the brute's hackles. The wolf lowered its leering head. For a moment, black lips touched the pup's muzzle, gentle as a kiss.

"God, it's—" Durand began—he was ready to confess surprise. He was ready to say he'd been wrong about wolves. But then the wolf's jaws sprang wide, swallowing the pup.

Durand said, "Hells!"

The word caught the beast's ear.

It stared, and blood welled between its yellow teeth. For a long moment, the wolf held Durand in its gaze, then it tossed its head back and gulped the cracking bones.

Impossible.

Durand wrenched the sword from his gear.

The wolf watched.

Bulges moved against the walls of its belly, kicking and pawing more slowly and more slowly.

"*Host Below,*" Sir Kieren said. "*It's a prodigy.*" His small hands twitched into the fist and spread-fingers sign that mirrored the true Eye of Heaven.

Durand gripped his blade. "*Aye,*" he whispered. A prodigy: a sign scrawled by inhuman hands, pointing. The lamp eyes blazed as the brute smacked its jaws. Then, as suddenly as the monster had appeared, it coiled behind its leer and sprang in a long arc that cast it beyond the branches—it might as well have leapt right out of the world.

All around them, Durand had the feeling that the Powers of Heaven and Hell were stepping between the trees, full of death and promises, with their eyes on his neck. A cold shiver passed up his sword, drawing the heat from his knuckles. Blood pounded in his throat.

Sir Kieren spoke. "What doom does this foretell?"

"I cannot guess," said Durand. "A priest might read something more in it."

"It's always something with you around. I remember the Patriarch, old Oredgar, he held you in his eye one time: always wondered what he saw." Durand was about to question the man, but the old knight set the subject aside. "Let's see if there isn't somewhere in this wood we can get under shelter."

They urged their horses on.

And rode onto the doorstep of a village, the first in twenty leagues of lost wandering.

"What is this place?" breathed Kieren.

Durand stared, and, quite suddenly, understood where they had arrived.

"—Gravenholm," he said. His own voice came like the wolf's rumble.

"*Your* land?" Kieren whispered.

After all this way, to strike his tiny inheritance after the wolf . . . Durand managed a nod.

"*Hells,*" Kieren murmured. His hands formed the Eye of Heaven.

There wasn't much for Durand to say. In the failing light, plowmen's furlongs crosshatched the fields. A stream meandered heavily toward the manor house. They called the river Plaitwater. He knew the house. He had stood in the hall, sat at the table, and listened to the old man's grief.

"Gravenholm . . ." murmured Kieren. "Your doorstep."

"One day." Now, however, the current owner still lingered inside, a widower alone at the end of a dead lineage. Durand winced.

"Bugger me," said Kieren in a cloud of breath. "Right, there's nothing for it. It's just a house. I want out of the weather. Come on. I don't think my heart can stand much more of this nonsense."

The knight urged his little roan into the fields and began to pick a course from bank to headland. Somewhere, far off, a fiddle was playing.

"Ah, listen there. That's better," Kieren said.

Durand could see the pale squares of the peasants' windows hanging in the mist. Closer, long-horned cattle stared over the Plaitwater. They looked as though they were drinking hot broth.

"And this must be Osseric's hall." A barn hulked by the water, flanked by a hall like a mountain of thatch on swollen timbers. "It's not so bad a place, though it would want a prop here and there if it were ever to serve as a fortress."

One day, Durand would live in that hall, but that night he felt like a housebreaker moving through the master's rooms. Dusk had caught them, though, and they really had no time.

Sir Kieren's eyes twinkled. "Which one's the barn, did you say?"

"Not sure," Durand said. "It'll do me, whichever."

"Surely. You are lucky to have the place. And I'd guess this moat is more to keep the stock from getting to the barley. Nothing unusual for a manor of this size. Not the mighty citadel of Acconel, but your father doesn't have a lot of liegemen. If it's all he could find . . ."

It was more than Durand had any right to expect; there was little left for second sons in Errest the Old.

"Good for ducks," the old knight continued. "Geese, a passing salmon, beaver. That sort of thing."

"And me," said Durand. He'd spent fourteen years working to earn the place. His father could give him the old widower's lands, but, among the Sons of Atthi, only a knight could inherit a knight's land.

They skirted the moat, Kieren setting a dawdling pace. Durand squinted into the heavy gray ahead where the gloom of sky and forest blended, thinking that Heaven's Eye would be there sinking beyond the clouds. They had almost run out of daylight.

"Sir Kieren," Durand said, "we'll have to ride hard to make my father's stronghold by nightfall, I think."

"Lad," Kieren said, "night's fallen. The baron must wait another night for his son."

"*It's hardly a league,*" Durand said. The sound echoed too loudly from old Osseric's walls. "It's a league to the Crossroads Elm, at most, and then it's straight on to the Col." They could be at his father's hall in no time.

"It'll be full dark before we cross the *fields,* lad." Kieren leaned close, eyeing the smudge of forest. "You forget that wolf-thing out there?"

"I'd be like a carrion crow at the old man's table."

"By the King of far Heaven, it's the Traveler's Night. When you're safe inside, it's all feasts and firelight with no doors closed to anyone, but when you're under the stars? There are more than mortal doors under the vault of Heaven. What do you think it means that there are no doors shut? We will be the only fools on the road."

"Sir Kieren, it is two leagues up a proper road."

Up in Osseric's manor house, a figure passed an unshuttered window. Durand pictured the silence yawning out across the table in the man's hall, no sound but knives and smacking lips. There were no fiddles in the manor house. He would not go inside, not to count the old man's teeth like a horse trader.

"With the Traveler walking and the tomb doors swinging, I don't plan to ignore the omen of the wolf. We've had our warning," said Kieren.

"It's a bloody league!" Durand replied.

And caught himself. This was not how a man spoke to either master or friend.

Kieren had shut his eyes. "I remember when I first took note of you among all those strays at Acconel. A few of them were picking on some smaller boy. But you stood in their way. A little black-haired scrap you were, down from the Col of the Blackroots. In the face of three larger boys."

Durand had often been in some trouble or another. He took breath. "Did I win?"

Kieren winked. "You might have done if we hadn't pulled you off them. Go home. I'll catch you up tomorrow. Does that suit you?"

Durand knew this was more patience than he deserved, and he knew he ought to apologize. But as he opened his mouth, a door clomped shut somewhere in the old manor hall.

And he said, "Yes. Yes, it does." He bowed his head formally in the old country style. The last thing he wanted was to shame this man.

"Done then, lad. I'll meet you in the Col of the Blackroots tomorrow if it is the will of the Silent King. Tell your father I hope to see him then."

"I will do as you ask, Sir Kieren."

Kieren inclined his head. "I will carry your apologies to old Sir Osseric. You give mine to the Traveler if you meet him."

As HE LEFT Sir Kieren, Durand threw Brag into a long gallop, storming past the fiddles of Gravenholm village to plunge deep into the misty forest once more. Finally, in a place as silent as a sanctuary, Brag jounced to a halt. The animal huffed at the thick air. Durand stroked the hunter's muscled neck, no horseman if he'd treat an animal this way.

Around him, mist steamed from the dark earth, thick as spirits. The Eye of Heaven had left him.

"Come on," Durand said, nudging Brag forward.

Ahead, the track meandered along the floor of a shallow and nameless valley. And, for the first time, Durand had a glimpse of how big a fool he'd been. The priests said that the Host Below swarmed every man's head, pulling and prodding. A tug of fear here and shame there. A night with poor old Osseric of Gravenholm would have done him no harm.

He looked into the dark woods; there were ruins under the leaves.

Since Durand could remember, they'd been telling Osseric's story back in the Painted Hall of Acconel. The man's wife had died in childbirth: a love story ending with oaths and sorrow. But the pages and shield-bearers in the Painted Hall fixed their attention on the son: a boy who'd lived in Acconel just as they did, who'd slept in the very same straw. He was brave. He was strong. But when his greedy master boarded a ship for the Inner Seas, he had to follow. And the winds off the Harrow drove their merchant-man onto the rocks where the bandy-legged fiends of that shore gnaw the bones of sailors.

Dreams of the wreck haunted Durand as a boy: corpses bobbing on bales of wool or following the ship down with the dragging weight of the tin heaped in its hold. Creeping fiends with iron fangs and skin smooth as sheep's gut among the dead. A thrill of fear went through him even now—an armed man, supposedly trained for battle.

But Osseric was a knight in the service of Durand's father. The lost son had been the only heir, and so in a realm where every stump was knotted with a hundred titles, Durand's father picked his second son's future from that shipwreck. With no heir waiting, all Durand must do, the priests said, was become a knight. And that had been Durand's duty for the last fourteen years: fourteen years of bruises among the page boys and shield-bearers in the Painted Hall of the Duke of Gireth in faraway Acconel.

Durand shook his head. He should have sat down at Osseric's table and been civil to the man. Osseric deserved to know his heir. After Durand had been to the Col, he would come back and do what was right.

Just then, some motion among the clouds smothered the Gleaning Moon, dropping Creation into utter darkness.

"Hells," said Durand.

Brag stopped.

It was dark as blindness. Durand tried to recall the branches and the sopping leaves over the roots and ruins, but tapped a flood of childhood memories instead. He had played in these woods as a boy, and now remembered crabbed trees, a castle mound in a village of graves, a tumbledown shrine full of blank-faced icons. He remembered roots and ivy fumbling over stone. The realms of the Sons of Atthi were ancient, and most ancient of all was Errest the Old.

As the gray stone icons floated before his mind's eye and the cold stitched ice through his clothes, a breeze skittered through the high branches. He remembered Kieren's talk of the Traveler and the open doors.

"Not clever to dredge up dead men and drowned heirs alone in the dark," Durand muttered, setting his jaw. He was almost home, and there wasn't a twig or stone for leagues that didn't belong to his father. Muttering a charm against the Lost, he waited for a break in the clouds to let a little moonlight slip down. And, with the return of the light, it might have been any evening.

Then he heard a sound—*tock*—hollow and distant above the rattle of the wind. Thoughts of gates and latches and tombs returned, and the dark poured in.

Durand grunted, but urged Brag on.

Tock.

He turned in his seat. The footpath behind him was black. The sound seemed to issue from somewhere beyond the curl of track ahead. It had a slow rhythm. It might be a length of old chain swinging somewhere—a lost trap or halter. It had to be some such thing.

Durand set his mind to tallying the coin his father would need for the dubbing in Acconel. He didn't much like it. So much silver for this; so much silver for that. Sir Kieren wasn't about to let his shield-bearer kneel in the Acconel high sanctuary in sackcloth, no matter that it might be easier.

Tock.

Durand froze.

The road might have been a black tunnel, a mineshaft. Heedless, Brag thumped forward. Durand reached for his blade, feeling as though he must move his hand with care.

Abruptly, the sound exploded under Brag's hooves: *tock-tock-tock.* It was the sound of iron shoes on stone. Durand threw his hood back and freed his blade. Cobblestones. It had been these cobblestones all along.

Right below him, the pale stones of the old Acconel road broke the skin of leaves. He likely traveled it a hundred times in childhood and had never heard. Now, every step scraped and clacked at the same note.

Brag must have noticed Durand's twitching; he had stopped dead. "Walk on," Durand whispered. And he heard the sound like a counterpoint beyond Brag's hooves: a staff's brass-shod heel, growing clearer, growing closer. What sort of man walked so blithely through the dark?

The trail opened, parting like curtains, and a huge tree spread black branches into the heavens. Now, Durand knew where he was. This was the Crossroads Elm, the hanging tree. Round the corner would be the open fields below the Col and no place for a man to hide. He could hear the staff still swinging just around that bend. *Tock. Tock. . . .*

Then there was nothing.

Silence chased the last report into the distance, skittering off like ripples on a millpond.

Durand jerked Brag to a halt, staring at the elm's old trunk. Not a whisper.

In his mind's eye, he saw the stranger stopped, waiting for him just around the tree.

Durand wouldn't sit there shaking. With a snarl, he spurred Brag on. The clatter of the hunter's hooves battered back the silence. With a wild surge, they swung round the great elm and into the open fields of the Col. Vast mountains reared into view. The empty road swung high to the old town between the peaks—and there wasn't a soul for half a league. Neither was there a ditch or a shock of hay to hide in between Durand's sword and the mountains. The stranger had vanished.

Durand gave Brag the spurs.

2. Homecoming

Brag got him home.

In the dark, Durand's birthplace resembled a madman's stronghold. The ancients had fixed the fortress in a cleft between two peaks; it guarded a pass, now little used. Crowded in that stronghold would be all the family and friends Durand had left behind in his long exile in Acconel.

Below the stronghold, the village was warm with hearth fires and filled with quiet talk from its open windows. Durand marveled at how small the village seemed after years away, and found himself touching the slate walls and hanging eaves. Almost before he realized, he had reached the wall of his father's stronghold.

Sucking in a deep breath, Durand nudged Brag under the gates and into an inner courtyard that stood empty as a drum.

Durand could hear voices up in the castle rooms: a hundred people gabbling. Firelight glowed down from every open window.

"Home," he said, rolling the word like a pebble on his tongue.

He led Brag across the courtyard and into the acrid warmth of the stables. Over the doors was the Col's coat of arms: the head and rack of three stags, two over one below. Durand took a few moments to scrub some of the water from Brag's hide while the hunter thrust his chin in the air. Durand grinned up at the brute, then, with a gentle slap, set off for the feasting hall.

In no time, he stood with his hand on the latch as voices throbbed beyond it, unnerved at coming upon a feast from outside and hearing laughter not shared. For a moment, he was like some lost soul blown in from the trees.

Durand turned the handle, and warm air poured around his wrist.

For an instant, no one noticed him.

He had a glimpse of Baron Hroc's liegemen sprawled in the smoky hall of his childhood. Wives sat in circles. Faces shone with grease. Some he knew; some sent his mind searching. A pair of tired serving men were levering one of the tables from its sawhorse trestles, while dogs prowled the reeds to the tune of a skald's mandora.

Then Durand stepped inside.

The skald's fingers stumbled, and everyone in the hall looked up.

"Durand." A black-haired man with an expression of astonishment had spoken. While the face was strange, Durand knew the voice. This was Hathcyn, his brother. The whole of the high table turned, and Durand's mother—strangely small and suddenly ancient—rose to her feet.

"Durand," she gasped. And there was hardly room for her smile in the white frame of her wimple.

THE SWIRL OF hands and smiles and toasts and questions kept the noontide feast alive late into Traveler's Night. The fifth hour found Durand staggering through the chill dark of his father's keep in search of the privy. He was swimming with wine and bursting with beef and crane and swan. He breathed a boozy plume of frost into the air, hardly able to stop smiling. These were his people. This was where he was meant to be.

Somewhere ahead they had hidden the upstairs privy—he was sure.

His palm scrabbled over a corner, then he fumbled into the darkness of a room: the privy, he hoped. A breath of pennyroyal and something rank told him he had guessed right. His scabbard clattered. The branding-iron cold of the stone was enough to make him regret an evening of warmth by the hearth fires, almost.

When he had finished, he pitched the washrag and a shot of water down the hole and left the little room.

Conversation swirled up the empty passage. Now that the feast's second life was nearly spent, the servants were back to dismantling the trestle tables.

Durand braced himself between the walls, yawning deep and thinking that all the forest omens had come to nothing.

A ribbon of light glinted in the darkness of the hall. As Durand leaned closer, it became an arrow loop crowded with the humped rooftops of the village between the mountains. Beyond the huddled flock of houses, he could see murky hints of the trees and the spot where the old elm would be.

Durand tore his gaze from the narrow window and descended to the hall, where he found Hathcyn weaving through the maze of limbs and tables, carrying a pair of cups. Though slighter than his younger brother, Hathcyn and Durand shared the same face: black mop, dark brows, blue eyes, square jaw—though Hathcyn's had been carved by a finer chisel.

"Here," he said, thrusting a cup toward Durand. "It's hot." Across the hall, the skald croaked out the end of a ballad.

Durand sipped hot sweetness from his cup.

"I was wondering where you'd got to," Hathcyn said. He looked round at the pallets and drowsy knights and their wives. "Girart and Lamis, you remember them? Sergeants? Sons of one of Dad's stewards? They were throwing daggers for clipped pennies. Every blade right in Mother's woodwork. She nearly spitted the pair of them." He winced. " 'Spat' the pair of them? Whichever, she nearly got Lamis."

"Now," he continued. "We ought to find you somewhere to sleep away from—"

"—I'm fine here with the others. Used to it."

"I suppose a straw pallet looks good after the roots and stones you've been bedding down on the last few days."

"The roof'll make a change," Durand allowed, grinning.

A pair of yawning serving boys were struggling to lift a heavy table from its trestles. Durand jerked his chin toward it, and, in a moment, the two baron's sons had plucked the thing from the boys' hands.

"All right you two, where should we take it?" Durand asked.

After a moment, one got up the courage to point down the hall toward the cellar door. "You two get the legs," Durand suggested. "We'll see who gets there first." The two boys nodded and were off, scurrying faster than if Durand had barked an order.

"Mother was pleased to see your face," said Hathcyn as they shuffled the heavy table down the hall. "God. It was a great surprise to have you walk in." Hathcyn stopped a moment, puffing. Blowing hair out of his eyes, he glanced past an unperturbed Durand. "If it isn't the woman herself."

"What are you two doing? Do you know where that's to go? Are you paid to carry it?" the Lady of Col demanded.

"The idea was mine," Durand said.

"And how are you, Mother?" Hathcyn said.

"You're drunk," she replied.

Durand raised his eyebrows. "And how are you keeping?"

She peered at the two brothers for a moment, her chin thrust toward them, then relented. "I'm well enough now all that's done." She shook her head. "Durand, it's good to see you back. What did you think of our feast?"

"Good, Mother."

"Well, I hope you managed to get something hot down you, at the least. You looked cold as drowning when you stepped through that door."

"Warm enough now."

At the far end of the table, bulging veins showed Hathcyn's strain.

"That's good," said their mother. "Your father's glad you came up."

"That's good, Mother."

"Can't believe how big you've got. Big as your father. Bigger!"

"Taller, anyway," Durand said. Hathcyn looked to the ceiling for assistance.

"Ah, it's good to see you." Her hand touched his wrist for a moment. There were tables to stack and pallets to arrange and arguments to settle. The stream of servants churned around them.

She hesitated. Out of her sight, straining Hathcyn shot a desperate look down the table—it was heavy.

"You'd best get them in order," Durand said.

"Aye, I suppose I'd better," she said and got back to the business of readying the hall for the night.

"God, Durand," Hathcyn gasped. "Let's get this thing put away." And they slipped the long table through the serving men and down the cellar stairs, where Durand could not help but pitch in, stacking and swinging tables and barrels with the rest.

When the worst of it was done, the two brothers climbed back into the hall. Hathcyn slapped his hands together and smiled up at Durand.

"You must be about done in yourself."

The last few men still working were stacking a heap of straw pallets in preparation for spreading them in the hall. Durand looked into one face, and asked, "May I?" and found his own patch of bare floor.

The two men sat cross-legged, while Durand set to unwrapping the mud-caked laces around his boots. The leather had gone at turns waxy hard and crumbling soft as flour. Other men were bedding down around him: guests and liegemen.

"I talked to Father," Hathcyn confided. "The harvest was good enough; he's got the coin to pay for all the trappings and whatnot. You can get yourself properly knighted. Imagine though: I was knighted out here under the mountains, and you'll be dubbed in Acconel with the duke right there by Silvermere of the Thousand Ships."

"It'll be a great show," Durand said, emphasizing his point with the boot in his hand—stiff as a clay pot. "Just me, the duke, and who knows how many other shield-bearers all lined up like nags at the horse-fair."

"And don't forget the thousand ships. The duke will bring them out, won't he?"

"If he can stay awake."

"Ah yes, I suppose he's getting on."

Durand set the boot down and made a thoughtful face. "The Blackroots up there are likely older. . . ."

Hathcyn laughed. "I missed you, you know. Always the sound one, no matter that I was older. I'd drag us off into some mad scheme, and you'd stare down the consequences."

"I meant to talk to you about that," Durand said.

"My earliest memories. You had this stern face. A stalwart thing on bowed legs. And now you'll be back to stay."

"Aye." Now, Durand was smiling. One last ride to Acconel, and he would be back to wait out his inheritance, maybe serving in Osseric's stead, if the king summoned the hosts to the Heithan Marches again.

The servants smothered torches.

Hathcyn glanced up from his haunches. "Well, I had better

bid you good-night." He gripped Durand's shoulder. "You know it's good to see you. Do you?"

Durand winked.

"Good," said Hathcyn, and was off.

Durand settled down onto one shoulder. His father's grand plan: the knighthood, the fosterage at the duke's hall. Each piece fit the next like a joiner's work, and now it was all coming snug together.

He closed his eyes.

"So you've got a place settled then, Lordship?"

A man squatted on the next pallet: the homely skald; his brown eyes glittered on either side of a saddle-backed nose.

"Aye, friend," Durand said. "More or less."

"I apologize," whispered the skald, mirth folding his face into a gap of missing teeth. "I've a habit of butting my nose in where it's not wanted. It comes with the trade. I'm called Heremund, by the way."

"Yes? I see about the nose."

After watching to see that his point was made, Durand closed his eyes once more, listening to lovemaking, farts, and snarling dogs until, finally, the weight of a long day bore him down into sleep.

HE WOKE IN the dark, surprised he hadn't slept through to Noontide Lauds.

The cold of the night had slipped in through cracks and windows, and he might have been sleeping in the hills except for the snoring liegemen all around him.

A mist of fleas jumped against his face as he shifted; he was dully aware of a dozen angry bites. But he had slept on the floor of one man's hall or another all the days of his life and a pallet swarming with fleas was hardly a new thing.

He wondered what had jerked him out of sleep.

Then a knock echoed through the black feasting hall: something else awake. Durand levered himself up on his elbows but could see no one in the darkness.

Nearby, a ribbon of moonlight glimmered on the wall. On impulse, he reached out, cutting light with his fingers' shadow.

As his fingers spread, he realized that the stone under that ribbon was huge for building work, taller than a man. But it conjured a memory. There had been a ring of standing stones around the well when the Sons of Atthi threw up this fortress. His mother had pointed to this one.

It was odd what a man could remember after years away.

Another knock echoed through the hollow castle, coming from beyond the hall. And another. Durand peered at the source of the light. Between the shutters, a silver thread of light shimmered and twisted as though slipping between some moonlight-spinner's fingers.

He left the blankets and fleas and crossed to the window. As he put his eye to the old boards, the last light of the Gleaning Moon struggled through broken cloud, silvering damp flagstones—and the figure of a man by the well. In his fist was a traveler's staff.

Durand's lips peeled apart.

The light swelled. The staff swung: *tock*. A battered hat turned.

Durand sprang back from the window. He had caught a glimpse of a knotted beard. It was the Traveler's Night. When Durand turned his eye once more to the narrow moonlight, there was only darkness below. Cloud had stolen the Gleaning Moon but, when its narrow sickle wavered back, the stark slate court was empty.

"Host Below," said Durand and resolved to learn what was going on.

Barefoot, he bolted from the hall with a naked blade in his fist, and skidded into the courtyard. Seeing no one among the doorways and arches, he searched the frosted flagstones for some sign, finding nothing but the curls of his own melted footsteps in the frost as he stalked round the well.

A shadow would have left more trace.

His lungs puffed fog into the still air.

THE NEXT DAY, Durand watched and waited.

While the others prayed Dawn's Thanksgiving and ate dinner over the Noontide Lauds, Durand composed himself as best he could, knowing that he had not left the omens behind when he left the forest. Atthians understood doom.

After noontide, a shape ran past his seat at the shuttered window, streaking off for the baron's chamber.

"Was that the gatekeeper's lad?" said someone close by.

As Durand glanced at the curious faces around him, it struck him that all the knights of his father's court looked as similar as cousins. He had never noticed before.

In a moment, the runner reappeared, this time chased down the hall by a pair of houseboys.

Durand opened the shutters; four horses stood around the well. He recognized Sir Kieren's roan and the jade that carried the knight's baggage. The other two animals were new to him—both saddled for riding. One was a fierce brute. The other looked every day of twenty years old.

Without warning, the skald slid onto the stone bench beside him, peering out. "Has the Fox come? Ah wait. What's this now?"

Doors flew open at both ends of the hall.

Durand's father loomed at the chamber door, while the courtyard stair brimmed with echoes. Finally, a gray head appeared above the stair, wearing a giddy smile: Osseric of Gravenholm. Durand could hardly believe it was the man he knew. Twenty winters of gloom had left his face, leaving a lunatic grin. Two shocks of white hair stood out over his ears.

Durand's mother broke the silence. "Good morning, Sir Osseric!" she called.

"Indeed," agreed the old man. "Yes. Yes, indeed it is! For . . . for look whom I have here." The old man hopped aside.

For a moment, there was only Sir Kieren climbing into view.

But Kieren turned. "Come on up. Your father has them all tied in knots," he said.

A stranger stepped into the hall: blond, tall, and as weathered as a plowman. The blade at his hip hung in a scabbard more worn than Durand's boots. There was something of the old knight's look in this stranger's face.

Durand felt the omen swinging down around him. *"He did not drown."*

At his elbow, the skald muttered something about ruining a perfectly good ballad.

"My son's come home!" said Osseric, tottering forward, smiling through his tears.

And, while Durand gaped at the sudden ruin of his dreams, the people of the Col shouted for joy.

Soon every sanctuary bell in the little barony was ringing.

DURAND SAT THROUGH dinner and prayers, scarcely able to think. He'd had his future a long time. For fourteen years he'd served in other men's halls, as page and shield-bearer. He had known beatings. He'd even broken a bone or two—always knowing that at the end of the road, he would climb back up the mountains to take his place.

At the head of the hall, baron and firstborn sat under the Col coat of arms: two golden stags over a third. Durand caught sight of his brother, face white as lard. The baron met Durand's glance for an instant, then looked away.

When a man is knocked from his saddle he lies still before trying to jump up. When the shock ebbs away, he can spit the dirt from his mouth and take a levelheaded account of the spot he's in. Durand understood this. Now was the time to learn if this was a stumble or a killing blow. He must think.

At first, his thoughts skittered over impossibilities. He was trained for nothing but Gravenholm, and there was no place in his father's narrow domain without it. Fourteen years were wasted. He took a breath and looked back to the high table.

Osseric and his son sat between the baron and his wife. The old man was beyond happy, and there were endless questions for the blond stranger. Durand noted that scars stitched the man's hands. There was a crease or two in his nut-brown face as well. The man who'd risen from the dead was a soldier.

Durand eyed the squat bearish figure that was his father and tried to think. He must begin to sort things out. He must learn where he stood. He needed a word with his father, but with the press of well-wishers around the high table, he could not get close. He began to feel as though someone had rammed a gag in his teeth.

Stifling this surge of unease, Durand resolved to act. While he couldn't get to the baron, he could reach his brother. In a few moments, he caught Hathcyn by the shoulder. And soon, they stood in the cellar stair, away from the crush.

"King of Heaven, Durand," Hathcyn said, dismayed by the whole thing.

Durand felt a witless surge of anger.

"Father tried, I think," Hathcyn said. "Did you see his face when he realized that it was Hearnan who had returned?"

"Who's—?"

"That's the name. I'd forgotten as well. He's been in Mankyria. Aubairn. Soldiering for clipped pennies, playing knight-errant all around the Inner Seas. It's taken him all this time to scrape up enough to travel north. He must have fought a thousand battles." Hathcyn sounded a little too excited by the whole thing.

Durand waited.

"And . . . I offered," Hathcyn added.

Durand pinned his brother with a narrowed eye. " 'Offered'?" There was nothing for Hathcyn to offer.

"I thought we might divide the Col between us when Father—"

Durand put his hand flat on his brother's chest. "You *knew* he'd never let you do a thing like that."

"I suppose I did, though I meant it when I asked. I thought it might be made to work."

"And what did he say?"

"He said that our kin's held the Col since old Saerdan the Voyager's day, father to son three score times without any man in all that line breaking it while it was in his hands, as old as the oldest family in the kingdom. That if we set to carving up our lands, our sons' sons wouldn't have enough to plant both feet on. That soon we'd vanish among our own peasants like a drop of wine in a rain barrel."

Durand opened and closed his hands.

Hathcyn's eyes were on his boots. "I think Osseric must have heard us," he confessed. "Father spoke loudly."

Now Durand shoved his brother, who shoved back hard. There was a moment of sudden violence in the narrow stairway, suddenly over. A stupid thing.

Durand rammed his fist into the wall.

"*I* didn't ask," Durand said. "The old man shouldn't have that to worry about."

"Queen of Heaven, Durand, I'm sorry," Hathcyn said. "I thought we had everything set."

"We did have," Durand said. It was too soon to panic. He had to remember that. This was still the time to pull himself together and find out how badly he was hurt. He needed to know where he stood. "I'll have a word with our lord father."

There was pity in his brother's face. Durand stalked back into the hall.

His father's throne was empty.

Durand caught hold of a startled houseboy.

"The baron. Where?"

"His chamber, Lordship." Durand freed the boy and mounted the stair to the baron's chamber. The door was shut, its dark oak shining under a cloud of wax.

As Durand raised his hand to the latch, there were voices.

"They're reavers. Mercenaries," said the baron.

And Kieren: "It's all that's left to him, Your Lordship. He's a knight-errant whether you wish him to be or not. He's a knight without land."

"He's no knight yet!"

Durand should have pushed the door then.

"Knights-errant," said the baron. "Fancy word for pigs on their hind trotters out for a trough. If they aren't butchering each other in some brothel sewer, they're marching for the man who dangles the most silver under their snouts."

"There's many a fine lord who hires extra swords. What else is the boy to do? He can't tag along with me forever."

Durand stared at the dark wood.

"Host of Heaven, but he'd be better dead after this," his father said. "What becomes of a man who fights for pennies and not for his house and lord and lands? There are rumblings against the king. Folk who still won't believe old King Carlomund just fell. Who knows what the year will bring? And these tournament games of theirs. The Patriarchs still hold that killing a man on a point of honor is plain murder." There was a murmur of dissent. "Deny it! And ransom: killing for pennies. It's greed and pride at best. I'd be throwing his soul to the Host Below."

"Baron, you must be sensible. It is a chance. There's many a lad who gets none. Half the men on your land: priest's sons, cotters. He might manage to cut his way out."

Silence stretched. Durand heard the shallow rasp of his own breathing.

"It must be said," Kieren declared. "He's entitled to nothing. He'll need to take what he can."

Durand stared at the door's skin of black wax.

"So many years, only to plant him with the paupers on some battlefield," his father was saying. "It would have been better if he hadn't been born. He was meant to be an honest knight-at-arms. A lord."

The weight of the words was still settling on Durand when, without warning, the door swung wide in his face.

Sir Kieren looked up at him, the idiot fox tails jumping. After a long silence, he said, "I'm sorry, lad."

Durand felt an idiotic impulse to take hold of the little man; his hands barely twitched. Silent, he stepped into his father's chamber.

The room was dark, its windows shuttered. As Durand stood on the threshold, he could make out nothing.

Finally, the shadows spoke with his father's voice.

"Durand. Come."

As Durand's eyes adjusted to the gloom, all he could see of his father was a brooding shape cut from the hearth's glow. Thin light from the shuttered windows glittered in his eyes, on the rings at his knuckles, and on the pommel of the blade at his waist.

"My son, what've you done to your hand?"

Glancing down, Durand realized he'd been kneading the knuckles of the fist he'd used to smack the wall. There was blood.

"Nothing, Father," he said.

"Talking to Hathcyn . . ." his father said.

Durand looked into the shadows at his feet.

"What've you heard?" prompted his father.

"Enough."

"There will be no inheritance."

Durand swallowed, and the shadow detached itself from his father's chair. The constellation of sparks—rings, eyes, and buckles—settled into their places as the baron stopped by the mantel. He said nothing.

"There must be something," Durand said. "Another post somewhere—"

"And who would you have me take it from?" snapped the

baron. "I am liege lord to four lordlings and a dozen knights. Each one has my oath, relic-sworn to the King of Heaven. If I'd known there'd be nothing for you, I'd have had you train for a priest."

"I'm no priest."

"No. You're no priest, I'll grant you that." His father would have heard stories of his boy, scattering black eyes and fat lips among the lowland lordlings at court. From the first day, he'd picked on the bullies.

Durand found the twin sparks of the baron's eyes.

"If I *must* try my blade—"

"And damn yourself? Is that what you wish? Your temper alone will put your soul in peril! If my petitions reach the Halls of Heaven, the Powers will hint at what's to become of you before the dawn. Until then, you are still my man. You will not allow anyone, no matter how they goad you, to drive you into another performance of the sort that grazed your knuckles or I'll turn you out. Do you understand?"

"Aye, Father," Durand managed.

There was a sigh in the gloom as Durand left.

In the feasting hall, Osseric's soldier son sat nodding to the others' stories, though Durand reckoned any story of this stranger's life could curdle the blood of any local knight. He felt the brass pommel of his sword in the palm of his left hand, wanting to take a swing at the man who'd taken his place. He was not proud of the impulse.

It was getting dark. Most of his gear had been thrown into a storeroom heaped with groundskeeper's tools. This was where Durand fetched up after leaving the hall. As he threw the door open, the light fell on his shield, with his father's gold stags— the Col's stags. There was a shovel. In an instant, he had smacked the shield across the room.

What old Osseric's son had found at long last, Durand had lost. It was as simple as that. Getting back to his feet was more important than picking scabs.

He gathered his bedroll—still damp—bundles of extra clothing, and the weighty roll of his armor.

Kieren's voice stopped him: "I see. You're not sulking after all. You're running off."

There was no privacy in a castle.

"I'm running from nothing," Durand said.

"Ah." Sir Kieren slid his knuckles along the blade of his jaw, his blue eyes glittering. "No, you're right. You're simply leaving in a great hurry. It's a different thing."

"Hear me, you—" he came within a heartbeat of saying something he could not take back. "No. Sir Kieren, I can't do this. Not now."

"Mmm. I'll have to remember to watch where I step." He pointed to Durand's battered shield. "If I find a priest, perhaps he will read the omens here; they are too subtle for the layman. I count one good split in the shield cover, right through your family's arms." His mustache twitched. "I've heard that, after an evening of gnawing bones by the Fiery Gulf, the Writhen Man will read his future in the cracks of scorched shoulder blades. I'm *sure* there's something to read here."

"Sir Kieren—" He had venomous words in his mind, but the Powers of Heaven saved him. "I must go."

"They will say that you have run away," Kieren said, quietly. "You might at least wait till the baron finishes his deliberations. You might be the richest freeholder in all the Atthias after your lord father is done with you."

"I'm a fighting man. I know nothing of pigs, or corn, or sheep."

"Durand, the land's unsettled. There are those who see our king's troubles as sign he stole the throne. Tax and famine. And there are those who worry—a weak king is a danger. There are spirits on the road."

"I must take my chances, Sir Kieren," said Durand. With his old friend looking on, he lifted his possessions and marched them into the courtyard, heading for the stable. While he had been packing, the Eye of Heaven had vanished from the ring of sky above the castle's central courtyard. As he stepped out, it was full dark between the mountains.

His father's crest hung over the door to the tack room. Durand walked through, and into the stone stable. A pair of stable boys started. He must have looked like some ogre down from the mountains.

"It's all right," he said. Their expressions did not change. "I'll need my horse. Brag. He's a bay."

"Aye, Lordship. We'll have him out right away." The boys were wide-eyed as rabbits.

"Don't bother about the saddle. I'll find it." Durand stepped back into tack room, peering up among the hanging saddles, and trying for a deep breath.

In that still moment, he heard a noise from the chill courtyard.

Tock.

He spun. The door was wide open, and a man in a dun cloak stood by the well. In the man's hand was a staff with an outsized head. The thing seemed to have been fashioned from the gnarled fork of a tree, cut close like a hand at the wrist. Its two wooden fingers jutted down, one cut short, the other stretching lithely for the floor. The tall man looked to have been walking, but now set the metal heel of his staff against the stone.

Tock.

Setting his teeth, Durand stalked from the darkness, hauling his blade from its scabbard.

The figure made no move. The shadows of a pilgrim's hat swallowed the features.

Durand stared, breathing clouds into the air. Then, instead of speaking or turning, the stranger sprang to life—leaping like a suicide down the well. For an instant, Durand was alone.

As he gaped, astonished, a childhood memory rushed back. There was a stair down this well: a forbidden place of greasy slabs, coiling into smothering water.

With a flash of teeth, he charged out and chased the stranger down a hole so black it might have been full of water. The stranger's hat bobbed two turnings below. Durand followed as gloom closed over both their heads. He found his way by the echoes of footfalls and slipping hands that rebounded from water and stone. He felt stair edges roll under boot-leather. The stranger was a vanishing flutter.

That stopped.

In a jumbled instant, Durand's foot shot out. Water exploded. His elbow smacked stone, and he slipped into cold blackness. But something hooked his collar.

"Not that crossing! Not at my hand," a voice rasped.

Durand coughed and spluttered. His collar tightened against his throat. Then he landed.

"Hells." He twisted on the stone. "What's happening?"

"You've fallen."

After another fit, he tried to right himself, damp fingers adhering to the frigid stone.

"Host Below!"

"Take care whom you call."

Durand squinted, pawing his forelock from his eyes. There was nothing to see. "I've had my fill of you and your stick, stranger," he managed. But as he gave his stinging fists a twist, he realized that the stranger stood feet taller than any man he had ever seen. He filled the well like a tree.

Now Durand saw the stranger smile: a thing of black pegs. The stranger swung his forked staff against the water. There was no splash. And the pool itself glowed—deep, aurora-fingers reaching for the roots of the world.

"Queen of Heaven." An icy plume rose as Durand spoke.

The light climbed the folds of the stranger's cloak and his staff's convolutions. Durand saw fingers like hog bones wrapped in twine. Under the pilgrim's hat, he caught the edges of a face: a thorn bush of knotted twine spilling from cheekbones where hairy cord knotted like a weapon's grip. Two cold pennies winked in the sockets of the man's eyes: one a nicked black, the other bright silver. There were teeth. They looked like shoeing nails.

"Better." The voice rustled.

It took a lot to square off with the creature.

Through clenched teeth, Durand managed a few words: "Who are you?"

"I am the Traveler."

Durand forced his gaze into that knotted face. Into the glinting coins.

"What?" he demanded.

"Prince of Heaven. Spirit. Lord of Roads. Warder at Crossroads. The Longwalker."

"You're a sorcerer," Durand accused, even as he realized that no breath steamed from the dry jaws above him.

Laughter leapt the walls. "My Brother dreams the World. He set his Eye in the Vault of Heaven, and you do not call him sorcerer."

The Creator, Silent King of Heaven, dreamt the world. Durand had stared into his warm eye every morning at Dawn's Thanksgiving. The brown iron pegs of thing's teeth meshed a fathom over Durand's head.

"You're mad," he said.

"No."

"Then *I* am!"

The stranger's head tipped abruptly in a gesture that seemed almost birdlike, and allowed the thin light to wink in its tiny penny eyes. "No."

"Host of Heaven!" Durand swore.

"No, no," the stranger corrected sharply. "I miss the days of the Old Gods in these lands, when my Brother and his children had not yet eclipsed the other lights in Heaven. Men *knew*."

The corded brow flexed. "Imagine a sea," it said, "—an *ocean!*—and in it each drop of water sits on the next without mingling. A rattling main of beads without the slightest connection holding one to the next." For a moment, its hand touched Durand's head in a mad, paternal gesture. "Such is the memory of man. I am more than a sorcerer, forgetful one, for I was never born."

Durand stared at the well and the man and the eyes and the staff. "Why have you come for me?"

"I have not 'come for you,' you have arrived. I haunt the crossroads, Durand of the Col." He fingered the burly crook of his staff.

Durand felt the grip of soaked clothing squeezing the heat from him. He felt the ache of his bruised elbow. His lungs were raw.

"What do you want of me?" he said.

"You are a traveler," the Power said.

"A traveler . . . ?"

"You do not see. You little ones are thoroughly trapped in this old dream of my Brother's—no matter that you'll leave it one day." A thousand knots slithered tight to pitch the creature's metal eyes toward the sky. "In my youth I was a wanderer. I walked the tracks of my Brother's Creation. I watched as old spirits preyed on young. And I spent an age at my Brother's side, no help to give, too far to reach. And now I am near." Again, the Power was all narrow chin and brown peg teeth. "But I must be quiet. Quiet or the Host Below must hear."

The knotted face twitched. What such a gesture portended, Durand could not understand. "You are a strange breed, you men, and I have learned that only the lost will heed me." Durand was too near, like a mouse on a blacksmith's anvil. Starlight sparked in the Power's eyes like lightning. This thing was brother to the King of Heaven. Durand could feel the Traveler's spirit thundering out beyond the castle walls, beyond the fields—the flash of a smith's hammer on the world.

The coin eyes fixed Durand's. "You must be a traveler or lost."

Durand had no answer. Every road that stretched over Errest the Old twitched under the weight of the same Power.

"What is to become of me?" Durand rasped.

"The question."

The Power turned toward the glowing pool. For a moment, the wide brim obscured its terrible face. The light seemed to reach fathoms down. "How deep?" Durand found himself asking.

The empty eyes turned on him, one winking, one suddenly bottomless. "It was old when the *Cradle*'s prow first scraped the shore at Wave's Ending to found your nation. It runs to the days of the Old Gods."

It had been more than twenty centuries, twenty-three. He spoke of a time before time.

"There are bones down below," the stranger said. "And jewels and swords and the brazen shields of chieftains; lambs for the wild gods, and fallen children. The water curls in every bone and hasp." The Traveler stretched his staff out once more and struck the surface. Again, the water rang. It turned, finally, to Durand. "What would you know?"

Durand clenched his teeth and forced himself to stare into the metal eyes. "Is there a place? Will I find a place?"

The Traveler said nothing, though its great limbs creaked in their knots. Its eyes hesitated on Durand's face, waiting, and as the flat metal glinted, Durand felt himself drawn to speak.

"Will I succeed? I—What point is there in striving if . . ."

The Traveler would not turn away, and Durand felt suddenly uneasy at what he was doing. Maybe he was wrong. Did he want the answers? It might be better to leave some things down among the bones. This thing called the Lord of Dooms its brother. What would Durand do if the Power spoke the wrong words? He tried to tell himself that it didn't matter, that when he came before the Warders of the Bright Gates of far Heaven, all that mattered was how well he had lived the life he'd been given.

And still the Traveler waited.

A question came unbidden. "Will I . . ." but Durand stopped. Surely some things were too much to say. But he could not help but think: What woman would want some vagabond thug, a tramp with nothing to offer.

"What of a family?" he said.

At this, the vast Traveler nodded. It turned to the wavering disk of water. As it passed its staff over the still surface, the light stirred below, moving in loose tendrils. Huge, glowing branches swept through the gloom, drifting in the current.

"There are answers here," the Traveler said. "Many answers."

Durand looked deeper, seeing finer and finer branchings weaving in the blue. He looked to the Traveler. The light shone in the knotted curves of its face.

"Ah. Yes. I see the place you crave. Yes. And a share of glory." The Power stopped suddenly, almost starting.

"By the Host," it whispered.

The Power's jaws opened, and a weak thread of vapor climbed the well like a wisp of incense, like a prayer. "There is success."

Durand tried to face the Power. "And the rest?"

"Yes," the great Power murmured, and it seemed angry then. "A beauty. Soon, you will find her." It withdrew its heavy staff, the dry fingers stroking whispers from the wood.

"Are these things true?"

"Yes," the Power answered.

"Without doubt?" Durand pressed.

"Yes."

They were so close that the breath of the stranger's words stirred in Durand's mouth. He tasted the earth. After a long moment, the great Power stirred. There was a stiffness in its movements as though it had only just remembered the Ages it had seen. It raised its staff and glanced down on Durand, its expression unreadable.

"It's no easy path."

The staff dropped and struck the water, leaving only blackness.

Durand knew at once: Both the Traveler and the light were gone.

⊛ 3. Between Fires

Durand bared his teeth, breathing hard against the chill of stone and water. He looked up at the circle of pale cloud high above and the mirroring ring down the well. It seemed as if the distant Heavens were reaching for him.

Then something dropped out of the sky—a tight black flutter.

He extended his hand, but the flutter missed his fingers and struck him—hard—taking a bite from his forehead. It clattered between his boots.

From the courtyard, Durand heard a strange metallic tapping—not the Traveler's staff this time. Confused and more than tired of mysteries, he mounted the stair.

At the well's edge was a boy, driving a nail through a dark, folded bundle with a shoeing hammer. For an instant, the child remained absorbed, then he took note of Durand standing over him and the hammer clattered to the stones.

"Host of Heaven!" His eyes were wet and wide.

Durand pictured himself, towering against the sky, hair dripping in oily rivulets. "Easy," he said.

The boy stared, paralyzed. His eyes followed Durand's shaking hand. It was, Durand saw, black with blood. He pictured himself, a blood-soaked monster rising from the dark of a well. He smiled, wiping the blood away between his hands. "I'm really no one to be frightened of," he said, almost sighing. "Flesh and blood. Less blood than before you threw that thing down the well, but still flesh and blood."

"What were you doing in the well?" asked the boy.

"What are you doing hammering past curfew?"

"Asking questions," the boy whispered.

"Well," Durand said, "one of your questions has struck me in particular."

The boy only looked at the folded question in his hand.

Durand crouched. "I fell in," he offered and tried the smile again.

The boy was not so easy to win over.

"May I see?" Durand ventured.

The boy opened his hand, revealing a small dark parcel shot through with an iron nail. There was blood in the seams of his palm.

"It's lead," the boy said.

"A bit of the roof, looks like," Durand said.

"You hammer a sheet, then write your question. Or your wish, or whatever. You scratch with the nail, and a bit of blood. And then you knock the nail through. Has to be the same nail."

"You write?" Durand asked. "I only read faces."

"You have to," the boy said.

"Who told you these things?"

"Everyone around here knows."

"You're from the Col?" He had never seen the boy, but he supposed that meant very little.

"No," said the boy. "My father is the priest."

"Oh." The priests had been trying to rid the peasants of their old, wild gods since the *Cradle* skidded ashore at Wave's Ending. "A priest taught you these things?"

"My father is a Vairian and a scholar!"

That might explain it. The Vairians were the strangest of priests, binding scraps of hearsay to stretched skins with knots of ink. They made good scribes.

"Your father is my father's priest-arbiter?"

The boy squinted. "Yes, *Milord*. He studied at the library in Parthanor. And he's a scholar."

"And he taught you?"

"No. I learned it from your mother's women. They know all these things."

The cold was overtaking Durand. He might have known. Patriarchs for law, wise women for birth and death and fortune.

"Why the well?"

"You drop them in the well so the Old Gods will answer in

your dreams. It is what the old priests did when the Col was standing stones."

The boy's eyes were full of suspicion, as though he expected a rebuke and didn't deserve it.

For a time, Durand said nothing.

"Cast it in," he said, finally.

The boy flung his message into the dark.

IN A FEW moments, Brag's hooves were clattering across the courtyard, past the well and under the long teeth of the portcullis. Durand wondered when he would ever see the gap-toothed fortress again.

Something moved under the gate. A small figure hugged the gate's blocky plinth: the priest's boy looking out at him. He raised his hand, and Durand saw a garnet in his palm—the mark of the nail. Durand raised his own hand in answer, not certain why. Whatever gnawed at the boy's mind, he must have seen a match for his own plight in Durand's. He wondered what the boy's name was, and gave him a sharp nod as he spurred Brag onward. There was nothing like an audience to give a man courage.

FOR HOURS, HE rode through the damp wilderness. At first, Brag galloped, then he cantered, and then he fell to plodding. Naked trees and muck gave way to long fieldstone fences that unraveled along the roadside, or undulating hedgerows that humped over the low hills. Durand drifted down between the hills.

He wondered at himself. What business did he have pushing Brag out on a night like this? And it was the wrong time to be on the road. Though Traveler's Night was gone, it was still the Gleaning Moon with all the harvest laborers on the roads. There were rumors of unrest. Winter stalked the wilds, and there was no more work for the hungry and the outcast.

He must build himself a new future, and he must be as careful as a carpenter about it. Gireth was an old duchy in an old nation, bound in oath and custom. From the lowest plowman to the king in Eldinor, a man did what he was born to. Durand imagined returning to the duke in Acconel. He could offer his services there, but what would they do with such an offer?

There wasn't a single sellsword in all the duke's retinue. A wellborn man could not beg charity, or—Durand laughed—a wellborn man refuse to offer it. Appearing in Acconel as he stood would shame the duke and himself both. The Barony of the Col had been in his family's hands since the first Duke of Gireth handed it to his shield-bearer, surviving the High Kingdom's rise and fall and wars beyond the Sea of Thunder. It was an ancient name, and Durand would not tarnish it. He could not go begging to Acconel. In any case, he did not have food enough to travel so far. He had a vision of himself stiff in a ditch like a stray dog as the snow flew.

Apprentices started at fourteen; priests were a different breed. Bakers, weavers, goldbeaters, and bookbinders were all guild crafts and all father to son. There was a reason some men turned to brigandage. But he would not turn up before the Bright Gates of Heaven with the souls of women and children howling round his neck.

Brag plodded on. Wrapped up in thought and a wet cloak, another of night's cold hours passed as he rode between the hills. He hardly noticed Brag's sudden nodding.

He looked up. They had blundered down some sort of ditch, and shapes were uncoiling from the darkness all around.

He saw men on every side, gaunt and hollow. He had blundered into some makeshift camp. Uneasy, he groped for his blade. Knives and knobbed clubs had already appeared from rags.

As he reached for his scabbard, he remembered his sword clattering down the well.

In that heartbeat, Durand judged his battleground. The thugs had moved in before and behind him while a knot of them were climbing out of a shallow cut in the hillside—just out of reach.

If they had waited another moment to spring their trap, he could never have got loose.

In an instant, he seized his chance. Spitting a curse, he wrenched poor Brag toward the empty hillside and set his spurs deep. The hunter vaulted out of the robbers' hands, up from the ravine, lurching high onto the hill above.

Below, the ragged line of pursuers spread across the dark

hillside, losing ground. The bay hunter quickly left them behind.

Durand stroked the big brute's neck. Dragging the hapless animal out into misery and the dark had been unkind.

They lost their pursuers, riding off among high-flanked hills that put Durand in mind of stories he'd heard about whales on the Winter Sea and how they dwarfed the ships.

He wondered about the men behind him, thinking of his father's words about knights-errant: masterless men roving between the halls of landed men. Some of the robbers by the track might have been luckless knights. But there were other stories about knights-errant. They were the heroes who got the maidens free of their ogres. Or so the skalds would tell you.

The Heavens opened and cold rain plummeted down from the dark, hammering a mist of mud into the air. His breath came in cold shudders, and the greasy hillside seemed ready to slump from under Brag's hooves.

Cursing it all, Durand searched for the hilltops, but could barely make out the joint between hill and Heaven. Poor Brag wallowed ahead.

As they crested a rise, Durand made out a dark smudge against the gray of the next "whale's" back. "Come on Brag, it may be there's some shelter ahead," he said.

As it loomed closer, the black smudge seemed to bristle with tattered branches: yew and bramble. A thicket among the bald hills. He rode close, though Brag lashed his head. "Easy." Durand splashed down the saddle. At the edge of the thicket, the leaves of the undergrowth lay like a blanket thrown over spindly branches. Brag nodded his fright at the wind and weather, but Durand felt the marrow freezing in his bones. There was no way to wedge a horse under the branches. His fingers stiffened in Brag's bridle.

"Hells," Durand said, and gave his cloak to the big hunter before pushing through into the darkness to lie panting until sleep took hold.

DURAND WOKE TO the sound of a screaming horse.

Real needles pierced his throat.

He coughed.

His eyes snapped open, and something jerked away from his

neck with a many-tined pluck. There was nothing but dark for an instant, then he made out a little cavern of branches. Starlight winked between leaves. He remembered the bramble.

Something rattled in his lungs, and he choked. The spasm jerked him upright and into the branches. After a moment, the fit gave way, and he took his hand from his lips. He wasn't dreaming: there was blood.

He looked around.

In the darkness where the ceiling of the bramble cave grew higher stood a mass of blackthorn like a column of knives and wire. And there seemed to be clots of darkness among the thorns. He peered at the shapes, unable to make sense of anything. Then the wind stirred the canopy and freed the glow of the Gleaning Moon to shine in a dozen pale eyes.

A moan slipped from Durand's throat.

The shapes unfolded, unwrapping themselves from stalks and branches. Wisps of hair floated over nut brown skulls. They were withered men. Ears as long and sharp as pea pods curled from the bare lumps of their skulls. Fingers unfolded and unfolded, armed with black needle claws.

"Host of Heaven."

The first figure set its hand on the ground to crawl toward him. Its talons sprang wide like a crab's legs, longer than any man's fingers.

Durand's hand scrabbled at his scabbard—empty—and he knew then that there could be no fighting them. He must break loose.

At the instant his hands touched the ground, the floor of the cavern came alive. Every fallen leaf was suddenly spinning, afloat on the backs of dark bodies. Spiders exploded over his arms and thighs, over and under wool and linen. A cloud of thread swelled around him.

He launched himself. His fingers touched the wall of leaves. The mist of silk clenched tight. It swathed his face and limbs, and his jaw pulped a hundred spindly bodies when he crashed down.

BOUND, HE ROARED until his throat was hoarse, and still he lay there rasping. He could not reconcile himself to this death; he would be pitched before the Gates of Heaven screaming.

Time passed where he and the wind made the only sound, and then the tentative blackthorn men surrounded him. Needles played over his back and sides.

"He is grown," a voiced croaked.

For a time, Durand thrashed like a landed fish. They waited. A talon knotted itself in his hair, jerking his head up. He saw a face. It was as brown and stiff as long-tanned leather. The nose was puckered like a rotten fruit.

"What do you want?" Durand breathed.

The face split, baring teeth like yellow knives. It turned to the others. "It speaks to us," it hissed.

"Who was he?"

"I do not know. It becomes more and more difficult."

"The old lines cross and recross."

"Not this one."

"No. This one runs pure back to the beginning."

The voices rasped and bubbled and whined. Durand closed his eyes and strained against the swaddling web as the brutes circled, stroking him with fingers that snagged at his tunic and leggings.

"Could he be Bruna himself?" one asked, speculatively. It was a name from the first pages of the *Book of the Moons*. First of forefathers.

There was a pause, then answers circled him.

"Yes."

"Yes."

"Another Bruna."

"Bruna of the broad shoulders."

"He was a strong man."

"Too strong."

"I remember his smile in those days after the first dawn," one said close by. Its long-fingered hand took Durand by the face and lifted his head until he gagged. He could feel the fingers meet and slither at the nape of his neck, long as a bat's wings. Then the leather-faced thing inserted its fingers into Durand's mouth, and pulled his lips apart. "Yes."

"Yes, Ilsander! I see Bruna in him."

"Do you think so? Bruna? What a chance! I remember him walking the hills with us when we were known to the Creator. Him smiling. Him with his brittle honor. Circling. Speaking hollow truths. And on the fields before our Maiden. And the Mother."

"She should have come before."

"She should have come in time."

"And here he is, Bruna of the broad shoulders. Bruna the slayer. Betrayer. He breeds true. And he lives in the light, while we must cringe in copses. He lives through this one while we wither among the thorns." The monster's eyes closed for a moment, in a kind of fixed rapture—suddenly a peaceful corpse. "I can see his face as though I close my eyes and return to the dawn of Ages."

Then the face soured, and the hand let Durand's head fall. He gasped for air.

"How she looked at him. I remember how he strutted. The gift of the Mother was full upon us. I remember how he struck. Oh, how I remember the scream!"

"Injustice, Ilsander. It is injustice."

"Perversion," a voice bubbled.

Fingers ran over his buttocks and back and played through his hair. Their claws were black, needle-pointed, and glistening. They seized him and rolled him firmly onto his back. Somehow, the sight of the things was worse than their voices alone. They minced around him, staring. Sack bellies swung between their shins.

He had felt the pommel of his knife dig as he rolled, and all his thoughts fixed on its angular hilt.

"The perversion."

One stepped in, and its talons skittered across his chest, finding his nipples through his surcoat and tunic.

"The Mother's mark is upon them all."

"The Creator ought to have known there would be death for us. He should have known there would be pain."

"Bruna and his ilk should not have been saved while we suffered. Who would fashion a world with one birth and a thousand deaths?"

"He did not know."

"The Lord of Dooms? The King in Silence? The Mother should have brought birth before so many of us were lost." The horror that spoke lifted its monstrous hand, curling its fingers. "Their blood lives while ours curdles and putrefies in our veins."

Durand worked his fingers under the tight threads.

"If she had brought birth to the world only a little sooner . . ."

"Bruna's blood is so warm in him. Oh, that Bruna's progeny still live, while I, so long ago, was slain. I can feel the blood mocking us. Spinning through these veins."

"Oh, Ilsander! It is an abomination!" one shrieked, overcome with despair.

"We are dead and he lives."

"Perversion!"

"We are separated from the world."

"So should Bruna be!"

Their eyes blazed. Wrath carried them in a dance like tempest leaves. He could feel the momentum of their anger push them to the brink of setting upon him. The copse shook with their screams, and a body landed on Durand's stomach. Orange teeth flashed, but Durand tore the belt knife free, gouging the horror.

It shrieked and sprang into the branches, spidering backward. Durand stabbed and slashed at the web cocoon, heedless of injury.

They tumbled, shrieking away from the iron blade, and he threw himself through the slashing thorns and into the open hills. The blackthorn spirits poured into the rent he left in the bushes like corruption from a flyblown corpse. Suddenly under the sky, Durand spun on them. He raised his knife, and those who had stumbled out froze where they stood. Every eye fixed on each movement of blade.

He held it like a talisman. "Mother of us all," he swore. The pinched, twisted faces sneered. Where they remained in the bushes, he could imagine that they were only a trick of the light.

"By the Warders at the Gates, you fear iron, do you?" he said. "You do!" Durand grinned wildly. Across the Atthias, peasants hammered horseshoes over their thresholds. Wise women circled cradles with iron—shears, knives, needles—warding off the Banished. The slinking creatures retreated to join their brothers among the branches.

Durand heard a whispering then. Or, perhaps, a rustling like any bushes would make at the passing of a breeze. It occurred to him that he might have blundered past such a gathering many times.

He pushed the thought from his mind, and risked a sideways glance in a desperate hope of finding Brag still nearby. "Brag, lad? You here still?" He began to circle the bushes, sidling with the knife between himself and the denizens of the blackthorn.

Brag stood two-dozen paces away from the copse, his eyes wide and flashing. Durand hadn't picketed the horse, but Brag had hardly wandered. Durand felt gratitude as complete as a child's.

He backed toward the animal, watching with queasy horror as the blackthorn fiends slipped into the grass. They came no closer, but neither did they let him free.

The horse whickered on the point of bolting.

"Good lad," Durand said, trying to hold the poor brute with his voice. Brown heads bobbed in the grass as if swimming. "Good lad, Brag. Just a moment and we'll be away."

Finally, Durand's fingers knotted on the bridle. Riding or dragged behind, he was leaving. After a last menacing wave of the knife, he turned his back on the blackthorn fiends and threw his leg over Brag's back. The horse screamed.

The fiends shot forward in an explosion of angular limbs as the knife went out of sight.

Durand locked his legs round Brag and charged their ragged line. The horse leapt at the last instant, bowling one brute into a tangle.

As they landed, charging the thicket, Durand twitched the reins, urging Brag into a hard turn. The horse leapt again, this time into a full gallop.

They put leagues behind them before dawn.

BUT DAWN WAS a strange thing, only a blooming light in the fog, at first dim and then painful as polished steel.

The weight of exhaustion crushed Durand to Brag's neck. If not for the horse's balance, fatigue would have pulled him to the ground.

———

HE WOKE SHIVERING over the saddlebow.

Somewhere in the mist, he heard a staff falling. *Tock*. Dry wood and a metal heel.

Tock.

Tock.

"God. No more."

After several moments passed . . .

"What're you two doing out so early, eh?" said a voice. "A rough night for a ride in the hill country. Now who's this balanced on your neck, eh boy?"

There was a hand on Durand's shoulder.

"Gods," a voice swore—the plural blasphemous. "Col's boy!" The homely skald goggled down at him. "What in God's name has happened to you, lad?"

Durand's gaze took in the man's smashed nose and the crumpled hat mashed down around his ears upside down and peering. He found himself laughing, like pottage on the boil. He could hardly stop.

"Here, we've got to get you inside somewhere." The skald turned, casting about. "Uh . . . Ah! The shepherd's hut. It's warm enough. We'll head back that way."

The small man's hand caught Brag's bridle and led them along the track.

The last thing Durand noted was that the little man had no staff in his hand, and that there were no cobblestones in the track they followed.

"HERE. HERE. GODS."

Each lurch of Durand's horse brought a gray stone hut closer. Three fieldstone walls erupted from a bank like a flash of gray teeth. As the skald flung open a door, Durand let himself slide from Brag's neck. He ducked under the lintel into what seemed little more than a damp cavity in the hillside.

The skald bustled ahead, kneeling at a hearth set into the earthen floor. Durand watched for a moment, then sagged against the wall.

"I'll have a fire ready in no time," the skald said. "Sod roof holds the heat as well as thatch." He glanced back at Durand and saw the open door.

"Best close that," he said, and stalked across to shut out

the light. Durand found himself amazed at the other man's mobility.

"Here," Durand protested. "I've got to see to Brag."

"It's a good horse you've got."

"Years," Durand mumbled. "Had him from Kieren. Too big, he said. It's a thousand leagues by now."

"He'll want more care than you're fit to give. I'll just get this started."

Soon, the skald had smoke rising from a clump of moss on the floor. A flame no bigger than a hatchling's beak filled the space with smoke.

"Here," he said. "Sit. Get some of that wet gear off."

Durand crouched over the tinder.

"I'm going to assume that you've left your father's hall in haste," said Heremund. "That's safe enough ground, I think. The rest, though, I'll have to work for."

The flame blossomed between the skald's hands. Then, as he fed twigs into the tiny blaze, the blush of heat swelled.

"Or you could tell me."

With an effort Durand murmured, "I left."

"Aye?"

"Got into the hills where the forest breaks."

The skald waited.

"And the rain," Durand added.

"I waited that bugger out in here," Heremund said, looking up at the blackened roots of the ceiling.

"Took shelter under a thicket of bushes."

"That'd explain the scratches."

"No," Durand said. He closed his eyes.

When he opened them, the skald had turned full to him.

"There was something under the leaves," Durand said. "Withered things. Long arms. Teeth. Pointed ears. Hands like taloned spiders."

"*Hosts Below,* lad."

Durand exhaled.

"How did you get free of them?" Heremund gasped.

"Skald. What were they?"

"I might've heard a story," the skald hedged. After a moment, he looked hard into Durand's eyes. Durand was too tired to look away.

"Not unheard of in the wilds. Creation's frayed at the seams. Sea and shore. Crossroads. Borderlands. Wastes." He kneaded his chin. "Ancients in the blackthorn, though. Those will be the First Ones, you've met." He looked into the knobbly rafters. "The priests will tell you about a whisper among the first pages of the *Book of Moons*. There are men in the stories of the Second Age and the coming of the young spirits to Creation. The *Book* only hints at their end, really." He looked up. "It's all First Dawn business. The wise women know that lot. They're prophets, your new friends, I suppose. That's what you'd have to call them."

Durand found it vastly easier to say nothing, and the skald explained.

"You see, they knew our first fathers. Way back before there was an Atthi or his Sons. Before Isle Kingdoms and High Kingdoms, all fallen now. And they know which a man favors. Which grandsire's grandsire's grandsire you're most like."

"How?"

"The Silent King's dreamed the world. Time before time. Right? Man's awake." Heremund made an expansive gesture over the fire. "Marvelous. No death. No suffering. No pain. And the little souls breathing and dreaming and walking. Stewing till they're done. Rising like loaves. Cooking till they're stiff enough to stand among the Powers. Wonderful. Yes?"

Durand drew a breath of mildew and smoke into his lungs. "You hungry, skald?"

"And it was wonderful, for a time, I reckon. But the King of Heaven wasn't the only Power in the Otherworld. Still ain't! The Hag, she worked the Son of Morning round: 'Why's He left you here to lavish His attention on these little souls? Has He no love left in his old heart for His own darling, His own Son of Morning?' That's how she turned him. And they wracked Creation. They fired the passions. Sowed disease. Spawned jealousies and grief. Folk died and weren't meant to."

Durand blinked, forcing his thoughts into order. "Skald. What's this got to do with those buggers in the bush?"

The skald smiled. "No death. Not in the plan. Yes? But men were dying—sort of. Right? No birth. None of that. But some of them died before the Mother was moved to join us. No Queen of Heaven. Check your *Book of Moons*."

No birth. No crying babes. No silver moons. It was non-sense.

"There was a time before the Queen came," Heremund declared. "Before she sorted men and women, birth and death. Right? So what happened to those who died before, eh?"

"I'm no priest, skald."

"What's become of the poor buggers who died then, before death? Then and in all the Ages since? The *Book* is silent. That's who you met."

Durand didn't much like the thought of those twisted men and their dark eyes festering in the Dawn of Creation. He had had enough. One explanation eluded him.

"And they're prophets?"

"No. Not exactly. They hate us, is all, and they want to know whose blood is in us. They want to know which of their old friends is laughing at them, living on. But sometimes they'll let slip. The wise women reckon you can divide us up by which of those forefathers we favor. The old buggers are accidental prophets."

Durand tried to remember the name he'd heard. "I was Bru—"

"—No!" snapped Heremund. The man actually clapped his hand over Durand's mouth—only surprise let him get so close. "Talk to the wise women. Tell your bloody horse. I won't hear it!" The man took a breath, lifting his palm. "Still, it's something you've met the old buggers. That's something. And it's something else that you've got loose. There ain't many alive." The skald was thinking now.

He smiled, waving the whole thing away. "The wise women make too much fuss over the First Ones. Most of us are muddled up. A bit of one, a bit of the other. Mongrel pups. It's only when the line pops out pure, you've got to worry. Then things can start happening. New songs chiming with old tunes."

Durand closed his eyes. "Why the blackthorn?"

"Hmm? Oh that? There's poetry in the old world sometimes. Blackthorn: the dark tree of fate, with its guarded, bitter fruit?"

Durand grunted, his head swimming. "My horse." Brag

was likely freezing. "Someone's got to do something about the horse."

"Yes. I'll see what I can manage."

HE OPENED HIS eyes on the cottage dark.

"It was you with the tapping as well, yes?" Heremund's voice was very quiet.

"What?" said Durand. He had been sleeping.

The skald abruptly bustled to make a meal of bread, cheese, and beer.

"So you're awake, are you?" he called across the low room.

Durand had no notion of whether it was morning, night, or noon. Little light found its way into the windowless hut. "Good morning," Durand replied warily, climbing to his feet. He was sure he had heard the other question, but his bladder was full to bursting, so he slipped out through the door into what did indeed seem to be a morning mist. Brilliance swelled the eastern Heavens. Durand thought of the King of Heaven and his perfect world all those Ages ago, and felt an urge to drop in the wet grass to pray the Dawn's Thanksgiving. Instead, he untied his breeches and did what he had come to do.

Brag whickered, likely thinking of oats. Heremund had heaped blankets across the horse's back and freed him of his saddle.

When Durand pushed back into the low darkness of the hut, the bow-legged skald's pack was loaded and he was busily grinding out the fire's last embers with his toe. Looking round, Durand discovered that the man had brought Brag's saddlebags inside. Bread and beer of his own was stowed away.

When he had finished eating, Heremund stood. "And where am I taking you?"

"What?"

"Well. I'm not one to leave a thing half-done, and I'd feel an awful fool if you died tomorrow after I saved you today."

Durand was legitimately surprised. "There's no call for that. You've business of your own, I'm sure."

The little man caught hold of the various bags and waddled past Durand into the light.

"Ah," said Heremund. "But you are a knight errant, are you? You are fixed on it?"

Durand called out through the low doorway. "I thought we'd agreed I was no priest." He curled and uncurled a callused fist. A decade of drills, sparring, hunting, and tilting at the quintain had given him the hands of a woodcutter.

Noticing, Heremund winced. "Or milkmaid either, I'm sure. Poor cows'd never forgive you."

"One thing is certain: I cannot stay here forever."

Heremund was heaping bags around Brag's ankles. Abruptly, the little man stopped, peering round at the close hills and mist.

"No," he agreed. "The shepherd will likely come back."

Durand ducked under the doorframe, and stood up under the pale skies, twisting his neck. "There's one way, as I see it. I must catch the train of some lord at tournament and show the man I'm worth keeping."

The skald was now busy, swinging saddlebags over Brag's back. Once more he seemed distracted, squinting off into the mist.

"If there's a wellborn man who needs another strong back among his retainers, you might hold on. Still, it's late in the year and an awfully long shot."

Durand, one eyebrow raised, had walked up behind the little man. He had to look up a good foot before he saw Durand's face.

"Of course," he said, "they're a practical lot, some of them."

"Where's the next tourney?"

The little man held up his thick-necked mandora, searching in vain for a spot on Brag's back. "I think I'll have to carry this. We should find you a packhorse."

Shaking his head, Durand swung up into the saddle, and extended a hand to the skald.

At the last moment, Heremund made a face. He snuffed at the air. "All right, what *is* that?" A night on the hills had packed Durand's head past noticing a stray scent.

"Awful, whatever it is," said Heremund. "We'll try for Ram's Hill. They have a good tourney there most years, come the Blood Moon. It's a bit of a trek, but we've got time. We should try to find an inn tonight, I reckon."

"Right." Imagining a dry room with a big fire, Durand urged Brag down the track.

He caught the reek nearly as soon as Brag moved. Heremund, right in his ear, said, *"Gods."*

NOT MORE THAN a dozen paces from the hut, a matted form sprawled in the bushes. As Durand drove Brag a few steps further, a bald-faced rook jerked its head from a wound and lurched into the air. There were white-tined antlers.

It was a red deer: a full-grown stag.

"Host of Heaven," Heremund muttered. "It was a wild night. I suppose the rut's just ending. He must have been driven out and died on the hills. Panicked in the storm."

Durand saw the great head in profile, neck ruffed like an eagle. Ten points. A match for the Col stags painted on his own shield.

"I—I'm plagued with omens," Durand murmured. "Now this, on setting out. What is a man to read here? A wild stag killed in the storm. Torn and lying. What doom am I meant to read here?"

Heremund was silent at Durand's shoulder, shaking his head: tiny convulsive gestures.

"You see something, don't you?" Durand said.

"I read no dooms," Heremund breathed.

"Tell me what you see."

"No." Heremund was whispering. "Once, in warmer days, I served at a court. A great man. And his wife was with child. They summoned the wise woman. But it went wrong, and, though the child lived, its mother could not."

Durand glanced to the stag, its gray tongue curled. "What has this to—"

"There—there was a prophecy. While the wise woman, she's rubbing linseed and balsam into dead mother and live son under the Paling Moon, there is a hard, cold glimpse of the babe's doom.

"Everything the lad did would come to nothing," Heremund said, quiet as thought.

"Hells." Durand remembered cringing in the well with that thing that might have been a Power. What would he have done with *that* news?

"Was it true, Heremund?"

"I have heard things lately. I have heard things that make me wonder."

🌀 4. The Hungry Leagues

It should be any time," said Heremund, peering down the trail. They hoped for a town.

Always, they were too late.

For two weeks, they had chased the skald's hunches round the south and east of great Silvermere. At Ram's Hill, they missed a tournament by three days. At Mereness, a pock-marked gatekeeper barked that there would be no tourney that year, someone had died. After a week, the few hard pennies in Durand's purse were gone with the last heel of bread. Now, Heremund was only certain of one final open tournament before the winter snows: Red Winding. Worse, a safe way around Silvermere might take them more than a hundred leagues through wild country, and they had only a week to reach it.

They rode hard. The king's messengers covered fifteen leagues in a day. But the king's men rode fresh horses. And they did not ride double.

Still, Durand knew that he must reach Red Winding. Already, they were waking hungry and riding tired. Durand feared that traveling in his company might kill the little skald, but there was no way a man could wait out the long empty winter.

Now, though, they were hunting the chill twilight for a town. Heremund had promised.

A dog barked somewhere ahead.

"What do you think?" Durand said.

"Aye," Heremund agreed, and, sure enough, between a pair of mud-dark hills, emerged the thatched hovels of a village.

Heremund leaned from his perch behind Durand's saddle. "Now, I'll see if I can't sing for our supper, eh? We'll—"

"You there, stop!" ordered a woman's voice.

Lean men filled the track ahead, billhooks and mattocks in their fists.

Heremund crumpled his hat in his hands, and called out: "We mean no harm."

"Fancy that. They mean no harm. Let them in," said the woman, and, when a few of the plowmen in the track glanced around, unsure, "Hold your ground, you daft whoresons!"

"Listen strangers," she advised. "It's after curfew, and we've had some trouble with lads on the road. Thieving. Filching livestock. We lost three wethers meant for salting just yesterday. There's no work here till the Sowing Moon, and we don't need no trouble from strange men now, do we?"

"Madam," Heremund called, "we ain't common laborers come scrounging for—"

"You'd say that, now, wouldn't you?"

"On a fine steed?"

"Riding double. And I've half a mind to ask where you came by the brute. He don't look too well looked after to me."

"My friend here has been at the court of—"

"Right! You've had polite, now it's time you were off. Lads?"

A couple of the long-faced peasants wound up with slings.

"Ride, Durand!" Heremund hissed. Stones whistled and zipped past them.

They rode safely up into the nearby hills and out of range.

"That was lucky," Durand said, having felt the stones pass close.

"Speak for yourself." The skald was rubbing the side of his head. "I think I'm going to have a thick ear out of this."

"You all right?"

"Aye. Or I will be. Always bad at Blood Moon, with winter coming on. And this year, with Mad Borogyn's uprising in the Heithan Marches, and the king's new taxes . . . Still, by the Bitter Moon, the mobs will be gone."

"Aye." He had no trouble imagining that the destitute laborers who staggered into the snows of the Bitter Moon weren't much trouble to anyone much longer.

Again, poor Brag was trudging through wet woodlands. Durand didn't know how long the hunter could stand the abuse. A well-fed horse didn't much mind the cold, but, lean and sopping, Durand worried about the animal.

The track mounted the flank of a wooded ridge.

"I don't suppose you know a hut round *here* somewhere?"

"Why should I need a hut when the people are so friendly?" He gasped at a lurching stride from Brag. "I swear, jostling around back here is going to split me in two. When you're trudging in the muck, it looks like luxury, but there's nothing left of me but a—"

The big horse had put a foot wrong. Poised on the slope, his legs shot out from under him. Without a lifetime's practice, Durand would have had his leg snapped as Brag slammed hard, then slid. Heremund yelped.

In a rushing instant, all three were crashing downhill, catching at saplings and tumbling. Bracken, gorse, and blackthorn lashed at them as they bounded through.

Finally, Durand was free and on his feet. A stand of dogwood had finally caught Brag in a black tangle of wreckage. Heremund was gathering himself up. They had torn twenty yards of bush. Brag thrashed his limbs.

"Oh God," Durand said and scrambled down the slope.

The horse was screaming. Heremund slid in close.

"Gods," he said.

Durand scrambled through the tangled stand of saplings and tried to reach the animal's legs. Durand had to feel for breaks. The hunter's stiff lashings threatened to brain him, but he slipped close and saw what he had feared. No horse was made for such a fall. There was a sick bend in the animal's right hind leg. The cannon bone had been snapped right below the hock.

"Ah God," said Durand.

The animal lashed harder for a moment, feeling trapped, no doubt, or scared by the pain.

Heremund's wide eyes were on Durand, fearful or hopeful from beyond the animal's flank. But Durand shook his head quick, half-denying what was in front of him. He had pushed too hard.

"Queen of Heaven," he said through clenched teeth. He remembered a thousand forest leagues chasing red deer and roe, driving the boar from his den, pounding through the sunlight with the hunters and liegemen of old Duke Abravanal's court by Silvermere.

The animal was screaming. Durand swallowed, seeing that Heremund would be no help with what he must do. While Durand had no sword, he still had his knife. He laid his hand on Brag's cheek, then, pushing to hold the animal, he made the butcher's cut where the blood pulsed in the big animal's throat. There was nothing to do then but hold on as the animal bled out.

When it was finally over, Durand stood, shaking. He gathered their belongings: bedrolls, mandora, and an iron roll of mail. Heremund watched, saying nothing, but then joined him.

Durand fought a fierce compulsion to return to the village and teach a few villagers the cost of turning travelers away.

EXHAUSTED, COLD, AND starving, the two men trudged west. The ungainly roll of iron on Durand's shoulder weighed on him like some Power's curse, but he would not abandon it. Tens of thousands of iron rings, tens of thousands of rivets, all hammered and woven and hardened in the forge. Like Brag, it was a gift from Kieren. A man could buy every ox in a village for the price, and without one a man was no knight. Still, he staggered under the iron weight when the track was uneven. It drove thought from his skull.

On and on they walked, under a dull Heaven. Red Winding dangled just beyond reach, but Heremund could not persuade him to relent. They tramped past stooped swineherds beating the branches for the last acorns, fattening pigs now that the Blood Moon was upon them. A field of women with their hips in the air bent to jerk blunt sickles through fistfuls of stubble. Where the land tended toward marshes, poor men waded barefoot in the muck to cut reeds. Leagues staggered past. The Eye of Heaven fled them west.

It was in a marshy ditch between hills that a pair of reedcutters nodded Durand's way, dragging wrists across foreheads. The mud in the hollows of collarbone and throat made them seem like dead men. Still, they smiled. One man tugged his forelock, somehow recognizing Durand's blood. Durand nodded.

He turned back on a worried Heremund. "No matter what I do, my lot is not the worst."

Heremund laughed.

"You could always wear that thing, you know," he said, jerking his chin toward the mail. "That's what they're for."

Durand laughed. "Walking all day in a hauberk and leggings. Then, perhaps, I *would* have the worst lot." There would be no skin on his shoulders.

They were low in a valley, and it was getting on toward evening. The first day's traveling was at an end.

Durand turned to the reed-cutters.

"Lads," he called. "What's this place called?"

The two men conferred a moment, then called back: "Balian's the village, sir." It was not a famous name.

Durand looked back to Heremund—this would tell him how far they'd traveled—but the skald's darting eyes told him more than he wanted to know.

"How far does that make it?" he asked.

"Three leagues, Durand. Maybe."

Durand nodded.

They must cover ninety.

Durand waved numb thanks to the cutters and tramped up the hill. If he did not find something soon, he would starve before he got his chance.

They reached the top of the rise, where a valley fell away below them, opening half a league around the silver course of the River Banderol. The low Eye of Heaven lanced across the valley, free for the first moment in days. It shimmered over black fields blushing green with the first shoots of the winter wheat.

Heremund stalked up after him. "You know, I wager those lads'd lend us a spot by their fire if we gave them a hand with the—"

Just then, light sparked on metal. Beyond the river, rounds of steel winked from the far ridgeline. Durand saw it: spurs, the pommels of swords, the high brows of helms all flashing under Heaven's Eye. A cavalcade of horsemen rode like something from a dream.

"*Knights,*" Durand breathed. As though his voice dispelled the dream, the column vanished, swallowed by some dip in the terrain.

"Durand, what is it?"

He waited for the glint of metal to bob back above the ridge, feeling the curl of his cloak in his fist. Here, at least, was a chance at something.

But the flash did not return.

He wouldn't wait. "Follow me, skald!" he said, and plunged down from the headland across the patchwork mire of fields. This chance would not slip from his hands.

Heremund chased him. "What in the Hells are you going on about? I'm not meant for vaulting bloody hedges."

Durand jolted down the slope past toiling peasants who gaped or shouted curses. Finally, the gray swell of the river loomed up in his path. There must have been twenty paces of deep water, and, left or right, Durand saw no sign of bridge or ford.

Heremund reeled up behind. "If you intend to escape me," he gasped, "you can't just *stop* here. I'm too quick for that."

"We've got to get across!"

"All right," the skald panted. "But I insist. Don't tell me anything. Not a word. Nothing that might. Drive off the thought. Some fiend of the forest. Has taken hold of your troubled mind."

The little man braced his weight on his knees, eyebrows up around his hairline, then gave up hope of getting an explanation.

"Right," he said. "I reckon I know where we are."

They squandered half an hour searching for the bridge, half the time walking backward. Durand kept his neck craned for a glimpse, but saw no more sign.

Finally, the skald gestured to a broad expanse of turbulent water where a thousand small stones had forced the river out of its deep channel.

"Here. The Ford of Coystril, I think," the skald said. "A battle was fought here long ago. Fetch Hollow's somewhere near." The little man peered up in turn at both flanks of the valley. The ruins of low walls mazed the slopes.

Durand needed to hear nothing more. Weaving under the weight of his armor, he splashed into the river. By the time he had jogged up the far valley wall, blood and blackness crowded his vision. At the top, he found nothing but an empty road. The riders were gone.

"There is some sign that men have passed here," said Heremund, sweating, and it did look as though something had churned up the road. "Not many," said the skald, "maybe a score. Some were on good horses, I think. Not peasants and oxen anyway. Shod hooves."

Durand nodded. "This is where I saw them."

"We weren't looking for oxen, then?" The little man paused. "Knights perhaps?"

"Aye."

"Glad you've seen fit to confide in me at last."

The road forked near where they stood, one branch heading overland away from the river. Heremund waded into the morass, fingering the gouges and sockets cut in the mud by the passing horses.

"We've got to overtake them," Durand said.

"They've taken the Tormentil road. A fair-sized town hunkered on the edge of the forest a couple of leagues west of here."

Durand checked Heaven's Eye, gauging that they had an hour or two before dusk.

"Of course," said Heremund, "they could be stopping before then or turning up another road to go somewhere else altogether."

"Tormentil," said Durand, feeling the sound of it. If it had a reputation, word of it had never reached him.

"Big enough there's likely to be a tavern of sorts most nights. Decent place. Nothing else close."

Durand allowed himself a crooked smile.

"They're heading for Tormentil, then," said Durand, "or we won't catch them."

"Three leagues!" exclaimed the exhausted skald.

"Aye, Heremund, but maybe when the Eye goes down, there'll be beer."

DARK AND DOUBT came on.

They slithered along the grassy verge of a track in full flood. Bald-faced rooks tumbled in bare branches, ill-omened things.

Durand wondered what he was chasing. A band of knights might be some lord and his men traveling to Red Winding, but it could as easily be nearly anything else. Still, he had not seen anything like a chance before this, and there were times when a man must take a stand.

The rooks could have been laughing at him.

"Durand."

It felt like he had swung poor Brag over his shoulder, instead of just his packs, and a fist of hunger worked its fingers in his guts. His eyes felt hot as candle flames. With every step his shield slapped him on the—

"—Durand. Hold up," said Heremund.

The little man hopped into the track and crouched low, careful not to sink his knees in the muck. There was no way to tell what he was after.

"Aye?" said Durand.

"I think we've got lucky."

Durand nearly laughed at the idea. "What do you see?"

"We'll have supper after all. I may even give you a share, seeing as you've been such good company."

Durand was about to interrupt when Heremund stuck a finger into the air. He made a show of snorting air up his nose.

"You smell it?"

Durand smelled nothing and scowled.

"Cow dung," prompted Heremund.

"How hungry *are* you?"

"It'll be a village close by, and I'll bet my eyes it's Tormentil." Heremund looked around himself and spotted something in the hedge a few strides off. "Here! That's clinched it for certain."

The little man had tramped up to what looked like a low roadside shrine. A squat stone construction slumped around a dark niche. As he reached the thing, though, Heremund stumbled back.

"Gods!"

Durand let his bundles down into the grass and waded nearer, swallowing an odd wave of panic. At first he could see little. There was a squat trunk of masonry, and a black gap at about the height of a man's belt. As Durand moved closer, the shadows kept their secret—for a moment. A scent touched Durand's nostrils. Sharp.

It was not uncommon for people to set flowers or loops of trail-woven grass rope at a roadside icon. Sometimes the thing might be given honey or bread. But what Durand smelled was the reek of excrement.

"King of Heaven," Durand murmured, wincing, but he did not retreat. The stink was foul, but there was more to it than the reek of a latrine pit. He clenched his teeth.

Within the niche, the light of the slivered moon glistened on round edges. There would be an icon in there somewhere, some Power's face staring out, likely rubbed smooth by the touch of many fingers. With the shrine at a roadside, there was a good chance Durand was staring into the face of the Traveler.

As he peered, the confusion of glistening points took shape. Over a knob of stone gleamed blood, buttery smears of excrement, and something else: a livid rag that obscured the face of the little Power. He looked; there was something about the shape. Then he saw: a narrow slit in the pale rag was feathered with short hairs. Durand stumbled backward, too late. There had been eyelashes in that scrap of skin.

"Mad," said Heremund. "Someone's mad."

"Who'd do a thing like this?" Durand said. Who would dare? Every soul in the Atthias had heard stories of lords who'd stabled their horses in sanctuaries and woken up blind. Or men who had offered coin to some shrine or other and then gone back on their word only to find themselves crippled or bereaved soon after. Durand could not imagine toying with the Powers of Heaven.

"Hells," said Heremund. "Let's get away from here. Someone's playing with the Powers. There's a town not far off, and I aim to be in it before I say another word about this place."

He got no argument from Durand.

5. Peers of the Leopard

Knowing there was a madman in the forest with them, they walked with their eyes on the trees. There was a murderer loose. Or a grave robber. A madman or a necromancer.

The howl of a wolf broke loose among the branches.

"Gods. Enough is enough," said Heremund.

Durand could hear the drum of padded feet and the huff of breath gulping round the loop of a long tongue. "Run," he said, and both men took off.

The pounding came closer still, and closer. The full, wild power of the wolf's howl screamed out. Any moment, teeth would snap in their throats.

Then, suddenly, there were buildings.

It was the town. Firelight swung ahead of Durand, and he bolted for it, throwing down his bundles. He nearly lifted Heremund off his feet.

And then they were surrounded.

A dozen armed men were lurching from round a bonfire. There were houses. The firelight seemed to slither on blade edges, and—for an instant—Durand could see that every man was scared out of his head.

"We've got you, you bastard!" someone shouted, and the whole camp of soldiers leapt on him. He had an instant to think of Heremund—the man must have stopped—then something stabbed a shock down his shoulder. Though he threw his fist, blows rained down on him like hammers on an anvil—he even saw the sparks.

Then it all stopped.

Durand breathed with his face in the muck. Someone was laughing. Clucking his tongue. When Durand peered up, there wasn't a soul looking his way, for every eye was on a small man beyond the bonfires. This was no giant who could stop a mob of soldiers, but a clerk or priest. A small man, all in black; the empty sleeves of his gardecorps robe swung nearly to the ground. The hanging robe and spindly shins made him look like one of the roadside rooks. He cocked a pale, bald head.

"Ah, yes. Fear and rage," the man cooed. "Two faces on one thin coin."

A leather brown soldier with a shock of blond hair turned on the Rook. "You'd best get inside before something happens to you, priestling."

Though Durand liked the soldier's chances against the stranger, the scrawny Rook showed no sign of fear.

"You will have noticed, I think, that a cur will snarl when he is afraid."

"Right," said the soldier. "We've had enough of you."

The Rook clucked his tongue. "You are so eager. Such a hurry. It comes to us all in the end, you know."

The soldier only slipped a mace from his belt.

In that taut moment, the door to the house burst open, spilling a rectangle of lamplight into the road. Someone stepped out, vanishing in the shadow of the building for a moment, only to reappear in the firelight: a square-shouldered man in the arms and armor of ten kingdoms.

"What is all this?" the newcomer growled—his eyes were all glints and creases: glass chips in a leather glove. "Have I got to watch you like your mothers?"

He narrowed one glinting sliver at the Rook. "You. That's enough. Old Mulcer's not so useless we can afford to chuck him."

With a shrugging flourish of upturned palms, The Rook bowed, and the blond soldier backed off. This explained things: The Rook was cocksure because he had friends. The newcomer's glinting eyes turned on Durand. "And you. I don't think I've had the pleasure."

Warily, Durand climbed to his feet, as the fierce old captain looked him up and down.

"Durand," Durand supplied. "Of the Col."

It was as he looked down on the captain that he noticed how the helmets shone full of firelight. He saw blades and pommels, and a good score of horses standing off behind the house. And, through all the bruises, he grinned: These were his knights.

"And you started this?" said the captain.

"Begging your pardon, Lordship." This was his chance. "I stumbled on your men here. I meant no harm. I can fight."

Around the circle of soldiers, there would be a half-dozen black eyes.

"So I see." The man eyed Durand a moment longer, then smirked. There was nothing between his eyeteeth but a black slot.

"I'm called Gol. Sir Gol of Lazaridge, and I serve Lord Radomor, son of the Duke of Yrlac who rules the lands west of the Banderol."

Durand knew the name "Radomor." The man was a hero. He had even married the elder daughter of Durand's duke, a wedding Durand half-remembered.

"And I reckon hired," said Gol. "It just happens that we're about to lose a man. But, friend Durand, ancient practice has it you've got to buy a round for your new comrades, 'specially when you've given them a fright and a few bruises."

Durand thought of the empty pouch on his belt, and wondered whether anything would ever be simple. "I've had some hard luck, this last moon," he said.

Gol chuckled. "That's easily solved, friend." He slipped something from his belt and sent it sailing through the smoke and firelight. There was a clink as Durand caught the thing: a purse, he saw as he opened his fist.

"Now you're bought and paid for, lad."

One of the men nearby fished the thing from Durand's palm, tossing it for weight. "One round?" he said. "It ought to do."

"Drink up," Gol said, and then to Durand: "You look hungry enough to work, but we'll see, I think. We're hunting a thief here in Tormentil."

This got a look from every man around the fires.

"Aye, lads. We've found the root of the trouble: why it's been so hard for these folk to pay the king's tax, why the harvest has been so poor lately. Seems our own bailiff has been cheating. Fining his friends and neighbors for this and that, and none of it ever getting back to His Lordship. And this bailiff, he runs the mill as well as all the rest of it. And His Lordship's peasants say this bailiff's been shorting them for two years. Every mother's son grumbling against his lord and master when it was this thieving whoreson responsible. Poisoning His Lordship's good name. Getting folks worked up against the king. And now this thieving little oath-breaker's got himself caught with his fingers in it."

Taking a thief might be a good start.

"Hey!" said one of the soldiers. "I've found another one."

Just beyond the ring of fires, Heremund stepped from behind a cart.

AS THE OTHERS drank up, Durand dashed off to collect his gear from the roadside. With a dozen or more armed men behind him, he no longer feared the forest. Heremund darted after him the instant Durand stepped from the camp.

"Durand, Gods, it's him!" he said, scuttling close.

"Who?" He thought he saw one of his bags up the track.

"The prophecy." The skald's tone was desperate. "It was Radomor."

Durand took an instant to recall.

"It was his father's court I was at!" said Heremund. "We've blundered right into it."

Durand ducked, reaching for a bag slumped in a pool of dirty water. As he caught hold of the thing, he realized that he had found his hauberk. It streamed as he wrenched it from the ditch.

"Heremund, this Radomor's practically a kinsman. I was at the wedding." He remembered now that the duke's girl had dark hair. "And he's a hero, isn't he?"

"Aye, but—"

"Nearly died saving the king at the Battle of Hallow Down," Durand recalled. The duke put on a great feast down in Acconel, and the skalds shook the rafters.

"Yes, Durand, but—"

"It's a noble house. There was a king, wasn't there?" Now, Durand argued as he stooped and plucked his belongings.

"Old King Carondas was his grandsire, Durand."

Durand threw his hands wide, his point proven. "Carondas's face is still on half the pennies in Errest. We've hunted a lord's train for a hundred leagues, and not had a sniff. I can hardly leave him."

"Lad, I don't—"

"Besides," Durand reasoned, "I've taken his money."

"I saw that," muttered the skald. "You won't go hungry with this lot."

Durand was not concerned. A new man must be tried. He had most of his things by now, bedroll to iron mail all sopping wet.

"I was never going to make it to this tournament of yours, was I? And how long would I last without a penny? I'd be dead or begging before the next moon. And it's done you no good traveling with me, has it?"

Heremund caught Durand by the tunic. "It was me, boy. Don't you understand? I was the fool with the vision. I fear I've done a terrible thing."

"Heremund! You've told me yourself. He's a hero. Think. What sense does your prophecy make?"

"No, boy. It's all coming back. All of it."

The frantic skald caught sight of something in the mud, and absently ducked to fish it out. It was some kind of strap.

Durand squared with the little minstrel. The alehouse campfires flickered beyond him. He took a breath. "All right, Heremund. Tell me what you saw. If it was so terrible, tell me."

Heremund blinked where he squatted with the muddy strap. "I remember snatches. Darkness and war. Gates and walls and towers. Fire. And the words. I don't know where the words came from."

At the camp, Gol was back among the men, bellowing and kicking laggards into motion.

"Heremund," Durand said, "this Lazar Gol has taken me on, straight from the wild forest. You saw it. The Powers have set this in my path for a reason," he said.

Durand reached down and took the strap from Heremund's hand. With a sucking plop, his shield burst from the mud. As Durand lifted the thing, Heremund rubbed at its face, baring stags' heads under the filth.

Down the road, Gol's tone was harsher now.

"They want me," said Durand.

Heremund was nodding as Durand left him and walked into the firelight.

"RIGHT," SAID GOL. "Most of you are pie-eyed, and you'll pay later. But I'll need a few lads. So, who'll I take on this little midnight stroll?" He peered through slit eyes, then reached out, tapping a man on the surcoat. "You. And you. And you."

He stopped, turning on Durand.

"And you, our new friend."

Gol swaggered through the others till he stood below the crossed arms of a giant Valduran, complete with jutting beard and wide shaven forehead. "And you, Fulk An'Tinan? You're still with us, ain't you?"

The big man stopped, thick lips stiff as a dead man's fingers. Durand wouldn't have been taunting him. He had heard it said that the Valdurans had held their mountain strongholds against all comers since long before Saerdan set eyes on old Errest. From their mountains, the warriors of the high passes watched nations rise and fall like tides round an island. And besides, the man's belt could girth an ox.

"I know it's your last night with us," Gol said, "but the night's not over yet. They'll all tell you His Lordship's hired me to play captain, so I'm here to squeeze every penny. And you, my friend, still owe His Lordship a few hours."

The Valduran hardly blinked. "It should have ended on Hallow Down. We, all of us, gathered to fight Borogyn and his Heithans. A little coin in the fighting season. Now we are this man's bond-warriors, bought while his last war-band were still cooling in the earth, his every bondman slain round him while he lived. It should have ended on the Down."

Gol turned away from the wild talk of the outlander, favoring his men with a mocking look. Durand wondered how a Valduran found himself so far from his homeland.

"It'll be just strong arms on this, lads," said Gol. "Shouldn't be anything fatal. A midnight stroll. Right? Now, if we're going to find a miller, we ought to find his mill. Come on."

The grim outlander shouldered his sword.

Gol cupped his hand at his ear, listening for the stream and spinning wheel.

"This way, lads!"

They tramped through the berms and fences of the village until they found the looming mill, its wheel bashing away out of sight on some tributary of the Banderol. A curt gesture of Gol's hand had two men at the front door. Durand was pleased to see that Gol's troop wasn't all drinking and bluster. They moved with speed and silence.

"We've come from Lord Radomor," shouted Gol. Inside

there was a slamming sound. "Break it!" Gol roared, but the door held.

Gol shoved his finger at Durand and the Valduran. "You two. Around back!" And they were off. Durand bolted around the mill, blundering through tangled bushes and a heap of eel traps on the way. There were one, two corners, and then a straight charge for river.

A gaping face appeared.

"Ballocks!" it said, and vanished.

Durand darted after. There was a sill of earth along the foundation next to the vast waterwheel flinging spray. The crooked bailiff had come out a back door, but Gol's men were already there—pounding at the new obstacle—before the man could turn. The bailiff was trapped between Durand and his own mill wheel.

"Come on then," said Durand, loud against the racket of the wheel.

The bailiff glanced once between Durand and the flickering blades, then—impossibly—he turned to the spinning flash and jumped. Men on the far side of the wheel roared. The bailiff soared. His foot touched a flying paddle, and he winged skyward so that, in an instant, his hands were on the shaggy eaves of the mill's roof and he was gone.

"King of Heaven," said the knights who appeared behind Durand. "Never seen the like."

Durand scowled up at the eaves three fathoms over his head. Letting a man slip through his fingers was no way to prove himself.

"What one man can do, another can match," he said.

With a breath caught in his teeth, he jumped.

And missed—almost.

His foot shot down a greasy rail. There was an instant of spinning horror. His knee caught. He clung, twisted, and the wheel carried him high. Torchlight flashed on wavelets. He saw eel traps under the river's skin. Then the shaggy eaves loomed like a bear, and he threw himself, heaving his chest over the roof's edge. The wheel under his heels looked hungry for bone.

"Champion of Heaven, teach me courage," Durand grunted.

Then he was up and peering over the humpbacked roof for the bailiff. He might have been on an empty island.

"Oh very good," Sir Gol announced from the road. "Come down you daft bastard." It took a heartbeat for Durand to realize that the captain wasn't talking to him. And that he must be able to see the bailiff.

Durand crawled the soggy rooftop toward the ridge. Spidery plants caught in the forks of his splayed fingers. It was a long time since anyone had paid a thatcher to mend this heap.

"Come down and give up the bloody coin," Gol continued. "Maybe I'll say I never found you. That was some trick, but the game's up, I think."

Durand peered over the roof-peak, picking out a pale shape sprawled over mold-black thatch. The man was staring down on Gol and his men.

"Come on, I'd hate to have to fire the mill, and you can't live up there forever. We've got you."

The sprawled form made no move. The thieving miller-bailiff judged that no one would be coming after him—not soon—and that Gol was going to wait a long while before burning down their master's mill.

Silent, Durand climbed to his feet.

"You should've been a sailor, friend," Gol said. "We've never seen anything like it." There was something said among the men that Durand couldn't make out—and laughing.

Durand stole down the slope of the roof, fighting against noise and bad balance. It was like walking on rotten mattresses, but he let the shouts from the street and the thunder of the mill wheel smother the little pops and crackles of the straw.

Finally, he could see over the roof's edge. Gol's men were pacing and staring up; they spotted him.

The bailiff must have seen the same thing. He twitched then, spinning onto his back, and Durand realized he wasn't in a good position.

He felt the bailiff's hands on him. The man's boot swung up for his guts—a wrestler's throw with a wild six-fathom fall at the end for Durand if he couldn't get loose.

They were locked together. For an instant, he and his victim were poised on the brink, then Durand's strength won out, and he wrenched the bailiff's shoulders off the roof and into the air. Durand's smile twisted, and he shoved the man up, pressing him high.

Gol's boys smiled up. A few flapped their hands, beckoning.

"Right," said Durand, and, with a chuckle, he pitched the fugitive down into a trio of laughing soldiers.

When he got down, the lads were shoving wineskins in his face and clapping him on the back.

"You, friend, are the most fearless squirrel in all the Atthias!" announced the blond soldier, Mulcer, who had squared off with the Rook. "Who needs ladders? He's a one man siege tower, this one!"

Gol laughed with the rest, before the whole lot of them rounded slowly on the bailiff.

"Where is it then, eh?" Gol said. "We went to a lot of trouble to get our hands on your neck. You think we're going to let you go without wringing the money out of you?"

They had circled the bailiff.

"Right boys," said Gol. "Let's hear what he has to say."

Two men caught the bailiff's arms and held him tight.

"The money's mine, Lordship," said the bailiff.

One of the men jerked his fist back, but Gol raised his hand. "No. I want to hear this."

"A man's allowed to save," answered the bailiff.

"Clever."

"It's true!" the bailiff protested.

"How'd you come by it all?"

"I get a share, don't I?"

Gol tapped his temple. "Ah. Now there's the trouble. You forget. I know what you're paid. It ain't enough, friend. Not nearly."

"Lordship, it were never that much!"

"But I've seen it, friend. Or as good as. Your little friends in town are telling tales. A penny here. A penny there." The bailiff's eyes hardened for an instant. "Don't you worry just who now. They lined up to do it. Nobody likes a bailiff. Or a miller. Especially one with his thumb on the scales. Buying short measure. Stealing the sweat off their backs. Fining them blue. A bit of advice: When you've been stealing pennies from your neighbors, you don't want to go jingling them under their noses, friend. They tend to remember. You'd have done much better robbing your master and spreading it about a bit. We'd never catch a man at that." He rapped a knuckle heavily against the man's breastbone. "Where's the money?"

"Let me go, and I'll tell you where it is."

"So you do have it," concluded Gol. "And you know where."

"*Let me go.*"

"Where?"

"Out the back. For God's sake. There's a bag. Please. I shoved it up an eel trap and rolled the lot into the river."

Gol glanced up to Durand and a couple of the others who went and pulled up all the traps, finding nothing but a half-dozen lashing eels. When they splashed back, Gol was squatting like a stone by his prisoner, and there was a rumble from the village road. For an instant, the glitter of Gol's eyes was the only motion.

Then there was a pounding.

From the dark came a tall stallion and a storm of cloak billowing about the shoulders of a horseman like a giant. Durand and the other trap-pullers stood dripping as the horseman's cloak settled, like great wings folding. He was bald as a skull, and a beard bristled round his lips. This was Lord Radomor. Some old wound—the one he took for the king—had hitched one shoulder, but he still had the look of a man who could tear up trees with his bare hands.

Gol drew himself up to face his master, but risked a quick look to Mulcer.

The blond man shook his head. "Nothing."

Gol muttered, "Balls," and bowed low to his lord.

"Lordship!" Gol said.

Radomor's voice rumbled: "Is this the one?" The lord's stallion seemed to have caught his master's mood. It looked ready to leap out of its skin.

"Aye, Lordship," said Gol. "It's him. He's admitted as much."

Radomor's dark eyes glinted as he turned on the thief, but then for a long time he said nothing. The bailiff was blinking, straining.

"You robbed them in my name," said Radomor. "You

cheated and swindled and stole and poisoned, all the while saying 'Speak to Lord Radomor. It is he who cheats and swindles and breaks you. It's he your children should remember in their curses.' "

The bailiff twisted, pinioned on his knees as his lord loomed from horseback. "No, Lordship! I swear it!"

"Swear nothing! You've broken oaths that set your soul at hazard, and now you would say more? You put treason in their hearts. I heard their rumblings in my father's hall, far off in Ferangore. Men speaking against taxes. Men speaking against their lord, and their duke, and their king in Eldinor."

Radomor turned to Gol. "Has this man returned what he has stolen?"

Gol spread his arms. "He has told us where it's hid, but there's nothing—"

Now the prisoner lashed like a gaffed fish. "God. It was there! I swear it!"

While the others jumped to restrain him, Sir Radomor's naked skull only tilted a degree or two.

"How does it feel to lose what you have slaved for? To be betrayed?" He stopped, drawing a gust of air through flared nostrils. For a moment, his eyes shut. When they opened, the time for argument had ended.

"It is treason to steal from your sworn lord," said Radomor. "Treason to violate a position of trust. And you have confessed." He hesitated then a moment. "These peasants of yours, do you think any of them will have starved on your account? Children. Women. Do you think it came to that?"

Durand glanced to the bailiff, and saw the man bent now, head sagging nearly to the road. They would take him to the duke's throne at Ferangore. They would summon a priest-arbiter, and he would be condemned before the law.

"Do you know what all this means?" Radomor pressed.

The thief began to look up, but Radomor had finished with him, and it was to Gol that Radomor spoke next.

"I am lord of this land. In my name he stole. In my name hang him."

———

WITHIN THE HOUR, a broad ring of peasants stood in the village green, wavering in the tunics they had slept in. They might have been specters. At the center of the green, Durand and the rest of Gol's men stood under a great tree. Some of the men were breathing hard.

The bailiff kicked over their heads, hanged without priest or law.

Finally, Gol set his hands on his hips and nodded.

"Right," he said, his voice pitched to the crowd. "Your bailiff-miller's caught."

Murmurs rose in the crowd.

"It's done. And Lord Radomor wants to make it right with the coin." The old soldier was pacing a circle. "Some of it's his by right, but he's ordered that every penny stays in Tormentil."

Now the villagers were waking up.

"But." Gol jabbed a finger in the air. "*But!* Some bastard's sneaked off with it all. Now. His Lordship's no fool. He understands temptation as well as I do. And stealing from a thief hardly seems a crime, does it? So, I'm giving you fair warning. That coin winds up in my hands by dawn, and every man and child gets his share, no questions. If not, if some bugger's got it hoarded away somewhere, I'll have no choice. Right? I'll tell Lord Radomor you're in revolt." He nodded toward the bailiff. "Treason against your rightful lord. And I'll torch this place. I will."

A murmur rose from the circle of peasants. Durand wondered how many there were—a hundred at least and not a few broad-shouldered. Gol had fifteen.

"I *know* it's a bad time. Harvest hasn't been good. There's been rumbling among the wellborn. But it'll be a bloody long winter with your stores burnt up, won't it? Yes? So that's why His Lordship's made sure I'm giving you fair warning. He won't be stolen from. Dawn. I'll roust the priest and have him call the time. By my reckoning, it's midnight now. That leaves you the last six hours of night to come up with what's owed. Look close at your neighbors. You know their hidey-holes. You know who's got light fingers, and who's got debts to pay.

"But if Heaven's Eye rises on this business without a bloody clear sign of contrition, you'll regret it."

There was not a soul on the green who doubted him; Gol had not covered the bailiff's head before hauling him up. In his features, the lesson was simple: A little man did not disgrace the name of a great lord.

⊛ 6. A Tower in Ferangore

"A rough night," said Mulcer.

Durand had found a spot to roll out his blankets. Most of Gol's men were sleeping in the yard. "It's not every night you see a man hanged," he admitted.

Mulcer winked. "You've led a sheltered life, then, eh?"

Despite himself, Durand laughed.

"I'm afraid our Radomor's past trials and arbiters. I reckon there's been too much of this lately: peasants sharpening their billhooks, the wellborn grumbling. A man can run out of patience."

"Will Gol really burn the town?"

"I used to be a man like you. Just starting. I used to half-expect dragons and princesses. But I've yet to see either. Where you from, did you say?"

"I'm from the Col. My father's the baron."

"You're what then, a bastard? A second son?"

"I think I'm more the latter," Durand said.

Mulcer smiled. "I'd say so. He couldn't find anything for you?"

"It's a small barony. He had a widower's land for me, but the old man's long-lost son turned up. He was supposed to be shipwrecked."

"*Damn me*," said Mulcer. "That's that Hearnan you're talking about, isn't it? Me and Gol served with him once or twice down toward the Inner Seas. Caravan guard, I think. There was a fight near Camberlee." He shook his head. "He was always mooning after some plot of land someplace, but it seemed a long way off. Seems he's found it at last. Has to be ten years!"

Durand shook his head. "Fifteen, I'd guess."

"Well, there's him happy at last. Maybe there's hope for us all."

"Maybe," said Durand.

Just then the Rook passed by, leering Mulcer's way. After a taunting hesitation, he vanished into the alehouse. Heremund looked on.

IT WAS FULL dark when Durand woke up, hearing sounds among the horses.

Someone was moving around the camp. He thought of how many villagers there were in Tormentil—of how many friends the dangling bailiff might have had. He was tired beyond reason, but he had taken Radomor's pay and wasn't going to let anyone slit their throats.

He made his way to the makeshift corral, but found no one. Still, the horses picketed in the yard were awake. One brute tossed its head as Durand peered in. A few others nodded or snorted in the dark beyond. Something had been among them.

Just then, he thought he heard the clop of hooves in the street, and he followed the sound around the building. Perhaps the man who had taken the money was slipping away. He had not heard enough to wake the camp, but was glad when a woodpile provided a convenient hatchet.

The sound lured him on through the black village. He tried not to remember the madness in the forest beyond the town, concentrating his senses on the road in front of him. As he heard the millstream ahead, he made out the calligraphy of leafless trees against the clouds. There was a pale shape moving.

Suddenly, he wished he had woken the others. He tested the balance of the hatchet.

A man stood at the flank of a big horse. He turned. Durand recognized the broad forehead of the giant Valduran, and Durand understood. The big man had been with them at the mill. He had seen the miller messing about in back. There had been time—while Durand was playing ape on the rooftop—to spot what the miller had been doing and stash the hoard in the trees.

"It's you," Durand said. "You've got it, haven't you? . . ."

In the gloom, the big outlander's face was as expressionless as the moon. He tugged the heavy saddlebags straighter.

"Did you not hear what Gol said? They're going to burn for this."

The giant squared with Durand. He was as big a man as Durand had ever seen. Small bones clicked in the knots of his hair. The pommel of an enormous sword projected beyond the slope of one of his mountainous shoulders.

Durand lifted the silly hatchet. He could not turn his back on an entire village. He could not slink off when he was challenged.

He wished he had his shield.

"The money's in your bags. Gol might not have hung that miller," Durand said. The words were a low growl.

Fulk only reached back, his hand moving for the hilt of the outsized sword. Durand planned to say more. The Sons of Atthi must speak a challenge, but, the instant Fulk's fingers touched the hilt, the razor wing of his blade whipped from its scabbard and through Durand's face.

But Durand had flinched away.

The foreigner blinked slow. He stood in some outlandish swordsman's pose. The long sword hovered overhand, and they stared at each other down the winking length of the blade, Fulk's dark eyes flat and pitiless.

Durand felt his heart beat, and then the pause was finished.

The big man caught his breath, then threw himself into motion, lashing, stamping, and wheeling, bowlegged in his baggy breeches. Each stroke sheared off another region of Creation, leaving no earth to stand upon and nowhere to run. Every instant flickered with death.

On a downswing, Durand found himself reeling closer to the monster, face-to-face. He jabbed the axe for Fulk's jaws, but, with a twist of hilt and blade, the axe was caught.

For a heartbeat, Durand hung from the axe handle.

Then a huge fist drove into his ribs, and, in a staggering moment, the moon flashed down to stab sick blackness into his skull.

The trees burst like clouds of soot.

He must be falling. Soft boots stalked very close.

He squinted against pain to see a sword glitter high among the treetops.

A voice said, "Enough!"

Durand could hear the giant's breathing, labored in the silence. He tried to focus his attention.

"Lemme guess." It was the captain . . . Gol. "You're not a man who'd go very far just out of rage, Fulk An'Tinan. You've got all the spark of a millpond carp."

Breathing answered, and a slow grind of gravel: Fulk's weight shifting in his soft boots.

"All this for a sack of pennies? If you'd stayed with us, you could have had a hall somewhere. Land. You would have made this miller's takings a hundred times over before you died."

Fulk grunted.

"Was it worth your life?" asked Gol.

Finally, Fulk spoke. "Is it worth yours to stop me, Lazar Gol?" His voice was thick and full of lips. The Valduran had a point, though. Gol had caught him, but any fisherman could hook a shark.

"Clever, Fulk. Put that sword down and we'll hang you nice and tidy. With your weight, it'll be over in no time."

"He is lost, this master you've chosen."

"It's not your business, friend, to judge your betters."

"I have seen it. The shadows are hard to read in these knotted lowlands, but my eyes follow them. He was lost on that field with his men. This is a cheat, all of it."

"And now you're running off."

The big man caught his breath. Durand knew the sound.

Grunts and scrabbling boots flurried. Then Durand heard a sound like a pitchfork biting straw—once, twice, three times, and a body fell. There was hardly any gasping—hardly any scrabbling at the earth and choking.

Hands seized Durand's head with enough of a jerk to make his guts lurch. Thumbs pressed, near to crushing.

"King of Heaven," Durand grunted.

"No such luck," said Gol's voice. A slap flashed sparks through Durand's head, and Gol grinned down.

"Your skull's in one piece. No soft spots. Bloody amazing. You'll live. And when you get up? Bury this gloomy bugger, right?"

Durand's head flopped back, and he heard someone smack a horse into motion.

Fulk was dead and steaming like a downed ox, and Gol had no mark on him.

DURAND WOVE HIS way back through the berms and fences of Tormentil, sick. On the fringes, among sheds and apple boughs, a black wind stirred. Durand felt the grip of eyes on him. In a moment, the wind had curled away into nothing, like a serpent of ashes. It was so dark.

"*Durand,*" said a voice. "This way."

With relief, he recognized the whisper for Heremund's. The blot of Heremund's silhouette stooped against the blank page of a wall. Durand must have reached the tavern.

"While you were gone—"

"What?" Durand breathed, exhausted. "What is it?"

"Another one."

"Host Below, Heremund." He didn't even have the hatchet. "Another what?"

"That man in the black gardecorps. The counselor or physic? On my oath, the devils must be twins. He just rode in from Ferangore. Caught like a black rag on the back of a wild horse." Durand saw Heremund's black shape twitch low. "Here. At the window."

As Durand lowered himself against the wall, there was a voice. "It is so, Milord." The speaker might have been in the yard with them; Durand hunkered lower. Heremund held a finger over his lips.

"Stop!" The word throbbed in the darkness of the tavern, deeper than cellars. Radomor was inside. "I have told you what it will mean if you repeat these things."

"Yes, Lord. Without proof."

"You know not what you say." The voice ebbed; there were footfalls. "My son. My wife."

"There is proof now, Lord. We cannot hold our tongues."

"I have known Aldoin of Warrendel since we were children."

"They have been seen together. She sits in her window high above your father's city."

"That she may do. She may do as she pleases."

"There is a sign."

"Oh no," said Heremund.

"A sign . . ." Radomor's voice was weary, but then it hardened: "I will see it, this sign. I'll see it with my own eyes, or you'll pay with yours! No matter what you've done in the past, all my debts to you will be canceled and you both will pay!" He paused. Durand imagined the man jabbing forked fingers at the Rooks' bulging eyes. If the Rooks were calling Rado-mor's wife an adulteress, it was the least they deserved.

Right above Durand's head, the shutters burst open. Plaster and splinters rained down his neck.

"Gol!" said the duke. "Rouse the men. We ride for Feran-gore!"

Durand dredged his memory for the dark-haired daughter of the Duke of Gireth. She was practically kin. He had been at her wedding. The Rooks were lying.

BY DUSK, A city bristled like a mountain in the midst of the plain before them. Lord Radomor raised a gauntleted fist, and the party jingled to a halt. Durand was alone on a borrowed packhorse, beyond his homeland, and riding to catch the daughter of the Duke of Gireth in adultery, riding to prove the Rooks had lied. Gol had set a firm hand on Heremund's chest, saying, "Whatever happens, there's no place for skalds where we're going. You can see that." It sounded bad.

Mulcer ducked close. "That's Ferangore," he said. Durand reckoned that whoever had thrown up the first walls knew his business. Caught in a fork of rivers, the city hulked atop a good steep hill: as natural a fortress as a man would ever find in the plains of Yrlac. And you could see it was old. You could see the hill fort under it, all banks and ditches. Now, though, that hill fort was girded in stone walls and ramparts. Roofs bristled in tiers, and the spire of the high sanctuary jutted like a lance-head where that first old chieftain must have sat his throne.

Durand sucked a sharp breath through his nostrils, eyes wide despite the bruises Fulk had left him. Night was coming on.

"There will be blood before morning," said Mulcer.

"Alwen did nothing," Durand said.

"You hope."

To the Nine Sleepers, and the Maiden, and the Mother, Du-rand had prayed that Alwen was blameless.

"My family's served the dukes of Gireth since Gunderic's

day. I lived in his hall fourteen bloody years. There are always stories about wellborn women."

"Not every marriage contract brings love with the land and titles."

"It's lies," Durand declared.

Ahead, Radomor pulled off a fine green traveling cloak, his breath catching as he swung the thing from his shoulders. The twist in the man's back and shoulder had Durand wincing. "Ever since the Downs," explained Mulcer. "They say it should have killed him." Grimly, the duke traded his cloak for a hairy rag Gol hauled from his packs.

"What's this?" Mulcer said. Some order rippled down the line. Mulcer listened, then explained. "We're to march in incognito. You're all right." Rough hands twisted emblems from bridles and stuffed them away. Hoods were pulled over scarred faces. A man blacked the white blaze on the nose of Radomor's rouncy. It bode ill. The road ahead swung over muddy fields toward the lowest gate.

Some tempting fiend turned Durand's thoughts to escape. With a little work, he could slip from Mulcer and take his chances on the road. He had sworn no oaths yet. If he left the packhorse he rode behind, his sin would be a small one.

Just then, Gol appeared. "All right Mulcer, I've got to talk to your new friend here." He grinned. "And, Durand, lad, I'll need that nag you're riding."

With a glance to Mulcer, Durand climbed down. Gol joined him in the road. The captain took the reins of Durand's packhorse, and offered the reins of his own gray hackney instead.

"Get up, boy. We're trading horses. You're to take us in."

"Sir?"

"They don't know you round here. Climb on, get up front, and lead us in."

Durand obeyed, cantering his borrowed horse to the front of the line where Sir Radomor had stopped in the process of changing cloaks. It was hard to imagine any trade of cloaks disguising this man. There was a banked fury in him that made a man think of savages beyond the Fiery Gulf.

"Lord Radomor," Gol said. "This lad's the one chased our monkey down from your mill."

Lord Radomor leveled his gaze on Durand.

"And it was him that heard our friend Fulk," Gol added. "Durand, from the Col of the Blackroots, he says. Knows no one inside. He'll take us into Ferangore. I don't think anyone will bother about the black eyes."

"Do it," growled the lord. His eyes were chips of flint.

"Yes, Lordship," Gol answered.

"Yes, Lordship," echoed Durand.

Bowing their leave, the two men rode to the very head of the column, past any hope of escape, where the captain made to leave Durand behind.

"What'll I tell the guards?" Durand asked.

"Something'll come to you," Gol said, and took his place in the line.

Two dozen hard faces stared at Durand, looking round the nasals of old helms or watching from under ragged hoods. Breath steamed in the air. And, for a moment, greater questions were driven from his mind.

At the head of a conroi of armed men, Durand cantered for the hill city. He guessed at what the gatekeepers might say: Who was he? What was his business? He cursed, seeing slammed portcullises and shot bolts in his mind's eye. A quick glance at the thugs behind him told him the truth: The sentries on the gates would be as likely to shoot as slam the doors.

He swore again.

And then they were at the gate, and an apish man in a brimmed kettle-helm was scrambling out of a low door inside. Helmets blossomed on the battlements twenty feet overhead.

"What in the Hells are you lot up to then, eh?" said the ape. "We was about to close up." There was a crossbow in the man's fists.

Gol's horse snorted steam, tossing its head.

"Well?" The ape gestured with his crossbow. Idly, Durand considered that at this range, the bolt would either blow right through his throat, or he'd end up with a wad of wet feathers tucked under his chin. Either would serve him right.

From behind, Gol whispered, "Go on."

The steel head of the bolt winked like a penny.

"What's your business here? You selling turnips? The duke don't like no trouble in his town. Right?"

The duke. Durand snatched at that flicker of inspiration.

"Right," he said. "No trouble. We're here to see the duke."

The crossbow wavered. Now, if the man's hand twitched, the bolt would snap Durand's femur or maybe just kill Gol's horse.

"What?" the guard drawled. "Looking for work?"

That sounded good.

"Aye. Work. We hear there's work."

The ape nodded. "Only the duke ain't here. He's off to Mantlewell on the pilgrimage."

Mantlewell. Durand stared at the little man, wishing he had a chance to punch him. Radomor would be watching. Gol was on the packhorse right behind.

"We'll wait, then," Durand snapped. "Or talk to the captain of this watch."

"By rights I should show you out. . . ." The gatekeeper lowered the crossbow, but remained conspicuously in Durand's path. Slowly, the fellow cocked his head.

And Durand realized that the man was after coin. Durand shut his eyes. He didn't have a penny to throw the whoreson. He could feel the hot pressure of Gol's stare on the back of his neck.

Durand had a flash. He turned to Gol. "Boy, throw this man a few pennies for his patience." There was a cool locking of stares for an instant, then the captain plucked the purse from his belt and tossed it to the man.

"Happy?" Durand said.

"Thanks very much, Captain," the gatekeeper said. "Go on through, but you be sure your boys make no trouble, or it'll go hard on all of you. This is a clean town."

Durand grunted and kicked Gol's horse under the heavy gates and into the city, wondering if Lord Radomor would string up the gatekeeper.

SOON THEY WERE high in the tiered city, standing before the black door of an alehouse, with Durand back among the ranks. Mulcer grinned with a glance at Gol.

"Where?" Durand heard Lord Radomor say.

"There is a room," answered one of the preening Rooks. "I think you will find the chamber perfectly positioned."

When Radomor and the Rooks had disappeared, the others walked inside. The building was empty on a night when it should have been packed. Durand eyed a wooden stair at the rear. He heard footfalls on the floorboards overhead.

The men were left alone. Hands rested on the pommels of swords as though any moment might bring soldiers in through the windows. It looked as though the Rooks had hired the whole building just to spot this "sign" they'd wagered their little black eyes on. Durand felt dizzy. He felt the memory of Fulk's forehead throbbing between his swollen eyes. He tried to believe that the Rooks had seen their last night.

To ease the tension, Gol sent a couple of the men down the cellar to haul up something to drink.

"It's a real inn," one of the men called up the cellar's trapdoor. "Not some alehouse. There's nought but casks of wine down here."

"One," cautioned Gol, and the men at the trapdoor nodded. He crossed to the street windows. "Bar the door, *boy*," he murmured to Durand. "We don't want no patrons walking in, stirring up questions."

Durand swept up a bench and wedged it tight between flagstones and door handle. There would be no interruptions.

Gol was watching the ceiling. Mulcer had noticed the same thing.

"What is he—" Durand began.

"Ssh," hissed Gol. He looked to the others—now wrestling a long cask up through the trapdoor. "Shut up, all of you!" Hard men stood like startled deer. Gol's eyes turned back to the ceiling.

Over the street-side windows, boards creaked, sifting dust into the common room. Gol half-nodded and crossed to the shutters there. With a glance to the others, Durand found his own shutter and squinted out.

The inn would have been high on the old hill fort, but when Durand looked out he could see nothing but the pale sides of the buildings across the street. There was one tier above them, and it belonged to the duke. Beyond that highest wall were the precincts of the high sanctuary and the citadel of Ailnor, son of Carondas.

Durand waited for the sign the Rooks had promised—whatever it would be, and whatever it might mean. In the street beyond the shutters, the air sat heavy and cool. He could hear the men behind him slurping at cups and murmuring. The floorboards upstairs creaked. For a moment, Radomor's voice throbbed through the floor, then, quite suddenly, it was silent.

Mulcer gripped his arm.

In the street, there was music: pure notes singing high over the roadway. Durand moved his eye along the crack of the shutter, peering among the rooftops, certain he could find the source.

As two rooftops scissored apart, Durand saw a window high in a tower. A figure leaned there, silvered by moonlight. He saw the oval of her downcast face. There was hair like sable. God, he thought, what was this? She held a recorder to her lips. The tower was high in the castle of the dukes of Yrlac. She looked out, and seemed to stop. There was a little clap of her hands.

A roar shook the rafters of the inn, and Durand's guts froze. Lord Radomor thundered down the wooden stair, the Rooks—or their black robes—flying behind him. "The bench, boy," said Gol, and Durand jerked the thing free just in time for Radomor to slam the doors wide and storm into the street. The frozen soldiers in the common room chased after. Few missed the dagger glint of the Rooks' wild grins.

At the uppermost gates, a man tried to hold the doors, but fell back when he understood whose way he barred. There was no one who would stand before Lord Radomor that night.

The uppermost tier of the city was a single courtyard: A hundred paces of cobblestones stretched below the tolling bells of the Ferangore's high sanctuary. Loping among Radomor's men, Durand saw the fortress beyond. Guards and servants ran to keep pace, some tugging on surcoats or hopping on one shoe. Soon, Radomor mounted the steps of the castle's keep, his Rooks swarming behind.

The fortress darkness was near total as Durand and the others chased their master inside.

"Where does he come?" Radomor's voice demanded.

"The well, Lord," simpered a Rook. "A shaft to the cisterns beneath the city. He enters at his townhouse. It's a bit of a swim."

"The well plunges straight into deep water." The Rooks were taking turns. "It might even be too narrow for a man to turn around."

"If we were to block it in . . ." offered one.

"And fire the house, perhaps," said the other.

"—An oubliette, Lord. A place of forgetting."

"He will arrive at any time."

"Do it!" Radomor commanded. "If he comes, he has condemned himself."

Gol spun, his finger darting among the men: "You, you, and you." Durand had been missed. "The keep? You know it?" As each of the men nodded, freeing Durand from this duty, relief was like open air.

"There's a grate on the wellhead. Drop it. Bolt it. And close the door to that room behind you." The men hesitated. "Go! And you'd best guard that door once you're out."

Gol's jaw knotted as he squeezed his eyes shut to think. The eyes opened.

"You two," he picked another pair of soldiers. "You know Ferangore as well as I do. Fire this Warrendel's house. As for the rest of you. I'll have four men on the front door. Draw the bar. The rest can keep the peace in the hall."

"I think," said one of the Rooks, "that His Lordship will want some men with him."

Gol nodded. "Mulcer, you, and you." This time he tapped Durand. "You'd best stick by me."

With his henchman finished, Lord Radomor stormed away, his cloak billowing to fill the hall. His wife, Alwen, would be somewhere in the dark castle, high above them, and unsuspecting. Durand tried to remember the dark-haired daughter of Duke Abravanal of Gireth. It must have been ten winters since the wedding. He remembered a girl saying something about how a yard had many yards in it, either explaining or teasing the younger boys. Durand remembered thinking she was lying. Now they were coming for her.

Only they had not moved.

"We are counting on you, Sir Gol," said a Rook. "A man who intends to be a power under His Lordship had best—"

"Come on!" barked Gol and Durand charged after.

Faces crowded the benighted keep: silent eyes, big and gray as mushrooms. On the stair, Radomor was like ghosts and warhorses, vaulting high into the ancient fortress. Durand and the others bounded after the slap of hands and soles through the dark. Finally, Lord Radomor stumbled into a tower where the air was thick with lavender. And, from the stairwell above their heads, a thunderclap of rending wood split the dark.

Someone darted out: a pale form with something clutched to its chest. Durand caught an arm. For a moment, a woman looked up into his face, eyes desperate and black as ink. It was Lady Alwen.

Radomor looked down on Durand and his prisoner both. Mastering herself, Alwen straightened and climbed back into the tower room with her husband. The bundle in arms struggled weakly, and cried.

Durand stared into his own callused hand.

THE WINDING STAIRWELL let out before a broken door.

The baby wailed.

Radomor said nothing, but, beyond the doorway, Alwen was speaking. Durand squeezed his swollen eyes shut in the narrow space. His head pounded.

She confessed everything. Radomor was often away, and Sir Aldoin had smiled upon her. It had been nothing at first but a friendship. Aldoin was a friend to both of them, but then something had changed. In the summer. While he was on campaign. While he rode out at the Downs. She never meant to harm him.

Durand and the others waited outside the door.

Durand listened for any answer from Radomor, straining to read the mood of the man, but Radomor never uttered a word.

Alwen begged his mercy, until finally she, too, subsided into silence. Ages after, Lord Radomor appeared in the doorway, his face so stiff and dark that he drove even Gol into the corner of the room. There was no sound behind him but the baby's crying.

When their lord had gone, Gol turned to the others. "Watch here," he said. "And, as you value your lives, don't be poking your noses inside. She's naught to any of you, and we'll know the worst of it before long, don't worry."

With that, the captain followed Radomor down, and Durand was left in an alcove before the broken door of a strange room in a strange fortress leagues from Gireth with two soldiers and the sound of weeping. He should have starved on the road.

No man spoke or looked into the faces of the others. Durand could not imagine the rage of this man. Lord Radomor had been a hero in the king's host. Now, he had lost the wife he had believed in, and a companion of his childhood. Where was vengeance?

The baby cried, and the three men stood. Two of an autumn night's long hours passed. The unseen woman, only a few paces away, murmured comfort to her child. Durand steeled himself against the desire to meddle, knowing his interference would do only harm. Distant sounds carried up the stairwell. Shouts of protest reached them from fathoms down. Men roared. Once, a woman shrieked somewhere.

Durand looked into his empty hand.

Then, just on the feathered edge of his hearing, Durand caught shivers of a panicked voice, different from the others—he knew what it must be: Somewhere beyond a guarded door, the voice pleaded from the mouth of a well. If there had been any doubt . . .

A belt creaked beside Durand. Its owner muttered "*God.*" It was Mulcer.

Durand looked into the empty arch of the stairwell and heard the metal racket of water. The well was the heart of the great stone keep. Even where Durand stood, at the top of the highest tower, he could hear. Frozen beyond the open door, Alwen must hear as well.

In the fifth hour of night, another pair of Radomor's men climbed into the mouth of the stair, saying, "Go. We're barracked in the undercroft."

Exhaustion weighed Durand down like a mail coat, but he made his way down the winding tower stair. Mulcer and his comrade rustled and clinked behind. Soon, the feasting hall glowed in its doorway before him. Hunchbacked Lord Radomor sat in his father's wooden throne, holding a silent court. There were guards on every door, penning twenty or thirty servants in the room with their master. The Rooks perched on stools, flanking their lord. No one had moved since the screams of the drowning man had rung in the keep. Every face was stiff with horror. All but the Rooks'.

On the way down, Durand and the others passed a nondescript door guarded by two more soldiers. He looked at the face of the thing: black nailheads, a ring pull, wrought-iron hinges, and a heavy bar on the outside. The well chamber. He glanced back to the feasting hall, only a few paces away, and could still see one of the Rooks hunched there.

The Rook turned to him and smiled a crooked leer, setting a silencing finger to his lips.

THE NEXT MORNING, Durand climbed back up the tower with Mulcer.

"What are we doing?" whispered Durand.

"Radomor will give in," Mulcer said. "He's been cuckolded, but he ain't the first, is he? He'll stew a few days. We'll pack the girl off to Acconel and her family. I don't expect Gireth will like it much, but who'll blame our Radomor?"

With love gone, it was only politics. "He'll set Alwen aside and keep the child," was Durand's grim surmise.

"A man of near forty years doesn't lose his heir lightly. Likely the mother will miss the boy, but Alwen's broken vows to the King *and Queen* of Heaven."

"Even the wise women will not step in."

"It will all be over soon enough," Mulcer concluded.

They had almost reached the top of the stair when a harried-looking burgher with knobbed wrists and a box of tools brushed past them, scrambling down. At the top of the tower hung a new door: iron nail heads, a ring pull, wrought-iron hinges, and a heavy bar on the outside. The image of the well-room door.

As Durand stood before it, he felt the eye of the Lord of Dooms upon him. Lead and stone and timber were no shield. But Radomor would relent; he must. He had been a hero at the king's vanguard. He had nearly died. He was a Son of Atthi, and a king was his grandsire.

Lady Alwen was nearly kin. He remembered her dark, desperate eyes.

Like mockery, the day crept by in silence. Nothing passed the door—neither food, nor water. Night came, and Durand lay all the hours of darkness in the deep undercroft below the fortress thinking of the woman in the tower somewhere above. What would he say for himself before the King of Heaven? They were murdering a duke's daughter. One of the crown's closest allies. Armies could ride.

The next day, he had guard duty downstairs. He thanked the Host of Heaven.

THE PLACE WAS hot. Uncannily hot.

Gol had him on the feasting hall with orders to make sure that no one left—no one got away. Waves of heat rose from the duke's naked skull like an upturned cauldron.

At noon, shouts erupted from the entry stair. One of Gol's men sprawled into the hall, landing on his backside.

And then, into the silent heat, tramped a double file of strange men in gold robes. They were priests, though a few had the fierce and bearded look of barbarous warriors despite their robes.

The most formidable was the last to enter: a man over six feet tall who sported a beard like a whole black bearskin. As the others took up positions either side of the door, this man strode slowly into the heat and darkness of the hall. He wore enough wealth for a prince. He was the Patriarch of Ferangore. Where the eye of the merest village priest could leave a man breathless and twisting, exorcism and damnation crackled in the Patriarch's eyes. He and those like him were the fist and heel of the Lord of Dooms in His Creation.

The Patriarch crossed his arms over his vast beard and surveyed the feasting hall, taking in everything. He grimaced at the unnatural heat of the air. Every soldier shunned his glance; they all knew about the girl and her child.

"I summoned you, Radomor," said this man, his voice filling the room. "You did not attend me."

The Rooks were moving, bowing and scraping like snakes and curs round Radomor's ankles. One raised upturned hands and smiled. "His Lordship has been occupied with other matters, Your Grace."

The Patriarch's dark eyes flashed toward the little man for an instant, but he stabbed his fingers at Radomor.

"I have heard what you are doing here! I have seen. My priests attended the fire in the city. You have murdered a man. You have burned his hall. It is enough. Your wife and child, you must free. Already, you have gone beyond the bounds of law and custom in this thing, taking matters into your own hands. Think of your grandfather who lies in the high sanctuary. Think of your father who prays at Mantlewell. I know you are a man who acts in earnest. I know you are an honorable man. A man who does not brook betrayal. But I tell you, there is more to learn from betrayal than hatred. Know that the Host Below watches the great ones of Creation." The man's eyes flared in a glance that took in the whole keep and the sickening heat of the air. "Know that the wrath of the righteous is a snare."

Radomor blinked once, slowly. He should not have been able to move under the stare of such a priest. The Rooks sneered up from his ankles.

"Radomor, son of Ailnor," said the Patriarch, "truly I tell you that no good will come of your association with these new counselors. Word of what happened at the Battle of Hallow Down has reached us here. The miracle of your recovery. And I tell you: Creation is a precarious thing. Man tampers with it at his great peril. Beyond the protection of Heaven's Host are things past imagining. As real as you or I, the Banished and the Lost are groping now." The man spread crabbed hands against the hot air. "Here. Hunting for the merest flaw in the walls of this Creation. Ask what these men do. Ask them how they scrabble at those cracks."

He stopped, lungs heaving. Sweat rolled and gleamed over his face.

"I have said what I have come to say, Lord Radomor. You have had your warning. Stop now and hope remains for you."

Despite the heat, Radomor's face was dry.

One of the Rooks beamed. "We are very pleased that you have come to speak with us, Your Grace."

His brother Rook nodded. "Yes. Very pleased."

Now the Patriarch held them in his eye. They should have frozen. They should have died.

"It has been most diverting," said one.

"Yes," said the other.

"And you have certainly caused us to think."

More nodding. "Yes. It is a great deal to think about."

"The thought of those things beyond imagining. Groping." He clawed his hands for a moment.

"Yes."

The two men stopped and smiled at the Patriarch.

The old priest grimly raised his chin and looked beyond the Rooks to Radomor, enthroned. "Remember my words," he said. And, after a long look at every man in that room, he abandoned the Great Hall of Ferangore.

The Rooks chuckled into the vaults.

ONLY THE ROOKS moved freely as the vigil wore on.

Though Durand was a guard, he had become a prisoner. This much was clear to him. And the longer he remained, the more certain he became that Radomor would never relent and that Alwen and her son were doomed. Gol had his eyes on them all, waiting for the first of them to move.

Once more saved from the high tower, Durand played guard now at the top of the keep's entry stair. The oven heat of the feasting hall was on his face and the chill dark of the steps on his neck.

Red blades of dusk had begun to probe the gloom when Durand heard an excited slapping of soles down below. The bottom door rattled, and conversation murmured. As Durand peered down, a stranger was marching up the stairway from the entrance with a Rook at either hand.

Sleek, agile, and armed, this was no Patriarch.

For an instant, Durand, the Rooks, and the stranger crowded at the top of the stair. Then one of the black creatures flashed Durand a grin and scurried into the Great Hall. The remaining Rook favored Durand and the stranger both with a grin as cordial as a corpse's leer.

Durand stood his ground, barring the stranger's passage. Though the man seemed half Durand's size, he stood poised on the balls of his feet, even at his ease. Black hair swept from a face of wide cheekbones and intelligent eyes. There were threads of gray at his temples. White linen slashes marked his black fighting surcoat. A sword hung from a knight's belt about his hips.

The Rook kept up his sickly grinning.

Meanwhile, the Rook's brother had bowed low before Lord Radomor.

"Milord, I am sorry to intrude."

Radomor's dark eyes moved.

"There is a guest," the Rook pressed. "A deputation. This one, I think, you will wish to see. Baron Cassonel of Damaryn."

Durand woke up at the name. The stranger raised an eyebrow.

"Baron Cassonel is high in the employ of the Duke of Beoran," said the Rook. "Was his champion. Now is his greatest liegeman. If you indulge us, Lordship, my brother will conduct him into your presence."

The stranger, Baron Cassonel of Damaryn, looked from Durand's face to the feasting hall of Ferangore, and Durand stepped aside. Every fighting man in Errest knew of Baron Cassonel. One in ten thousand, he had fought his way from knight-errantry to a place at a duke's side. The sword at his hip was Termagant, a High Kingdom blade of a thousand winters. There was a story of him at the prince's tournament in Tern Gyre, when Durand was a boy, besting every fighting man in the retinue of the Duke of Beoran, one after another. Now he was a baron and the duke his liege lord. As the man stalked out, everyone in the hall held still.

Cassonel bowed.

"His Grace, Ludegar, Duke of Beoran, sends greetings," the man said. His voice fit him well: circumspect. "He bids me to offer his respect and admiration to his cousin the Lord Radomor, heir to Ailnor, now Duke of Yrlac."

Radomor leveled his gaze upon the newcomer and uttered the first words Durand had heard from the man since the tower. "Not to my father himself?"

"Your Lordship," Cassonel confirmed.

"And you ride messenger?"

"I believe His Grace chose his messenger to demonstrate the esteem in which he holds his cousin."

Radomor closed his eyes. "What would my cousin have you say?"

Cassonel glanced around the room, even meeting Durand's stare for an instant. Some twenty people would overhear any word that might be uttered. Some men shifted.

"You may say what you will, Baron Cassonel," Radomor said. "It does not matter."

The swordsman-lord made a slow, shallow nod. "Among the magnates of the kingdom, there is concern over the policies and practices of His Highness, Ragnal, now King of Errest: his intervention in the Heithan Marches, the debacle in Caldura, the patrols on the far borders of the East. In five short years, they have emptied the treasury and thrown the king into the hands of moneylenders."

"I fought in the Heithan Marches, Baron Cassonel."

"Last survivor of the king's vanguard at Hallow Down. Your heroism is well known."

"Since my grandfather's time, many men have come to this court," Radomor said. "Always, the answer has been the same."

Cassonel nodded a grave and shallow bow. Durand found his gaze drawn to the man's blade. Cassonel rested his hand on the pommel.

"I am sure it is so, Lord Radomor. But I am bound to press the case. Your grandsire, great Carondas, is a king of cherished memory. Only in his winter years did he set aside the Evenstar Crown, childless and fearful that Errest would suffer if he should die without issue. It was for the kingdom that he passed the Evenstar to Bren, his brother. It was for the kingdom that he married the lady of Yrlac and took this seat. He could not know that he would father a child so late in his life. Many wonder at the miracle of your father's birth, and its meaning."

Radomor shifted. "And still, Ragnal is king."

"A king who, I am asked to explain, has stripped the domains of minor heirs in his wardship beyond recovery. Who has sold possessions, stolen moneys set aside for the maintenance of the land. Orchards have been sold for timber. Forest and common lands have been put to the plow."

"Many times," Lord Radomor said, "my father was asked this same question."

"Duke Ludegar bids me remind you that he has seen widows forced into disadvantageous marriages as merchants and freed peasants buy their way into land and titles. The sons of our countrymen are made to pay extortionate fines to enter the lands of their forefathers. The wellborn of Errest are taxed without consent to the ruin of our lines."

"And I, Baron Cassonel," said Radomor, "am not the Duke of Yrlac."

The baron took a moment to glance over the faces standing round, just a fingertip now on the pommel of ancient Termagant.

"I am bidden to say, Lordship, that a window is opening that may not remain so for long. His Grace, the Duke of Cape Earne—a man of thoughtless fidelity—is gravely ill. His son has already been informed of the fine he must pay to enter his inheritance." He inclined his head a fraction toward Radomor. "I am asked to say that it is a sum both beyond reason and beyond the ability of the boy to pay."

Radomor's thumb curled in the carved arm of his father's throne. "The balance of the Great Council shifts."

"This I cannot say."

"My father would never agree."

"My duke bids me remind you that yours is the blood of kings. Yours is the sacred lineage unbroken, through invasion to the *Cradle* and the fall of the Shattered Isle. With respect, he asserts that the realm cannot long endure a profligate ruler."

The baron bowed, gaze firmly on the face of the man in the duke's throne. Even in the heat of the hall, a chill passed over Durand. It was patricide they suggested. It was high treason.

"Even now, arrangements are being made," said Cassonel. "Duke Ludegar can make an easy way."

Lord Radomor held his fearsome silence.

"Your men will know how to send your answer," Cassonel concluded. "I must leave you to consider. But remember, the Great Council meets before the snows."

With this, Cassonel stalked toward Durand and the entry stair. Durand ought to have cut the man's head from his shoulders—no matter how futile the act. Instead, Durand stepped aside.

The Rooks followed Cassonel down the stair. Durand stood

in the dark with his fists knotted. It was treason. He had seen and been seen, and he was trapped. More of Gol's men watched the door downstairs, and a room full lurked in the hall behind him. He would never get free.

Then, from that hall, Durand heard a whisper. "I'm not sure I like this."

Durand caught his breath. The voice was familiar: Mulcer's whisper skittering down the vaults from somewhere in the Great Hall.

"For God's sake, do as you're told." Durand could hear Gol's clenched teeth.

"I don't know, Gol. All I thought was we're finally catching hold. Getting a place in a lord's retinue. Now, I wish we'd left these two skulking wretches back on Hallow Down."

"You've got no bloody choice."

"What are we doing? Eh? We hire that new lad on. What do we look like? A pack of monsters out of some children's tale."

"We're bloody well doing what we're paid to do. It's too late for backing out now, friend."

There was someone dying upstairs.

As Durand listened for another word, he believed himself to be alone in the dark. Like sorcery, then, two grinning faces emerged in front of him: the Rooks. They held him in their eyes, then each raised a hushing finger to his lips. It was all Durand could do not to bolt.

WHEN THE RED fingers of dusk left the arrow loops, Durand left the feasting hall and joined the others sleeping in the undercroft. He worked at his hand. Exhaustion pinned him to the stones and held him asleep.

HE WOKE, HOURS later, to a voice, purring, "It is dangerous to be a little wise. Better to be a fool, I think. Too late now. We are sorry to lose you. Oh yes."

Durand's eyes opened in the black vaults of the undercroft. A voice growled. Durand recognized Mulcer.

Shapes were moving: a black figure—one of the Rooks— squatted over the blond soldier. Mulcer moved, but the Rook raised a hand—just fingertips—though their touch struck the soldier like a pickaxe. He writhed, pinned to the floor like a man in the throws of a seizure. The Rook bent low, close as a grandmother over a cradle. Durand had a dagger; he would use it.

The Rook was lowering his lips, smiling over Mulcer's rigid face. He reached with his fingers—both hands now—peeling lips apart and prying jaws open. Durand made to snatch the dagger, but, sudden as lightning, a spasm clamped him, too. He looked up into the leer of the second Rook, crouching low over him now, as though he had seen into Durand's mind. A finger of the creature's right hand, the longest, sat on the pulse of blood in Durand's throat, and with each heartbeat Durand's muscles wound tighter, creaking his clenched teeth and popping the stitches in his boots.

Through it all, Durand could hear something whispering. Not the Rooks. Many voices, like a rumor passing over a crowded room. He could almost feel the breath of their conversations.

His eyes bulged. He strained to find Mulcer. The man struggled with the Rook locked on his mouth. Rhythmic convulsions pried Mulcer's shoulders from the floor, and the Rook was a puppeteer, riding him, drifting above him, pulling with long fingers. Never did he let go. The man's back arched higher and higher, cracking like knuckles.

All the while, the whispering grew louder. Durand could feel their words. The whisperers were coming. An uncanny glow swelled into Creation, filling the room. Durand's eyes rolled to find the source. From every sleeping mouth a tongue of pallid flame now wavered, as the Rooks' pull was drawing out their souls. Any moment, it would all come to pieces.

Then, with a hollow groan, Mulcer collapsed.

There was silence.

The Rook grinned to his brother. He seemed to notice Durand, and his smile broadened. A grotesque bulge in the Rook's throat distracted the man a moment, then he set a silencing finger over his lips.

The nearby twin released his grip, and Durand sagged free. Mulcer was dead.

And Durand could hardly move.

He was on the door again.

He was never alone.

Two days had passed with the door shut. From time to time, the baby's piping cry stirred. He knew the door would never open, and that he could not face the King of Heaven if he allowed things to stand as they were. Too much was happening. He would not help Lord Radomor murder his wife, no matter how she had betrayed him. More than Cassonel's treason, *this* ate at Durand's mind.

His first impulse was to grab the bar and rush the woman and her child down the stair. The guard standing beside him would have to be put down, of course. Durand could take the man's sword. There would also be the men at the bottom of the stair, the guards in the feasting hall, the men on the keep doors, and a whole city kicked alive like an anthill.

The sword would help there. Oh yes. A smart man wouldn't take on an entire city without, at least, a good sword.

Another tack.

He eyed the dull curve of the guard's helmet. If he knocked the man down and yanked opened the door, he might be able to lower the woman and her child to the courtyard from her window without worrying about Radomor's retinue in the keep. It worked for skalds: heroes with bed linens shinnying down towers.

He tried to picture it: fifteen fathoms to the cobblestones with a woman and her baby twisting at the end of bedsheets. A good bedsheet might get him five feet. If Alwen happened to have twenty stout blankets in that room, he stood a chance.

He closed his eyes, mentally changing tacks once more. He must set aside the hopeless heroism. A man might reason with Radomor. Confront him. He saw himself, a stranger in that dark feasting hall, ranting about the man's adulterous wife. It was hopeless, but he could think of no one in all the realms of Creation who stood a better chance. Poor Lady Alwen could not do it. Only the Rooks spoke to the man now.

But Durand had forgotten: This wasn't Radomor's land. Ferangore and Yrlac didn't belong to him; they were old Duke

Ailnor's holdings. This was Ailnor's house, and, by all accounts, the Duke of Yrlac was an honorable man who must see all this for the insanity it was.

Sadly, the duke was not in his city.

Durand pawed the back of his neck, grinding out the frustration he must hide from the other guard.

What use was the duke when he was leagues away? Durand looked at the ironbound door. The duke might return at any time, but there was a real danger that Lady Alwen could wait no longer. And how long could the baby live? A few days more, at most. If there was no water locked in that chamber with them, it must be less.

Before he could work out the odds, Durand turned to the other guard. "Going downstairs." The man blinked back at him, more surprised than Durand—just. "You'd best watch here till I get back," he added, and slipped into the stairwell.

This time, before Durand reached the oven heat and armed guards of the Great Hall, he ducked into a side passage. Here, he found himself in a corridor lined with arches.

Taking a breath of free air, Durand glanced down the first of these hollow arches, and found himself looking down on the bald head of Lord Radomor himself. Both Rooks twitched from their perches at the touch of his glance—black robes trembling like the legs of spiders. Durand flinched back. They would kill him but that was the least of it: There was more than just his life at risk.

With a slow breath, Durand set off once more, searching out a route that would take him into the lowest levels of the fortress. Every keep had a sneaky postern door somewhere down below. As he searched, he wondered how long his partner upstairs would wait. The man would think he'd gone to have a piss. Soon he would wonder.

To make his way down, Durand stole close to danger, prowling past turned backs and clinging to shadows. It could be in the lowest levels that he might find his door.

His knotted path led him groping down among the largest stones of the keep: clammy giants in the dark. The air tasted of cellars. There, he found a narrow passage cut into the thickness of the walls. If there were going to be a back way out, this would be it. He stepped into the blackness.

"Right," said the gloom. "Where do you think you're going?"

After a moment, a face and knuckles floated in the spitting glow of a candle: another of Radomor's soldiers.

"You're relieved," Durand ventured. The soldier squinted despite the candle, and Durand used the time to walk nearer. The soldier wasn't a big man.

"By the Powers of Hell. Who's that? The new lad? Durmund?"

He was almost on the man.

"Something like," Durand said. "They leave you down here all alone?"

"Aye, and all they give me's this hog-tallow candle." Durand could smell the greasy smoke and the bite of onions on the soldier's breath. The man's face was full of bristles. "But I've just got on duty, friend."

Durand stared at the wizened face. In that instant, he was very tired of lying.

"I'm not your relief, friend," he said. It felt good.

"Then what are—"

"—I'm not going to stand by any longer." Join me, or stop me: an honest challenge.

The soldier raised a knowing eyebrow. "Leaving old Radomor while he's in a bad humor?"

"Aye," Durand said. The man had missed the point; he was smirking.

"Well, it's not His Lordship you ought to watch out for. It's old Gollie-boy. He don't much like folk who take his money and turn their backs. 'Specially after what a man might've seen the last while. I think His Lordship's counselors have got Gollie right jumpy: afraid to make a mistake. And you swanning off now would count as a mistake, friend, in case you're wondering. Embarrassing for His Lordship. You'd cause our Gollie a whole pack of trouble." His too-familiar smile broadened. "I suggest you just turn around and forget the whole thing. In fact, I might forget it ever happened, if you've got the coin."

"I haven't got a clipped penny."

"Well, not on you, but—"

Durand struck like a tiger. The candle flashed out as he

clapped one hand over the man's mouth and rammed him high in the angle between ceiling and wall. He pinned the soldier there, thinking of knives, dreading a brawl in the dark. But the moment stretched. The soldier didn't struggle.

Releasing his grip, Durand felt the man slump bonelessly from his shaking hands. Some Power of Heaven must be watching—he hoped it was a Power of Heaven.

Durand pawed the walls until his fingers slid over hinges and rotten timber. Another moment's work found the bar, and then he was through the door and out into another cool space between walls. This time, however, the only vault above his head was the open evening sky.

Durand stole out, daring to feel relief. As he slid in close to the massive foundations, he heard the croaking of birds. He thrust his head round the corner, and found the courtyard teeming: rooks, ravens, magpies, crows. The stooped things lurched and cackled in all directions. Atop the stained walls of the high sanctuary, the creatures heaped every spire and cornice, sliding on the rooftiles and spilling out across the yard below.

Durand jogged for the stables—where he caught hold of a piebald nag no one would miss—and he clattered through a storm of black wings and down into the city.

IN THE STREETS, he slowed his pace, passing strangers in the twilight: laborers trudging homeward, watchmen waiting for the curfew bell to slam their gates. One even commented. "You're lucky. The bloody sanctuary bell ought to have gone an hour ago."

Durand thought of the birds, and the fouled icon near Tormentil. He wondered what had become of that fearsome Patriarch. He wanted to spur the stolen horse, but he forced himself to ride easily, pulling the mask of a laborer's boredom over dread. He must reach the last gate.

Finally, the thing swung into view, and Durand knotted his fists a little tighter. He was almost free.

The gate passed overhead.

But as he had this taste of freedom, someone laughed.

Durand twisted. The gate's mouth gaped empty behind him. Another laugh barked out, this time clearly from above his head. A pair of dark blots peered down from the battlements: rooks.

Durand spurred his stolen horse for the horizon.

THE FIRST NIGHT, he rode blind, thinking that the duke's Mantlewell was south somewhere. There was no one to ask. All night, the carrion birds tracked him.

When the Eye of Heaven rose over Creation, Durand threw questions at every bleary line of threshermen or gleaning peasants he passed, asking where he must go, and, at every twist, the rooks were never far away. Sometimes the things came near enough for him to shy a rock. He would turn a corner to find them on a signpost or perched and chortling on the stocks in a village green. At other times, they hung so high above him they seemed a pair of black letters inked on the clouds.

Toward noon, he found a boy standing in the road, a blue rag in his hand. Durand reined in his stolen mare. Time had cut the track deep between fields banked up on either side. The boy's mouth hung slack. The blue rag was a sling.

An older man slithered down the bank, his beard and tunic full of chaff. As he reached the boy, he noticed Durand.

"Oddest thing I ever saw," the man muttered. "I've got the boy flinging stones to keep the crows off."

Durand said, "You should get under cover."

"This one. It was a lucky shot. Hit the thing square on."

"Is there a shrine or sanctuary you could hide in?"

"And it just come to pieces."

Durand felt a chill. "Came to pieces?"

"Like it was all full of maggots. Blowflies. It just come apart. Whack."

Durand made the fist-and-fingers sign of the Eye.

"Yes. Broad daylight. Whack. Bits and grubs and feathers." The boy spoke. *"Right through it."*

Durand peered hard at the older man. "You say 'crow'?"

"I don't know," said the older man. "Raven. Crow. Rook. Something like that. The bastard didn't know it was dead, I guess. A bad sign."

Durand shook his head. There was a rise a hundred paces off. In the crook of a tree up there, he saw a black shape that could have been the bird. One rook remained, and Durand didn't like the thought of these poor peasants getting caught up in things bigger than they were. "Get to a priest," he said. "I'd hurry."

"Aye." The man nodded and made to take his boy by the collar.

Durand said, "A moment. I am bound for Mantlewell. Can you point me to the road?"

"Yes. Aye. My wife's from that way. You're looking for a stone cliff on the Highshields road. Highshields is sort of up on that cliff. With all the mines and that. Things kind of step up on the way to the mountains. The Well is . . . cut into that, like. The road goes straight for it."

Durand nodded, thinking of Alwen in her tower. It sounded as if he was getting near.

"May the Warders protect you, and the Champion grant you courage," Durand said and, as father and son nodded goodbye, nudged his borrowed horse into motion. He hoped that one of the Rooks was dead—killed by a little boy with a bit of blue rag—but he didn't fool himself. They were on him. He was a dolt for choosing a swaybacked nag instead of a proper charger. He imagined explaining himself before the Gates of Heaven. "Mother and child died, sure. And sure I am a thief, but it wasn't an *expensive* horse." The Warders would hurl him straight to the Host Below.

He could feel Gol's men barreling down the road behind him. If he could reach the duke before they caught him, everything might still work out.

Driving the nag on, he soon struck the oak forests of the south where the land began to change. These were not the chalk hills of Gireth. In Yrlac, the land rose in waves of stone. The trail took wild angles, and water ran cold and rusty in the crevices.

Above the forest, on a hill as gray and bare as an oyster shell, he heard voices. At first, nothing moved among the scruffy trees behind him. Then, almost under his feet, a flock of starlings exploded into the air, a few whistling over his head. Gol was closer than he had feared—only a bowshot behind.

Durand pitched horse downhill, abruptly spotting a gray bank a league ahead. A line of cliffs rose over the forest: the step the peasant had spoken of. If he could get that far, maybe Alwen lived.

The track spooled onward—he heard hooves on the stone behind him—but no matter how he drove his horse, the cliff yielded no sign of monastery or village ahead. He had images of fighting it out with Gol's thugs against the stone because he'd missed a turning. Abruptly, the track shot sideways across the face of the vast wall, and before Durand's eyes, the wall seemed to uncurl like a sorcerer's fist, revealing an echoing place of ferns and mosses.

A stream poured out of the rock, and Durand's nag splashed into the shallow water, startling a hushed score of pilgrims. They had the look of neighbors whispering at a sickroom door.

Durand slipped down from the nag's back, wondering what he had stumbled onto this time. He walked past the staring pilgrims into the gorge. The stream ran over the stone floor, filling it with a sound that sent Durand back to the keep at Ferangore and its well. Here though, no grate blocked the sky. A few fathoms over his head, ivies clung in the sunlight. It was like walking in a snail's shell. He teetered and balanced over the cool water. Otherworldly voices played in the air.

At the heart, the gorge opened into a cavernous granite well soaring over a pool. Bushes clung to the higher walls, knotted with strips of linen. They might have been swaddling clothes.

He faced the backs of a half-dozen tall men—wellborn by their surcoats and stature. Beyond them at the pool's edge, a figure knelt. The instant Durand's eye fell on the long back and flowing silver of the man's head, he knew he had found Duke Ailnor, the son of King Carondas's winter years.

"Your Grace—" said Durand.

Though there was gray in the hair and beards of the duke's men, their fists had twisted in Durand's collar before he could flinch. Blades glinted. Faces glared, tight-lipped as skulls.

"It is almost noontide when it is said that the light of Heaven's Eye falls on the water of the pool." The bent duke sighed. "But, this day as the last, clouds obscure the Eye. There will be no healing."

The kneeling man stood. For a moment, he was the image of all holy men and kings—a face on coins from the loose silver of his beard to the unflinching stare—but then he seemed to find something in Durand's eyes.

"You!" Ailnor tottered, alarming the guards locked on Durand's arms. For an instant, Durand was a steer in the butcher's hands. The knights twisted their blades.

"No! No." The duke steadied himself. He waved his wary followers back and stepped close until he cupped Durand's face in his hands. His eyes were gray and full of something like awe.

"Such dreams I have had," he breathed.

Durand had no answer.

"I have seen your face. As it is . . . and much changed. I have seen terrible things, so that now I would sooner lay my bones in the crypt of my fathers than sleep. I sought to escape them." He shot a glance at the pool, then returned his avid gaze to Durand. He looked like a man trying to read his future in a stone.

Durand forced himself to remember why he had come. "I bring grave tidings, Your Grace."

"I think it is beginning," whispered the duke, close as kissing.

"Your son . . ." Durand said.

The gray eyes closed. What was Durand meant to say? His long night's ride seemed to take hold of him. How could he go on?

"At Tormentil we had news," Durand said. "From Ferangore. Aldoin of Warrendel—"

"They played as children. Hobby horses. I remember young Radomor battering Warrendel from our stable with a wooden blade."

"He is dead," said Durand.

Cool air turned in the empty well above their heads. Eyes still shut, Ailnor said, "Drowned." Cold fingers slithered in Durand's guts. *"Was it drowned?"*

"Yes," Durand said, though no one could know. "He was drowned."

"And Alwen?" the duke asked.

"It is why I've come."

"The child. My grandson?"

"In the Lady's bower. Locked inside."

"It was my wife's chamber," Ailnor said.

Durand took a breath, forcing himself on. "He has them locked up and guarded. No one comes or goes. It will be their tomb."

The duke nodded. Durand would have said more. He would have spoken of Cassonel and Beoran and the plot, but Duke Ailnor staggered back, his shoulders tilted like the yard of a broken ship.

"I must think," he said, and waded past Durand toward the mouth of the gorge. For Durand and the duke's aged retinue, there was nothing to do but follow.

THE STRICKEN DUKE walked into a spray of flying water as Gol's horses hammered down the streambed. Durand saw the old man throw up his hands, then the duke's guard had barred Gol's way with flashing swords.

Gol raised a fist, holding his men at bay. Durand could not believe he had ever been one of the leering fiends behind that man. They were not knights, no matter how they styled themselves. The duke's guard stood in a semicircle around their lord while the water flowed.

"What is the meaning of this?" demanded the duke.

"We were tracking a fugitive," Gol snarled, jerking his chin toward Durand. "I see you've found him."

" 'A fugitive,' " the duke repeated, advancing a step through the line of his guards.

"Aye, Your Grace. Worked for your son. He'd hardly started, and now he's deserted his post." Durand's nag was tied to a bush right at the bank. "That's the horse he stole. And he killed one of my men. Hagall. Crushed his skull." Durand wondered if this were true.

The duke stood like a sorcerer before a storm.

"He has brought me news, this fugitive of yours."

"I'm sure he has, Your Grace, but think on who's telling the tale before you go too far believing it."

"I will, Sir Gol."

The old captain made a face, this game of courtesy not coming easily to him.

"Your Grace, I've been charged with taking this man back to Ferangore," said Gol, though it seemed more likely that the man had planned to string Durand up the instant he laid hands on him.

"Events draw me to Ferangore as well, Sir Gol," said the duke.

"Well then. You have an escort, haven't you? We'll keep an eye on this Durand for you. Make sure he doesn't find a chance to slink off. Keep everyone nice and safe."

The duke narrowed an eye but nodded nonetheless.

"To Ferangore," he said.

As THEIR UNEASY company rode, Gol watched Durand like a dog at its chain's end.

By evening, the leagues of riding were wearing hard on Durand, though he was not about to ask for rest—he regretted each instant he had spent standing in that tower. He could have ridden for Mantlewell on the first day.

As he blinked at exhaustion, the track turned sharply around the roots of an enormous stone. He lost sight of Duke Ailnor's men, and, in that instant, he felt a razor edge catch at his throat.

"Now," snarled Gol. "You've made a fool of me, boy. In front of Lord Radomor and those two bloody counselors of his. I'll wait a lifetime for another chance like this. I've waited longer than you can know, so I'm telling you: You've shown where your loyalties ain't. You think His Lordship wants folk running around who know what's happened? Hmm? Think on it, pig."

Then Durand was free. They'd snaked back into sight, and one of the duke's guard had turned, his lined face all suspicion. But there was nothing to see; Gol had chosen his time well. Durand remembered Fulk and digging the shallow grave in the woods for the outlander. There were three wounds like harlots' mouths on the pale body: hand, chest, and back. Gol had not even been breathing heavily. Durand touched his neck; his fingers came away slick.

As THE EYE of Heaven rose over the plain, Ferangore seemed a fortress island. From Durand's spot in the line, he could make out the keep and, almost eclipsed by the spire of the Patriarch's high sanctuary, the tower prison of Alwen and her son.

Duke Ailnor was like a man in a dream. Something shivered in his gray eyes that shot chills through whoever looked at him. Durand recalled the horror of recognition in those eyes when they first saw his own face.

"No bells," the duke said, his voice loud in the dawn stillness. "The Patriarch should be ringing the dawn."

"It could be a wind, Your Grace," said one of his knights.

His mind was not lost now. He said with grim certainty, "There were no bells."

8. The Night of Two Hills

The folk of Ferangore watched their party with sidelong glances. Now, the gatekeepers held their tongues. To Durand, the people seemed like sailors hunkered down on deck, staring up at the belly of a storm.

The duke's party scattered the carrion birds in the courtyard round the high sanctuary. A thousand black-beaded eyes stared down from every roost. As the party climbed into the keep itself, Durand felt Gol's soldiers all around him.

A Rook popped into the arch at the top of the entry stair. The men stopped as the Rook grinned down.

"Your Grace," he said, and bowed with a flourish so low that the sleeve of his robe licked the threshold.

"Where is my son?" said the duke.

"In your feasting hall, Your Grace. He expects you."

The duke made no answer, and they pressed on into the feasting hall, Durand counting eight more of Gol's men. Some smiled at him. Every one was armed.

Radomor had not left his father's throne.

The duke stood before his son as he had stood before Gol's soldiers at Mantlewell.

"My son."

"Father." Radomor did not move.

"Where are the bells of the high sanctuary?"

Radomor said nothing, though his two Rooks shared a knowing smile.

"I have come about Alwen and the boy," the duke said.

"Yes."

"Yes. I must see them."

The duke's guard were wise enough to have their hands on their blades.

"That will be difficult, father."

The duke's head turned an inch. "Tell me I am not too late."

One of the Rooks spoke out: "Oh no. Not too late. Not the way you imagine. He has been advised to relent. He has been told it was wrong of him to keep them here, but you must understand that he was angry. Alwen wished to leave Ferangore. The country seemed a better place. She could let the scandal pass. Lord Radomor's impulse was to contain the news, but this man, Durand, made him see that it would be difficult."

The duke returned his gaze to Radomor.

"Where is she now?" he asked.

Another Rook answered. "She is traveling to her dower lands in Gireth."

"And the boy?" asked the duke. "My grandson?"

Now Radomor answered. "He is with her, father."

"Then we will go to her."

"You may do as you wish."

"Yes, my son, and you will come with me."

Now, Radomor stood. Durand looked for rage or triumph in the man's features but found nothing there he could understand. Then Radomor's eyes turned on him, dark as lodestones.

DURAND KNEW THEY must be dead.

They rode east as though Alwen and her baby might be waiting. It was a game, or the last verse of some skald's saga. Durand couldn't see the end, but he could not stop. He massaged his hand. Until the game was over, there was still a chance that he had killed no one, and it would all end. But he wished he'd stuck with Heremund in Tormentil.

Armed men surrounded him. There were two parties: knights, soldiers. They glared under the ornate brows of iron helms, eyeing each other with the tight attention of wolves and dogs.

"Here." Duke Ailnor stopped the column as the Eye of Heaven sank below the hills behind them. Daylight's twelve hours were gone, and now a hill rose in the gloom, swathed in ferns and long grass. It looked to have a high flat top. The duke pointed toward the crest, and they rode for it, ready to make camp. Durand could not argue. He had to sleep. It was no longer a matter of will.

At the top, the party stared over a wide, dark river. To Durand's surprise, he knew the place. This was the Banderol. It had been his road from Acconel, and he had waded it to follow Radomor's train. He must have seen this hill.

Duke Ailnor joined Durand at the ridge, saying nothing. His gray eyes were on the shadowed lands beyond the river: Gireth.

Men were climbing from their saddles, dropping into the grass. As Durand rested on horseback with the duke, too tired for courtesy, the Rooks took the chance to approach, half-bowing as they cringed forward.

"An intriguing stopping-place you've chosen, Your Grace," said one, peering up. The man's gaze fell on a cluster of standing stones nearby: lichenous slabs rising from nests of small boulders. There were sockets of darkness caught between, places that must have been chambers. "Very intriguing indeed."

Duke Ailnor made no answer.

"Oh," the second Rook said. He fished in his gardecorps, grinning up at Durand. "I think I have something here for you." With a flourish like a conjurer, the little man drew a long blue rag from his robe. As Durand's stomach lurched, the Rook jabbed the rag into Durand's palm and passed a hand by Durand's ear. "And what have we here?" With another flourish, he produced a small smooth stone. Just the thing for shying at crows. "Don't worry, my friend. They are yours now. You may keep them."

The two men bowed once more and said, "Your Grace." Durand remembered the boy.

Before settling, Radomor and his henchmen had taken themselves off a couple of dozen paces. The duke's steed nodded.

"It is an old place," Ailnor said. He didn't ask about the rag.

"Your Grace," Durand agreed.

"These stones. Tombs from the days before the *Cradle*'s landing. They say Gireth was named for a tribe. Savages stealing among the birches as Cellogir the Pilot sailed into the Bay of Acconel. You can see it in the villagers even now, I fancy. That knowing silence."

Durand knotted the boy's sling round his fist, not in so mystical a mood. From what he had seen, plowmen knew hardship. It had likely been the same all those winters ago.

"Your people are from Gireth, yes?" the duke said.

"Yes, Your Grace. My father holds the Col of the Blackroots."

"Ah. An old line. Like mine. Shipmates, maybe, on Saerdan's *Cradle*. What do you think?"

"I would not guess, Your Grace." Ailnor's line was Saerdan's.

"Bloodlines matter. We Sons of Atthi. The wise women, the wellborn, we breed our children like horses. But they matter." The old man's eyes were on the camp across the hill. "If not in the ways most imagine."

He nudged his mount a step forward, his long beard and hair flashing as cold as silver. "Do you know this hill, boy?"

"No, Your Grace."

"They call it the 'Fetch Hollow.' They can see it from the Banderol. There was a battle." He stopped. "Somewhere here . . ." He was looking downhill, toward the river. "I can hardly make it out. We are standing on the great bend of a horseshoe. The two points swing down for the river. Between is the Hollow. It's a ravine, full of oaks." Durand thought he could make out the place. "Some ancestor of ours drove an army into that ravine, and a skald will tell you that no one came out. There was a monastery, as well, later and for a thousand winters, right where we are standing, but it burned."

"Our lines were old even then."

With a familiar nod of his chin, the duke swung down from the saddle. Durand followed. "When they have all bedded down, I want you to get away." Durand had not expected this. "I must play out this game. As long as there is any hope, I must go on. I cannot give up my grandson. But you. You are young yet, and I fear my son will not permit you to live. You were not meant to survive this long, I think, and some way will be found. Perhaps that cur Gol will come smiling to breakfast, saying he caught you trying to run off. Perhaps he'll kill one of my men and put the knife in your hand. My son is proud, and you have run across his land carrying tales of his shame."

The duke looked over the camp. Somewhere, he could see Lord Radomor.

"They say he led the vanguard of the king's army. On the first day, Borogyn and his Heithans surged down upon the king's men like a sea. My son and his vanguard held them back but at great cost. Heroes. On the second day, King Ragnal held the vanguard in reserve. They were to recover. Radomor was wounded. So many were dead. But the battle shifted. The Heithans ground hard. They drove a slow advance against the king. Borogyn seemed ready to turn the line, and so, I am told, my son rose from his sickbed and threw his broken vanguard at their heart. They struck deep and drove themselves deeper. Ten men died for every step, but they reached Borogyn—or Radomor did—and hamstrung the Heithan advance. Borogyn's young princes turned coat. But so many died. All of Radomor's men.

"My boy lost himself in that battle. He is gone," the old man concluded. "I still remember when my wife was alive. The future was so very different then."

"Your Grace," said Durand. "I don't know if it is my place, but a messenger came from Beoran. They are trying to move your son to treason."

The long shadow of their hilltop stretched leagues into Gireth. Ailnor said nothing.

"You are in danger," Durand pressed.

The ancient lord looked Durand in the eye. His voice was a rattle.

"When they sleep," he said. "Take the Hollow down. I think they will not follow."

THAT NIGHT, DURAND dreamt of blood. The whole hilltop covered in it. Thick. His hands came away as if caught in pitch. He heard clashing weapons. Someone was whispering. The syllables wound around each other, coiling and uncoiling in the dark.

But he woke into stillness. He picked out a pair of sentries on either side of the camp. It was time. First, he must get a few things together. He knew well how far a man got with no money and no supplies.

The baggage bulked under a tarp behind Duke Ailnor's pavilion. Durand padded quietly past sleeping men and horses before scrounging for a couple of loaves and a wedge of cheese. Most important, though, was the iron roll of armor he had salvaged from the barracks hall at Ferangore. He had lugged it for leagues, and was still not ready to leave it and all it meant behind, though part of him wondered at his greed in keeping the thing.

The two parties had tied the horses in a sort of trough between the camps, right above the Hollow. Keeping the touchy animals between the camps was like keeping geese in the yard, the poor man's substitute for a guard dog. Durand set his gear down and began the awkward job of picking his nag from the rest. Horses nodded and spluttered, identical in the dark. He tried to keep his attention fixed on the task at hand and soon spotted a swaybacked brute that looked familiar.

"Durand," said a voice, close.

Like a knife, the word stuck in his back. Shadows rose from the grass as men stepping out from behind horses.

He jerked the dagger from his belt.

"Brave," the voice said: Lazar Gol. A glance revealed five, or maybe seven, others. Durand called upon Heaven.

"But brave'll do you no good," Gol said.

Durand prayed again. There was nothing for it. He couldn't beat Gol alone. With another half-dozen men thrown in, he wouldn't even get a chance to shout.

They moved.

He bolted.

In an instant, he had rolled under his stolen horse and was up, blocking and dodging like a plowman in a football match. The horses made a tangle of invisible ropes and a barricade of bodies. He cut and dodged, making for his gear on his way to the ravine. He saw a white face and mashed the heel of his hand in the middle, and then he had his bundle and was plunging into the steep-sided ravine called the Hollow.

Almost at once, he fell. His heel struck the slope and cart-wheeled him over. There was nothing but the breakneck pitch and tumble, and the certainty that trees and dagger branches waited below.

An earthy darkness swung up around him.

He struck, hand and head first, ending up against a scabrous bulk he took for a tree trunk. There was iron in his mouth, and he knew that if his fingers hadn't caught between the tree and his temple, the Hollow would have done Gol's job for him. As it was, his hand and head throbbed.

As he lay there, he became aware of a sharp odor spiking above the loamy dampness of the ravine and its tangled oaks. It was a slit-bowel smell: the piercing reek when the huntsman nicks something deep in the guts of a stag or boar.

Durand forced himself to move. Gol's men would be on top of him any time. With a pair of fingers stiff as a rod, he jabbed at his guts, making sure the stench wasn't his, but there was no pain.

He sat up.

It was black as the bottom of some dark pool. Carefully, he climbed to his feet. The ground still sloped. The reek caught him when he tried a deep breath. Knowing only that downhill was safer than up, he resolved to make for the river. The Hollow led straight for it, so he set off, moving as quickly as he could in the tangle—sometimes falling, sometimes picking his way.

As his eyes groped the blackness, pale shapes floated out of the dark. He began to think he should have taken another way down to the river. The shapes flickered out of sight at the pressure of his glance. There were things in the trees: round shapes. Lines glinted.

Toward the bottom, the ground leveled out, but the catching branches crowded close, making every blind step a matter of tearing clothes and gouging skin. For the dozenth time, he lost his balance. As he caught himself—imagining he was grabbing a branch, his grip closed on something else. It was flesh.

In that first instant, he thought of Gol's men and tripped himself jerking back. The pale shape of a man stood before him, and he had nothing but a dagger.

But the shape didn't move.

Durand got back to his feet. His eyes told him it was a sanctuary icon, some marble Power lost in the ravine, but he remembered the feel of skin under his fingers. Durand squared off with this strange figure, and, as he looked, he realized there were others around, all still as idols.

He forced himself closer. He saw a spear's shaft and up-raised arm. Sinews stood under the skin. The eyes were open, like glass beads. The stubbled face was twisted as though the man had suddenly turned. He wore a bare tunic, but there was a shield in his left hand. Durand looked round to see the cover of the shield. Curled around an iron boss—a cupped guard for the fist—was a stag painted in the old style, all curves and knots. He had seen a thing like it once, hanging in the Painted Hall in Acconel. Only a skald—or a grave robber—would know how old.

And there were others.

He had no time.

Though he could hear nothing, Gol's men could be stealing through this wood even now. As he moved on, however, he could not help but puzzle at the uncanny scene around him. It was as though he moved through a frozen instant in the battle for Fetch Hollow. He passed dozens of warriors. Some men wore only their breeches. There was a brass horn curled at one soldier's hip, the metal hammered to resemble a lion's roar. Men's mouths gaped. Wide eyes shone like pearls.

Then, as Durand looked into one set of those eyes, the whole of Creation suddenly throbbed—a bell tolling—and the eye twitched round, spinning like a leech in a glass. The bell's memory shook the trees and moaned in his lungs. And, for that instant, he was face-to-face with a screaming man.

For all his years of sparring and brawling and meeting omens in the dark, Durand was off like a startled rabbit. He slithered over corpses, leapt, and bounded on. He tried to remember the river. No matter how mad the place got, it ended at the river. And the Lost did not cross running water.

These were the men of Ailnor's tale: Sons of Atthi, despite their antique gear. Here were his kinsmen—Atthians meant to be driving an army into the Hollow. He saw emblems he knew, twisted by years. But it was backward.

And it was an Otherworld thing. Even as he blundered through the maze of paralytic corpses, he fought to touch nothing, ducking around and stepping over arms and legs. The

Otherworld had endless strange and fatal rules—names must not be uttered, food must not be eaten. A slip, and a man's soul might be trapped beyond reach of Heaven.

The bell tolled again. And, in that instant, he saw blades flicker like the workings of some Hellish clock.

Fires winked through the screen of oaks and frozen war. Durand stretched his stride, bounding through the tightest, most savage knots of the fighting. The world reeked. Men hung spitted on silent lances. Helms burst under the bite of blades.

He careered onward, understanding against his will that here Atthian men fought Atthian men: hundreds of kinsmen knotted together, motionless and trapped in their raging. There were no tribesmen in the Hollow. Upon the shields were slathered Atthian charges. Some were men of Gireth. A herald would know them all. It was civil war.

This was the kind of madness that Cassonel's masters proposed.

The bell tolled again, and, with its titanic throb, shadows twitched across a hundred shields. In the back ranks, many of the warriors looked high beyond the field. Durand could see a fire glittering in their massed stare. Behind him, the dark hilltop was gone. A village was blazing. Spires and broad windows dripped lead. He remembered the monastery. Men pouring down the hillside into the Hollow.

The bell tolled again. Then, high in a monastery tower, the great bell tumbled. They had fired a holy place. He knew how it must have been. One lot of these fools had seized the monastery—a makeshift fortress—and their foes had set it alight. And this was their curse. Both sides were here now, forever tearing in the dark.

Durand ran like a leaf before a storm.

EVEN SCARED WITLESS and running for his life, Durand found there were limits. For a time he blundered through camp stools and bonfires, but soon there was nothing but unending forest, league after league. Finally, he wove to a halt, the jouncing weight of armor overcoming him. He was not sure how far he had traveled when he stopped, and so he turned back to the hill.

There was nothing: no blaze and no battle. Somehow he had run out of the horseshoe and never touched the river.

He was shaking.

A wineskin had been slapping around his neck since Gol's men made their grab, and he decided that it would be safe to drink what he had brought with him. He drank deep, then dropped to his knees, the mail coat landing like a body beside him.

He fought to breathe, shutting his eyes. He had left old Duke Ailnor to the mercies of his son. He had abandoned his search for Lady Alwen. Even though he had stood outside her door when her baby was crying, he had left her now. It was hard to see how this was what he had intended.

For a time, he listened to his heart pound, then, like an echo of his own imaginings, a cry came out of the dark. He blinked hard, setting his teeth, but the cry came again: a woman's voice. And he stood. He knew it could not be Alwen, but, equally, he knew that he had seen a hill vanish. There was no choice but to follow the sound into the dark.

A man spoke. Though Durand couldn't catch the words, he could tell that the man thought he was funny. He might be drunk. The woman spoke again, her voice pitched high and loud. Splashes and sloshes rang out through the trees, and Durand knew that he must be near. He tore through a close-woven screen of willows and out into a bed of reeds. The sound and smell of running water filled his head.

Now, he peered through the curtain of reeds. Over the water of a stream, he saw a pale shape. It was a woman, her back straight, and her skirts spread on the glassy surface like a water lily.

He looked with a shaky sort of wonder.

Then someone laughed, coarse. "Host of Heaven, if she ain't a river maiden." A fat man on the far bank bent and swung big hands. He already had a black eye. Other shapes moved among the trees. They had driven the woman into the water. She was backing away, getting closer to Durand with every step. Running water was a treacherous thing, and this was no shallow ford.

"You're a pretty thing to be out alone like this," the fat man said. "Hrethmon, would you let a thing like her out like this? You wouldn't, would you?"

Another thug stepped closer to the bank. He was young, and white-blond hair flashed in the moonlight. He was shaking his head "no." Durand heard chuckling from the gloom—too many voices.

Now, the girl spoke, her voice a clear note. "I'll warn you once more. The pair of you had better get yourselves far from here quick, or you'll regret it." The dark volume of her hair bobbed at her shoulders. She held herself straight as a lance.

But they had her in the river up to her hips, and the current was hauling.

"Right, lads," the fat man drawled. "He'll be along any time. The water maiden's man." His head rolled mockingly. "If I had a thing like you, I'd keep you under lock and key." The man was hardly over five feet tall, and his paunch made his tunic stand out like an apron. But there was a mace. "Why don't you come here, and me and the lads'll show you?"

The girl breathed a curse; it would be over soon.

No matter how many there were, Durand knew that he would not step aside.

The girl's hands settled in her skirts, a subtle movement. To run, she would need to tear the dress from the water. Durand saw her fingers closing. The black-eyed fat man looked as though he had also seen her grab her skirts. He waited, smiling. Three more thugs stepped onto the far bank, leering. There were dark shapes in their fists: hatchets, truncheons. Finally, the woman snatched what she could from the water and ran.

Five pursuers launched themselves from the far bank, beginning a wallowing rush for the woman. She was moving, but Durand settled low in the reeds, unarmed and knowing he must have surprise.

She hit the deepest part of the stream, but fought through, and, in an instant, was in the reeds and past Durand, scrabbling up the bank.

The sopping length of skirts caught and dragged.

She couldn't get far, and the two thugs saw it. As they hit the reeds, faces shining with lust, Durand exploded.

The blond passed closest. Durand caught the man's shoulder, and hooked a heavy punch into the side of his head. The fat man wheeled. His forearms bulged like hams, and the iron mace blossomed in his fist.

"Are you this man we've—" Durand clapped his jaw shut with a hooked fist. The blond thrashed in the reeds, downed but not unconscious. Three more were coming on. Durand risked a glance to the girl. All he could see was the batter-white of her dress spread against the bushes.

The fat man swung the mace, and missed by inches. A mace was an awful thing when swung by a strong arm.

The others were nearly upon him.

Behind Durand, the girl was on the move—circling or falling, Durand couldn't see. But the fat man glanced, too. Durand launched himself into this moment of distraction. He hit hard and high, leading with a driving fist against the man's jaw and knocking him sprawling into the reeds. The mace was in Durand's hand.

To fight, he needed solid ground, but to win he needed to keep the whoresons off-balance.

He surged forward into the river, skittering the mace-head over the water and roaring like an outlander. He caught one man a blow on the elbow. And, in a pell-mell moment, they were all on the run.

The fat man was up again, shouting "coward" at his comrades. But Durand rounded on him. They were alone, and, now, Durand had the mace. Water flew as the true coward joined his friends across the river.

And the stream ran cold around Durand's legs.

He heard hooves from the gloom over the river. The men were gone.

Suddenly, he was caught in a sopping grip, tight and cold. It was the girl. She squeezed, and Durand felt a sudden flare of unexpected lust. But then a shudder passed through her. There was a catch in her breath.

She staggered free.

The young woman who faced him did not seem half as tall as the one who had challenged the brigands, but it was her—and not the daughter of Duke Abravanal of Gireth. She fixed him with a long look he could not decipher.

"Why did you? . . ." she began.

"I could hardly leave you there."

"They didn't know you were there."

"I heard you calling." The young woman was close, off-balance. Durand found it hard to catch his breath. She looked up at him, her lips parted. "We should get away from here," Durand said. "If any of them can count, they'll come back."

Now she nodded, glancing over the water, and then leading him up the bank. Her sopping dress dragged over sticks and forest earth. And it clung over the curve of her hips. As she climbed away, he couldn't help but look.

She turned.

"I have seen you," she said.

Durand was about to stammer some apology.

She shook her head. "I have seen your face. Long ago. Or dreamt it."

Wary, confused, she peered at him until a shiver took her.

Durand took a moment to shut his mouth. "You'll catch your death," he managed. "I haven't even got a cloak. I'd best see you're safe, anyway. I'll just get my things. I'm up through the trees that way. Then we can be off. Stay a moment, and I'll see you safe wherever you're off to. Do not worry." Strangely, Durand felt he'd stumbled on some kind of purpose.

She was still watching him, her face indecipherable in the gloom.

"Right here," Durand said. He blundered up the bank and scrabbled after the bundle of armor, hardly thinking. This was something to put in the scales against Ferangore. In a moment, he slid back down the riverbank, carrying everything he owned.

She was gone.

HE SEARCHED FOR a dark hour, then forded the stream, half-wishing he could believe it was the mighty Banderol. He wished now that he had asked the strange woman where in Creation he was. He might be anywhere, though she had spoken the tongue of Atthi with no strange accent, and he supposed that must be something. On the far bank, a track shot off through the forest, running left and right. Deep ruts tore down into the earth. It was no animal trail. Still, as far as the young Blood Moon overhead would let Durand see, he found no trace of the woman from the stream.

"Host of Heaven, where is the Banderol? Where have I fetched up? I have been a fool. Worse than a fool. Lord of Dooms, where have you sent me?" He half-wondered if this was Heaven's curse upon him.

He took the left-hand path, staggering between the ruts. He tasted pooled water, trees, and earth on the air—a breeze added cool lakeshore. Then, as a high bank began to rise on his right hand, a fouler smell: wet horses, dung, and latrine trenches boiling over. Here was the smell of civilization.

Looking for an uphill track, he struggled through what felt like half a league of sliding muck. As he walked, he could see trees against the vault of Heaven ten fathoms up the bank. It could have been the hillfort at Ferangore, freed of its stone shell. Finally, fatigue and desperation convinced him the track would never turn for the hilltop.

With a deep breath, he crashed up the slope, hauling at the hillside brush like a bear. Firelight dawned at the crest. There was indeed a camp on the hill. Trees and tents ringed the flat top of the promontory, while, in and out of the firelight, shield-bearers and serving men trudged. Every kind of horse stood in the dark, puffing steam. Shadows played over the walls of bright tents.

Just as he began to wonder what he had stumbled into, a snarling shape of iron and wool exploded from the brush. Durand crashed flat into the branches, with someone's fists hammering his ribs as he rolled.

"Sneaking bastard!" his attacker roared, stamping a breath of garlic and beer round Durand's ear.

Durand rammed his elbow into the weight bearing him down, feeling teeth clack. "Hells!" More garlic. This, he would not endure. For an instant, Durand managed to plant his foot. He drove himself upright, balancing the struggling weight of his attacker on his shoulders. He tried to get hold of hair or hood, but his nails scrabbled over iron rings.

"Host of Hells!" the attacker swore. "Not so easy, you sneaking bullock." The man's fingers caught the hair at the nape of Durand's neck and pitched him suddenly forward, his chin biting the ground like a plowshare under all the weight.

He couldn't free his arms.

Now a stubbled muzzle brushed his ear, huffing, *"Right, you murdering pig, now I'll slit your throat with your own knife!"* There was a hand groping at his hip. The blade came free. Durand couldn't move.

"Sir Badan!"

It was a new voice, and it came from a few paces off. Durand's jaw was creaking at the hinges.

"Badan!" a second voice shouted.

"I've caught someone behind the tents, haven't I?" said Durand's attacker. "Likely some whoreson's sent him to spy out our lordship's little secret, eh?"

"And will you slay him for it? Think on what you do. This is a tournament."

"He's a spy!"

"And the heralds? What would they do, if you killed a man beyond the lists? If you broke the King's Peace, what do you imagine they would do with the rest of us? His Lordship would not be pleased if you had us banned. Not now."

"Mind your business, Agryn," said the voice at Durand's ear, "or maybe I'll open your gullet, too."

"Others have tried."

There was a snarl.

"Badan!" said a third speaker. "I can't have a man of mine threatening another member of His Lordship's retinue."

The weight on Durand's shoulders rolled off.

"Oh! Coensar."

"Aye. . . ."

Durand took his chance to peer backward. He saw three men and three bare blades.

"I haven't broken the Peace," said Badan. "The whoreson lives. I caught him nosing around back of our tents. Don't know him, but he's no peddler, that's plain enough. He is too well grown for a peasant. Broad shoulders. Got me in the teeth."

The one called Agryn spoke. "He wears a sword belt and his surcoat is slit for riding."

"He's someone's pet soldier," Durand's attacker, Badan, finished.

Durand kept still. He had heard of a Coensar.

"Get up," Coensar said. "Slowly."

Durand stood. A tall man stood a few paces from him, the Blood Moon gleaming down the long blade in his hand, and from the weapon issued a faint moaning. In this light, his hair, blade, and eyes were the same steely shade. It could be the Coensar Durand had heard about: a tournament captain. He had taken scores of men.

Durand made sure the men could see his hands. While he had nearly shaken this Badan character, he didn't like his chances against three, especially if one were Coensar.

Of the three, Sir Coensar stood furthest away. Next, a long-faced man with bowl-cut hair watched like some carved knight in a sanctuary. Both of these men were still. The nearest, however, sneered like a wolf, holding his jaw. This would be Badan, and he was bald to a fringe of red hair that ran long over his shoulders. As Durand watched him, he worked the jaw in what looked like a very painful yawn. It served him right.

Coensar fixed Durand with a challenging stare. "Who are you?"

"I'm called Durand. Durand of Col."

Badan interrupted. "Wha'? From down in Gireth?"

"And who sent you?" Coensar said.

"No one. What is this place?"

Now Badan laughed. "You have just happened to stumble across us, of all people? Coen, let me give him his dagger back." He waggled the blade, its point glinting.

Coensar's clear eyes never left Durand. "I'm not inclined to believe you."

"King of Heaven," said Durand. What could he possibly say? If there was a clever answer, he did not have it.

"Milord, I'm past tired. All I meant to do was find the bloody round of tournaments. Where am I?"

"The tournaments . . ." Coensar said.

"Aye," Durand said. "I never meant for anything. . . ." For a moment, Durand covered his face with both hands. He mastered himself.

When he looked up, Coensar was still watching.

"You're looking for the tournament," Coensar said.

"I was."

The long-faced knight—he had been called Agryn—was shaking his head, back and forth. Something was happening.

Coensar eyed the man.

"Where am I?" Durand asked.

"Red Winding," said Coensar soberly. "The tournament at Red Winding."

"But . . ." Seven day's march in seven hours. Creation seemed to pitch like a ship's deck, but Durand forced himself to stand. "And you're fighting?" he asked.

"We are." The clear eyes looked deep.

Here was a chance; here was Durand's heart's desire. The Powers had dropped a prize into his hands. He must not let it fall. "I can fight," Durand declared.

Badan barked, but Durand tried to match the captain's stare. "I'm no thief. I'm Durand Col. Hroc's son. Ask anyone who's been to Acconel; they'd know me." This was his chance do things right, they must believe him.

The one called Agryn started the headshake once more. Each man checked the others' faces.

Durand heard movement from the tents. Someone was coming. Through the tent ropes, a man wove toward them, a lantern swinging in his hand. He was only a few yards away when he raised the light to reveal a face: ink-dark eyes and sable hair, the living image of Lady Alwen.

Durand couldn't close his mouth.

"Heavens," the man said. It looked like he hadn't meant to greet company.

Coensar smiled. " 'Acconel,' you said?"

Hands closed on Durand's elbows, and Durand turned his eyes to Heaven.

9. Trial above the Mere

They dragged Durand into a tent where they stood him like a moth in a canvas lantern. Heavy chests lined the walls and a swirling carpet from the Inner Seas had been rolled over the grass. There were knights all around: big men with arms folded, some just returning blades to scabbards. All eyes were on Durand, including the dark eyes of the black-haired young man with the lantern: his judge.

Dressed all in red, this man who so looked like Alwen of Gireth settled into a camp chair and gave Sir Coensar a bantering look. Bits of brass winked at scabbard and buckle. "Well, who have you brought me, my captain? Introductions seem in order, at the very least."

Who was this man?

Coensar said nothing.

"Well, then," the young man pressed, "Sir Agryn, perhaps you will tell me?"

Agryn blinked once and bowed a fraction. "Lordship, this man claims he's known in Acconel."

The young lord leaned closer. "Hmm. He's a big lad. Dark mop. Eyes look blue . . ."

Now Badan grunted. "I think a man'd remember him, *if* he's ever been to Acconel." But then the young lord—still the preternatural image of Alwen—was looking into Durand's face, considering. A homely footman stepped close to slop claret into his cup.

"Says he's come ninety leagues round Silvermere to join the tournament," Badan added. "Says he comes from the Col."

The young lord raised his empty hand, saying idly, "I suppose if you've no boat, you must go round."

They were playing with him. Durand eyed the circle of fighting-men carefully, thinking he should catch what he had missed—baffled. Most looked far more displeased than their lord, who now regarded Durand with a narrowed eye. And threw up his hands.

"All right, then, I concede. Tell me who you are, and perhaps that will tell me what I must do."

"I'm called Durand, Lordship: son of Hroc, Baron of Col."

Now the impossible young lord sat back, hooking his thumbs under his glinting belt. "Whom do you say you served?"

"I served Sir Kieren, Lordship. Kieren of Arbourhall."

The man let a long moment slide past.

"I would have thought he was past playing knights and shield-bearers by now. The Fox must be older than Coen here, and God knows how long *he's* been at it."

Coensar closed his eyes. Something had gone wrong for these men.

"Well, I know nothing else about him," the young noble said. "But he's fully as daft as he says he is, and I would guess that he's served in Acconel."

There was something in the man's voice—this uncanny resemblance, this knowledge of Acconel. Alwen was not an only child. The Duke of Gireth had two daughters and two sons. His heir and his youngest daughter had always been in Acconel. But the youngest son . . . He never came home. Only that summer, half the court had packed themselves off to Mornaway for his wedding and come back silent. He was never anywhere to be seen. Durand tried to remember that name.

"—*Lamoric*," Durand said, and men all around cursed.

"That's it then," said the young lord.

But Durand could hardly hear them all. Before him sat the youngest son of the Duke of Gireth, brother of the woman he had thrown in that Ferangore tower, uncle of the infant child lost beyond hope. Durand felt the Powers circling him, mocking, watching, weighing.

Lamoric twisted in his chair. "You wouldn't think this should be so difficult," Lamoric said.

"*Lordship*," Durand said. He managed a very shaky bow.

"Yes," said Lamoric. "It has been a long while since I set eyes on Acconel, friend." He knuckled his chin. "I wasn't even born in the place. Father was doing the rounds."

No one laughed.

"So you are Durand Col, son of one of my father's lesser barons. You served a knight of my father's household. And I am Lamoric, youngest son of Duke Abravanal. Now you know. Why are you not with Sir Kieren? Why are you not at Acconel."

"Your Lordship." Durand forced his mind back to distant, half-forgotten things. "I was meant to inherit a fief called Gravenholm, but now the heir . . . They thought he was—"

Lamoric looked baffled. "What are you saying?" Then he seemed to realize. "The shipwreck? Hearnan? They've found him?"

He should be explaining about Alwen, about the man's infant nephew. "Hearnan was the name, yes," said Durand.

"By the King of far Heaven. That was to be yours, then? His father's land. What did you say? Gravenholm?"

"Aye," Durand acknowledged.

"And now?"

"What?" Lamoric's sister was surely dead. He remembered her face in the high window.

"What now? Without this Gravenholm."

"Nothing, Milord," Durand managed. "My lord father, he will not displace a sworn man."

"God save us from honorable fathers. But who has sent you to this place? Kieren sent no word."

"Kieren?" The Silent King alone knew what Power had thrown him into this man's lap. "He does not know."

"Do you mean to tell me that you just left him?"

"I . . ."

"I can hardly take on a knight who would abandon his sworn lord. Really, you are—"

Knight. "Lordship," said Durand. He would not compound his crimes by pretending. "I'm no knight yet."

"A shield-bearer then? By all the souls below, man, what am I meant to do with you? The heralds would have my ears if I let you fight. You know my face, but you're no use to me. By rights, I should flog you skinless and have you dragged back to Acconel. I don't know what I should say. You're no knight, you swore to serve old Kieren, and you left him?"

He had no answer. He could not tell the man what he must.

Lamoric clawed a black forelock from his eyes. "Host of Heaven. I can spare no one to take you as far as Acconel. Not now. The mêlée begins in the morning." He paused. "And I'm not letting you out of my sight. For now, you work for Guthred. He can always use another hand. Guthred?"

The homely footman stepped forward. "Lordship?"

"I think we've found you some help."

"Durand," said Lamoric, "you're to do what Guthred here tells you and keep quiet about who you've seen here this evening. I am not myself tomorrow. A season's blood and sweat will come to worse than nothing if you forget that. Do you understand?"

Durand nodded. Whatever the game they were playing, he understood that he should keep his mouth shut.

"And Guthred," Lamoric said, "remember, the Herald of Errest is out there. We are being watched."

Durand eyed the circle of knights once, then stumbled after the old man. He said nothing about Yrlac or dead sisters.

OUTSIDE, THE HOMELY footman, Guthred, rounded on Durand.

"I'm Lamoric's man, right? Though he's pulled together this lot for this season, I've served him ten winters, and I was a soldier with some of these boys before that," he said. "I'm watching you. You'll do nothing against them. Right?"

"I swear, I—"

"Swear to it all you like. I'll *see* to it. Anyone could know old Kieren's name." The man scratched an imposing nose, then made a dry laugh. "But you don't see many who can put a mark on Badan when he's watching for it."

"I had no choice."

"You can have that carved on your slab if you've got a penny for the stonecutter. Old Badan don't forget." The old shield-bearer had stopped laughing. "We sleep over this way."

Where Guthred left him, Durand sank to the rutted ground. His eyes dwelled on the wide ring of blue, red, and yellow tents: more canvas lanterns glowing at the dark pasture's edge. Horses huffed and tossed against their pickets.

He had killed a woman—though he had tried to save her. Now, he was in the camp of her brother. The man must know.

Damp oozed through his hip and shoulder as knights and pages across the hill blew out the motley lanterns, one by one.

"YOU SAY SOME odd things in your sleep, friend."

A shock of rotten teeth puffed into Durand's face. And, for a heartbeat, he was on the road with Kieren, or starving with Heremund Skald—wherever *he'd* gone—or locked in the keep at Ferangore with Alwen dying in her tower.

But it was Guthred scowling down.

Durand thought of all the wild things he might have muttered in his dreams: murder and treason. Guthred peered close.

"I don't know how you've come here, or what's rattling in that head of yours, but there's a mêlée to fight. If His Lordship's to get his shield in the Herald's Roll, you've work to do. Come."

Durand pulled himself up, following the shield-bearer through a camp now choked in mist. Hazy shapes were on the move and only coughs and clearing noses assured Durand he really was in Creation.

Somewhere, if Durand understood, the silent Herald of Errest carried his Roll of Errest with its painted shields under this same blanket of mist. They said the man had served every king since Einred's son and the Battle of Lost Princes: three hundred winters. What blot would they put on Durand's shield when the world learned his secret?

"Mooncalf! Remember, he's not Lamoric while he's fighting here. They've taken to calling him 'The Knight in Red.' No name. Forget that, and I'll remember," Guthred warned, and they were off.

It turned out there were nearly a score of shield-bearers trailing Lamoric's retinue. Guthred, though a commoner, seemed to be in charge of the lot of them. He issued orders, sending some down the hill for water and others to look after the fighting men.

"You and I are going to look after Milord Lamoric's armor. I'm keeping my eye on you. And don't worry about breakfast, you ain't serving it."

Durand had not thought.

"I like to make sure of the equipment the morning of," said Guthred. "I leave it to someone else, Host Below knows what'll happen; I keep track, nothing goes wrong.

"Load everything that's mail into that cask there. I've got it half full of white sand from the mere near the town. And vinegar. Roll it till I stop you." When Durand didn't jump to work quick enough, the shield-bearer spat. "Or stand there shaking the cursed thing if that's your choice. And don't think I won't know if you slack off. I'm watching. Don't go wandering too far. Don't think of running off. And don't think of spilling His Lordship's name."

Durand loaded the barrel with the best mail he'd ever handled: supple rings, forge-hardened. Out beyond the hill and the town below, Silvermere lay like a specter in the predawn twilight. He booted the cask along, but couldn't keep his eyes from the water. In one night, he had skirted the greatest lake in the Atthias. And there was no short way round: on the west shore was cursed Hesperand; on the south, haunted Merchion; and on the east, the Halls of Silence and its giant lords. The night before, he had been in far Yrlac searching for Alwen. Now, he stared at peddlers' carts winding their way up from Red Winding. What Power had done this, and what did it mean?

Lamoric appeared—black hair, dark eyes. Across a dozen yards of turf, the lordling had stopped to talk with Guthred, who gestured to Durand without looking his way.

He had everything he needed: the last tournament of the season, and a chance with a tournament lord. But he was stealing a place he had no right to. One that he couldn't possibly keep once he'd done as he must. But this was the chance he had prayed for. How could he throw it away? What Power had brought him to Red Winding?

THE NEXT HOUR was consumed in preparation, and there was work to be done with a full conroi and all their horses to be armed and ready.

While shield-bearers ran, a fresh wind bowled the mist out over the waves. Mobs of hawkers arrived to cry the virtues of meat pies and beer to fighting men and to the gawkers up from Red Winding. Longshoremen had hammered together a reviewing stand by the lists, and now old men, burghers, and noblewomen jostled on the benches like pigeons in a coop.

At the last, as Durand and another shield-bearer threw one saddle over a dun charger, Durand felt the saddlebow rattle loose. With no time to spare and no thought of secrets or confessions, he went hunting for a saddler with a hammer. The man he found worked for the Duke of Mornaway's son but nailed the thing together without a word.

He could see heralds making ready.

The ranked banners he passed put Durand in mind of the blazons in the depths of Fetch Hollow. How many of these men would ride for Beoran's rebels if it came to war? He imagined sly looks among the highborn. How many waited for Radomor's answer?

Hawkers and beggars worked the crowd. In their midst,

Durand nearly stepped on a blind man who thumbed the wide, stained pages of a *Book of Moons,* somehow reading aloud. Next to him, a pockmarked child was swallowing an entire basketful of adders, somehow coaxing them, live, into the pit of her stomach. A man in a breechcloth sat with something in his hand, purple and sloppy: his own heart pulsing for all to see.

As Durand made to pass, a hand caught his elbow. The adder girl faced him. The blind reader turned his way, saying—reading?—"Second among them was Bruna of the Broad Shoulders. The wrath of the righteous was his vice. Betrayed and betraying. Treachery taught him mercy. Treason taught him understanding. Beware his line when it runs true. There is little such a man learns that does not cause pain."

Durand tugged his sleeve free of the little girl. The saddle was in his arms. He had no money to pay. "What are you saying?" The blind man smiled like a sanctuary icon, and the girl was looking up with adders in her throat. Was he doomed to betray? Did that explain Ferangore? Was that the root of his silence? He broke away.

And stumbled right into Guthred—who squinted from Durand to the girl. "What's going on?" he demanded. After a moment sizing Durand up, he took the saddle. "Give me that and get with the others quick."

DURAND TOOK HIS place behind the lines of mounted warriors glaring across the hilltop pasture. All told, there were three hundred knights: fighting men of every ancient house. Men and warhorses trembled under their panoply, ready to fly.

For now, these men needed Durand more than wild truths. He snapped up his own coat of mail and fought his way into the mob of serving men at the rear of Lamoric's conroi, hauling the rusting thing over his head.

Guthred stood before the shield-bearers, raising an eyebrow at the mail coat. The old man himself wore only a quilted canvas gambeson. He'd stitched a steel bowl in his skullcap.

"This is His Lordship's very last chance to make this Red Knight game come off. The old Herald's watching, and you'll do your bit. You're each to make sure that none of our lads ends up without a weapon. No one wants for a shield, no one falls because you didn't see. A man drops his lance; you put a new one in his fist before he knows it's gone. He can be in the worst of it, and you'll be there.

"Now, get to your man. Keep him living. You've one last chance to make sure he ain't left something behind, right?" The shield-bearers hesitated. Guthred flapped his arms. "I mean now!"

The others shoved their way through the press. Guthred caught Durand by the arm. "Now, you. Kieren didn't go in much for tournaments. Right?"

"They hold one at Acconel when they drive the bulls. I've watched, but—"

"The old bugger. And he missed the Battle of Hallow Down last summer, too. I'll not leave Lamoric in your hands. Blind seers or no, you'll be with me. We're looking out for Coensar."

"But I thought you were Lamoric's—"

"You don't worry 'bout that. I'll have a man on Lamoric, but you—you'll be looking after Coensar. I see no reason to trust you, and plenty not. If you ain't so useful, the captain's got his wits and he's got Keening. High Kingdom blade. There isn't a man here who can—"

"—What's that?" the shield-bearer said.

Durand heard nothing. Then realized: The lines were silent. Seven score warhorses stood shoulder to shoulder on Durand's side of the lists. The lances were poised like a line of flagpoles.

Guthred started to move, getting a better position, and Durand followed. "Coensar's wearing azure with terns in silver," he said. He jabbed splayed fingers into Durand's chest. "Blue with three white birds on. He'll be at the head of our lot when they charge out."

"Who're we fighting for?"

"His Lordship's lined up against the Duke of Mornaway's boy, Lord Moryn, His Lordship's brother-in-law."

"His man fixed that saddle. Lamoric's pitted *against* his brother-in-law?"

Guthred grunted. "Moryn's heir to Mornaway. His bodyguard are hard men fresh from Hallow Down—but our lads will fight harder for a chance at his ransom. Trust greed."

Durand shook his head—but there was money in Mornaway.

Guthred pointed. "That's him, so watch. A greyhound-lean man coolly stalked the line of his knights on the far side of the lists. His shield bore a maze of diamonds in blue and yellow, the dizzying design repeating on his surcoat and the trapper of a blood-bay warhorse. "He fights these things to keep sharp for the king's next call."

"I see him," Durand said.

"Clever boy," Guthred said. His attention had turned to the reviewing stand where the Herald of Errest would be watching.

"Hold there," Guthred said, raising his hand. "That's the heralds."

Someone was speaking. All Durand could see were the backsides of horses.

"That's it," Guthred concluded.

Durand turned—about to say, "That's what?"—when he heard the first note of a trumpet, and Creation exploded. Sevenscore warhorses launched their weight of iron and muscle into motion.

The line thundered away, a hundred-forty haunches, fast as falling. You couldn't get so many men on the field at Acconel. He had seen nothing like it.

As Durand staggered, the line of horses' backsides struck; the impact stamped across a hundred paces. Tournament lance-heads—three-knuckled crowns—bit, their shafts detonating. Men roared. Horses collided. Strong men flew like rag dolls. And the remains of the enemy line burst through. Horses dragged riders.

"Bad one," Guthred grunted. "The bastards always take the first charge at a gallop." He shook his head a twitch. "Daft buggers."

With a grunt, he turned to the shield-bearers. "Watch for our boys!" Blinded by leaping mobs, Guthred turned to Durand.

"You see the captain?"

Durand searched the chaos of three hundred knights careering in three hundred directions as the charge splintered, then some lodestone's pull imposed itself upon the confusion and the lines took shape again. The last few slashed back and forth between the lines roaring curses. "Nothing," Durand said.

"Lines met badly. Some bastard must have taken his opponent on the right, or sheered off, or some cursed thing. Bad pass. It'll make a short day for some. I don't see any of our lads."

Durand swept the churning throng but saw no one. They could all be sprawled in the muck or disarmed or surrounded. "No. There's—"

"Hells. Stick by me, mooncalf. We've got to work round the side. There might be time." Guthred turned to the others. "Take as much as you can carry and follow me!" The shield-bearers and a thicket of lances bolted around the field, heading for the sideline under the crowded stands. As they ran, though, the ranks of horsemen drew themselves together. "Hells, they're going straight back at it!" Guthred shouted.

Despite the struggling men in the field between them, the two lines charged. The heaving formation of iron and muscle rumbled past Durand and Guthred's clattering mob.

They struck while Durand and his fellow shield-bearers were shoving their way through gawkers. The crowd jumped to life, but when the ranks thundered apart once more, the field's slaughterhouse madness was laid bare only a few yards from Durand. Stallions floundered like hooked fish. Bloody men dragged themselves toward safety. Some lay still.

Guthred pointed. *"Coensar!"*

Durand looked for a body, but then spotted a blue and silver figure riding through no-man's-land. Sir Coensar circled one of the crawlers, Keening leveled.

"He's got that one," said Guthred. "The fellow's lamed himself somehow."

The downed knight rolled onto his back.

Meanwhile, the lines swept together at either end of the field. Horses still churned, knights were roaring.

"Right boy," said Guthred. "We're getting Coen's fish. If he dies out there there's no ransom!"

Durand blinked as Guthred broke from the crowd and charged out between the lines. Two or three hundred lances jostled, ready to charge. The man had to be mad.

Durand gritted his teeth and ran.

Seeing Guthred take the field, Coensar gave a nod and broke for Lamoric's ranks. The wounded man moaned behind the mask of a battle helm, "To the Hells with you!" Pitiless, Guthred took hold and began to drag. "Grab an arm, boy!"

Durand took a fistful of surcoat.

Suddenly, the turf shuddered to life.

"Son of Morning," Guthred croaked. He let go.

In a sick instant, Durand realized that Guthred had misjudged. They were too far from the fence. A glance took in the leveled points of a hundred lances bearing down. A double tide of iron and muscle surged toward them. In a twist of panic, Durand flipped the prisoner over his shoulders and ran, the lines slamming shut at his heels. He dove.

The lines flew apart. Durand and his cargo hit the turf by Guthred's side. The crowd roared.

Guthred spat dirt from his mouth. "How many times do the buggers mean to do that before they get to business?"

Gawkers hauled Durand to his feet. A beaker of something was dumped over his thigh. He had torn his knuckles when he locked his fist in the prisoner's hauberk. Despite the press, Guthred managed a word in Durand's ear. "Clever. Three hundred pounds of man and armor there." He peered up into Durand's face. "A thing like this might get a new man noticed—if that's what he's after."

In the fields, the last great charge had devolved into tangled skirmishes. Swords flashed over a storm of grunting men and beasts.

"God!" the downed man moaned. "You whoresons. I think you've separated me from one of my arms. Ach, some bastard's stepped on my hand."

Guthred moved his heel. "You're lucky you're alive, Lordship." He was busy keeping an eye on every shield-bearer and every rider. Durand watched the faces change with every heartbeat. He couldn't imagine tracking it all.

The prostrate knight wrestled his helm off, gasping, "Oi! Back, you bastards. There's a man still alive down here." An older knight, past forty, grimaced from a tight mail hood. A graying beard bristled nearly over his cheekbones. For a moment he worked his shoulder, eyes squeezed shut, but then he looked up—one eye remained an empty pucker. "Who owes me the arm?"

"That's him that's looking over you," said Guthred, taking his eyes from the lists. "I dropped you."

In front of them, a man flew from his saddle. He hit the turf like an ox dropped from a wall.

"Ah," One-Eye said. "Gimme your arm, friend." He reached up, and Durand caught his hand without thinking. The man levered himself up. "There," the stranger said, "you're settled. Arm for arm. I still owe you a life, though, I think." He was smiling. "Tell me where I'm to stand till they're done. I could use a drink. This will ruin me. I'm Berchard, by the by."

A conroi of men in blue swung past, the leader with a kicking enemy slung over his saddlebow.

Guthred looked to Durand. "Put your new friend by the fire pit. We'll start a pile."

Abruptly, Coensar was before them. He brought ancient Keening up in a salute—maybe to Durand, maybe to the crowd. The mob was loud behind them.

But as Durand glanced at the throng, his gaze fell upon a woman's face. She stood straight-backed, looking down on him from one of the wellborn boxes. Half the crowd was looking right at him, but Durand knew her; she was the one from the stream. Under the Eye of Heaven, her hair was not dark at all, but red as new blood. She wore it uncovered in the style of a maiden.

"Aw no," Guthred was saying. Somewhere across the field, a group of knights in stained gear was walking from the lists, disarmed.

"I'm afraid they're taking the polish off your grand performance there, boy. That's three of ours just yielded."

AN HOUR LATER, Durand and Guthred were catching their breath among the tents, having just hauled a knight—big as a carthorse—to safety. One of Lamoric's men, the giant had taken a blow to the forehead. The needle pulled, then popped, as Guthred's man worked on the knight. The wound bristled with eyebrow and stitches as the big knight took a pull from his wineskin.

While Durand watched the surgeon's work, Guthred kept an eye on the field.

"Aw. Aw no. Aw no!" He ripped the skullcap from his head

and whipped it to the ground. "Not another! This'll break us. Lamoric's getting a good show for the Herald."

Out in the lists, a knight Durand did not recognize was on his knees. "Does that make eight?" Durand asked.

"Or nine, friend. It might as well be nine. This will cost us." It could mean the armor, horses, and weapons of every man, all lost to ransom. Guthred bent to collect the iron bowl of his skullcap. "We haven't had a day like this in ages." He looked at Durand, and spent a long moment still and staring. "You're a real good luck charm."

The day had been long, and frustration had Lamoric's retainers snapping and snarling. An hour before, Durand and the other shield-bearers had to scuffle with the men of another retinue. One of Lamoric's knights had hit the turf right at Durand's feet. They could hardly watch another man dragged off.

"Come," said Guthred. He nodded to the carthorse knight. "He don't need his hand held. You'll see, he'll be up and surrendering like all the others in no time." A thread of blood slithered from the big man's brow to his beard.

Abruptly, the crowd was howling. "Hells, what's this?" Guthred said and bolted for the lists, elbowing a path to the front row with Durand in tow.

As Durand stepped out, Lamoric, easy to recognize in solid red, swung down from his warhorse. In front of him, a lean knight was getting up from a hard fall. He levered a shield from the muck.

It was covered in diamonds: blue and yellow, azure and gold.

"Host of Heaven," said Guthred. "Lamoric's knocked Moryn Mornaway on his arse!" Moryn's ransom would buy every man they'd lost. But Guthred's face was tense.

"Can he take him?" Durand asked.

"Shut up," was Guthred's reply.

Lamoric did a good job playing the grave knight-at-arms, waiting for Lord Moryn to collect his sword and shield. Some of the crowd were shouting, "Get to it!" and "Past time for kissing now!" There was laughter.

As Moryn stood, Lamoric raised his blade to the red face of his battle helm. When Moryn answered, Lamoric moved: gallant salute turned murderous attack as Lamoric wrenched his blade into a high slash. In the wheeling moments that followed, the two combatants sent a flickering exchange to nick shields and test distances.

The Lord of Mornaway was swift and supple; Durand spotted something in the man's gait: he'd done something to his hip. An opening like that could be enough.

The two combatants danced apart, reeling to catch themselves in clean guard positions. Lord Moryn assumed an outlandish pose, coiled with his sword cocked over his off shoulder. Durand had never seen the like.

"Come on. Coen's shown you," Guthred muttered.

Moryn waited like an adder, poised as Lamoric jittered out of reach. Suddenly, Lamoric saw some chance. He lunged close, jamming his red shield high. The Lord of Mornaway uncoiled—a fraction too slow.

In a confusion of shields and blades, Lamoric's sword clapped over Moryn's armored knee.

The lord of Mornaway sprang clear, clutching at the pain. The steel cap over the knee had blunted a maiming strike, though God knew what had become of the bone behind it.

Some of Moryn's men made to jump in. Durand braced himself to throw his fists against their swords, but Moryn snapped his hand into the air, stopping it all.

Gravely then, the Lord of Mornaway stood and raised his blade in salute.

He was brave, but no man could fight if he couldn't move.

Lamoric prowled in, sure to throw speed and mobility against his opponent. Astonishingly, however, the hobbled Lord of Mornaway kept the Red Knight at bay, twitching stop-thrusts into Lamoric's path. Mornaway was a skilled swordsman, and he had seen a dozen violent winters before Lamoric was born.

But Lamoric circled, forcing lean Moryn to step and turn, each time on the bad leg, and each time in the ruts and troughs of the torn ground. The Lord of Mornaway could not last long.

Inevitably, he staggered on the knee.

Lamoric leapt into that moment. He beat Moryn's blade wide and crashed bodily into the knight, pitching him off guard. Red and diamond blue stormed around each other, then, from the midst of this hail, one tight backhand slipped through: Lamoric's blade caught Moryn's helm. Then, with a wrenching twist, he rang another tight backhand from the steel. Moryn's long hands fumbled at the face of his helm, his shield loose.

The crowd was silent.

And, after a wavering moment, Mornaway collapsed.

Lamoric set his point at the lord's throat.

"Do you yield?"

Two or three of Moryn's men leapt down from their saddles. Durand and a few others jumped into the lists. Impossibly, Moryn's hand waved them back yet again. Lamoric leveled his blade. "Lord Moryn Mornaway, do you yield?"

"I do." The warped helm tumbled free and a brutalized older man winced up at his captor. "You have fairly bested me. And, on my oath, I am your prisoner."

Durand was not the first to charge into the lists.

He saw the girl again from the thick of Lamoric's men as they carried their Red Knight master back to camp. Until Durand looked up, he was an unthinking participant in the mob, but when he glanced from the crush and saw his Maid of the Stream looking down, he forgot the others. Eyes dark as a faun's, but staring through him.

The mob gave Durand a shove.

He spotted the red flash of her hair as she walked down the benches toward a set of plank steps not far away. Durand broke away from the rest and reached the steps just as she arrived.

"Hello," Durand said, and she looked. Her eyes were enough to stop his breath.

"Do you remember me?" he asked.

She said nothing.

"You disappeared. I am glad you are well."

The eyes held him another moment, then darted. The crowd jostled him closer. Like a child, Durand wanted to ask if she had come to see him, or if she had seen him hoist Coensar's prize from the lists.

"A fine day," he managed, instead.

"I shouldn't—I shouldn't be speaking with you," she said, and she was already turning.

"Wait! Who are you?"

"A lady's maid," she said.

A tiny thing, it took her only a moment to slip off into the crowd. Durand could not follow.

THERE WAS LAMORIC, stalking in circles and swinging his crimson mantle. The great red helm was still on his head. When every man in the camp had a drink in his fist, Lamoric planted his foot on his chair, and turned on the only somber man in the camp: Moryn Mornaway.

Already, one of the swordsman-lord's eyes had closed, swelling tight. But his back was straight as a spit.

"Welcome to my camp, Lord Moryn," said Lamoric. "I am very pleased to make you my guest."

The lean knight nodded a shallow bow. "I must be quicker in the future."

"Or face a less fortunate opponent."

Sweat plastered hair against tall Moryn's forehead like ink on wet parchment. He blinked, narrowing his better eye. "Do I know your voice, Red Knight?"

"I have chosen not to use my own arms in the lists," answered Lamoric.

Lord Moryn paused, then said, "A novelty."

"Well, I am forced to avoid the feasts, I am afraid."

"And if I encounter you once more, I may not know you."

"Regrettable," Lamoric allowed.

"I should like to face you again," said Moryn. "I should like that very much. If you will not give me your name, you must be sure to wear this red helm when next we meet. A satisfying prize, it would make."

"Lord Moryn," said Lamoric, abruptly. "You are an honorable man?"

Moryn stiffened. "It is rarely questioned."

"And I have never heard it said that you ran off when paroled or struck a man unawares."

Moryn was still as a drawn line; he took a slow breath. "Half-a-thousand knights are sworn to fight in the name of Mornaway. The house of Mornaway is as ancient as any in this realm. I do not take the honor of my lineage lightly." He narrowed his eye once more, looking close at the red helm. "I ask you plainly, Knight in Red. Should I know you?"

Lamoric took hold of the great red helm and, after a good

showman's pause, lifted the thing from his head, and there he was: Lamoric of Gireth, youngest son of the duke, sweaty and grinning.

"You?" said Moryn. The word slid like a blade of ice, even as Lamoric smiled.

"And I will have your word now that you will tell no one."

After an astonished moment, Moryn wheeled to the on-lookers. "Sons of Atthi witness. Before the Host of Heaven, I, Moryn Mornaway, heir to the lands between Lost Hesperand and the Westering Sea, swear that no one shall learn the true name of this Knight in Red by word or deed of mine." He turned stiffly back to Lamoric. "Will this suffice?"

"Lord Moryn," said Lamoric, setting the slot-eyed helm on his knee, "I find myself quite satisfied just now."

Moryn fixed Lamoric with a smoldering eye. "I would welcome the opportunity to redeem my honor."

"And I do not feel it necessary to repeat our confrontation. It was quite decisive, I think, brother-in-law."

The wounded lord drew himself to his full height, saying, "Then we are finished. Our men will arrange the ransom. I must appear at the feast, and there is little more for us here."

"Again I am satisfied," said Lamoric.

At a look from Mornaway, the startled knights of Lamoric's entourage parted and allowed him to walk from their circle.

"You see?" said Lamoric. "That is but a taste of what will come when we succeed. We will open their eyes!" He grinned. "Poor Lord Moryn, he never liked that a wastrel of my ilk married his sister." Durand remembered some scandal; no one spoke much of it.

Stiffly, Coensar answered, "No, Lordship."

"He liked that I bested him even less. I am satisfied indeed."

"Yes, Lordship."

Lamoric chuckled. "Well then," he said, "how have we done, all in all?"

"My Lord, not well. We've lost nine men to ransom, which will likely cost us half our mounts and armor. Moryn's price may save us. And I only managed to take one hostage." Coensar looked around. Suddenly, Durand realized what the man was searching for. The one-eyed knight was missing.

"Where's the new man?" demanded the captain.

Now, Guthred turned. "Durand!" Durand stepped forward. The one-eyed man had fled.

"Your friend?" said Coensar.

"I've seen no sign of him, Captain. Not since we brought him here."

"Did you have him swear out a parole?"

It had never occurred to him. They had left the man right in the camp. He must simply have walked out. Coensar looked tired. "No, Sir Coensar."

Guthred's fists were white.

Just then, a strange voice broke the silence. "Ahem."

Quick-fisted thugs like Badan caught hold of the stranger before he could utter a proper word, though this did not stop the man from shouting.

"Bloody whoresons! Set me down!" Durand saw fists and heels and a bearded chin as the man kicked and snarled in the hands of his captors. With Badan in charge, Lamoric's lads planted the stranger before their master's chair.

He had only one eye.

"You were saying, Sir?" Lamoric prompted, gesturing that Badan should give the man room to breathe.

"Bastards!" the stranger spluttered. "My leaving was square in line with the ordinances of chivalry. There wasn't one of you whoresons had time to make me yield, let alone vow not to wander off, and I ain't planning to climb back into the bloody lists today to give you a second crack at—"

"*Hells!*" Badan leapt from the one-eyed knight, as if the man were a knot of serpents. Stumbling among his comrades, Badan snatched his sword free, horror in his face.

"What is it?" Lamoric demanded. Half the men had their blades drawn.

"*Berchard,*" Badan gasped.

The stranger looked up, narrowing his good eye as though he were surrounded by madmen—but then he seemed to realize.

"Ah!" He pointed. "It's Badan, yes? Where's all the hair?" He smiled.

Badan was shaking his mostly naked head.

Berchard nodded up to Lamoric, confiding: "You'll have

to excuse my old friend here. He thinks I've risen from the dead."

Badan made the Eye of Heaven.

"He and some mates of his left me hanging in Pendur, is all."

"Oh, did they?"

"It's an old story now. And, with luck, I'll get a chance to tell it, as I can see you're a decent fellow who wouldn't want to kill a man just to stop his tongue wagging. I've seen that face of yours, haven't I? What with this setback here today and all, you may need another hand, and I'm a free man with no hindrances." He smiled. "And—"

Durand felt a sharp pain at the nape of his neck: a twist of fingers in the short hairs. Guthred snarled in his ear. "Oh, you're a luck-charm, that's certain. You mind I'm watching."

10. Death and Dreaming

Only Coensar took the city track down to the feast.

With Lamoric playing Knight in Red, he kept to the abandoned hilltop as night fell. The Heavens swung above them, scattered with stars. If they turned from the fire, they might look down on the hall of Red Winding, where tall windows winked over the black glass of Silvermere. They scraped together a simple feast of their own with beer, hot sausage, and cold meat pie. Most fell to bragging and laughing. A few of the group were watchful, waiting.

Durand took himself to the firelight's cool fringes—the first chance he'd had to think in all the hours since dawn. He could not believe that only one day had passed since Fetch Hollow. He still bore scratches from those oaks. He still had not spoken to Lord Lamoric: He still had not confessed.

While the men laughed at one long story, Durand noticed Lamoric standing without a word and step into the dark, a strange look in his eye.

Berchard's voice drew Durand's attention back to the fire. "I've told you, not till I've finished my supper."

"All right then," said Badan, lurching to his feet. "Then I've got one. While you buggers weren't looking, I'm out there. You should have seen the bastard." He mimed a lance under his arm. "Hit him square on the shield. Dead center. Tore one of his boots off throwing him down, the whoreson." His yellow teeth sparked like a dry fire.

"He got up barefoot, the mooncalf, blinking and stumbling about, like." Badan reeled around the fire, mimicking his victim. "Any case, he could have surrendered right there, but he pulls his sword and starts waving it around." Badan followed suit, drunkenly hauling out his own razor-edged blade as the others flinched and swore. "What could I do? There he was, armed, and would he hand his sword over to me? Ballocks! So I circled him a few times." The sword flickered round a few circles. "Still on horseback, like? Not about to let him take a free poke at me." He jabbed the air, missing ears and elbows.

"Hells, Badan," Berchard swore.

Durand grimaced.

The blade swished.

"I kept shouting at him: Yield! Yield, you whoreson. But he would not. He just kept working his mouth and blinking. And I'd had enough."

Badan grimaced, abruptly distracted. "—Filthy jaw." He spotted Durand beyond the circle of his audience. "Your bloody elbow's broken a tooth for me, oathbreaker." There was some laughter. Durand didn't join in.

"Anyway, I spurred my horse at him and swung," Badan declared. "Started high and swung underhand." Again the crowd flinched from his blade. "I caught him on the back of the head." His teeth glinted. "Now, I swear I was trying for the flat of the blade. I just reckoned on putting him out for a while. But . . . Poor bastard. No ransom now, but my boys dragged off his armor, and his horse looks all right." He stuck the long blade into the turf, swaggering. "I couldn't believe the look on his face, though. Standing there with one shoe off and one shoe on, like. His head wide open. He looked a fool."

Badan leered at others, waiting for guffaws, but none came.

"Hells, Badan," said one man.

Long-faced Sir Agryn actually stood.

Badan appealed to the others, plucking his sword from the

turf. "It was just the sight of him there, that's all. Just that bare foot and—"

There was a sound like cut silk; Agryn parried Badan's waving blade.

"Badan. You have struck a peer undefended. You have struck a peer undefended from horseback while he was on foot. And you have struck from behind. By the Silent King and his Host both, this is a tournament only. And you have compounded your madness by looting his person. I concede that you are ready to leap into the Hells, but do you mean to turn the Eye of Heaven from us all?"

Under the huge and empty sky, this threat seemed very real.

But Badan jerked his sword free, staggering a drunken step backward. "This is not your Septarim now, monk," he snarled. "We're fighting men here. Not ghosts. Not damned bloodless priests."

Durand climbed to his feet. He was not the only one.

But Agryn said nothing.

"It was bad luck," snarled Badan. The sword glinted. "And he was armed. It could as well have been me! If you've no stomach for a fight, maybe you ought to go back to playing under your habit!"

The somber knight twitched his cloak aside, freeing his sword arm. A glance told Durand that none of the others knew what to do. But, at that moment, Coensar strode into the firelight. His hand was on Keening. Lamoric followed behind.

"What is the matter with you?" snapped Lamoric. "Badan? Agryn?"

Badan snorted.

"Put that sword away, Badan," Coensar ordered. "Put it away now!" Badan obeyed.

"Good," said Coensar.

"I'm in no mood for this." The young lord stalked around their circle. "I did not hire you all to watch you pick at each other. I've had to ransom nine men today. Nine! You had good reputations. Hard men. Good in a fight. I'd like to know what I hired you for, if I'm the only one can best a man."

He stopped himself, touching his face. "Never mind. The season has been long . . ." He fumbled with a smile. "You. It was Berchard, yes? I am going to sit down, and you are going to tell us all how the dead come to life."

"Ah." The one-eyed knight scratched his beard, surprised but recognizing a command performance when he heard one. "Yes, Lordship. We was fighting down in Pendur. South. Badan here had more hair."

"Right," said Lamoric. He flopped into his chair.

"We ended up on the losing side of a row down there without a friend for thirty leagues and no one left to pay us. And after two days of slinking from hill to hedge, walking our horses like a pack of spaniels, our food ran out. So, without a penny between us, my lot decided we had better find a likely spot and get ourselves some provisions."

Durand watched glances exchanged around the fire. Agryn and Coensar gave a sober nod. Guthred took it in, shaking his head. Lamoric leaned and listened.

"Well, we *were* on enemy land, after a fashion," the bearded knight said. "In any case, the next village we found, we came in riding. I remember it felt cursed good to get off my feet. And this village, it was one of those type you find built like a wheel round a well or river or something—with long spokes of field jutting out into the trees. We charged straight down the track. And all was well. The place was deserted." He shrugged with his palms upturned.

Durand watched Lamoric. His hands clenched and unclenched. He looked to Heaven. Coensar, meanwhile, stared snake-steady into the fire, his eyes gleaming.

"But we had no idea what we should take," Berchard was saying. "This was no burgher's mansion. A barrel of beer if we could find one, that was sure, but other than that we had no notion.

"So, me, I cantered my horse up to the mill, dropped over the fence and made for the door. Just in case, I made sure my sword was ready. Some miller might have been waiting with a scythe or a mattock or some cursed thing, ready to knock my head in. Bastards, millers." This drew Durand's attention. He nearly laughed. "So, I was careful. But I needn't have been. The mill was empty, too. Dark and thick with dust inside, with nothing in the place but corn and the racket the mill wheel was making.

"I ducked in and made for the larder. There were oats, dried peas, flour—that kind of thing. I even found beer. I thought sure I'd set us up for days."

Badan laughed.

"Now," said Berchard, a thick finger in the air, "all this took some time. I don't know how much exactly, but some. And I couldn't hear much but the big wheel squawking and rattling. So, when I got outside, my arms full of corn and peas and whatnot, what did I find but this whole bloody village lined up looking at me? And they were all kitted out like madmen. Armlets and anklets and circlets of leaves and sticks. I might have laughed right out if it hadn't been for the hellish grim look in their faces. Hells!

"I reckon they'd trooped back from some forest festival to find my friends riffling their crofts. Badan and the rest jumped on their horses and made for the hills."

"We didn't know we'd left him!" Badan protested. "There was no time!"

"No time for me. I'll give you that. Those peasants hauled me out to the edge of town and this monstrous great oak. And this old brute had this one great bough stuck out over the road like a long arm pointing nowhere. And I peered up at this notch in that long bough, and saw it smooth-polished and shining, and I knew that I'd be in front of the Throne of Heaven before nightfall.

"They threw a rope up and over that thing and snapped it down into that old groove and started to haul me up. And they were dancing, the bastards. I was strangling and they'd got back to their festival. I think I actually kicked another life into the thing—unless they came back because of the noise.

"So, I was hanging there, all my weight on the cords in my neck, knowing if I stopped straining the rope would pinch my windpipe flat, and the bastards were dancing. I'm spinning slowly, round and round, sucking air through my teeth. And I know I should be thinking on what to say to the Warders at the Bright Gates and dying well, and all that. But I am so angry. I start throwing myself side to side, trying to pop my hands loose, I think. Trying to get at them.

"Then that rope made a tearing sound. A little *critch* sound inside." He appealed to Lamoric, adding, "Lordship, my eyes must have bulged right out of my head."

"I'm sure, Berchard," Lamoric managed.

Berchard spent a moment looking back at Lamoric, but then pressed on. "So, with the cords in my neck stiff as broomsticks, I started kicking, jerking back and forth with lightning flashing through my skull."

"We should have stuck by!" Badan said. "You must've looked like a pike. A fat bearded pike."

"Then there was a short drop, a great flash, and the rope went altogether." He puffed out his cheeks and sighed wetly. "I ran faster than I ever ran. I must've made the woods before they even knew I'd gone. But I remember looking back over my shoulder, and there was this long ragged line of charging peasants swinging like a scythe across a fallow field, pounding up this boiling wave of dust."

He stopped, peering up into the rapt faces of shield-bearers and peers alike. "Really. I've still got something of a scar under all this somewhere," he offered, tilting his head back and scrabbled at the brown bush of his beard. Any scar would be conveniently difficult to find.

Moaning arose among the sceptics. Berchard held up one hand, flat.

"I went on pilgrimage after that. To the shrine of the Warders at the Pale City." Three hundred leagues across the Fiery Gulf.

"Aw, ballocks," said Badan.

"In Atthia herself, near the Mere of Stars where—"

Abruptly, Berchard's mouth hung open. A tall, narrow figure had stepped from the dark and now stood as still and black as a storm-blasted tree. Every knight leapt to his feet, drawing steel. The fire luffed in the silence.

"You've minstrels at your feast, brother." It was Lord Moryn, looking leaner still without the bulk of his armor.

"Brother," acknowledged Lamoric.

"Your man Coensar was at the feast this evening."

Lamoric inclined his head, his expression wary. "Yes, brother."

"I watched your man."

Durand saw Coensar shift, slouching behind his snake's gleam.

"Did you?" Lamoric prompted.

Lord Moryn moved a step closer to the fire, forcing Lamoric's men to give way. Though he was tall and grave, his face had ballooned around the tight seam of his right eye.

"Aye," Moryn affirmed. "And *he* watched Kandemar the Herald until the ancient drew the Tern Gyre roll from his satchel."

Durand leaned closer, feeling the Knight in Red secret being teased apart.

"I expect he was interested," murmured Lamoric.

"There was a look on your man's face when the company stood over the roll, peering down at the blazon painted there. He took in every shield called to the prince's tournament. Then he spun on his heel and marched from the feasting hall."

"Aye?" It was a sour word.

What had the man discovered?

"Your red shield," Moryn said, "it is not there. I have run my finger down the list myself. Despite the Knight in Red's victory under the eyes of half the peers of Errest, he has not been summoned to the prince's tournament at Tern Gyre. And if there were ever a stage for a man to show himself better than most believe, it is Tern Gyre. But if he is not on the roll, the Knight in Red cannot join the peers."

Moryn stopped, the fire's glow lapping at his surcoat. This was Lamoric's game, and he had lost it.

But Moryn pressed on. "A second thought."

"As many as that?"

"Our season is at an end. No more opportunities remain for the Knight in Red to attract the Herald's eye. Red Winding is—was—the last tournament of note before the great and the chosen gather at the Gyre."

"You amaze me," said Lamoric.

Moryn raised an eyebrow.

"And you are on the point of abandoning this Knight in Red game as a lost cause: all the silver you've wagered, everything you must have sold, and everyone you've bought to be here, lost. You are waiting the right time to tell these men that you must scatter them to the four winds even as the winter moons come upon us."

The men around the campfire shifted uneasily. A few turned their attention on Lamoric.

Moryn had them all in his fist, Durand included. "And yet?" Lamoric pressed.

"It is the custom of my house to hold a small tournament each year at a hunting lodge on the River Glass: High Ashes. It is fought in one week's time."

"I had never thought that you, of all men, would bid me to return to your father's domain."

"If your brother had not spoken for you, you would still be there now." Dead.

"It is not so large an affair," said Lamoric. High Ashes would be a brawl among Moryn's future liegemen.

"And still," said Moryn, "the Herald of Errest will be there."

"You will excuse me if I was under the impression that High Ashes was a tournament for your father's men. Friends. A private thing."

"And yet it has been arranged."

"I must take your word."

Lord Moryn let the statement hang between them. "You wish another chance to prove your mettle. If I wish my chance at your red helm," Moryn concluded, "I must furnish the opportunity."

"A chance to reforge my honor where it was broken?" was Lamoric's wry reply.

"We leave in the morning. The mêlée begins at dawn six days hence. I tell you plainly: You will provide me my chance, and you will not best me a second time."

Lamoric got to his feet, seizing Sir Moryn's hand. "I will see you at High Ashes."

The fire shivered in Moryn's one good eye.

THE CONFRONTATION KILLED their little feast and had the men sitting with their mouths shut. Durand watched a furious Lamoric for a while—this was not the best time for confessions—then took himself off and spread his bedroll over the ruts. For a few moments, he crouched there alone, beyond the reach of muted conversations.

The Red Knight business was a new thing. He wondered at the bad blood between Lamoric and this Lord of Mornaway. There had been whispers about the wedding when the host rode for Hallow Down. And secrets tended to slip out.

Durand winced at the thought. Images roiled up: hunchbacked Radomor and his Rooks, Alwen in the tower stair, the girl and her snakes.

The last silhouettes at the fireside kicked out the embers and straggled off toward their tents. One walked toward Durand.

"I saw you with my prisoner." The voice was Coensar's. Durand imagined that he could see the captain's eyes like two new pennies in the shadow. "You had no sword." He jabbed a long blade into the turf. It swayed. "This one's yours. You'll need it before long."

Durand glanced back to the man's face, but the captain had already turned. Durand reached for the sword, gripping it hard before sliding it into his gear. He tried not to think of his own secret. He felt the unsteady gratitude of a castaway whose raft skids onto an alien shore.

LYING THERE IN the ruts, Durand dreamed: The darkness was heavy with the scent of water. Night breezes moved through willows.

He stood on a riverbank.

The muck mashed between his toes. He wore only his linens: a long tunic and his breeches.

A river, like ink under the moon, curled off into wooded darkness a few hundred paces away. Something winked out there. A faint light was moving on the waves, drifting closer. In a few moments, he made out the profile of a skiff against the slippery glints of the water. Low above the gunnels, a single candle flickered.

The prow of the boat turned with the course of the river. Something about the scene probed the locks of his memory. The blond lines of the gunnels looked like something carved by a maker of mandoras or lyres.

Then he saw her—a flared cuff, a drape of white sleeve.

Without a thought, Durand stepped down into the river slime. She lay with the candle clasped in small hands. Her skin glowed as pale and soft as a dove's throat. He could feel the cold weight of the river, chest deep.

And the boat was passing him by. He reached, straining his fingertips into the path of the craft, but it was no use. Veils of weed caught his fingers. Dark curls tumbled over the square stern. He thought he knew the place now. This was the Maidensbier. A story. Her name was lost to him, but she was the maiden of the river's name. It was an old story. Standing in the water, watching the retreating skiff, he put his hands over his face.

Here, the story was real. This was the Lady of Gireth, wife to Gunderic, the founding duke, who had fallen in love with one of his lieutenants. Loving both and wishing harm to neither, she lived a precarious summer until the duke's shield-bearer stumbled on the lovers where they lay by the riverbank. The shield-bearer was a steadfast man bound by strong oaths to keep no secrets from his master, though compassion compelled him to wait for the morning. Durand watched as the skiff carried on, and knew that this was that long night.

They said that the girl drank foxglove, setting herself adrift upon the river, finally to pass below the walls of the duke's capital. Afterward, Duke Gunderic and his line abandoned that first capital and took his court to Acconel, far to the west. The skiff was almost out of sight. He could still just make out the fan of black curls—dark as sable.

The loyal shield-bearer, as Durand recalled, was made first Baron of Col: a spot as far from Acconel as could be found. His shield bore the three stags.

A SECOND TIME he woke, like a drowning man breaking the skin of a lake.

He found a different darkness: one of ruts and chill drizzle. His sopping blanket lay over him like dead flesh. In his first blinking moments, the dream rain and mud and memories of women explained the dream away. He lifted his hand. A green veil of slimy weed trailed from his fingers.

Then voices reminded him that he was not alone.

Beyond the tents, a white shape drifted through the gloom.

As in the dream, he was in motion without thought, tripping through guy ropes.

Someone—a dark shape now—stood in his path.

Durand and the stranger staggered apart, and a sword whisked from its scabbard. Durand's new blade was rolled up in the blankets somewhere in the mud behind him.

"Hold there," Durand gasped.

"Oh, it's the new man, Durand, yes?" It was Lamoric's voice, rattled and breathless. "I don't—Watch yourself. The latrine trench isn't far off." He said nothing for a moment, hanging like a specter in the dark. "With the rain you don't smell it."

"I thought I saw—"

"She's dead."

"What?"

"My sister." The man was fumbling his sword into its scabbard. "You grew up at Acconel . . ."

"Alwen." He fought to keep the horror snaking through him from reaching his voice.

"I—I can hardly say it. They've found her. In the river. Drifting past the citadel at Acconel, then off for Silvermere. It is not possible. It has to be a mistake. My father. There was a priest writing for her every *week*. It will kill him."

Durand wondered about the white shape he had seen. Was there a messenger out here in the dark or someone else who shared the same midnight vision?

"You knew her?" Lamoric said.

"She was older than I," Durand stammered. "Married."

"Ten winters, aye. To Radomor of Yrlac. And now she's in the river. What in the Hells does it mean?"

Though Durand knew, he did not answer. The Rooks had sent her home. "She is on her way to her dower lands in Gireth," they had said.

But this was not all. "Was there any sign of the baby?" he breathed.

"God, I . . . I never thought. She never mentioned. Just Alwen sprawled in a rowboat."

Only the dark hid Durand's shudder.

BY DAWN, COENSAR had hired a merchantman to carry them across Silvermere to Acconel where Lamoric would see his sister buried. No one asked how he knew. But Durand remembered that pale figure in the dark; Lamoric had not been wearing white.

As they sailed, the night's drizzle swelled into a wild gale that beat Silvermere into a realm of surging mountains. Back and forth across the face of the wind, the ship's master set a reeling course with straining giants at the steering-oar. Through the screams of the horses below and the wind above, the men on decks watched Lost Hesperand and the Head of Merchion pitch into view and out again—places where no man would land. Men saw monsters pitched up from the depths by the waves. Even the creatures of the deep could do little in such a storm.

Through it all, Durand watched Lamoric clinging like some bleak figurehead in the merchantman's forecastle, though the bow swung and crashed down like Creation's end. Durand hung on with the sailors in the ship's waist, tethered like a dog to the rail. He fought with the others to keep the horses upright and alive. Lamoric haunted him, and, from time to time, he would catch Guthred watching.

Finally, as light failed them on the second day, the great port of Acconel hove into view. The rain had returned to its steady drizzle, like some guard dog curling back into its kennel. Every man aboard was left soaked and pale.

When pinpoints had swelled to arrow loops in the dark face of the city's walls, the captain's mate hallooed until they sparked some action on the quay. Men came running along the wharf, leaping into boats to meet the ship and haul her in. The boatmen shouted their astonishment to the sailors who threw them lines and bragged about their passage.

Among these men, Lamoric appeared like a specter. As each man noticed the lord among them, they shut their mouths, some snatching hats and skullcaps from their heads. Lamoric bent over the rail. His voice, when he spoke, was quiet.

"Were you here when they found my sister?"

Most of the longshoremen scratched their necks or turned to tie off lines; one bow-legged man, braver than the rest or in charge, answered.

"Lordship. They brought her here. They say little Almora spotted her."

"Almora?" She was his youngest sister, a dark-haired child.

"They say the girl rose from a sound sleep, Lordship, went off through the passages of the castle and fetched up at a window high in Gunderic's Tower." Durand flinched at the likeness: Alwen in her tower. "Could see her clear. All in white, she was, sliding over the water. Laid out like she was sleeping, a candle in her hands."

Lamoric hardly breathed the next words. *"You saw this?"* His hands shook.

"My grandmother. My sister, Lordship. The wise women of the fourteen duchies knew before morning. Your brother sent fishermen scrambling out to catch the boat before it was lost on the mere. The lads and I, we helped getting her in."

Lamoric was nodding. He was fighting with tears.

"I've come to bury my sister," he said, finally.

Now, the longshoreman closed his mouth, and Durand had a premonition of what was to come. None of the men in the boat wanted to look Lamoric in the face. Every hand was still.

"It is done, Lordship. Your father's buried her this afternoon," the longshoreman said.

Lamoric blinked. He pushed himself upright. The men had taken a half-step back, as though the group were inhaling.

"The high sanctuary then."

LAMORIC STALKED OFF between upturned dories and drying cordage, a few of his men in tow. Most of the others remained behind, keeping an eye on horses and supplies. Durand could not be one of those—he had to say something. He was glad when Guthred joined Sir Agryn and Coensar to follow their master.

Lamoric stalked under the cavernous Fey Gates as the curfew bells tolled, Durand and the others hurrying after. Shopkeepers hauled great shutters over their windows; alehouse signs hung swollen in the drizzle. They passed one called The Waterclock on Fishmarket Street where Durand had passed long evenings. The city smelled of privies, dung, and the rain: everything the same, nothing familiar.

They wound their way through the stone warrens of the

citadel. Walls crowded overhead till the streets seemed little more than damp passageways. Pigeons stormed and swirled between the eaves.

At more than one corner, Durand was ready to turn for Gunderic's Tower and the Painted Hall of Lamoric's people, but the young lord's twisted course led only to the high sanctuary. White spires rose from the midst of shops and guildhalls: a relic from the days of the High Kingdom when the kings of Errest ruled all the Atthias.

There was a double door: oak enough for a warship carved with all the writhing vines of a forest. Low in one door, Lamoric found the hidden outline of a smaller portal. The young lord took hold of an iron knocker half-concealed among the carvings.

They stood for twenty heartbeats, waiting. Lamoric never turned or said a word. A hundred yards of empty street stretched at Durand's back. Suddenly, the carvings split as the wicket door creaked wide. A crabbed hand beckoned them inside.

Beeswax candles filled the vast nave, glowing over ancient columns and throwing shadows over interlaced branches and running beasts. An entire forest of tapers glittered thirty paces down the aisle. Durand could see the long shape of a plain sarcophagus. He thought of the long white form in his dream.

The acolyte who opened the door pointed to Oredgar, the Patriarch of Acconel himself. In samite and gold, the tall priest might have stepped from the mists of the lost High Kingdom a thousand years before. There were private rites and vigils long after the public ceremonies were finished.

Durand and the others let Lamoric proceed alone, and waited, dripping on the entrance tiles, under the undulating sheet of a dark window. Durand rolled his eyes at himself. What was he if he held his tongue?

The silver-bearded Patriarch set his hand on Lamoric's shoulder, then stepped back as Lamoric crouched low among the candles. Durand found he didn't know what to do with his hands.

Guthred was watching him, his face sour. It was as though the man could look into his soul. Finally, he relented.

"God," he said, peevishly. "Long time since I been in a place like this." He peered up where the slender pillars criss-crossed among the vaults and arches, high at the limits of candlelight. In the dark, the thousand thousand panes of the windows were black and glinting.

Agryn snorted. It was more a sigh.

"You can feel Him," the old shield-bearer said. "Watching you. Watching, but not saying nothing. My dad was a great one for that. Had a way of looking at you till you knew you must be up to something."

"The King of Heaven watches always," said Agryn.

Guthred grunted, and Durand winced hard.

In the high sanctuary, you could feel the Lord of Dooms, like some vast thing rising from the sea.

"It is a sanctified place and older than the kingdom," said Agryn.

Guthred grunted once more.

The Patriarch shot a scathing glance down the aisle at their chatter, his tiny eyes as piercing as a sea eagle's.

"All right, men," murmured Coensar.

As Durand writhed in a fool's agony, he glanced up in time to notice something strange in the high glass sheet beyond the others. One of the tiny panes of glass didn't have the same sheen as the rest. Something was moving beyond it: an eye slipping away.

Something moaned—nowhere near the window, but high above. The sound throbbed again. Down the aisle, Lamoric had struggled onto one knee. The Patriarch was turning, his long mantle swinging out. Every bell in the sanctuary tower moaned in doleful warning.

Snarling, Durand leapt past the others, springing low through the wicket gate and out into the dark. The spy had been at a side window, so Durand pelted for the corner, knowing he had taken too long, and that any spy worth his wages would be gone.

As he careered into the dark yard, however, he saw a figure stooped some twenty paces away. The man wore a black gardecorps robe. The sleeves swept the turf like black wings.

The Rook lifted his finger. "Shh."

Durand charged headlong, but the little man spun from him, darting off in a riot of cloak and sleeves and shadows, until there was nothing left but scattering darkness.

With nothing to chase, Durand skidded to a halt, his gaze raking every crevice and shadow among the tombs and trees and distant houses. And then he heard voices. Swords were rattling from scabbards.

"There!" Guthred shouted. Coensar and Agryn followed him, looking up toward the roof of the high sanctuary. The throbbing of the bells had ceased. "What's he done? Is there something here?" Guthred was saying.

It was Agryn who approached Durand first. His eyes were on the yard, as he murmured, "What did you see?"

Durand did not know how to answer. What unwholesome impulse had drawn the Rook to Alwen's tomb? What was he doing in Acconel? Durand could not lie, but what could he say that would not destroy him?

"Someone. In the dark. Watching," he said.

Coensar had stalked over to the flawed window. He thrust two fingers through the space of the missing pane.

"I gave chase," Durand continued, "but he'd gone before I could lay hands on him."

"Now you've got us chasing shadows?" Guthred said.

Oredgar the Patriarch stalked around the corner with Lamoric following behind.

"No," said the Patriarch. He stalked straight for Durand. "It has gone. But there was something here. Unnatural, but held at bay by the wards of the Ancient Patriarchs." He turned, robes bright against the darkness. "It had its eye on you all."

Lamoric's retainers stared out into the streets of Acconel. No one said a word.

"My sister is inside," Lamoric said.

THE OTHERS WAITED in the dark sanctuary, as nervous as a lost troop in a hostile land. A man could not draw steel in the high sanctuary without barring the Bright Gates, but each of them had his fingers on his blade's hilt. Durand clutched his new sword with the same hand that had seized Alwen's arm.

Their clothes dried where they stood.

In the third hour of night, Lamoric completed the cycle of

prayer for his sister and took the long walk back to his men. Durand avoided his eyes.

"You will want to be with your family," was Coensar's surmise.

"We will go to High Ashes," Lamoric answered.

Coensar tucked his chin a fraction. "Lordship, we have lost two days. And, from Acconel, half of Lost Hesperand is between us and Mornaway." It was too far.

"Then we must hurry."

Coensar fixed Lamoric with a steady stare, then nodded. "Aye, Lordship."

11. Ride to the Glass

The company crowded the courtyard of an inn, men and horses jostling for space. Though Lamoric had wanted to be gone in the night, the men had been desperate for sleep. Now, though, it was nearly noontide and still they lingered in Acconel. Durand slung the last of the saddlebags just as Lamoric stalked from the inn doors, heading straight for Guthred.

"Where did those whoresons go?" he demanded.

"Still down at the barber's," said Guthred. "Badan won't be fit to ride till—"

"—Then we'll haul him on a bloody cart!" snapped Lamoric.

"We'll get him," said Durand. Guthred rounded on Durand. "Find a damned wheelbarrow; it was your elbow cracked his teeth."

Out they went, jogging over mud and cobbles to a market in Haywarden Street. Durand's empty wheelbarrow boomed like battle drums.

Drunken storefronts and canvas stalls leaned over the heads of a mob of townspeople. There was no sign of the two stragglers.

"Hells. Should have been here," said Guthred, out of breath.

Durand surveyed the stalls and caught a fleeting glimpse of a pair of soldiers reeling past the mouth of an alley. One had a patched eye. "There!"

Guthred was off, bowlegs pumping. They charged through crowds and alley rubbish, Durand shoving the wheelbarrow bounding ahead.

In a few moments, Guthred had hold of Berchard's sleeve. The one-eyed old campaigner had Badan braced like a drunk against the wall.

"Are you finished, Sir Berchard?"

A wide grin split the man's beard. "Oh! You should have seen our Badan."

The stricken man sagged, his eyes like two slices of boiled egg. There was a butcher's gutter down his shirtfront.

"We have to get back," Guthred said. "It's bloody leagues to High Ashes. We're losing time."

Berchard nodded. "Here," he said, "let's get him into the barrow." Durand took Badan's ankles, and they swung him in. Durand lifted the handles.

Berchard whacked Durand's shoulder. "Durand, boy, you ought to have come along."

The face looking up from the barrow was swollen as red and hard as an apple. The man had deserved it. Durand set off, pushing as fast as he could.

"Anyway," Berchard continued cheerfully, "the tooth-puller pried open our man's jaw, and what's he reckon? He'd best yank seven. Not one. Not two. Seven!" Berchard shoved a blunt finger into his mouth. "Everyshing on zhat shide." The finger smacked free. "A penny a piece."

Guthred was shaking his head. "He pays the puller by the tooth," the old shield-bearer muttered, disgusted.

"I'll tell you this for nothing, friend Durand," said Berchard. "It's a lucky thing you've still got both eyes. You'll have to sleep with one eye open if you want to see your next Naming Day."

Durand gave the man a pained grin, preoccupied with the wheelbarrow. Badan was no lightweight, and, at Guthred's pace, the barrow's wheel dove down every rut, careering for walls and alleys like a living thing.

"Anyway," said Berchard. "I take Badan into the little tent." He waved back toward the market. "It's in a tent. Just a pair of stools and a box of picks 'n pincers. The man looks into Badan's mouth, staring right into the reek. And Badan opens as far as he can, only it's nowhere near far enough. You couldn't ram a knifepoint between his teeth. So the puller sets his hands on Badan's face, real gentle. Badan hardly noticed. Then the fellow yanks." They passed under a sort of bridge between two houses, and the old campaigner's laugh racketed around the arch.

"I thought Badan was going to crack his skull between his heels, he jerked back so fast. Lucky thing Badan was drinking since sunset." He tapped his temple with one knuckle. "No fool him."

There was a louse on the back of Durand's neck, pricking like a needle. He couldn't stop to claw at it.

"Truth," Berchard swore, jogging sideways with his hand in the air. "I swear, I think he bought half that innkeeper's claret. He figured the red stuff had to do with blood, and that he was going to lose a fair bit.

"Anyway, we start to pick Badan up, and, when he realizes what's happening, he shakes us off. He doesn't want to look like any coward. He sits down on his own. No help. His fingers are digging into his knees pretty good, though. His chin's up. I thought *he* was going to be first to draw blood. The puller pries our boy's mouth open. And—oh!—the tears are squeezing from Badan's eyes. But he takes it! He lets the bugger work."

Durand nearly walked the barrow into the legs of a carthorse. Guthred had tramped right through a crossroads.

"Then the examination commences," said Berchard. "Our puller's got this iron needle. I say needle, but it's longer, more of an awl, and it's blunted on the end. Squared off. Badan doesn't open his eyes. The guy starts probing, and you can tell when he hits a bad one from the way air kinda sniffs—sharp—up Badan's nose. So he's prodding and prodding and Badan's all hisses and whistles."

Guthred cursed. Durand's shoulders and fists were burning.

Berchard held off the interruption with the flat of his hand. "But then the puller starts *talking*! I don't know what was going on in his head. Me, I'd've got in and out quick as I could, but he started up: 'This man I knew—in Eldinor—he was working on this woman once. Pretty thing. And the worms had had one of her teeth. Too many sweets. It was near gone.

Just a ring. Nothing in it. And he told her what he had to do, and he went in with his pliers, and he started to work on her. Pulling and pulling. You know? And then the tooth popped. He had the pliers too high up, you know? And the tooth just snapped shut under the pliers. Now. He went one way, and she went the other. Knees up, if you follow. From the waist down, bare as the day she was born. And he's looking at this—arse, dimpled knees, thighs—staring while she blubbers on—when, all of a sudden, he feels this greasiness under his hand, and he looks. His hand's all blood. He's used to blood, of course, being a tooth-drawing man, but, when he looks close, he sees something else. He thinks one of his fingers is bent down—broke probably—and when he looks even closer. Kind of turning it over? There's naught there. Naught but this little white chicken bone sticking out of the blood, halfway—' "

Durand winced.

"Hold on now. You've got to remember; Badan's hearing this the whole time. He hears every word, and I can see sweat standing all over his face. I can smell it. He lets go of his knees. Quiet. He's all restraint is our Badan. And he slips his hands up, while the fellow's talking, and poking, and he slides his fingers into the greasy collar of this fool's tunic, and just as he got to the part about the chicken bones, Badan jerked that collar tight.

"That fellow froze, and Badan gave him this look." Berchard took a moment to make a mocking fist and finger sign over his heart. "I've never seen anything like it. Drawer's eyes are bulging out, and Badan's are just these puckers of yellow bile.

"When he lets go, this puller, he isn't about to say another word. You could see him shoving all his stories about wrong teeth pulled and broken jaws and wisdom teeth and rusty pliers and all that sort of thing into a big old strongbox, and tipping the lot into a river. I swear. He even brought out the good stuff. Must have been poppy or ivy or mandragora. Let them *both* settle down a bit. I swear though, the vein in that man's neck stopped jumping the same time Badan's eyelids shut.

"Once he got going, though, he seemed to know his trade. Badan didn't stay out once the drawing started. I expect it's hard to doze with a man up on your chest." He shook his head thoroughly, valiantly suppressing a laugh, when a moan from the wheelbarrow broke his will.

The inn swung into view. There was a shallow hill to climb, but Durand clenched his teeth and in a few moments they were at the door.

"He'll be right as rain now, though," said Berchard. "Puller's told our man to wash his mouth with malmsey and brine to draw the evil. When he comes round."

Guthred nodded. "They'll go for blood every time, but the spirits love a lick of wine or salt water."

Sir Agryn was waiting at the inn doors.

"He would be better," said Agryn, "to think of the Host of Heaven. But he is Badan."

Coensar noticed the new arrival.

"Hells. Get him in a cart. Lamoric's already headed west."

HALF AN HOUR later, their train jolted through the cavernous Gates of Sunset and out over the West Bridge after Lamoric. Durand fingered his new blade as they rode over the span, thinking that the road to Mornaway led through the domain of the Duke of Yrlac: father or son. During the night, he had looked closely at the sword, noting every notch and ripple in the well-worn blade. While it was neither new nor ancient, the blade was straight, and its apple-wedge iron pommel lent it good balance. He would have to work to deserve it.

His latest borrowed horse stepped down into the Ferangore Road, and they were off.

Coensar guided them north and west as much as he could, fighting the grain of the country to avoid the many routes to Ferangore itself. Each farmstead and hamlet they passed seemed a ripe hiding place for Gol and his thugs. Every rider they passed had Durand twitching for the sword, and every gatepost raven had its eyes on him. In weeks or days, this might be the heart of a civil war.

It was also, however, a lovely day.

The Eye shone in a pale, crisp Heaven. The stony farms of north Yrlac were rich and black after the harvest. On their right hand, the wasteland of granite hills called the Warrens crawled slowly by, dull as cloud in the distance. It seemed impossible that this was the land of Radomor's madness.

Durand glimpsed Lamoric at the head of the company, dark and furious—almost as wild as Radomor.

Guthred was grumbling. "No time. Too far."

Durand smeared his hand over his face and observed the men of his half-stolen company. He could see the backs of all the knights. One-eyed Berchard slumped, asleep as he rode. Sir Agryn used a winking pendant sundial to scry out the precise hour, so that he might say the Noontide Lauds from horseback. Other men honed great swords like belt knives or fussed with the length of reins and stirrup leathers. Badan bled and moaned from the baggage. No one spoke. No matter how badly Lamoric wanted it, they could never reach High Ashes in time.

Every little road-straddling village was empty, except for barking dogs—and babies wailing indoors. Eyes peered from shuttered windows.

They rode through a night as black as a midnight mine, following each other half by sound.

Sometime before First Twilight, a mist or fog descended invisibly, shrouding Creation and turning the wide world into a muffled chamber.

To the north, Durand glimpsed empty lands. No longer the Warrens now, but something stranger in the shifting gray: the Lost Duchy of Hesperand, a region of ghosts and rumors. More than once, Durand watched Sir Agryn draw his dial from his tunic only to drop the useless instrument once more. Twice, buildings swelled from the mist on either side of the track. Durand heard doors thumping shut.

Conspirators, Rooks, and the Host Below could all be circling in the roiling gloom.

As the last hours of this twilit day bled away, the track jogged down a slope of rough pasture and out of the mists. They had come upon a sheep-dotted valley. Half a league away, a gray keep perched on a conical mound with a village sprawled around its feet.

The keep might mean food and warmth.

"Look," said Berchard. The man's finger pointed steadily

beyond the valley and its castle toward a lead-dark smudge against the distant mists. It could have been forest. *"That is Hesperand out there,"* he said.

Coensar called a momentary halt.

"I want to know how far we've come and how much longer we've got. We'll ride for that castle, see if we can't get a hot meal, and find out what's what."

There was a murmur of assent.

"Guthred, take a few of the boys down to announce us."

Durand volunteered. He would have thrown himself at anything.

HE FOLLOWED GUTHRED and a few shield-bearers down into the valley. Though it was hardly time for curfew, there was no sign of life. At the village boundary they jounced to a halt, scattering a flock of pigs in the road. The streets ahead were empty and still. The horses whickered, and Guthred crooked his fingers into the sign of the Eye.

The horses walked now, passing houses with hanging shutters until the gray keep at the center of the village brooded over them.

"Don't like it," said Guthred, and men climbed down from their horses, casting about for any sign of the villagers. Durand dropped from the saddle.

As though he'd stepped on some hidden trigger, his landing sent a drawbridge shuddering down in a din of chains. He had hardly got his sword free of its scabbard when a knight on horseback erupted from the castle gate. The knight pitched his horse down the hill at a wild gallop—careering straight for Durand. There was no time or space to step aside. The stranger had a shield tight by his horse's neck and a murderous lance under his arm. Guthred's shield-bearers leapt aside, but there was no time for Durand.

Teeth clenched, he flinched his blade into the knight's path, but caught only the hail of grit as the stranger jounced to a halt. The horse's muzzle nodded an inch beyond the point of Durand's blade.

"Who are you to come armed into the lands of Duke Ailnor of Yrlac?" roared the mad knight.

A huge mustache spilled over his chin, and his eyes bulged like hen's eggs. With a lance at his neck, Durand had to reply. "Sir, we're travelers only. We mean no offense to your duke. I am called Durand."

The egg eyes darted as the stallion danced.

"You would have hospitality?"

"I am a shield-bearer, sir. My captain is Sir Coensar," Durand said, remembering to conceal the Red Knight's name. "On the rise, you'll have seen his men. We're bound for Mornaway."

"I am Beornic, His Grace's steward of the castle and lands of Ydran you see about you." The lance bobbed in his hand. "You'd best come inside."

Durand nodded, keeping his eye on the skittish steward. "I will summon my masters."

THE FEASTING HALL was silent but for the tramping of their boots on its floorboards. A broom lay abandoned by a heap of straw. Tankards stood on the table. Lamoric keeping out of sight, the whole company filed in.

"Sir Beornic," Coensar said, "your village. It is very quiet."

The man nodded, his eyes darting still. The others gathered around the table.

"They have all gone."

Coensar frowned, but Berchard spoke. "What do you mean 'gone'?"

"It came yestereve."

" 'It'?" said Berchard.

"Word that Duke Ailnor has disinherited his son in favor of his infant grandson. Our wise women stood up right then."

Durand caught hold of this bit of news. The old duke had disowned his own son. Would it be the end of Cassonel's conspiracy? Perhaps the hard warriors around Duke Ailnor had set things right.

"I'm sorry," said Coensar. "I don't understand."

Beornic was nodding. "There was a court held two days past. A great storm blew up, like the world was ending. It was as the wise women had seen."

"I'm sorry, Sir Beornic," said Coensar.

"A year ago." Beornic's voice was a hollow scrape. "At the Turning of Winter. We sat the vigil in the sanctuary, then midnight came. Out in the snow we went, and the Paling Moon was soaring full, like a cold Eye of Heaven. But, as we passed into the yard, the snow shimmering, we saw . . . we saw another village. Every man and child, staring back at us beyond the sanctuary wall. Naked they were. Very pale." They could almost see the vision passing before his mind's eye.

"But it was not another village. It was Ydran. My bailiff was there. His three daughters. Everyone. Each of us saw himself standing in the Paling Moon's light, naked in the snow. No one spoke. It seemed as though the dead were reaching, wanting to speak. Then a cloud. A rag of cloud passed, and they were gone.

"Some townspeople were closer to the wall and heard things. Next year and this, face-to-face. The wise women knew. And it would start with these tidings from Ferangore."

"Host of Heaven," Lamoric said. "Agryn, what do you make of it?"

"I cannot say. The Turning is a time between times. Midnight is a time between times. We are granted glimpses. We are under the eaves of Hesperand here."

Berchard was nodding. "I've heard men say it's mad to go in the boneyard at the Turning of Winter." His good eye turned on the dry gray sockets of the arrow loops. Light bloomed into the hall from the west, out over Hesperand.

"I could not follow," Beornic was saying, staring off.

"Where have they gone that you could not follow?" Coensar peered close.

"They saw it coming. The old king's line breaking in Yrlac. That is how it begins."

"Where did they go?" Coensar pressed.

"The wise women gathered them up. They've gone into the forest."

"*Hesperand?*"

"Aye." They would step from Creation to escape the doom they saw for themselves. "But I could not follow. I am His Grace's steward of the castle and lands of Ydran. I have sworn it on my soul, my hands between his hands."

"They've gone into Hesperand." The man's eyes were wide. "To stay and to stay. They will drink the water and eat what grows."

No one breathed.

Coensar was the first to catch hold of himself.

"Guthred, lads," he said, "take Sir Beornic out of here. Find him strong drink. Get him out of this fool hauberk." For once, Guthred gestured to another shield-bearer, and Durand was still there as the little man shuffled out.

Lamoric put his head between his hands. "Nothing to do with us."

Coensar muttered something about wise women.

"What do you think is going on?" Lamoric wondered.

"Things like these," said Agryn. "Each man must respond to an omen as he will. And who is to say what will happen here? I would have said that a man cannot slip his doom. The wise women know much of dreams. Birth and dying."

"Radomor is disinherited and my sister is dead," said Lamoric. *"What has happened?"* He pressed his palms tight together, and turned a fierce look on Coensar. "Where is this place, Ydran?"

"We've not come very far yet, Lordship."

Quietly, Agryn drew out his sundial, moving into a shaft of light. The little pendant glinted. "The day is not yet done," he said. "I read it the eighth hour under the Eye of Heaven. And, though the hours of night are longer, we might yet put five leagues or more behind us."

Lamoric nodded; they must go.

GUTHRED LEFT A shield-bearer, called Eorman, to stay with the mad steward until some arrangement could be made, while the rest set off once more. They followed the rutted track west where they must veer toward Hesperand before heading round it. Everyone was uneasy. It was misty as a mountaintop.

Guthred squinted like a mariner into the fog. "Don't like this weather." The forest seemed to loom close and then sink into the mist like a shape under the skin of a lake. Durand was sure he was not alone in seeing the villagers of Ydran before his mind's eye, shuffling into the trees to be lost forever. Or staring back from the mist.

After an hour or two of this eerie march, a tug of the north wind hauled the great curtains of mist wide, and the company faced the forest eaves of Hesperand. Men cursed. Durand set his teeth. Above and beyond them was the Lost Duchy. The wind was full of the sound of branches.

"Hold up," said Coensar. Horses were already rearing, one cart jerked half out of the roadway.

The rutted track under their feet veered sharply from the face of Hesperand, running south for Ferangore and the long way round. Ahead, the wall of trees that was Hesperand opened into an arcade of green archways over a wide road that ran straight for Mornaway.

Lamoric looked down the Ferangore track in the pasture muck. "South then," he said. "The Ferangore track."

"There is a great arm of woodland between us and High Ashes," said Coensar.

"It will slow us down?" It was hardly a question.

"It is Hesperand," said Coensar. "We'll be days getting round it."

They would miss Lamoric's tournament. Every man there must understand it. Right there, they were deciding whether to disband and scatter themselves on the winter roads of Errest, or to press on—no matter where they must ride.

"So we ride harder and get around it," Lamoric replied.

"Lord Moryn said six days."

"And what are *you* saying, my captain?"

"It is sixty leagues, Sir Lamoric. Skirting it will be days, not hours."

"If we left the packhorses?"

"We might borrow arms. But, after Silvermere, none of these animals is fit for heroics."

There was a long silence. Every man was listening closely.

From his place in the line, Durand could see Lamoric bend. There had been enough moisture in the air that his black hair hung streaming.

"Sir Agryn," Lamoric began carefully. "I have heard that men have passed safely through Hesperand."

It was like some play; they might almost have rehearsed it.

Austere Agryn was very still as he regarded the forest. There was a strange quality to the light in that green corridor.

"Yes, Lordship. Men have come and gone. Some see nothing but wastes and foundation stones. Those who keep the King of Heaven firmly in their hearts can—"

Berchard was standing in his stirrups. "—If they take no food and drink no water. I mean no offense, brother Agryn, but this is the Otherworld, or close enough. What's us is us; what's them is them. There are rules and rules and rules inside."

"It is true," said Coensar. His words steamed in the clammy air. He had been staring into the tunnel ahead, remembering or marshaling himself. Now, he looked back to the others. "I've seen it. Years ago now. Me and my lads rode in, and we rode out again, and I am here to speak of it."

Lamoric nodded carefully.

"I do not wish to turn back," he said.

Now, the young lord turned to his retainers. Somewhere, they must have known that this had been in his mind since Acconel. Somewhere, they had already consented. Still, Lamoric had to speak.

"Lord Moryn has called me out. You, all of you, saw it. And he's promised that the Herald of Errest will be there to witness. Unlooked-for, we have been given a last chance. There will be no others." His eyes took on the gaze of every man, even Durand's. "There is providence in this," he said. "We must go on."

Not a man said a word.

Lamoric spurred his horse and rode into the tree-lined path. Every man followed.

A SEA OF leaves whispered and set the Eye of Heaven to winking.

Durand happened to turn his head. For an instant, the world swam, and he might have been a drowning man at the bottom of a flooded world. Then it settled.

"Keep your wits about you," Guthred chastened. "I can see it lulling you. If we're to get through, you can't be dozing. I've talked to poachers in Hellebore. They'll slip through now and again. Treat every leaf like a scorpion."

At the head of the party, Sir Coensar was grave and watchful. The sword and shield in the man's hands told Durand more than any spoken warning. Still, the place was green and bright. He could understand why the peasants of Ydran would choose to hide here rather than face whatever doom awaited them in their hovels. The air even smelled better. In Yrlac, it had been dank, full of sopping grass and muck. Here, a man's mind turned to the warm days under the Reaper's Moon: the last days of summer. Here, there were green leaves; in Yrlac there were none. Still, Sir Coensar went armed.

But, as every sentry knows, any danger grows routine in time. After another hour, Durand felt as though he had slept last night under a summer moon and woken to greenery and humming flies. The track climbed down into a winding maze of stony hillocks where the scabbed trees twisted toward the sky. The jostling of the trail had shuffled the riders. Wide trails narrowed or bent tight under the trees. In the process, he and Guthred had fetched up near the head of the column, just behind Coensar, Agryn, and Lamoric. Durand felt now that he was bodyguarding them all.

"I don't understand what it means," Lamoric said. "Why would he disinherit his son? And what happened to Alwen?" After a silent moment, he changed tacks. "Poor father. His masterstroke is ruined now."

Coensar kept his eye on the convoluted trail.

"Lordship?" asked Agryn.

"Sorry. That wedding. I'd seen hardly thirteen winters— still a page in Windhover—when Father announced that he would give Alwen to Radomor of Yrlac. I thought that it was nothing but politics, tying loyal duchies and old bloodlines. With one wedding and another, he'd bound Mornaway, Yrlac, and Gireth all together for the king." He gestured with the edge of his hand. "Then I saw the man.

"I was home for the Sun Wheel at the Turning of Winter. Alwen, she had a bit of a sharp way of speaking, and one of my father's liegemen, Sitric Gowl, he muttered a name: snipe or shrew or some such nonsense. I remember thinking he was a whoreson, but Radomor! He loomed up like a thunderhead between Sitric and my sister. It ended in the tiltyard with Radomor lifting Sitric right up from the ground. By the neck. Hanging the fool like a one-man gallows, just with his own two hands. That wedding was more than noble houses among the Sons of Atthi. He knew her, he married her, and he fought for her."

Durand looked up between the trees. He thought of the Eye of Heaven upon them all.

"Now old Ailnor's cut him off, and what kind of death does my sister have? Almora seeing her in that boat? Mockery. I thought she must be happy, when I thought of her. There was a child."

Durand had the key. He knew the source of Radomor's fury. He knew that he had played jailer to mother and child. He knew it all. If he meant to call himself a man, he could not stand mute.

"My mind's turning round and round it," Lamoric said. "And now we are *here*," he finished, looking into the trees.

Finally, Durand could keep silent no more.

"Look to her husband."

But the voice was not his.

In an instant, Lamoric's men were in motion: blades and shields and swiveling helms.

A stranger stood in the track: one of the Fetch Hollow men, or one like them. Tall and lean and lethal behind a haunted stare. Cool brass scales glinted under his cloak.

Coensar landed with Keening at the man's throat, and the old sword moaned.

"Always the same," murmured the man. He showed no sign of having noticed the sobbing blade at his gullet. Like a sleep-walker, he looked through them.

"Let him stand, Coen," Lamoric breathed.

Coensar did as he was asked, but kept Keening's point at the man's throat as he gave ground.

"Who are you?" asked Lamoric.

The stranger paused. His eyes narrowed.

"There have been many like you. A great many," he announced.

"What business have you telling me about my sister?"

"Always the way." It was as though he was not talking to them. "You go to the tournament," the stranger added.

"I don't know what—"

Coensar raised his hand. "You aren't speaking of High Ashes, are you?"

"The tournament," the warrior corrected.

Coensar snapped the flat of his hand into the stranger's sternum, but the man seemed more bewildered than injured. He had broad shoulders.

"What tournament?" Coensar said.

"The Bower. The tournament on the Glass."

Now it was Sir Agryn's turn to interrupt. "Ask again who he is."

"What of it man?" said Lamoric. "Who are you? My captain'll kill you where you stand if you don't answer."

Now the stranger seemed to notice the edge still flickering at his throat. "I am called Saewin. I search." He blinked, giving his head a half-shake. "You go to the tournament?"

Incredulous, Lamoric turned to his captain. "What of this tournament? This Bower?"

"I have seen it, Lordship," said Coensar. "Once. Every seven winters, since the High Kingdom. There's a tournament in Hesperand."

"But . . . but we have no time. We must reach High Ashes." His horse seemed to pick up its master's mood, nodding anxiously.

"We may still try," said Coensar.

The man called Saewin was nodding. Then, as fluid as a fish, he stepped from Coensar's sword to the shoulder of the hill. His hand darted deep, and he pulled from the earth the weapons of a fighting man from another age. First, a long and straight-bladed sword flashed into the twilight. Durand judged that there was hardly another like it left under the vault of Heaven. Next came an oval shield and a helm, gilded like a reliquary. The last, though, was the strangest of all. Deep in the ground, the warrior caught hold of something, then pulled, drawing out a long shaft of some dark wood. Hand over hand the weapon came, until a blade popped like a fish from the depths. It was a lance or long spear. As the stranger switched the blade high over his shoulder, a weird rain spattered over the men. A drop landed on Durand's cheek.

Guthred's eyes locked on Durand's face. Durand reached

up, and found that his fingers came away red. The old blade was bleeding. Dark tears sweated from the edges to curl down its blood-dark shaft.

Saewin stood then, a mad warrior from a thousand winters past, looking for all the world like he meant to join them.

"You're mad," Lamoric said.

Berchard spoke out. "Lordship, think carefully about what you do."

"You'd have me bring this madman with us?"

"I just say think on it. This is no ordinary place. Turning aside strangers. Nothing good comes of that."

Agryn knuckled the skin under his nose. "There is something about that name 'Saewin.' "

"Fair enough then," said Lamoric. "I won't turn a stranger away in this place, but neither will we slow our march for him." He turned to the man. "Keep up, Saewin of the forest, and you may travel a while with us."

Saewin nodded slow under his antique helm, looking for all the world like some brass creature of the sky.

THEY HAD COVERED another league when Durand spotted a glint among the trees. "What was that?"

Heads swiveled his way.

Knights from ahead and shield-bearers behind all watched as he pointed. "There." A shape moved beyond the trees.

Something clattered—Saewin had dropped his war-gear in a heap and now scrambled up an old beech, hands and feet finding holds more easily than Durand could find rungs on a ladder. Five fathoms high, the warrior looked out like a sailor.

"Armed men," Saewin breathed. Everyone heard.

Berchard's face twisted. "Armed men? What's he on about?"

"*Quiet,*" said Coensar. "Everyone. Your shields and your swords."

Durand hooked his scarred shield from his packs, and turned back to find that he had a long clear glimpse of the other party: Soldiers and horses had halted in a clearing only a hundred paces from where he sat. Every horseman wore a coat of mail. Just then, Durand's borrowed horse shifted, and, with that tiny motion, the trees eclipsed the other company. He tried for another glimpse, but no matter how he moved, he could not find the chance window that had let him see.

"They're gone," he said.

Coensar nodded sharply. "Quietly now, gentlemen. And eyes open. I won't send outriders in this mad place, so each man must be his own lookout."

Saewin dropped the five fathoms from the branches, and plucked his gear from the track.

As THEY LOST the light, they saw more and more of the wandering strangers.

For leagues, the trail sank, and, in the earthen walls rising around them, muscular tangles of beech roots became the ribs of small caverns. Durand found himself imagining the wink of buried hoards in the hollows. High above, the elephantine trees knotted like a sanctuary aisle.

A voice from the back of the ranks called out, "Now *I* see them." The men winced. Troops had been sighted in all directions. Now, Coensar did not even bother to call a halt. It seemed that the forest was crowded.

Durand worked his shoulders, his hands lumbered with sword and shield. A louse took its long chance to prickle the back of his neck.

Just as he let the straps go to have a scratch, the bushes exploded. A mounted rider plunged into the track. Sunset flamed in the knight's face and the yard of steel in his fist. Durand uncoiled, catching at his own sword and shield, sure he was too slow.

Though he was so close that Durand could see the stubble on his jaws and the blaze where the wind had burned his cheekbones, no blow fell.

The knight simply stared down the track, seeing nothing. His head turned once more, and then he urged his horse up the bank.

This time the column had stopped, and the eyes of every man were wide and fixed on Durand; some men were lowering the sign of the Eye.

"You."

Saewin stared up at him, the bleeding spear in his fist. The man's head tilted, causing the shadows that brimmed in his eyes to turn.

"*I'm* the one."

The rest of the company were nudging their horses into motion. Durand tapped his mount's flanks, but the stranger kept pace.

"Me. Though the search has been long, we are very near now," said Saewin.

Even as the madman spoke, Durand was conscious of Guthred watching him.

"I don't know what you want, friend," Durand said, "but, whatever it is, you can have it."

"My Lady awaits me." There was something about his hands: blood oozing up between knuckles locked on the old spear. "*Me.*"

Berchard jounced in between them. "Here," he said. "Leave the boy alone. Whatever old snare you're worrying at, he's nothing to do with it."

Durand heard a new sound: running water. Somewhere ahead, a good-sized stream rolled through the leaves. It would have to be nearby and quick for him to hear it over the din of hooves and harness. Berchard was nodding.

"What is it? Why do you look?" Saewin demanded. "What do you hear?"

Durand had no time to answer. The stranger's head whipped round. "*What do you hear!*"

The men of Lamoric's company hesitated, catching the stranger's rising frenzy.

"Ride on," Coensar ordered.

"What is it?" Saewin had turned from Durand, appealing to anyone. Durand spurred his horse. The company rode at a ragged canter now.

"Hells," snarled Guthred. "Get to the river. The river or we're *all* done for!"

Berchard called to Durand: "Ride, boy. Ride!"

"Stop!" Saewin shrieked. They were leaving him behind. "Not like this. Not again!"

Durand had a glimpse of the arcane warrior springing up on a great stone behind them, the veins and sinews of his body standing stark below a face that seemed nothing but rolling eyes. Creation fell into darkness. The trees roared their horror.

The men sawed their reins like plowboys. A wind snapped around the galloping company, snatching at cloaks and sucking at the breath in Durand's mouth. He was standing in his stirrups, and his horse was flying. Behind them, Saewin lunged, hurling himself around trees and shaking the earth. Great husks of bark came free in his hands.

The forest was unraveling before them. Beyond the shoulders of the men ahead, Durand saw a narrow span. A bridge like something carved by a bowyer swung from the gloom. There was light beyond: green banks and shining leaves. The hot blast of Saewin's raging burned on Durand's neck.

They rode out. Saewin screamed, and they hit the deck of the span, vaulting in an instant onto the high arch.

Durand shot a glance back. The ancient warrior twisted, launching the long and bloody lance from his fist. Between eye-blinks it flew; the blade was a glint set to splay his collarbones like a great carver's fork.

But it never landed.

The weapon hung in the empty air where the bridge arched highest. Durand's borrowed horse had taken one step farther than Saewin could reach. The air hissing through Durand's teeth was warm and full of cool summer. Beyond the bridge, Saewin was gone, and the standing blade of the spear was faint as a stroke painted on glass.

🔘 12. The Lady's Bower

In this new Creation, the company creaked on the high, timber span. Every one of them looked as wild as any roadside madman. Finally, Coensar spoke into the stillness, "This river. They call it 'Glass.' We are riding to this tournament of Saewin's. It draws us on."

Far below, the river rumbled, bounding between mossy walls, its flood as clear and green as a knot of crystal. The air above was cold. At a glance, Durand imagined falling into the gelid flow, tumbling leagues through the forests of northern

Errest, past Tern Gyre and into the misty Winter Sea—a place he had never seen. It could easily have happened. Saewin could have thrown his lance one frantic heartbeat sooner.

"There's no going back with this madness in the woods," Lamoric said. "The whole duchy seems a funnel to this place."

Uneasy men nodded and spurred their horses forward.

On this new side of the Glass, another aisle of great beeches led on, and they pushed on. The nave of trees opened wide to reveal what might have been the chalk-gleaming crown of some giant from Creation's Age of Powers.

"Just as it was," Coensar breathed. "Bower Mead."

"God," Durand whispered.

The crown was, in fact, a shell keep of flawless white limestone where the gray pillars of the forest gave way to a glade. Walls rambled over the grass enclosing an area as large as the duke's castle at Acconel. Hard men craned their necks like wondering peasant boys.

"We should try to slip past," said Lamoric, but even he was fascinated. They rode into the shadow of the keep, every eye on its walls as though fiends might leap from the windows. Sheep grazed here and there, but there were hardly fields to feed the castle's people, if any people there were. Soon, though, he had his explanation. Beyond the shoulder of the castle, a slope fell away toward the setting Eye of Heaven. In the red blaze, he made out fields and distant cottages. Plow teams toiled, the moan of the oxen carrying from the valley with the dull reports of mattocks, as men and women swung hammers against the chill earth.

"What is this?" said Sir Agryn.

"Getting set to plant?" Lamoric offered.

"Aye," answered Coensar. "It is just as it was. They sow the winter wheat tomorrow."

"What?" said Lamoric. "Always? What if it's a cold year? Surely they don't hold off?"

Sir Agryn was shaking his head. "It's an older power than seasons, I think, Lordship." His long fingers spread into the fist and fingers sign of the Eye.

"Marvelous," said Lamoric.

"I cannot be more precise, Lordship," Agryn said. "The

story is dark to us, though this Bower Mead may answer before long."

At these words, the gatehouse came into view.

A glance that Durand couldn't read passed between Coensar and old Guthred.

"We should leave it be," said Lamoric. None of them made a move to depart.

"Durand," said Guthred. "See if you can find a porter. Maybe there's a porter's lodge in the gatehouse. Tell your friends we've come."

"I will see who I can find," Durand answered.

With the eyes of half the company on him, Durand swung down from his mount. There was a big barrel vault, its blue shadow cut from the white wall, almost a tunnel to the doors inside.

Durand stepped under the arch. Sunlight probed murder holes and arrow loops.

"Hello?" he said. His voice rolled around the masonry.

No one answered.

"My captain, Sir Coensar, is at the gates. Is there anyone—"

Something hissed—a foot on bare stone—near and far, in front and behind. As Durand twisted, he caught sight of Guthred and Lamoric and the others all watching him twitch. He took a firm step into the tunnel and out of view.

The shafts of light slid over him. Now he was alone with whatever had hissed beyond those arrow loops. He turned and quickly spotted one loop in the western wall that stood dark where the others shone. He looked away.

"I can't believe these gates would be unguarded," he muttered, allowing an idle step to carry him back toward the loop. "The castle's in good repair. . . ." A second step. "Peasants in the fields."

Another step brought him within a yard of the stoppered loop. He stabbed his hand deep, locking his fingers in something tangled and fibrous. He pulled. A brow and cheekbone flashed against narrow gap. A great nacreous eye blinked against the stone, its owner hissing like frying adders. Durand had pulled his fish out by its beard.

Durand leaned close to the pearly eye.

"Come on, friend," he said. "My captain and his men are waiting outside."

But the eye only blinked, and Durand had no choice but to twist another racket from the adders.

He let his victim free. "Open the gate and announce Sir Coensar."

The pale eye remained at the arrow loop a moment longer, then there was an explosion of hisses and slithers, and Durand was alone.

For several heartbeats, he stood in the gloom with his jaw open, wondering how he would explain himself, but then the doors creaked open. A bent, ragged man stood against a slash of bright lawn. Above a beard like a winter-killed sheep, his pearly eyes were wide and fixed on Durand.

"Lordship," the strange man said.

"I'm only announcing Sir Coensar," Durand explained. "If you'd tell your master he's here?"

The stranger's mouth twisted wryly. "Yes, Lordship. Well. Yes and no." With that, he turned and trotted away.

The man was gone, and the doors hung open. Durand took his chance to tell the others that they were free to enter.

INSIDE, THE COURTYARD was wide and green. As Durand followed his masters inside, he peered at the perfection of crisp masonry and green lawn. In the slanted light, he picked out the silhouettes of eerie guardsmen, statue-still up in the parapets. If the men of this place were anything like old Saewin, he was lucky he let the gatekeeper loose.

Filing in and finding themselves alone, Lamoric's travel-stained company spread in a ragged line. Berchard gave Durand a questioning look, but Durand could only shake his head.

"Well, now I suppose we'll meet the master of this place," Lamoric said, making as though Otherworld castles were nothing new to him. The rest of retinue curled their fingers round the hilts of their weapons. Durand scanned the walls, searching the shadow of each arrow loop.

Abruptly, there was a clatter. For an instant, Durand thought of crossbows, but, instead of feathered bolts flying, a pair of tall gray doors swung wide across the yard.

The party stared.

There was nothing but gloom between the doors.

"It's going to be one of that Saewin's kin, ain't it?" Berchard muttered.

Something moved in the doorway. A shiver of tension passed over the ranks, then there was a flash of yellow.

"What in every Hell?" said Berchard.

A double file of young women walked into the courtyard, each wearing a fortune in good silk. They stopped in two facing lines, and, though they stood silent, every one had the ducked-chin look of a naughty child. They wore their hair uncovered, letting plaits and tresses shine in shades of copper, gold, and raven's wing. For a long moment, none of Lamoric's men moved. Durand found that a pair of these maidens seemed to be looking at him, up and down, and doing a bad job concealing their amusement. Durand thought of his matted hair and his hard-worn surcoat—green gone the gray of peas-pottage. Beside him, Berchard slapped dust from his robe.

With heroic composure, Lamoric stepped forward. "Um," he said. "Good day to you, fair ones." No one else could have done so well. "I am Sir Lamoric, the leader of this company, second son of Abravanal, Duke of Gireth."

There was a lot of smiling and no answer.

Lamoric returned their smiles, baffled. After facing a few moments of their silence, he seemed compelled to press on. "I apologize for our intrusion. We travel to a tournament in Mornaway." No one said a word. "I have spent the season fighting as a black knight in the lists—the Red Knight, you understand—planning to—"

Abruptly, the smiling maidens turned from a stammering Lamoric to the doorway behind them. The attention of everyone in the courtyard fixed on the empty arch. Finally, a woman appeared. She wore green. Her eyes were clear and wide, and her hair, red as new blood, swept from her face into a thick plait. The double file of maidens curtsied low as she walked out between them.

"I am the Lady of the Bower," she said. "These are the handmaidens of my court."

The women—the handmaidens—returned their knowing glances to the men of the company and executed a slow curtsey.

"It has been my pleasure to attend most of the courts of Errest," said Lamoric. "And still I have never seen anything to match the beauty of this place or its inhabitants." He bowed with a flourish. Some of the other knights tried the same, in a creak of straps and clink of mail.

Pleasure shone from the Lady's eyes, and she stepped closer. With a teasing languor, she walked down the ragged line of Lamoric's men, stirring a wake of discomfiture among the threadbare knights. Durand felt one ridiculous needle of panic, but mastered it quickly. The green silk of the Lady's gown rippled as she moved. Her hair was red on the pale snow of her neck. Then her eyes were on Durand's, looking up for a long moment before setting him free.

She turned to Lamoric. "You are welcome beyond the Glass and to Bower Mead. All of you. You have arrived in time for the festival. The earth has been turned the last time, and so the tournament will begin tomorrow."

"Yes, Milady," Lamoric said.

"We eat only lightly today, but tomorrow," she said, "we shall feast. You may make your encampment among the others on the grounds."

Lamoric seemed to be on the point of protesting. They had to be in High Ashes.

But the Lady only waved them good-bye and turned. Even Lamoric could not force himself to stop her. Durand followed the veiled movement of her thighs until he noted the eight women who remained. Two or three were staring at him in playful accusation. He swore under his breath, and, as one, the women wheeled, following their mistress as she glided back toward the keep.

It was only as the last woman stepped out of sight that Durand realized the grass was in motion. Though it had been mown short, the lawn rippled like the green silk of the Lady's gown—quietly impossible. Slow eddies played in a wake of turning spirals. He watched as wavelets lapped at the scarred toes of his boots.

"I meant to make my excuses and go," said Lamoric.

BEYOND THE WALLS once more, Lamoric rounded on Coensar. "We'll never make High Ashes now. I can't believe—I've as much as promised that we'd fight here. We haven't time!"

Coensar was still as stone in his saddle, his eyes on the castle and the yard. "It is the same as it was," he murmured. "I half expect to meet myself in the lists. A younger man."

"I should turn round and explain. Host of Heaven, I've wagered my every penny and all my holdings on this Red Knight trick. What will Moryn think of us now?"

"The mêlée will be below," said Coensar. Where the land fell away toward the Eye of Heaven, snatches of amber mist curled in a broad green. A perfect battleground.

The horses plodded on.

"There he will be," said Lamoric, "waiting with the Herald of Errest, passing snide remarks and pointing at the empty seat. I should still be in Acconel—"

First they saw a corner of bright cloth, then, around the flank of a corner turret, a camp of a hundred garish pavilions huddling under the wall. The tents crowded like gowned and drunken dames in the twilight. Mist coiled around their ankles.

Agryn interjected, "There is doom in this, Lordship. To step through this place on the very day when seven years lapse between tournaments. It is not to be—"

Abruptly, Lamoric gasped, *"Hells."*

There was a shield-bearer on the fringes of the camp. He lugged a horse's trapper. And, before he vanished into the maze of tents before their eyes, every man had seen the pattern on the canvas: diamonds, blue and yellow, azure and gold.

"We're not the only fools to save steps between Red Winding and High Ashes," Lamoric murmured. In one of those tents, they would find the lord of Mornaway.

Guthred was nodding. "All right, lads. There's a flat patch off toward the wall. If I've seen it, you've seen it. Get the gear off the horses, and see your man's comfortable. Doesn't matter where we are. I shouldn't have to tell you."

Durand made to join them.

"No, no, Durand. You come with me. I think I'd best check on Sir Moryn."

"Guthred," said Lamoric, "I think I'll see the man myself."

"A moment, Lordship," said Coensar. "You may want to send your shield-bearer after all."

"I don't plan on hiding from him," said Lamoric.

"No, Lordship," said Coensar. "What are you thinking, Guthred?"

The ugly man nodded. "I'll tell His Lordship we're here, and, if Lord Moryn's got the Herald of Errest with him, I *might* mention our Sir Lamoric wants a word." He raised an upturned palm.

"I see," said Lamoric.

"Doesn't pay to chase them," Coensar said.

DURAND SHOOK HIS head.

"Stiff-necked fool," said Guthred.

Moryn remembered them and was *just* civil. Still, Guthred had taken an obvious pleasure in announcing that Sir Lamoric was at the tournament, but unable to receive visitors, what with the arduous journey and all.

The Herald of Errest was not in Hesperand.

"Why under Heaven would we be mad enough to let him at Sir Lamoric now?"

Tramping through the tangled rows of tents, Guthred ducked guy ropes and tethered horses. The place was quiet, but its many crossroads were busy with men on silent errands.

An enormous saddle bobbed into Guthred's path. The groom attached to the thing only eyed them, as Guthred made a show of waiting. At the next crossing, a yoke of buckets reeled out, splashing Guthred and the shield-bearer carrying it.

"Hells," spat Guthred, slapping water from his leggings. "Why don't you go first?" So Durand took the lead. "You're tall enough you can likely see our way."

Beyond the muddled confusion of canvas alleys, the white battlements of the castle played signpost. Durand tried not to notice the pale soldiers on those battlements, or how each man glowed like the neck of a wax candle, and soon Lamoric's pavilions were in sight.

Then Durand stepped into the path of a massive horse, snatching his boot from under one sharp hoof just before it broke his foot.

He made to throw the rider a good hot look, but found himself back in a Ferangore passageway, toe to toe with Cassonel of Damaryn. The plain, worn hilt of the High Kingdom blade Termagant was at the baron's hip. For an instant, Durand could see the baron's eyes narrow. There were shadows. The man didn't know him at once.

Then there was recognition—a lifted chin—and something almost like regret.

Much too late, Durand bowed and stepped back.

After a few heartbeats, Cassonel clicked his palfrey into motion.

Durand drew himself up. He and the baron held each other's secrets, and, with them, each other's lives. Durand checked a staggering step backward and was surprised to bump into someone on his heels.

Guthred looked into his face, his expression cold.

"He nearly ran me down," said Durand.

Guthred didn't blink.

"It's a dangerous place," Guthred said, finally, his tone laden with menace.

WHEN THEY GOT word of Lord Moryn and the absent Herald, the others laughed with relief. There would be no battle with Moryn until Moryn produced the Herald. They were late for nothing.

As the others fell to brawling congratulations, Durand noted that Guthred slipped aside to say a few words in Coensar's ear. The captain, straightening to his full height, glanced up, searching the jagged skyline. Guthred took a moment to make certain that he caught Durand's eye.

The man had long since lost patience with his new shield-bearer. Durand, spotting one of the other shield-bearers carrying a pair of empty water buckets, stepped in the boy's path and held out his hands. The lad blinked up at Durand and handed over the buckets without question.

A string of men trudged back and forth toward the forest with buckets in their fists. Durand set off, putting the others behind him for a time. Against the forest, he saw folk bent round a well.

He thought of Cassonel somewhere among the tents. The man knew Durand had worked for Radomor. He likely knew about Alwen and might find it odd that Durand worked for the dead woman's brother. Durand had been there at Ferangore; he had said nothing to his new comrades. His career could be smothered in its cradle by a single word.

And he would deserve it.

But Cassonel might have another thought in his mind: Durand was a witness. He had been in Ferangore with all the silent listeners.

In the midst of that alien field, Durand hesitated.

He had gone a long way to protect his hide and pride. But the troubles of one man did not have much weight against the kind of treason Cassonel's message portended. A word from a magnate like Yrlac or Beoran could throw hosts into battle—and slaughter the toiling people of the countryside by the thousand.

Although Durand had warned Duke Ailnor, it was hard to believe that Ailnor alone could stop the intrigue. He must remember that his own neck was not worth much compared to a kingdom. He must watch Cassonel.

The sidelong glances of passing pages and shield-bearers goaded Durand back into motion, and he soon reached the black depths of the well. Two men were already there: a sturdy fellow in green and a tall, gangling youth.

The taller man reached the bucket windlass first.

"Good day to you," he said, from under a fringe of rusty-brown hair. He looked too young to be a knight.

Durand nodded a fraction.

The more stocky man smiled. "Evening."

The youth gestured toward Durand's camp, using his chin while he worked the crank handle. "You're with this Knight in Red?"

"Aye," Durand replied, though he wondered how long this would be true.

"How long?" the youth asked, surprising a dry laugh from Durand.

"Not long."

"God," the tall youth said. "I don't know how to speak in this place. Who's king in Eldinor?"

Durand scowled, suddenly on his guard. "*Ragnal* is king."

The stocky man laughed.

"And we're under the Blood Moon?" ventured the tall youth.

"Aye. . . ." said Durand.

The youth's teeth flashed, and he eyed the silhouettes among the tents. "Who knows with this land? A man might have been here a hundred winters. Or arrived from a hundred winters past. I was riding the verges with a patrol of my father's men. Then there were these hounds. I've never heard the like. Then the forest was tossing like a man with fever. I fetched up here."

The sturdier man laughed. "I was hunting, me. Riding. I saw a stag, the like of which I'd never seen. Fourteen points. And then there was the tournament." He shook his head.

The tall youth smiled. "It will be only my third time in the lists," he said. "Oh. I'm Sir Cerlac," he said, freeing his blade hand from the chore of cranking the windlass and extending it across the well.

Durand was taken aback. The awkward figure was a belted knight. After a moment's hesitation, he took the man's hand.

The shorter man made a lopsided grin. "I've been in the lists a thousand times. Sir Abern, I'm called." He offered his hand as well.

"Only my second," Durand conceded. "And as shield-bearer."

"Aha," Cerlac said, finally hauling a full bucket from the chill darkness below Hesperand. He passed the bucket first to Abern.

The squat fellow nodded thanks and tipped the bucket, drinking deep.

As Cerlac took the bucket and lifted it to his own lips, Durand saw something strange pass over Abern's face—a slithering of moonlight, it seemed. Durand lashed out, catching the bucket's rim in his fist. "Don't drink!"

Cerlac froze, holding the black water before him as though he'd found an adder. Coils of golden sunset slithered on its surface.

"Hesperand," Durand said, explaining.

"Eating and drinking. King of Heaven, I'd forgotten."

They both looked to Abern. The Eye of Heaven seemed not to touch him. His skin glowed with a pale light.

"Abern?" said Cerlac.

"I've drunk from this well a thousand times," he said.

Like dun and ochre shadows, there were others coming. Not from the camp. Two or three dozen peasants appeared from the forest edge. Sturdy, silent men, they surrounded Abern, who simply smiled. Durand felt a peculiar horror as the peasants came near.

Brown hands curled round Abern's arms. "A thousand times," he said, and the peasants withdrew with him, vanishing into the shadows of branches.

Cerlac set the bucket on the wall of the well.

"You must tell me your name," the shaken man said.

"Durand."

As the Eye of Heaven left the western sky, Sir Cerlac shook Durand's hand for the second time.

SUCH STORIES MULTIPLIED. Guthred, pissing into the bushes at the forest edge, saw a pale hound the size of a colt staring back at him. One headstrong lordling tried to leave the Mead with his people. Only two of his men made it back, and both were torn as if by beasts and the wind.

Trapped and under siege, the men preoccupied themselves.

Though someone had lit a campfire, Durand found a stump of firewood on his own and sat down to work the edge on his gift sword. The ill-fitting scabbard had let fingers of damp insinuate themselves into the spaces around the blade. Already, webs of rust bled from the steel.

The others laughed; he polished.

Durand considered his strange place among these men. There were mistakes. There were small victories. But it was all built on rotten ground, and a word could destroy it all.

Under the circling pressure of his oily rag, the red webs seemed to give way, though it was hard to be sure in the dark. Little light escaped the ring of turned backs around the fire. He felt the nicks and scratches in the steel as he rubbed his way down the blade. His fingers found deep, puckered notches where edge had met edge on the battlefield. Long scores chased the blade where split chain links had screamed down its face. A great many men had likely wielded the thing, and many were likely dead.

Shouts erupted in the circle. Black shadows were wheeling.

Durand was halfway to his feet when the uproar collapsed into laughter and groaning. Two swordsmen swung and danced in the circle.

"Very good," Coensar's voice said, quiet but clear. The captain was circling, a wooden sword in his fist.

"You'd best shut up, Captain, or he'll have you," a brave soul jibed.

Frantic clattering leapt over the whoops of the crowd.

One-eyed Berchard glanced over his shoulder, and spotted Durand, waving him in.

Beyond the blaze, Coensar stood with Sir Agryn lying at his feet. The captain thrust his ashwood sword into the turf, and, bending, offered the man his hand. "I think you let me have that one, Agryn."

"You're wrong."

Coensar hauled the one-time knight of the Septarim to his feet.

"I forget how dangerous a man you are."

Berchard shouted in: "For a priest."

"Those old ghosts taught you a few things."

"Little to do with the sword, if truth be told," said Agryn. "It has been a long time."

Coensar quirked a rare smile, and, as he stood back, spotted Durand's arrival. "Durand, shield-bearer," he said. The wary eyes of the others settled on him as well, shadows cutting deeply. Coensar stood for a moment, his hand idling on the butt of the ash sword. "I hear there's a horse tried to take you from us."

"Aye," Durand said. Guthred had said at least that much. There was a snicker or two. Someone coughed.

"But you are well enough now?" Coensar said.

"Aye. . . ."

Coensar held out a hand to Agryn who gave up his wooden sword to his captain.

"Everyone tries me one day," Coensar said and held out the sword, its handle suspended between them. Whatever the game was, Durand closed his hand around the hilt.

"Best of three touches, then," said Coensar.

The gang leapt on him. Grinning shield-bearers tugged and

jostled him from all sides, and suddenly he faced one of the most infamous swordsmen in the Atthias.

Durand raised the hardwood blade, thinking that it didn't take much to drive thoughts of magnates and treason from a man's mind.

"Good," the captain concluded, and crouched, facing Durand over the fire. His eyes took in every hint of stance and style Durand betrayed.

Durand circled behind a borrowed shield. Practice swords were good for cracking heads and breaking elbows—teaching hard lessons. Coensar's cool, glass-splinter eyes flickered above the fire, while Durand waited.

"If he waits long enough," Berchard rumbled, "old Coensar may nod off."

The circle laughed.

The fire's heat tightened Durand's face. Striking first with an opponent like Coensar was charging blindly into a house of snares. Unfortunately for Durand and his sound strategy, Coensar would not attack, and the mockers were not on Durand's side.

Durand stared over the rim of his shield. Knowing better rarely did a man much good.

"Have we time to fetch a bench?" someone said.

With a muttered curse, Durand changed his grip and darted. He used speed and reach to dodge the fire in one careering lunge. As the wooden bat whistled down, Coensar wrenched his shield high. The whole crowd flinched at the shock of the impact.

Durand had hardly started his grin, when he felt a punishing jab under his ribs. It might have been a horse kicking him.

"One," was all Coensar said, stepping so that the fire was already between them once more.

Durand sucked a lung full of air and forced his attention back to his opponent, only to catch a subtle wavering of Coensar's shield. Durand might be winded, but the captain looked to be working a set of jarred fingers.

Coensar circled backward to keep the fire between them, and Durand waited, taking a lesson from Lamoric's fight at Red Winding. Suddenly, he saw a misstep. In an instant, the captain's shield boomed yet again. This time, the wily swordsman's hissing counter clapped Durand's jaw shut.

Durand staggered through real sparks and the ones behind his eyes. His tongue felt thick as dead fingers in his mouth.

Coensar, however, had stood up. "Hmm. I think I see it." Durand fought to stay upright, watching the other man warily.

"You're a sight quicker than I'd have guessed, but you're missing something." His voice was quiet.

Durand couldn't muster his thoughts to make any sort of reply.

"Long ago, I learned that when you must attack, the first swing rarely scores. A good swordsman shows you two faces. Get on him. There's no harm swinging first, but you're not going to reach past a shield—lest your man's drunk or asleep. Every peasant knows to plow before he plants.

"Here." The captain dropped into his fighting crouch once more. "I ask you: try my head."

Durand had heard hard-jawed sergeants say the same in a thousand bruising lessons, but he hefted the sword regardless.

Coensar said, "Do it now."

Durand steeled himself to make a good show of it. Tugging a sharp breath, he hauled the wooden bat high and yanked it whistling down to clop the captain's skull shut.

The shield's edge caught it.

The captain nodded coolly.

"You knew what I must do. Yes? The ground is poor. We're in a tight spot. There's hardly room to dodge a cut like that. I had no choice but to take it on my shield. You forced my hand. With my shield up there, I'm half blind. If it's a feint, you've got my ribs. My knee. If it's not; my eyes?" He inclined his head.

"If you know what I've got to do," continued the captain, "you've got me. Force and anticipate. Show the man an opening, but be waiting for him when he tries to take it."

Durand nodded.

"Now," Coensar said. "It is best of five touches."

Durand raised his shield.

And, though he managed to make Coensar work for each of his bruising "touches," he lost.

The captain shook his head. "You're quick for the size of you."

Durand grunted.

Coensar raised an eyebrow. "Call me a liar, ox, and it's real blades next."

"Now that's an idea." Lamoric grinned from the circle, and Durand took a prudent step into the background. "Sharps might add a thrill to the proceedings." He slipped his sword from its sheath and held it, his palm inverted, high over the rest. Durand wondered if the man were drunk.

"Any takers? Agryn?" The blade seemed to flicker, now pointing at its prospective victim. "I have hired the best. I'd like to see what I've bought. Come along, Agryn. Let's see what those ghosts of yours have taught you."

Agryn blinked once. He seemed to eye all the others for the briefest instant, as though deciding whether any of the others might be better suited. There was Badan, Berchard, Coensar. Instead, Agryn hauled his own blade from its scabbard. Lamoric's face split in a smile, and both men raised shields.

"Right then," said Lamoric. "On your guard!" He started his sword into a series of wheeling lunges, drawing flame into the glittering eddies of the blade. Agryn skipped backward, scattering the crowd. This was a thing that got every man's heart pounding. Agryn's sober demeanor belied great agility.

Lamoric put more and more behind each leaping swing of his blade until he could hardly stop himself. Then Agryn struck, hopping inside one fiery arc, his shield high, and, in an instant, Lamoric's weight poised on the tip of Agryn's sword. Everyone watched for blood to well from the neat slit in the man's surcoat.

None came.

"Two swings too many, Lordship," Agryn said. Lamoric grimaced and made a great show of extricating himself from the sword's point.

Coensar nodded, his manner serious. "You must be as quick to abandon a trick as you were to try it."

The young lord's fingertips found the split weave of his surcoat for the first time, and the wild glint left his eyes. He was panting. "Yes," he wavered. "I do see. These mock combats.

I'm not sure I can trust myself these last few days. A man dares too much." With a sharp intake of breath, he bared his teeth in good humor.

Durand caught Guthred staring at him from among the men standing across the fire. The man did not look away.

"Would anyone else like to try their master's sword?" Lamoric said.

He glanced around the circle, then spun back on Durand. Scarred and stubbled faces turned. Durand felt a jolt of fear. He liked the sticks, if he had to choose. Real blades were another matter. It was not that he was afraid of the edges—everyone was afraid of the edges. You couldn't swing. A shield-bearer who maimed his lord did not live long.

"If you insist, Lordship," he answered, eventually.

It seemed Lamoric had noticed Durand's slow response. "Afraid you'll hurt me, are you?" asked Lamoric.

Something in Durand's face must have answered.

"Very well then. Commendable loyalty. But I mustn't let the new man off so lightly. Perhaps we can find someone else for you to play with." A touch of the playful glitter returned to his eyes. "What about Sir Ouen? I don't think Ouen would be much offended by a scratch or two."

The scarred faces laughed.

At first, Durand could not match the name to a face, and, for a moment, there seemed to be no one answering to it. Then something moved in the circle of smiling knights. Huge hands settled on shoulders, and a knight like a carthorse strode into the circle. His shaggy, grinning head loomed over the others as he stepped into the firelight. A knot of stitches still held one eyebrow together.

Durand had dragged this giant from the field at Red Winding. When the man smiled, every one of his front teeth flashed gold.

Guthred was still watching.

"Yes," Lamoric said. "Now we'll see what our man is made of." The grisly pun registered. "Well, Heaven forefend. But it can be so hard to tell in the chaos of a battlefield."

Though Sir Ouen had a lean chest and a potbelly, his arms looked to have been strung with the bow-cords of a siege engine. He drew a sword of war, four feet long.

"I suggest," said the man, "that you get yourself into a good thick gambeson. I don't play gentle."

"After you," Durand said, and, as the smirking giant gave a nodding bow, he followed the man from the circle.

In the dark, Durand decided that he was insane. This was pride, and nothing else. He had seen Guthred's eyes on him, knowing. Coensar had beaten him. Now, Lamoric had singled him out to meet this Ouen.

While Sir Ouen found his tent, Durand dug among the tumbled packs where Guthred's lads had heaped the shield-bearers' and servants' gear. Finally, his hand closed on the weighty bundle of his armor among the blankets and loose tack. Ouen had said "gambeson," so Durand could wear nothing more—not without showing himself to be a coward. Leaving the security of iron mail behind, he hauled the stinking padded coat over his head.

Beyond the meadow and its rings of firelight, something dark was moving—a midnight storm prowling like some soot-gray cat around the Bower. There was no sign of wind or bad weather over the meadow itself. He was trapped and trapped again.

He tugged the cold stiffness of the canvas straight and turned back toward the fire to find that the gap-toothed ring of knights and shield-bearers had multiplied. "Hells," Durand said. This was not just another knight or two gathered from the neighboring camps. There were flashing gowns around the fire now. Three of the lady's maids from the castle stood in the growing circle. Ouen stood, smoke boiling as he limbered his arms, whipping the shield and massive sword around like toys.

It had turned into a fairground wrestling match—or a public whipping.

"Host of Heaven," Durand muttered. For a stolen instant, he closed his eyes. When he opened them, he saw a new figure in the crowd, small but straight-backed—beyond the fire was a familiar face framed in crimson. The girl from the stream, leagues and worlds away, held his eye. He could hardly breathe.

Durand stepped inside the waiting ring.

Ouen bared his gold teeth, lowering his frame into a ponderous fighting crouch. "On your guard," he rumbled gleefully. Durand saw the girl look fully in his direction. Her foal-dark eyes were suddenly wide.

Then light snagged in the razor's edges of the giant's long blade, and Creation sagged away. There was only the giant and the sword and the fire.

Everything began.

Ouen swung the winking razor-edges like a sledgehammer. The blade flashed in circles—the same wheeling assault that had just failed Lamoric. Durand waited, suddenly in Agryn's shoes. Finally, when the giant reached with a long swing, Durand ducked in, shield high. Ouen caught his counter, the big man's knee ramming Durand in the ballocks. Durand rolled, knowing that Ouen and Lamoric were not the same man.

"He's got a better memory than that!" Badan said. The wolfish knight was in the circle with him. Before Durand could untie himself, gleeful Badan levered him roughly to his feet.

Ouen bowed slightly, the fire shivering in his teeth.

Fighting for air, Durand raised his sword. In the pain and sickness after the heavy blow, some part of his mind noticed the wink of his own blade, and it sparked a realization: In this game, the sword was nothing more than a distraction. A peer could hardly hack a man dead at a campfire sparring match. But Ouen was not Agryn to play some sort of touch-and-talk match. No. This was a fight. Ouen wanted Durand to leave this game black and blue.

Durand understood.

The big man crouched, this time advancing until he became a monstrous breathing shadow between Durand and the fire.

Between one step and the next, Durand darted in, throwing out a flash of steel to cover his real intent. At the same moment, he locked his fist in his shield straps and threw a punch straight from the earth. The tight arc buried the corner of the shield in the knight's kidney.

But that was not the end. Durand leapt in, ramming his shoulder under the big knight's ribs. He bulled forward. With all his might, he lifted, legs pounding down. The bonfire exploded under his feet. And, as they burst out the other side, Ouen finally toppled backward. The man slammed into the turf among the feet and shins of his scattering audience with Durand's full weight bearing down on his chest.

The giant's wind was gone. The crowd stood in shocked silence.

Exultant and more than a bit startled, Durand began to extricate himself, but felt a fist lock in the back of his gambeson. Ouen trapped him face-to-face.

"Well done," Ouen gasped, baring his big glinting teeth despite what must have been suffocating pain. "But look here." Something wiggled like a trout below Durand's chin and a razor's edge scraped his throat. "A draw, I think."

Durand looked back into the man's eyes, the sprawling hair, the matted beard, the glinting grin. He had to laugh.

The hand released him.

As he swayed to his knees, curtains of silk and fox fur swung shut around him. Though it was skirts that surrounded him, he might have been kneeling in the midst of a four-post bed. Clear, clear eyes looked down.

"Impressive," said the Lady of the Bower. She reached a tiny hand, and Durand climbed to his feet. As he stood, the scentless warmth of her breath touched his forehead. He blinked into her eyes, taking in lips like dusty cherries and skin without fault or blemish.

"Thank you," Durand said.

A minuscule crease appeared where the arc of the Lady's brow approached the bridge of her nose. "There is something about you," she said. Her eyes held his, as though he were a cipher to be puzzled out. "Broad shoulders. I wonder who you will be. Who you are." Durand's lust stirred as her gaze moved over him, though he saw no arousal in her manner. She was so close. He could see the night air moving in the red down at her hairline. Her lips were not quite closed.

"I am Durand of Col," he said, carefully.

"Yes." His answer had been insufficient. Irrelevant.

She smiled—like an apology. "You are welcome here, Durand." Her fingers pressed his arm, conducting a wave of warmth. She looked up to the others. "All of you are welcome."

For a moment, as he held her in his eyes, it was all Durand could do to swallow.

🔯 13. The Price of Secrets

Guthred put him to work.

While the others drank or rested, he lugged barrel after barrel to the forest edge. Eerie howls made their way through the branches. The sky churned silently. He saw eye-corner shapes on the move. He worked until something appeared from the trees.

"Where in God's name?" the doubled shape said, and pitched backward over a barrel of flour. There was a sharp crack, and a white cloud billowed high.

Setting his teeth, Durand stooped to pick a man out of Guthred's supplies. For an instant, the man's face was covered by a shapeless hat. He grumbled and pushed it back.

"Heremund!"

Durand might have laughed, but for the skald's look: wide-eyed through a mask of flour. The skald's expression was one of horror.

"Durand?"

"Aye."

"Oh. I don't like this. Not at all. What're you doing here?"

"I'm with Lamoric of Gireth."

"What? I thought you were serving Lord—"

"No." Heremund must not mention the name. "I'm with Lamoric now."

"Bloody Hesperand," Heremund grumbled. "I was a half a league from the borders, I'm bloody sure I was."

"Heremund!" Durand said. He found his hands shaking. The homely skald was like a rope thrown from the past. Durand could hardly speak. "Good to see you."

"I was bound for Mornaway and Hellebore. There were riders in fine cloaks skittering from hall to hall all through Yrlac, and rumors of Lord Radomor and King Ragnal and—"

The skald stopped, taking in the tents and the castle and the wide expanse of grass.

"Oh no. It's the tournament, ain't it? We're over the Glass. Gods."

Durand heard shouting. He followed the skald's glance and

was astonished to see the last few men carrying torches out of the camp.

"I suppose it's underway now," said Heremund, and, muttering like a wise woman, the bowlegged skald marched off toward the light.

WHEN THEY RETURNED to the field, everyone was gone.

Durand and the skald stood under a full moon framed by silken billows of cloud. An alien moon in an alien Heaven. The tents were still as the bottom of some brown lake, and the pale watchers from the battlements were the only signs of anything resembling life.

"Queen of Heaven, Heremund, I just left them."

"Must have started."

"In the dark?"

"This way, I reckon." The little man tramped off in the direction of Durand's well. Durand stalked after.

"It's a particular sort of vengeance, this," Heremund muttered.

As they crossed onto the broad shoulder of the green, a scene out of legend stretched before them.

Gleaming in the preternatural half-light, the Lady and her maids waited below the crest of the long slope to the village, standing as though on a stage. Heremund and Durand hesitated a dozen yards behind the women. It seemed the Lady was carrying a sheaf of flowers. It was hard to make out.

Below these figures, knights and shield-bearers and grooms and servants waited in two silent ranks, marking an aisle from the salt white castle down to the village fields. Every man wore his full panoply: armor, surcoats, and tall leather crests on the helms under their arms. Everything glittered as cool and colorless as the glacial moon.

"There was hardly time," said Durand. He had not been lugging barrels so long.

"Come," said Heremund. "Is that Lamoric there on the left? We'll slip in behind."

They descended the slope.

Finally, Durand picked out Coensar's silver wing of hair. "Here," Durand said. It was his turn to lead, bringing the skald into the back rank of Lamoric's conroi. The young lord wore his red helm. Every man was rapt, looking uphill to the Lady and her handmaids, so, with a glance to Heremund, who had nothing to say, Durand slipped forward, compelled to see for himself.

As he stepped into the front rank, the Lady and her handmaids looked up, though not at him. They stared beyond the double file of knights to the plowed fields of the village below. The peasants of the manor had silently gathered at the far edge of the manor's fields, separated as though waiting on facing shores of a black lake.

At this glance from the Lady, one old man among the peasants nodded and stepped onto the plowed earth, crossing the field for the castle. Although his feet slipped and slithered among the furrows, he kept his balance and his stiff-necked pace never wavered.

Durand did not, at first, see what was happening nearer to hand: Both the Lady and the maids of the Bower had set out from the hilltop. But he straightened as they passed, bright and solemn as children at a grave.

Heremund shook his head.

Just at the edge of the field, the company of maidens met the lonely figure of the old man. He reached up from the mud as the Bower's Lady bent, extending the bulky bouquet she had been carrying. Durand could hear the crackle and rustle of that bouquet—no pale flowers, but rather a moon-silvered sheaf of wheat. The old man reached up and, with wordless dignity, accepted the sheaf as though it were a swaddled child.

"The Spring Maid," said Heremund. "Seems the Lady of the Bower was a devotee of the women's cults. The full moon and the harvest rite. Last corn. All of it rings of the Spring Maid." He peered into the Heavens. "It must have been the Reaper's Moon when they left."

The skald's whisper was the only voice. Durand could not have made a sound.

The villagers on the far bank had dropped to their knees. No one moved. A shiver crawled through Durand. The only things in motion on the whole face of Creation were those nine women.

But, somehow, Heremund continued to speak. "The Maid's like your blackthorn boys."

The skald's voice seemed a desecration, wild and impossible.

"Everything was dying. The Son of Morning and the Host Below had set themselves to ending Creation. Tines of frost slid through the flesh of the world, as the Eye of Heaven guttered. And the Mother finally came. She set the moons over the darkness. She set the wheel of life moving in Creation, drawing man and woman apart, and together. But there was fear. It was not enough. The world was still falling into night. Freezing to the end of time."

"Heremund," whispered Durand.

The skald frowned, but continued. "The Maid, she was the first woman. Or one of them. And she grieved for the death of the living things. She cried out, and every living thing heard her."

Durand understood the silence then, or thought he did. It was the memory of that cry.

The village elder bowed toward his Lady. The Lady nodded. With the sheaf in the crook of his arm, his fingers caressed seed from the brittle head. He bent. A shiver of his hand sowed the first seed of what must be the winter crop. He stroked, bent, and sowed.

Durand saw that some of the knights had shut their eyes.

The man made his methodical progress down the length of the furlong, and, finally, when he had finished his journey, there was nothing left of the sheaf. He turned to his Lady, and she nodded low in reply, she and her maidens all turning back toward the castle. In silence then, the procession of maidens made the walk back between the lines of armored men.

Heremund was shaking his head as the women disappeared into the mouth of the pale castle. "It was the Reaper's Moon. Full. And the cross-quarter day. It is just what the Masters would have chosen."

All around Durand, the knights began to sag out of their rigid lines. Coensar, apparently loath to step into the path that the procession had so recently taken, stepped out behind his troops.

"Just as before," he said.

He seemed to scan the crowd for a moment. His cool eyes fell on Durand, then Heremund. He paused a moment.

"He came from the forest," Durand supplied.

"I am called Heremund. A skald."

A trace of something touched the captain's features: hard mirth. "Then you will have sung my song."

The skald was mystified, then he blinked, suddenly flustered. "Aye, well. There is a story," he admitted. Durand tried to remember.

The captain nodded, then left them to call for the attention of Lamoric's conroi. He sounded tired as he spoke to them all.

"I remind you if you've forgotten, or tell you if you never heard: No one sleeps who means to fight. It's the rule of this place."

While it was a mad regulation, Durand was not alone in nodding. What room was there for doubt under the weight of the presence poised over Bower Mead?

THERE WERE SHEEP and wolves as the assembled company broke up, and Durand noted both sorts of creature among the bleary knights. He saw Cerlac wipe his forehead—in bewilderment or relief. Berchard smiled under comically raised eyebrows. Then there were wolves: Guthred giving Durand a hard look, Badan baring his few teeth at Durand's glance, and Baron Cassonel moving through the murmuring flock, as watchful as any stalking beast.

Though Bower Mead seemed an island out of the world, he had brought his enemies with him. At the prospect of retreat, his mind turned to Saewin and the spear over the bridge. There was nowhere he was safe.

"You are a shield-bearer here, then?" said Heremund.

"What do you know of this place, Heremund?"

"Ah," said the little man. "Not enough. A skald's curse: There are more songs than a man can learn even in *twice* seven winters trying."

"Heremund," Durand pressed.

"It's the story of Hesperand the Lost, Durand. The duke and his Lady."

"The duke?"

"And old Saewin, of course."

Durand stopped, taking hold of Heremund as the man tried to trudge on. Thinking he must gain control of something in all this mess, he nearly lifted the skald off his feet.

"In the name of every Power—" the skald spluttered, his protests drawing glances.

Durand released his grip. Then, as indifference replaced disapproval among the passersby, he bent close at the skald's ear.

"Saewin."

"Aye, Durand. Saewin."

"Tell me." And, as the other men slumped about the bonfires, struggling against the dragging weight of sleep, Durand tugged Heremund off to the castle wall.

"Now, Heremund. Please."

Just then, a cloud fluttered at the moon, sending a ripple up the wall toward the feet of the pale watchers overhead. A night breeze curled over the dark green, pulling a whispered roar from the trees.

"Tell me," he repeated.

"It might've been an accident," said Heremund. "But I reckon there's a curse in it somewhere. It has the touch of the Powers about it."

There was a slap of leaves in the wind.

"It was the days of the High King after they'd moved the capital east to the Jewel of the Winter Sea." Heremund winced at a lashing of wind. "But—though they'd not been seen since the *Cradle* sailed—the Sons of Heshtar had returned. They'd crossed the Sea of Thunder and were marching up the Gray Road. There were rumors and rumblings. But their legions. They outran the screams."

Behind Durand, the men in the camp had begun to run through the dark, catching at tent flaps and guyropes. Each gust blew the bonfires down, like a breath of darkness. Durand held his ground. "On, Heremund."

"The High King: Allestan. He felt it! The falling of cities in Aubairn. The death of liegemen. The sack of sanctuaries. He called them up, the war host of the High Kingdom. Ships sailed from Parthanor. Armies rode from Vuranna. From Caldura. From Errest the Old!"

Heremund staggered at a gust. "And here in Hesperand, at the heart of Errest, Duke Eorcan. He stayed behind. Folk wanted a home guard. Someone to hold court. The thousand other small things. He kept a household guard. That's your Saewin, one of them. Saewin's brother; he rode south!"

Durand held fast to the thread of the story despite the rage of Hesperand.

"We should get under cover!" said Heremund.

But Durand needed to know. It was Hesperand trying to stop them. "Finish it!" he said.

Heremund shook his head. "God. Saewin and that brother, they were close. They cut lanccs. The same ash tree. Each a twin of the other's. They cut their palms. Made vows."

Above them, clouds swept across the moon, pitching the fields into darkness. Durand could hear shouting from the camps and the scream of horses. The wind hauled at his cloak.

"Gods, lad," said Heremund.

"Tell me!"

"The younger brother. He rode off. No one knew how bad—there'd been no word.

"But that first host. They rode straight into it. The thralls of Heshtar. Maragrim. Writhen men. Braying men. Whispering giants, stooped like oxen. Nightmare things not seen before or since. They had come in creaking ships by the tens of thousands. Wild things. Spirits. Slaves.

"The Atthian armies. They came piecemeal. They died. The men of old Errest most of all.

"And no one knew. Beyond the Blackrooted Mountains, there'd been no battle. The Sons of Heshtar wove darkness over the battlefields." The skald winced into the wind. "The Hidden Masters. They dreamed empty dreams. They saw nothing in their quicksilver but their own long beards. But Saewin's lance. It told another story."

Durand had to lean close to hear over the wind of Hesperand.

"It wept, Durand. Fresh blood! Oozed down the ashwood's grain. Saewin's, his brother's, the blood of the thralls of Heshtar, it bled. And Saewin knew: His brother and with him half the Sons of Atthi were in mortal danger. And, worse—as Saewin leapt up ready to hazard his life—three hundred leagues away.

"Imagine Saewin talking Eorcan into it! Showed him that spear. But Duke Eorcan, he called on the Hidden Masters. More than whispers, then. Any wellborn man could find them. And they tapped the deepest powers. The powers of the duke's land. And set a great sorcery in motion. Every peer in Hesperand made ready. Five battalions. Their mounts and arms. Three hundred leagues to meet the thralls of Heshtar.

He clung against the wind.

"But it went wrong! Terrible oaths bound the duke to his land, and his men to him. Then as now. Bonds and bonds knotted men and lands tight. It was them the Masters used: pulled Eorcan's host into the spell. And those bonds. They caught Hesperand and its hundred villages. They tore it all from Creation."

"It went as planned. The moon—the Reaper's Moon— rolled into place. The Eye of Heaven swung round. The cross-quarter day of Harvest dawned," Heremund said, pointing with a chop of his hand toward the black horizon, "Errest shivered. Then there was desolation!"

With a single crack of thunder, the wind collapsed.

It dropped cloak and tent and tree. Bower Mead filled with silence.

Heremund looked off toward the distant village and up at the pale fortress. Men scattered around the valley did likewise, stooped among their ruined tents.

Heremund laughed, short and hollow. Durand shook his head.

"There's precious little left of the rest," said Heremund. "They took it with them. But somehow, Saewin and the duke, they weren't ready. Since then, most reckon there was a tournament held on the night, though no living man knows why. And this tournament, this tournament all around us is, maybe, an echo of it. At the Lady's castle of Bower Mead."

Durand remembered Saewin's ranting. Accusing. "My Lady awaits me," he had said. What had happened?

"They say Duke Eorcan still rode at the head of his host. Still rides there—and there's a place for him saved at the Great Council wherever they sit—but that he and his men were all of them spirits, sleeting through the thralls like a killing rain.

"And Hesperand came adrift. Shaken from the heart of Errest as the bonds of oathtaking snapped tight around it. And so now it is as you have seen it: sometimes there, sometimes not. A place of ruins, or a place of living men—and every child is more ancient than the oldest elder of the Atthias beyond."

The light was returning to Bower Mead.

"Heremund. When you saw me ... why were you so shaken?"

"It happened here." He pointed to the earth. "Right here. This is the heart of the heart of it. Something grim enough to tear Creation at its seams. I cannot say how great a magic is required to accomplish such a thing. And every tournament at Bower Mead, it kills a man."

Durand nodded, slow. The death fit the place, and the Harvest ritual. His mind filled with the face of Saewin in the forest as the warrior raged against his doom—whatever that was. There was a great secret moving around them.

The stories of this place. He had heard of men walking safely through empty woodlands. Hearing voices. Men wandered into meadows humped with green ruins or stood in the halls of castles surrounded by living strangers. They were lost here forever or fell to bones and ashes when they stepped on mortal soil.

Durand resolved that there were secrets enough in Hesperand.

"Heremund," he said stiffly, "I've been short with you, and I'm sorry for it. I've seen things. Done ... things." He stopped, sucking a breath through his nostrils. "I am not the man I was when I left you at Tormentil."

"Lad—"

"Join the others if you wish, Heremund. I have to think."

He left Heremund then and walked to the empty ground beyond the camp and its firelight.

Alone, he looked out over the village from near the green brink where the Lady of the Bower had stood. It was as the priests would say: The Son of Morning and his Host snare a man by his pride or greed or fear, and draw you in until you can no longer see your way out. Until it is easier to go along.

But a man must make choices.

He stopped in the gloom.

"My man Guthred," said a voice. "He'll wonder why you're skulking out here in the dark."

Durand spun. A faint trace of firelight caught the hard edges of a man's features, and set tiny points alive in his eyes. It was Coensar, hardly ten paces from him. The captain was playing with a stone.

"Well done with old Ouen," he added. "Lucky. If you hadn't trapped his blade at your own throat, he would have looked damn foolish, and you would have made a new enemy." The captain paused. "It's a mistake to make enemies. . . ."

Durand nodded and silence hung between them. He could feel Coensar's eyes on him still.

"Has he told you?" the captain said, finally. "This skald friend of yours?"

For a moment, Durand was lost, then he remembered Heremund's brief confrontation with the captain. There had been a story there as well: another secret. But there was no time.

"Sir Coensar—"

"It's a dry old joke now." Coensar turned a wry smile. "Baron Cassonel's story." Coensar turned his attention square on Durand. "Do you know it?"

Cassonel was famous for one thing only. "He took on a conroi."

Coensar nodded. "At Tern Gyre. His Grace, Ludegar, Duke of Beoran, refused to fight Cassonel in the lists."

"You were with the duke?"

There might have been a smile.

"Cassonel was young. A boy. There he is, throwing down the gauntlet. The duke laughed. Then we got word that something had gone wrong down at the quay. The ship. Every man's fortunes in armor and horses all sinking. The whole lot of us ran down, but found nothing but seagulls and sailors with blank looks. When we climbed back to the postern gate, there was Cassonel. It was hardly more than a door at the top of the stair, but Cassonel threw his gauntlet at Beoran's feet a second time. The only way His Grace would pass was as Cassonel's prisoner. The duke sent every last one of his men and Cassonel defeated them in turn—like the Warders at the Bright Gates, standing his ground in that narrow doorway. There were twenty-seven men, and finally the duke."

"Lord of Hosts," said Durand.

Twenty-seven battle-tested knights. Who needed Hidden Masters and legions of darkness to be a hero?

"I was Beoran's champion at the time. He was talking about an heiress—a baron's widow—who had sixty manors. Damaryn. She needed a husband. She did not look so bad to me. In the hall beyond that postern door stood all the peers and heroes who had gathered to honor the Lost Princes that year. King Ragnal was there, though he was only a young prince at the time."

Durand noted the creases around the iron glints of the man's eyes and the dead silver of his hair.

"That Termangant sword of his is quick," the captain said.

"How long?" Durand murmured.

"Hmm. Seven winters I fought to gain Beoran's favor; fourteen since I lost it."

"Hells." Twenty-one years: Durand's lifetime.

"And now he's here, old Cassonel, Baron of my Damaryn, the rung that slipped from my hands. It's been a long time. I've been waiting."

"This is the first—"

"No. But nearly. I met him here seven years ago." His face twisted in a wry smirk. "He should never have been at a tournament, let alone this one. Beneath him, really. But then we were thrown on the same side of the mêlée, and I could not honorably oppose him."

"You've found other chances?"

Coensar's teeth glinted. "He's a baron now. He fights for Beoran. There's no need for him to risk his neck in a tournament. He has sixty manors. Ponds of fish. A hundred mills. Sanctuaries. Hunting preserves."

"And now he's here . . ." Durand said.

"Lady Damaryn has a mustache like a Heithan prince," Coensar said.

But Cassonel and the tournament explained every look Coensar had given him since they'd made camp. Guthred was his own man and slow to trust by his nature. For Coensar, it was all about Baron Cassonel. In light of this realization, Durand saw that his secrets had poisoned everything around him.

"Sir Coensar," Durand said, "I was with Radomor in Yrlac. In Ferangore. Cassonel came. He spoke treason, trying to convince Lord Radomor. It's Beoran and others. I don't know who. They are moving."

The captain hefted the stone in his palm, smiling into the dark.

His eyes glinted Durand's way, and he pointed into the

green. "Do you see that?" The grass was soft and gray under the moonlight.

"Captain?"

Coensar nodded at the green, and then he threw his stone. The rock soared out, and, when it landed, the field came alive. The uneven gray slope broke into thousands of round bodies, scattering like beads on a stone floor. It might have been Creation crumbling away.

Durand stared.

"Rabbits," said Coensar. "I don't know if it's the storm around this place. There're always rabbits here in moonlight."

HE SAID NOTHING more. Durand turned back toward the fire-lit camp, numb. He had made his choice and confessed. Now, there was nothing left but to allow the world to mete out the consequences. There was a little more to tell, but he felt a shaky sort of peace, like a man waking from a broken fever.

The jumble of pavilions seemed like black silhouettes clipped from the glow of bonfires, every one empty despite the hour. He wondered where Cassonel was among them. The baron would be sitting at one fire or another, in a squad of soldiers. Durand could hear laughter.

He had just begun to smile when a shape darted among the canvas alleys near Lamoric's camp, conspicuously bent and careful. Durand thought of Moryn and Cassonel and Saewin and the shapes beyond the forest edge.

Wrestling his sword free, he rushed toward the thing: an inky figure against a canvas wall.

Only a pace beyond the reach of Durand's blade, the shadow turned. Red hair flew around a face he knew. It was the woman from the stream, now wide-eyed with terror.

"God," Durand said. Quickly, he lowered the sword. "I . . . I am sorry. I—"

"Is it *you*?" the woman faltered.

"It is. Durand. From the river. And Red Winding." He spoke gruffly, trying to think. Surely, she had followed him. How else could she come to be there with him in the middle of this accursed land?

"Yes," she gasped.

Durand looked to the sword. "I thought . . . someone so

close to . . ." He realized he couldn't name his master, and concluded lamely: "I would not have frightened you for the world."

He slid his sword home.

And found they stood very close, unobserved by the world, her eyes looking up at his, dark and wide. Durand stepped closer, and felt a pressure to say something. "You will watch the tournament tomorrow?"

"Yes," she said. Wary, thinking.

The scent of her hair filled his head: a flower—purple swathes on summer hills.

"How . . . how did you come to be here?" he asked.

"This place," she said. "We could not have found it for our lives. Lady Bertana . . ."

She was very close now, her eyes like the flash of the moon at the bottom of wells, of an animal on the point of bolting.

He stretched out his hand, just brushing the warmth of her shoulder.

His near touch broke the spell that held her.

She gave her head a shake, looking at nothing. "May the Queen of Heaven protect you," she said, and darted off between the tents.

Durand stood alone. Dark shapes loomed around him: tents and angles. The sounds of conversation distant. The silent storm beyond. He was like one of the rabbits on the hillside, with Coensar's stone dropping out of the dark.

He closed his eyes, and heard, from among the voices throbbing in the dark, Heremund. The skald, it seemed, was already entertaining.

"All right, all right," the skald shouted.

Durand stole into the ring of bleary soldiers, feeling the heat on his face.

The men leaned in close; the skald hunkered down. "My first time, I was thirteen. She was a big girl. Skin like milk. Reddest lips. Just a scattering of tiny pimples over her forehead. I remember her lips were chapped, and there were little blades of skin like corners of parchment. A taste of iron. She stopped everything, and she knelt over me. My back was on the straw, my tunic rucked up and my breeches around my knees. She struggled her kirtle up over her head. It was this heavy, heavy wool, and narrow. I remember watching as it pulled her smock up behind it. I caught a glimpse of dimpled knees. Round stomach. Big solid thighs. The smock came off in one pull, and there she was standing over me. Big breasts low. Nipples standing in brown, spreading bruises.

"And I couldn't help myself, on my back with my breeches down. It had been standing there the whole time. I couldn't wait. And sweat gleamed over her chest and sides. And it was too late."

The circle of men erupted, rearing back. Ouen bellowed and shook his head. Berchard rolled onto his stomach, burying his face.

Coensar appeared at Durand's elbow.

Across the circle, Lamoric slipped between two men. Durand was surprised to find the young lord's eyes on him, staring across the circle, hands on his knees.

Berchard was speaking: "Heremund, my friend, if that's your first time, you're pure as fresh-fallen snow. You must go farther than that."

"Ah," said Heremund. "No. You see, it was the first time with my nose."

"What?" Berchard demanded.

"My nose. You see, she saw what was happening, and, well, she was not happy. There were breasts and a big, round arm." He shrugged. "And I was on the straw.

"She was gone, but I was on my elbows with this sticky pool of blood under my chin. My nose was running, I thought."

There were grimaces of recognition around the circle.

"That," he explained, "was the first."

"Mine was in my helmet," Ouen said, screwing up his face at the thought. The big knight's nose was little better than Heremund's.

The skald cocked his head. "You don't go in for the kissing much then, eh?"

"I wonder," said the giant, "if those dogs folk are seeing out there like a bite of cocksure bastard now and again."

"Now, now," said Berchard, waving the company to order. "So then. When was your true first time, Heremund Crookshanks?"

The bowlegged skald Heremund mimed dismay. "Sir, as a gentleman of breeding I could hardly speak of an affair so private and personal, like. The honor of a lady is involved, after all, ain't it?"

Men fell about the fire.

But Durand's glance met Lamoric's. The young lord did not laugh as the others rolled, and there was no shaking his glare. Coensar had told him.

Among the others, Ouen was striding over the blaze. "That's enough from you, I think." His huge hands caught Heremund as if the skald were a naughty child, and the two disappeared toward the trees, leaving cheers behind.

Every face waited, and there was a crash from the branches. Ouen returned, slapping the dirt from his palms.

Durand looked up, only to find that Lamoric had disappeared. His voice was at Durand's ear in an instant.

"Come with me," hissed the young lord.

HE WAS BARRED from the light by both Lamoric and the more distant figure of Sir Coensar. So, as the awful conversation began, there was nothing but forest at his back.

"Durand, tell me why I shouldn't have you hanged here and now."

Durand said nothing.

Lamoric shoved him, and then paced before him like something in a cage.

"My captain tells me you've just come from bloody Radomor of Yrlac. Did you not think to mention it when I took you on? When we sailed for Acconel? When we stood vigil over my sister in the bloody high sanctuary of Acconel? What is wrong with you? Are you mad? Are you in his pay even now?"

Durand held his tongue even when Lamoric glared up at him.

"For God's sake!" Lamoric lunged, shoving Durand. It was half-hearted. "For God's sake . . . just tell me. Tell me what you know of my sister."

Durand took a breath. "It will not be easy to hear, Milord."

"Say it!"

Durand nodded. "Lord Radomor was told she'd been with a man called Aldoin."

"Sir Aldoin. Warrendell. My Alwen?"

"The man was his friend."

Lamoric spoke, not looking at Durand. "He was at the wedding. Radomor believed this?"

"He did. Sir Lamoric, he had what he took for proof." It was hard to speak.

"Proof?"

"There was a sign she made . . . to call him."

"What are you saying?"

"The man, Aldoin, I know to be dead. Your sister . . ." He felt his face burn in the dark as he remembered catching the woman's arm and turning her back into that tower room. "I cannot say what happened, only that Radomor was angry."

" 'Angry.' "

"Aldoin drowned. They could hear him. We could hear him down the well."

They stood in silence then. Lamoric was bowed and staring at the earth. The shaking knot of his hands touched his mouth.

"Durand. I ask you, as your kin has served mine since the Gunderic and the *Cradle*. Do you believe it? This proof? *Do you believe it?*"

Durand forced his eyes to meet his master's gaze.

"She confessed, Lord."

🌀 14. Where Dance the Shadows

As the Heavens rolled above them, every company sank slowly into a drained and shaky silence. Alone, at first, Sir Agryn prayed First Twilight when the coming dawn silvered the eastern sky. Soon, the others joined him, watching the cool glow swelling in the Heavens above the castle. Even Badan could not resist the call to his knees. Agryn continued his murmured prayer until the needle of Heaven's Eye split the horizon, and he could stand to give thanks for the dawn.

Durand kept his hands busy with horses and harness, knowing he was a traitor awaiting his sentence. His time with these men was finished, but still he checked long limbs and mended cinches. He curried twitching flanks. It kept him awake.

While the men waited out the night, villagers built a reviewing stand overlooking the green, hammering, at first, in darkness. The knights would fight where Coensar's rabbits had scattered only a few hours before. The path the castle women had walked would divide the lists, north from south.

With the coming of the dawn, every conroi creaked into motion. Belted knights yawned and shivered like boys. Grooms threw parti-colored trappers over the heads of warhorses. Men struggled into hauberks and surcoats. Shield-bearers raced with forgotten shields and battle helms. Soon, the whole company struggled out to the lists, half to the north and half to the south. They were tired, and one man among them would die.

As Durand passed lances and shields between the crowded horses, he wondered. Each man that reached could be the one.

No one spoke of shirking the strange duty that had been imposed upon them. They must fight.

As Durand slipped through the close-packed horses to check the crupper-strap on Sir Coensar's mount, all the rustling and muttering subsided. Looking up from the shadows, Durand spotted a knight in black and silver facing the captain.

Baron Cassonel of Damaryn sat in a tall fighting saddle. His expression gave no hint of his emotions.

"Sir Coensar."

"It is."

"It has been a long time, I think."

The others were watching; no one spoke.

"A very long time indeed."

Cassonel regarded Coensar with a dispassionate stare.

"And you are in Hesperand once more?" said Coensar. "It has been seven winters."

"I did not intend it," the baron said. "My lord wished haste."

"How fares the Duke of Beoran?"

"Well enough."

"Good. I wouldn't wish him ill. I've my own lord to follow now."

"This Red Knight," Cassonel said.

"Yes. The Knight in Red."

Lamoric touched his helm in mocking salute. Coensar changed directions.

"You were caught on the road?"

"I had no intention of coming here."

"At least the weather is fine." Coensar smiled. "How does the wind blow in Ferangore? Old Duke Ailnor fares well, does he? Or did you miss the old man? It can be hard tracking a man down. You can go years without catching sight."

If Cassonel was surprised, he hid it well. He did shoot a glance to Durand where he stood among the cinches and stir-rup leathers. "The Duke of Yrlac is hale, Sir Coensar."

"I had heard rumors. His son . . ."

"The duke is hale. And you may find that he outlives some of us here."

"God willing," said Coensar.

"You fight on the north?"

"Aye."

"I think it will not be long till we meet once more," Cassonel said and led his men to the southern company.

Durand felt a hand grip his shoulder. He looked up and saw Coensar grinning down. "That, I enjoyed." And Durand took some comfort that he and the captain, at least, would not part on bad terms.

As Cassonel and his retainers took up their place in the line across the mist-steaming yard, nine long shadows fell over the battleground, stilling the men. Into this silence, horns brayed from the reviewing stand. Durand winced at the shiver they sent through his bones. The Lady of the Bower and her hand-maidens looked out over the chaos of pennons and horses, then they mounted the rough steps into the stand and took their places—nine silhouettes against the green canvas of the stand's back wall.

There were others in the stand: travelers lost in Hesperand. His Stream Maid must be there as well, somewhere behind the green canvas awnings—a woman he had simply let walk away from him. He had not even asked her name.

Again, there was fanfare.

"The Lady of the Bower welcomes the peers of the realm to this festival in honor of the Maid of Spring."

From his position among the horses, Durand made out

warriors in green surcoats. Each man carried the coiling horn
of some fantastic beast. It occurred to him that, although they
looked every inch a fighting man, each must be a herald to
the Lady of the Bower. He wondered who they were, and
how they had come to be in Bower Mead. A graybeard herald
was speaking.

"To further honor the Maid, her ladyship enjoins all free
men who are of age and not infirm to take part in a display of
skill at arms to begin before this hour has passed." He narrowed
his eyes and set a fist on one lean hip. "Let no man shirk his
chance to demonstrate his devotion to the Maiden of Spring."

He raised the coiling horn. Silver fittings glinted against the
dark curl. "The next blast upon my horn will mark the beginning of the combat." With this, the herald bowed sharply and
dismissed them all to prepare.

"Well, you others, have you heard him?" said Coensar. "A
surprise, eh?"

Durand caught himself staring up from among the horse's
arses, gaping like a fish. Hesperand was an old duchy, and this
tournament predated knights and shield-bearers both. There
had only been fighting men. There he was, standing in mud
and shirtsleeves, expected to climb on horseback and fight armored men with real blades.

Guthred grunted: "I'm bloody infirm."

Lamoric twitched around, his red battle helm oddly menacing.

"The rest of you," he said. "No excuses."

"Right," said Guthred. "You're on horseback if I've got to
tie you there. Get to it."

And the crowd broke.

Every man of age meant twenty-one or more, and rank didn't
matter—shield-bearers and grooms charged in a sudden storm.

Durand wove through the anxious mob. He'd planned to
keep out of sight, and leave as quickly as he could. Now, he
was hunting up tack and saddles to join the battle line.

"Hurry, you drove of goats," barked Guthred, "or you'll
fight as you stand!" A horse screamed—the wrong horse—
and the man spun. "Get out of there, you daft bastard! You
think Lamoric wants you bashing around on his good bloody
palfrey?" One of the grooms ducked a hasty backhand.

Durand rooted his hauberk and shield from the packs and hauled a good sturdy cob from among the horses. The brute was no warhorse, but it looked strong enough.

"The riding saddles, you stupid whoreson," Guthred was shouting. "How many fighting saddles you reckon we've got? Throw an extra cinch round."

With a few quick slips of strap and buckle, Durand urged the cob to the line. He would be lucky if the brute didn't break his neck running away. Around him, the companies took shape, reinforced by scores of raw men on bare horses. Wide-eyed beasts threw their heads. Grooms in gambesons hunkered over saddlebows, clutching spare lances.

Coensar was speaking. "—a second rank. Or third. And tight. Knee to knee. There shouldn't be room to drop an apple between us when we're riding out."

Coensar's head swiveled as he looked over the crowd. Lamoric, beside his captain in line, sat low, his battle helm red as raw flesh. After the night before, Durand wondered what turn the man's thoughts had taken. The helm neatly masked any trace.

Durand was left riding at the man's back. If he had never seen Ferangore, this might have been his chance to win favor with the young lord. Now, though, he owed Lamoric a debt, and would throw his whole will behind it.

A hairy fist clamped his knee. Guthred peered up at him. There was a spear.

"Here boy. You asleep? Even you won't do much damage without a bloody lance."

Durand took the spear.

"Point it at their lot," Guthred added, helpfully. "And move this bag of bones." He slapped the cob's rump. "I've got to have a word." He barged his way past Durand and through the close-packed horses toward the front.

There was movement among the heralds.

There were a lot of bare blades in the hands of scared men. Durand swallowed. A night without sleep had skimmed his face over with grease. His mouth was dry right to the back of his throat, and, somewhere along the line, he had missed his last chance for a piss.

The cob shifted its weight, side to side.

"Durand?"

Behind him, red-haired Cerlac rode at the head of a straggling column, looking more like a knight-at-arms now in mail and surcoat.

"Your chance, eh?"

"I suppose."

The man seemed to notice something.

"Hells. Are you riding bare-headed, then?"

"I'm lucky I've still got my hauberk." There were plenty of men on the verge of riding against lances wearing nothing more than quilted canvas.

"I reckon I can manage another lucky stroke for a comrade at arms. Here." The young knight called back down the line behind him, and soon a boy ran up, holding a helmet over his head like a plattered roast at a feast. Cerlac plucked it from the boy's hands.

"It's a bit rough." The thing looked like a hammered iron bowl, but there was a broad nasal bar to blunt any slash across the eyes. "The webbing's still good, and the iron's sound enough."

He held it out, and Durand gladly took the thing. "You're generous."

"Now you've got a fighting chance, eh?"

"I'll do my best to get it back to you in one piece." Durand put the thing on his head, blinking at the sharp smell and the unfamiliar weight.

"I owe you my life after that bucket last night. Good luck."

Durand touched the brow of the helm in salute. He felt free. Cerlac nodded and rode for his place down the line.

Suddenly, Durand was jostled. Coensar was bobbing and twisting in his saddle, looking up and down their line. Durand saw pointing across the lists, then Coensar was shouting back. "All right, you lot. Back them out." There were moans of confusion. "Get them out of line!"

On the field, the heralds were already tramping out to get things started. But the conroi wallowed back, tearing itself loose of its astonished battalion.

Coensar stood in his stirrups. "Follow me. We haven't much time!" They rode, swinging round the whole field. In the midst of the enemy line, Cassonel, in his black and silver gear, stood in his stirrup irons, watching them come, incredulous. In a moment, they would join Cassonel's battalion, losing Coensar the chance he had bled for.

Only as Coensar led their conroi jostling into the northern company, did Durand see the explanation: The heir of Mornaway had taken up a place in the ranks opposite Lamoric's men. On opposite sides, Moryn would have had his chance at Lamoric. Now, the man was forced to be an ally.

Arranging it had cost Sir Coensar dearly.

They settled into the line, horses twitching. Their erstwhile allies stared back in astonishment.

The Lady's heralds walked out into the lists. One of the men passed down the ranks in front of them. It would be any moment now.

There was a heavy ripple running through the opposing line: more jockeying. Men and horses jostled to make way for a new conroi, and a sober Baron Cassonel emerged in the front rank. The man regarded Coensar steadily. The Baron of Damaryn would give Coensar his chance.

The green-clad heralds took up places at each of the four corners of the field. Across the way, Durand spotted redhaired Cerlac who shrugged back with a smile. Now they would fight against each other. Durand checked to be sure that his sword was free in its scabbard. He touched the pommel of his misericord dagger. He tried to find the balancing point of the lance. Each breath snapped his throat dry as parchment.

Durand could still not see into the reviewing stand, but a shadow had risen against the canvas. The long figure's arm was raised. The heralds noted it as well, each of the four raising a horn to his lips.

Horses stamped. Durand gripped lance and shield.

There was a wispy something in the Lady's hand, and—as soon as Durand had seen it—it fell.

The line surged into motion with the blare of trumpets.

THE MÊLÉE WAS a wild and furious thing. After the long night under the silver moon, the climbing Eye of Heaven set every streaming color ablaze.

For hours, Durand fought to stay with Lamoric's conroi and not to get himself cut from the group and taken. There were collisions and screams and pitched battles as conrois clashed. Men fell and ran. In the confusion, blows clattered in from wild angles. Men bobbed in and out. As the bright Eye climbed, Durand took a lance against his shield and uncounted slapping blows over mailed limbs. As far as he knew, no blow of his own had so much as bruised another man.

In the day's third hour, a lance jabbed big Ouen from his horse, but Lamoric and Berchard together swooped down. In an instant, the giant knight was flying over the field, suspended between two horses with his feet churning the air.

Durand and the whole conroi swept in to cover their retreat from the lists. The big man hit the ground beyond the palings, tumbling from the hands that had hoisted him out of harm's way, and laughing as he rolled to a halt among a crowd of startled shield-bearers.

It was while Ouen tumbled that things went wrong. Coensar was howling an order. "To me, to me! Reform! Reform!" From the churning, wheeling chaos of the mêlée, another conroi had broken loose. In racing for the edge of the lists, Lamoric's men were strung out across two-dozen paces with the slowest horses and poorest riders straggling and exposed. Enemies leapt to seize the advantage.

Durand, on his stolid cob, barely had time to spin as men and horses sleeted through the fragmented lines all around him. One grinning villain picked him out, rushing forward behind the long blade of a lance. The attacking point howled up Durand's shield, as his own lance shot the gap between his attacker's horse and bridle, wrenching ten feet of spinning lance from Durand's fist.

Lamoric's conroi flexed, twisting like a pit bear—blades, armor, and lances lashing to drive off any new attacker.

Suddenly safe, Durand shook a stung hand. His lance was a sharp angle in the mud, ashwood snapped like a reed. He felt blood slick in his ear. With the rest of the conroi bristling, there was room for Durand to slip out, pull himself together, and collect another weapon.

The quickest route took him past the reviewing stand, but, as he slipped into its shadow, a knight in red dragons spotted him. The man's gilded helm and its tall dragon crest twitched Durand's way. Though the whoreson must have seen that Durand was unarmed, the Dragon jammed his spurs home, his warhorse's trapper rising in a red storm. The pennon of the Dragon's lance lashed like flame.

"Hells," snarled Durand.

In the instant that Durand understood that he must run, voices gasped behind him. Several of the young women were standing now, many with their hands at their faces. He saw wide eyes and excited grins. If she was here, his Stream Maid was among them. He could not run.

He spurred the cob down the Dragon's throat. There was no time. He got one gulp of air, then Dragon struck, lance glancing from Durand's shield—slamming Durand over the back of his saddle. But Durand swung: the slapping overhand blow caught the Dragon's helm—staving it in with the force of charging horses alone. The dragon crest flew on, spinning.

There was a shriek among the women as the leather crest flopped down among them.

The Dragon himself crashed from his saddle. As the downed man's mount flounced to a halt, Durand hauled himself back into his seat and turned to the stand. The maids were smiling and standing and staring. His Stream Maid was there, in shadow. The Lady of the Bower flashed her teeth. The Dragon struggled on the ground, like an insect, half-crushed. Durand felt he should do something. He should get help. Or he should take the bastard prisoner.

The heralds winded their arcane horns: a long hollow note that skirled above the field.

Durand twisted. The din of blades ebbed away.

The Lady stood as placidly as she had been when she started the whole event. In the lists behind Durand, only a few straggling clatters continued to ensure him that it was not sorcery that had stilled them all.

Every streaked and muddy soldier on the field looked to the Lady of the Bower and her handmaids. Durand felt a fool, caught by mistake on the same stage before all the others. With a nod to the Lady, he gave ground, bullying his carthorse backward, as the gray-bearded herald strode out in front of the stand.

The man bowed stiffly to the crowd.

"You have each acquitted yourself well this morning, and

my Lady thanks you for your spirited participation. The Eye
of Heaven has reached its zenith. The general mêlée is at an
end. When every man has sung Noontide Lauds, the tournament will continue; this time to be fought by chosen men
alone. The Lady's selections will be delivered to each war
band. Let each fighting man be ready for the call." The man
paused. "When next the horns sound, it will be the seventh
hour."

As the old herald departed with his mistress for the castle,
Durand closed his eyes and breathed deep, careful breaths.

It was over.

For a time only men-at-arms and villagers remained.

After a few awkward heartbeats, the fighting men turned
from the lists, moving without orders toward the pavilions.
Someone collected the battered Dragon.

One-eyed Berchard swung in beside Durand's cob.

"Durand! Bravely done." He smiled. "And you've found
hidden virtues in that old cob horse." He extended a wineskin
to Durand. "May you both sire great lines!"

Durand took it, surprised that any of Lamoric's men would
speak with him. "I thought the thing would be scared out of its
wits."

"Too daft to notice, more like. And I'm not sure he isn't
blind," Berchard said. He took back the skin. "You did well.
Taught a couple of them, I reckon. That last one anyway." He
grimaced. "He'll think twice next time he sees a rough country lout on a plow horse." Then he offered the skin once more.

Durand took another swig from the bottle and a good
breath of air.

"He deserved worse," said Berchard.

Glancing around, the old campaigner leaned close. "And,
as for me, I talk to whomever I like." The man leaned back
and nodded. "For what it's worth.

"Here's your mate," he added, with a glance toward the
edge of the field.

Heremund took the reins of the plow horse as Durand
climbed down, his legs like sacks of sand.

"You're alive," the skald laughed. "What a brawl that was.
Like no mêlée these eyes have seen. Half these fools are lucky
they didn't kill themselves, let alone anyone else. There were

horses bounding off like hares, every which way. Men on backward. Upside down. Boys on pigs have more grace."

They trudged toward Lamoric's tents, Durand eyeing his future. It was Blood Moon in the wide world beyond Hesperand, and winter was in the wind. He would be making his own way once more.

Heremund produced a loaf of bread. "Don't worry. I stole it from Guthred," he explained. "Nothing baked or grown in Hesperand."

There were bruised men sprawled everywhere, most too tired or battered to even think about speaking. Heremund winced at the worst of them. "Looks like a wagon wreck on market day."

They found a dry spot in the grass and sat down. The earth felt like earth. The Eye of Heaven was as warm as always. Slipping his arm from the straps of his shield, Durand tore a chunk from the loaf with his teeth—a few loose. His right hand was stiff and swollen.

Heremund smiled around a long sip of claret. "I might have missed your ugly face, you know."

"You saw that scrape with the Dragon, then?" Durand said.

Heremund handed him the wineskin. "He should never have come for you with that lance."

Durand didn't argue.

"Dragon's a baron," said Heremund, "I think. I can't remember which. Hardly fair, and what's he gain besting a foe like you?"

Durand smiled. "Thank you, I'm sure."

"Your gear is nothing he'd want as a prize, and you weren't fairly armed. He made a fool of himself losing. No money. No honor. Little risk, no reward. I wonder what the rules would be if you'd have caught him? He'd have to yield to a knight."

"I thought I was going to end up skewered."

Heremund laughed. "Aye. Whack! A bolt through a pigeon, right in front of our lovely hostess. I'm beginning to think I should train you for a skald like me. I don't even lance boils."

Durand raked his helmet off with the bad hand, the leather webbing peeling away from a paste of brown blood.

Heremund winced, but, looking up, spotted something over Durand's shoulder. Durand turned to find eyes on him. Toward

Lamoric's pavilion, dour Guthred was staring. Lamoric's helm faced their way as well.

Heremund touched his shoulder.

"I suppose though," he said, "*you* really *ought* to seek out the uneven battle."

"You want me skewered?" Durand said.

Heremund's eyes narrowed, considering the proposition. "No, I imagine you'd be a bit tough for my teeth. Though I suppose with the kind of malleting you took today, you're likely halfway tender by now."

Durand allowed himself a smile. There were a hundred bruises waiting for him, he was sure.

Heremund jabbed a stubby finger toward Durand. "Everyone likes the dashing hero who wins despite overwhelming opposition. Yes, overwhelming opposition's the only way. You'll have to keep an eye out."

"I'll need a better helm," Durand said.

"Skill."

"Aye, and a coat of plates, while I'm at it." Durand laughed, swallowing another tart mouthful of wine.

Someone whooped toward Lamoric's camp.

"What's this now?" said Heremund.

Durand thought he heard his name, and stood to find Berchard marching toward him.

"Here! Durand! The Green Lady. She sent this along for you." He slapped a hard yellow lump into Durand's torn right hand. He caught a whiff of lye. Durand didn't understand.

"What is it?"

"They've announced the chosen men, and, God save us, you're one. We'll have to clean you up a bit."

In different ways, every man in the conroi looked as astounded as Durand—all but Sir Coensar, who wore an expression that might have been amusement. The captain had a scroll of cream vellum in his hand.

Coensar lifted the scroll and quietly read: "From the company of the Knight in Red are selected the Knight in Red himself, Sir Coensar his captain, and Durand of the Col."

Berchard grinned. "Well done, lad," he said, taking the soap back and giving the hand a good pump. "My horse is yours, if you need it."

By Agryn's dial, the seventh hour was almost upon them. The strap on Durand's helmet was tight enough to crack his teeth. He swallowed against the knot. The green and yellow shield of his family was torn in a dozen places. Berchard's horse, a sooty brown, tossed its head fit to break its neck. Durand snugged his grip on the reins.

There were thirty chosen men. All the fighting men north and south had been reduced to two tight conrois. Peasants had uprooted the palings and driven them into the turf much closer to the reviewing stand, staking out an area fifty paces on a side. There would be no room to breathe out there.

Durand waited in a line with the north fifteen. He was the only man on either side whose horse wore no trapper—and the only man whose face was bare.

"When it starts, stick close," hissed Coensar. Lamoric, as Knight in Red, sat beyond the captain.

Durand nodded once, sharply. With Lamoric at risk, the captain wasn't pleased that a novice had stolen an experienced man's place.

Opposite their conroi were fifteen visored knights; helms, and shields, and trappers all matched.

"I'm the saltire cross. Take the green."

There was, indeed, a man in gold and green opposite him. Durand slipped his lance higher in his hand, accidentally provoking the blue knight to do the same, raising his lance in a mocking salute. He could feel the garter below his knee binding.

The Lady of the Bower stood. In one delicate hand, she held a bit of green silk. Durand glanced for the champing conroi opposite. He saw Coensar's "saltire"—a white cross on sable: Cassonel of Damaryn. His black helm turned to the stands.

The Lady raised her arm. Durand locked his teeth and tore his eyes away as the green fabric fell.

The avalanche of their hooves buried the call of horns. The line charged as though every knight had leapt from a cliff. Durand aimed for the green and yellow shield that bobbed toward him but, at the last, the head of his lance slipped over the rim. Green's point struck Durand's three stags hard enough that Durand nearly lost his shield.

Reining in as the thunder passed, Durand shot a glance at Coensar.

—And saw the captain's horse galloping riderless, Coensar himself still tumbling.

While Coensar staggered to his feet some twenty or thirty paces from help, the Baron of Damaryn drew Termagant and set his spurs.

Durand pitched his mount into a headlong gallop as the whole rumbling charge of Cassonel's sword and armor and barding flashed down to skewer the captain's heart.

There was just a chance: Durand hoisted his lance overhand and stabbed into the blur of sable and silver like lightning from the empty air. The lance splintered as he flashed by.

He heaved the brown into a savage turn to find Cassonel's warhorse lolloping away, and the Baron of Damaryn himself rolling across the turf.

Durand pulled up where Coensar swayed. The man was blinking. Keening dragged in the grass. He was still on his guard or trying—unsure if Cassonel was alive or dead.

Durand ripped his own sword from its scabbard, but the Baron of Damaryn lay sprawled in the skirts of his surcoat. He struggled to get his hands underneath him, tried to shove himself upright. He couldn't.

Now, Lamoric—the Knight in Red—joined Durand, putting himself between the captain and anyone who might think to pick off a stricken man. Cassonel was still on his face.

"That was well done," said Lamoric. Riders from Cassonel's retinue were swarming out. If they chose to fight, there were too many. But they leapt down around their leader, ducking low like dogs around a corpse. For a disjointed moment, Durand thought they were sniffing and picking at his clothes. Soon, though, they gathered their master up, and carried him from the lists. There were no shouted challenges or threats of revenge.

Lamoric was watching Cassonel. "He's finished for today."

Coensar laughed from the ground. "And I've missed my chance."

And Durand realized. "I'm sorry," he said. "You might have taken him. I shouldn't have."

Coensar's eyes darted to Durand, beads of lead in a face gray as wax.

Then Lamoric's men surrounded them. Guthred pulled Coensar away. Berchard took the bridle of his own horse. "No one's fault. It was no one's."

The others gathered Coensar up and carried him off to safety, Berchard nodding up at Durand. "Watch His Lordship, Durand. There's no one else."

The next charge of horsemen began.

HE FOUGHT IN the hope that Coensar would clear his head and rejoin them. They took no prizes. They won no duels. Though Lamoric hissed and snarled, Durand guarded him closely, riding hard to stick by allied conrois and refusing to let any screaming knight goad them into a fight they could not win. Durand watched and rode, teeth bare and eyes wide, cutting like a shepherd's dog between Lamoric and harm.

With no time for any goal but survival, Durand scarcely noticed that his shielding tactics won his master the advantage. While they ducked and dodged, other conrois tore at one another. Puffed-up thugs hared off at every insult; knights dueled like alley bravos. Soon, there wasn't a single three-man conroi left in the field. Every other group had lost at least one rider, and the desperate air of men hard-pressed was on them all. It was then that Lamoric took charge.

"Curse you, Durand, I'm my father's son, not his daughter, and that's the last I can stand of hiding. Get out of my way, and we'll take a few prisoners before this cursed mêlée's done." With a stiff gesture of his sword, he broke away. Durand charged after. The young lord, with Durand's help, forced a knight in yellow to surrender, then turned toward a pair of horsemen. Durand recognized one as the knight who had nearly unhorsed him at the beginning of the afternoon's combat. His shield was checked in gold and green: Durand's own colors.

Just as Durand set his spurs, the herald's horns moaned out. Durand's borrowed warhorse fell out of its gallop.

Sir Gold and Green took his helm in his hands and lifted. Durand was startled to see the rusty hair of his acquaintance Cerlac. He waved an exhausted salute, and Cerlac grinned back.

But the Lady was standing, her face the model of playful indignation, and, climbing down into the lists before her, came the graybeard herald.

"Her Ladyship has no interest in watching men tear one another to pieces in mismatched battles. Let each man-at-arms who remains within the lists prepare himself for the deciding contest of the day's fighting. You will fight singly. One man against another until there is victory."

NOW THE FIELD was narrow and lined deep with spectators. At one end, Durand stood in a shadowed knot of nine horsemen, wishing he could see past the iron mask of Lamoric's helm. Near a hundred knights made up the first rank of onlookers, cheek by jowl, silent, and bloodied.

Beyond them, the peasants of Bower Mead had closed upon the field, standing like a solemn host of specters. Grimy faces, homespun garb: hairy wool and nettle. They numbered more than a hundred.

The sound of the place had changed. Someone sniffed a running nose. Tack on horses at the far end might have been pennies rattling in Durand's hand.

It was here they would have to fight.

The graybeard herald, his face like a carved icon, stepped into the narrow lists. Down the long ground, Durand could see another knot of horsemen.

The man spoke now, his voice pitch low: "Eighteen of you remained within the lists when the horns were winded. Nine," he said, "and nine. Now, you must now decide who will enter next."

The herald looked back to his Lady, who nodded once very slowly and took her seat.

"The first combatants must enter the lists."

"Right," said a voice.

A knight Durand had never met swung up into his saddle and erupted from their ranks, lance in hand. At the far end of the lists, another stallion pranced into the long alley. The men loved a joust. Everything a man did was seen.

The first knights lit out. The grunt and slam as they collided sent a flinch through the horses all around Durand. Both men hit the ground before the Lady's seat in the stands. You could hear the two combatants hauling breath through suffocating helms as they fought. Finally, the far champion fell, bludgeoned over the shoulder till he couldn't lift his sword.

Durand watched the women. They were seated close enough to flinch at every blow.

When the first pair of knights had been dragged from the lists, a man in black shrugged off the others at Durand's side to barge into the narrow field, his warhorse high-stepping. And again the ground shook under the Lady's eyes as he rumbled out to meet another champion from the far camp. You could see the shock twitch through the fabric across the black knight's back as his lance struck home.

At Acconel, Durand once saw a standing man struck by a charging horse's shoulder. He landed five paces away. And here there were two horses, with all their speed and all their weight balanced on the point of a lance. Idly, he thought that it was amazing no one had died.

Then he remembered this tournament's rule: *There was always one.* And it must happen soon. There were only seven pairs left to fight.

Before Durand could finish the count, another knight tore out in a swirl of green. Again, the ground rolled in the narrow place like battle-drums in a bedchamber. Neither man died. The handmaidens sighed for the vanquished man, but were giddy as the green knight bowed and handed up the captured crest of the loser's helm: a gilded lion. A breathtaking woman accepted the mangled leather head with care.

By now, the others were all on horseback. Durand felt Lamoric's hand on his shoulder. It was ridiculous to fight in such close quarters. There were too many people too close to breathe.

Another pair rode out, catching Durand by surprise. He had hardly noticed the last pair fall. They had all been quick. Another knight rode out. There was a crash that left both riders struggling like foals in the grass.

There were only a few of them left now, all lined up.

"I'll go now," said Lamoric.

"Lordship," Durand acknowledged, taking a sharp look

down the alley of faces to the horsemen at the far end. And saw Moryn.

The Lord of Mornaway tugged at gauntlets and seated his helm. Durand actually glanced to see that the man wasn't beside him as well. He had changed sides after the fighting began. To play such a trick, Mornaway must have felt very ill-used by Lamoric's evasions.

Now, one bad pass could throw away Lamoric's chance at the Herald and the prince at Tern Gyre. And Lamoric was about to ride out.

"No," said Durand, and caught Lamoric's arm, half twisting the man from his saddle. There was no time to explain. He slapped the rump of the next man's horse, sending the animal lurching into the lists. The rider, a knight in blue slashes, twisted around, but he was in too far to retreat without looking a coward.

Durand could see Lord Moryn falter, his horse falling off stride. Then Moryn spurred the animal on, and the two knights met with a crash that sent the blue knight skidding from the lists, hauled by one stirrup.

As Moryn left the lists—with a long look for Lamoric—Durand noted that no one had died.

"Now. Keep off!" growled Lamoric, nudging his mount into the lists and charged a knight in marine hues. On their first pass, each man's lance detonated. An exchange of fierce cuts ended with the enemy disarmed by a hacking strike across his knuckles. The green knight fell on his knees, vanquished. Lamoric, after gravely accepting the man's surrender, bowed to the Lady and remounted to ride from the lists.

And still no one had died.

"That's you," Lamoric said, jouncing past. And Durand was next—he was also the last. And the tournament had not yet claimed its victim.

He looked down the corridor of faces: a hundred peers and a hundred peasants. He guided Berchard's sooty brown between the palings and into the lists. Heremund was among the faces. The skald's hat was a knot in his fists. No one said a word.

Durand closed his eyes. Someone might already have died, passing in some surgeon-barber's tent. He looked down the long alley.

At the far end, he saw gold and green. Cerlac's green and gold. With dull astonishment, Durand raised his lance and watched Cerlac answer, his expression neatly shut behind the slit mask of his helm.

Gold and green.

The Silent King knows all dooms, and a wise man does not grumble.

The women of the castle leaned in. The joust would end on the blood-soaked ground right before them. Cerlac was having some trouble settling his horse. The women talked and pointed. There were a multitude of eyes on him. Durand shut the women from his mind and fixed his attention on Cerlac.

Man and horse both were one shifting maze of yellow linen and green diamonds. Durand watched as the shield bobbed—moving squares against the field of diamonds.

He cocked his own Col stags.

Someone was leaning in—astonished, foal-dark eyes, and a fringe of red hair. The Stream Maid.

But Cerlac nodded.

Durand snatched a lungful and spurred his horse.

They were off. Walls of staring faces rippled past. As the green edge of the stand flickered by, Durand swung his lance into line. The big brown charged like a bull. At the last, Durand clamped the lance tight against his side.

Twin shocks: shield and lance. Splinters flew. His thumb-knuckle punched his own ribs like the beak of an anvil, but he held his seat.

He ended his rumbling charge in the southern camp, fighting for air. He gulped and swallowed. Men were close around the horse's flanks. There was no time. He needed a weapon. Fumbling his sword free of its scabbard with a shaking hand, he spun. He spotted Cerlac, still in his saddle, also hauling his blade free.

He charged. Cerlac pitched toward him, his sword catching flame in the red dusk. At the last, Durand swung, but there was hardly room. At the point of impact, Durand's knee met Cerlac's. Cerlac's helm struck the cross-guard of Durand's sword, the knight's head snapping round. Durand's blade flew over the crowd. Cerlac hurtled to the sod in a hail of chain skirts and scabbards.

Durand halted the brown as a desperate Cerlac bobbed up, weaving across the turf on all fours, groping for his own sword.

Durand dropped from his saddle—empty-handed, his knee barely taking his weight. The wall of peasants had closed over his sword. One look at their grim faces told him that he wouldn't get it back. Cerlac was already on his feet, blade in hand. The man reared back. Durand stood before him, defenseless. But Cerlac checked his swing. He gestured, thrusting his chin toward a snapped lance. A good four feet remained—and a point.

The crowd was close enough to whisper as Durand picked up the lance and faced Cerlac. Both men wavered then. Breath hissed. Before Durand's throbbing eyes, Cerlac was a masked shape of gold and green and eye-slit shadow. Durand tried to fill the bottoms of his lungs and stamp some feeling back into his knee. Finally, they stepped into a circling dance.

Durand forced himself to think. The lance would make a passable bludgeon, and the point was sound. He would have to pick his chance. As he circled, his shadow swung over Cerlac, and Cerlac came into the light. In that instant, he saw clear ribbons of freckled skin and red lashes through Cerlac's visor. Durand struck, jabbing high. The point squawked from the top of Cerlac's shield and caromed from the diamond helm.

Cerlac launched an iron hail, and, grimacing under his shield, Durand lashed back. Razor edges flickered between them quick as willow switches. Blows sparked and scrabbled over mail and shields. Durand caught a cross cut below his ear that dazed him, but managed to bash another stroke against the iron cask of Cerlac's helm. Then the first flurry was over, and there was no air left in Creation.

Durand staggered free, stooped as a baited bear. In the lull, Cerlac's sword twitched, drawing Durand's eye. They circled. He could do little more than react, following his partner wobbling through the blazing sunset, blind and blinking into the brilliance or stumbling into shadow.

There was no time to get his wind back. He had thrown too much into those first moments. Cerlac darted. A strike against his shield shuddered through the bones of his shoulder. Cerlac's blade flickered like an adder's tongue. The point jabbed

at Durand's hauberk, faster than he could stop it. He wondered if, even now, some injured man lay in his tent breathing
his last. Cerlac's point shot for Durand's face, but a flinch sent
the blade raking at the mail over his ear. He would not survive
much longer.

Abruptly, Cerlac swung. The shearing overhand bit deep
through the lime planks of Durand's shield and stuck. Durand
yanked, but couldn't pull free. For an instant, an animal panic
gripped him. Cerlac wrenched the shield, twisting the blade—
it was a chance. With jaws locked, Durand hauled on his
shield and tripped Cerlac in a fairground wrestler's throw that
sent the man sprawling even as the Col Stags split—the shield
useless.

Cerlac hit the ground.

Durand blinked at the wreckage in his fist, knowing he
could block nothing now. His shoulders smoldered like hot
lead. But Cerlac was down—helpless for a moment. They
were gasping in the stands. Women's voices. Doom turned on
this heartbeat: One of them must die.

But Durand closed his eyes. A man cannot choose the time
of his ending, only the manner of it. He let the ruined shield
fall from his arm and Cerlac get to his feet.

Tense and still, Durand raised the broken lance in salute.
Cerlac was looking at him. What they began, they must finish.
Cerlac nodded and raised his sword.

The ending began with Cerlac. He reeled forward, casting
his blade into a looping sledgehammer's swing. Durand beat
the blade aside with his bit of lance, warding his face with his
free hand.

Cerlac swung again, forcing Durand to weave and stumble.
There was no time to counter. He could scarcely breathe. With
every step, the swinging weight of his hauberk pitched and
carried him.

Finally, Cerlac aimed another sledgehammer swing for Durand's head. Durand could only bull himself inside, trapping
Cerlac's blade high. The other man skipped back. Durand
lurched clear and hurled a scything blow at his opponent's
shins.

With what fire remained in his blood, Durand barged close
yet again. Lights burst in his eyes. He could hear Cerlac's

breath rasping against the face of his helm. Durand crashed the broken end of his lance against the painted diamonds there and held on, hammering again and again, almost losing his grip in desperation.

They staggered apart. Durand had nothing left. Cerlac was clawing at his helm. Round pennies of flaked paint glinted where Durand's blows had fallen. For a moment, Durand thought something had happened. Some blow had got through. Then the man caught himself, flinging the helmet aside.

In the final assault, Durand caught blows on his forearm, his shoulder. Staggering, Durand covered his face. Something raked down his head. His ear. There was blood.

And there was a moment. Durand's eyes focused. Cerlac's bare face was a mask of blood. He held his sword high, the blade flashing its image in Durand's eyes. Then he brought it hurtling down.

Durand remembered leaping inside the arc, trying to bring his lance up.

There was a scream.

MEN PULLED. DURAND heard a high whistle ringing in the air over the field. There was iron and earth on his tongue. A blade of dry grass had found its way into his mouth. There were voices.

Suddenly, a horizon of trees was rolling like a dropped platter around him—sky the cool pewter of encroaching evening. Hands pressed at him. Shouts. Suddenly, against his will, his stomach was turning itself out. The horizon ducked and spun—its trees like black teeth.

Then he was above everyone, hanging between two men's shoulders. He clawed at the roughness of the iron mail under his fingers. Something swung from the wetness on his cheek and jaw.

He looked up and saw the face of a woman. Then the woman's eyes, clear and full of pain. They trembled, pale amethyst. He wanted to touch the down at her hairline where the cool air played. She reached up, and her pale hands wrapped something round his neck. His bearers bent. Durand's feet slid. They were kneeling. His gaze passed her chest, the jeweled strand of her girdle, and the silk of her tiny slippers.

Her breath was in his nostrils, and he felt a pressure of lips on his forehead.

WHEN NEXT HE woke, he was lolling in a bath.

Scented oil burned from the many necks of the brass lamps suspended about the chamber. Rose petals drifted on the water, spinning under the pressure of his breath, rocked by the beating of his heart. Durand stared. Somehow, the heat and buoyancy conspired to render him insensible of his limbs. He seemed to exist only in two aching points: a jagged knot in his skull, and a much duller throb in the arch of his breastbone.

He stared across the sea of petals to a tapestry across the room. In the weave was a girl in a white chemise. She cradled a rabbit in a bed of hay. It was not just hay, though. Each stalk ended in a drooping head of barley. The rabbit seemed to look up from the world of knots and stitches, favoring him with a knowing stare.

STILL STRUGGLING TO pull his thoughts together, he soon found himself in a white hall within the castle of Bower Mead. Score upon score of mailed knights stood along great feasting tables. Silver lamps of sweet oil filled the air with scented vapors.

Standing, he rocked on his feet, facing the shimmering ranks of warriors. He was at the high table. A few of the leading knights stood with him. They were all rich men. The others were the ladies of the Bower. A few smiled his way. He could think of no response.

Everyone seemed to be waiting for something. Down the table, the Lady of the Bower raised her hands above the room. Her voice chimed in the air.

"Most gracious Mother of All, Empress of Heaven, we humbly offer our thanks. We pray on this night that You may hold us in Your heart wherever we may travel in all the lands under the Moons. We remember Your sacrifice, and we thank You for the gift of life which You have given and will give. Now as then; now as always."

The men stood silent.

"Maiden of Spring. Once born, never dying. Most Holy Sister. Maid of spring and harvest, we offer our thanks on this the night of Your cry in the darkness. We who bear and are born, honor Your taking up of the burden of Creation. In Your memory we undertake to do likewise."

The men intoned: *So be it*.

After the rumble of voices ebbed away—when the room stood again in silence—Durand saw the Lady nod once. A knight of every conroi made his way to the space below the high table. Each one bowed in his turn and offered his thanks for the hospitality of the Lady and the thanks of his company for the lives and good fortune of his men. When this ritual had been completed, men entered the room from every side. They were the pale knights from the castle walls. Scores of them. Durand had never seen living men so pale. Each one carried a steaming tureen of pottage.

With a great moan of wooden benches, the guests took their seats. Gray hands set bowls before each man. Durand flinched as a long-fingered and bloodless hand slid a bowl under his chin. Then the gray knights retired to the walls.

Along the high table, the Lady and her handmaidens drank, though no one at the tables below moved. Durand could not imagine eating.

Durand left bread and pottage alone. Goose, duck, veal, chicken, and pork followed, baked in pies or minced in herbs and milk. Durand's head ached. There was a hammering ache in his ribs. Dish after dish passed him by, his tongue a bloated thing in his throat.

Durand stared into the rippling silver of the goblet set before him. Finally, he reached out, taking the cup in his hand, raising spiced wine to his lips.

A hand caught his wrist.

The lean face of Moryn of Mornaway was looking back at him. The man would not let go. *"Do not drink."*

"Host of Heaven," said Durand. Looking out, he now saw that on all the long tables in the hall, not one platter of the hundreds carried from the kitchens had been touched. Gingerly, he set his goblet down.

Quite suddenly, the Lady of the Bower spoke: "Our feast is at an end. As is this longest of vigils for our warriors. Know, all of you, that on this night, the world is under the eye of its Mother. No creature under this moon may do another harm. A lamb could lie in a leopard's fangs. A hare in the jaws of a wolf. You need post no sentries, and keep no watches. All the lands of the world may sleep at ease on this night. Go now in peace."

The men rumbled thanks to the Queen of Heaven, and each conroi presented itself to the Lady of the Bower in turn, offering praise and thanks before departing. Lamoric bowed low, red helm in place. Moryn stood, straight-backed, and bowed. Cassonel—hale now, though with a limp—bowed as well. When they had finished, Durand stood and climbed down from the dais, feeling like a ghost.

"Durand?" It was Heremund. "Here. I've got him."

Berchard shouldered his way against the current of departing guests. "Here. He held out the hilt of a sword to Durand. "After the fight, those peasants just turned and melted off, silent as deer. This bit of steel was left lying there. Coen figured you might need it again if you came around."

Heremund clapped Durand gently on the shoulder.

Berchard shook his head. "If you'd been a step further back—half a step!—that man would have split your head like a cabbage. It was mostly the hilt he hit you with. I'll admit: I had my good eye shut when that blade started down."

Durand touched his forehead.

"I've never seen a sleeping man stab anyone," Berchard continued. "It's easier the other way round. Ouen was saying that lance caught right there."

The man reached out, pressing two fingers against Durand's breastbone. A bruise, a broken rib, throbbed under the man's stabbing fingers.

Then his expression faltered, and he withdrew his hand.

"Durand?" said Heremund.

Berchard nodded, suddenly more serious. "A good knock on the head. Strange things. You lose a few moments. Never remember exactly. A moment before, and then the floor."

The skald had taken hold of his sleeve.

"Let's get him out of this place," Heremund said.

Durand's chest ached. The pressure of something hard lingered in the arch of his ribs.

They walked through the gloomy castle courtyard and into the chill air beyond the gates.

"You've won, Durand," Berchard said. "No one could fault you."

"Sir Berchard," Heremund said, "I'm sure he'll be fine when his head clears. I'll make certain that he's all right."

Berchard nodded, ready to leave them. "Things like these, they happen at tourneys, Durand. Your friend knew it."

With that, the man departed for the tents.

Durand felt the skald's eyes on him. "Tell me," Durand said.

"You won, Durand."

He probed at shadow-clotted memory, dreading what he might find. "I won."

"What do you remember?"

"I remember a blow. The blade coming down." It winked in his mind's eye. He could see nothing after that.

"Aye. That one shut your eyes. But you got that lancehead up between you, jutting like a stake. The lunge. Cerlac drove himself onto the point. I'm surprised the broken end didn't go right through you."

"Hells," said Durand.

Heremund nodded, continuing quietly. "The pair of you just stood there a heartbeat. Then the blade slid."

Durand shook his head. Under his fingers, he could feel the angular bruise over his breastbone—the phantom of that lance balancing its weight against his ribs. It throbbed like a second heart.

"He died before last twilight," answered the skald.

"Host of Heaven," Durand murmured.

"Are you all right?"

Raising his hand, Durand answered, "I must think." And he left Heremund, setting off down the track the maidens had taken toward the fields. It had all been so strange. Lamoric's men might have ridden straight to Moryn's little tournament if Hesperand had not pulled them in. Lamoric's father might have waited to hold Alwen's funeral. Gravenholm's heir might not have stumbled home from the sea. He thought of his long vigil in the keep at Ferangore. There were many things that need not have happened.

He had never meant to fight. He should have been passing

lances and running broken equipment to Guthred. Now, he had met a man and killed him all in the space of one long day.

The churned earth of the lists stretched before him, and he stepped into the rectangle of matted grass where the stands had been. Now, the battlefield might as easily have been turned by plowmen as by armored knights.

Alone, he sank to one knee a few steps from the ruined acre. He was as tired as he had ever been. The ribs ached. And he had fetched up right near where Cerlac must have gone down. He thought of his father's savage warnings: A knight-errant was a man in danger of losing his soul.

He blinked hard and breathed. Berchard was right; he had done nothing wrong. Every man knew that when he stepped into the lists, death was waiting.

Against the trees, he caught sight of an angular shape: the well's windlass. A shock of cold water was what he needed. He staggered off toward the well. The air prickled with ghosts, but soon he had his hands on the well's cool stones. There was no bucket, only the rope running down. He looked over the rim and found the moon hanging below the earth, shining in deep water. His own reflection was like a black keyhole.

He turned the windlass, sending shivers over the image— swinging the whole sloshing moon to his hands. Icy blackness crashed over his eyes and down his chest.

"You are called Durand?" a voice said.

This was not a place to be surprised. Streaming, Durand lowered the bucket.

A dozen paces across the green stood the Stream Maid, her skin pale in the moonlight. She seemed small, her face white under a green veil. A breeze tugged at the cloak around her shoulders. He could not look away.

"I . . . I ought to have foreseen." She looked down, and Durand felt as though a light had been tipped away from his eyes. "I am afraid I did not anticipate—"

Abruptly, Durand realized: this was not his Stream Maid.

"I'm so sorry," she said. The Lady of the Bower.

Durand could not look away. He could not answer. His stare. The stiff mask of his face. Could she see condemnation there? These things registered on his mind, dropping into the balance one by one.

"No," he said.

"I saw something in you," she murmured. "I did not think it was this. I didn't mean . . ."

She was beautiful and very sad. He raised his hand. Her cheek cool as snow against his palm, though his fingers found heat where they slipped into her hair. She seemed very young and very delicate. He could feel the calluses of his fingers catch.

She stepped closer, seeking comfort. Her eyes looked straight up into his. "Durand?" She set her hands on his shoulders, and they kissed, sinking down together by the broken ground.

He could feel the stubble of his chin rasp at her throat. Her hands darted over him as soft as pigeons' wings. He couldn't breathe fast enough. He could feel the ghosts of charging knights even as her gasps swirled in his nostrils, in his mouth. It was like the black water of the well once again, pouring over him. The ghosts of horses pounded the earth on every side. He couldn't see. He couldn't think. He could not be close enough.

By feel, he caught at her skirts, pulling them up, baring her white legs without ever lifting his mouth. Her hands were at his waist, pulling at his surcoat and tunic. He felt her cold fingers fumbling against his stomach, at the cord of his breeches. He wanted more of her. On his knees, he slipped his hands under her chemise, sliding them up her sides. In a moment, she was naked against the ground. He kissed her. He nuzzled her chest. She strained her neck to kiss him. He balanced himself over her and brought his weight down. Her heels touched his calves. Her thighs brushed his sides.

When he finally rolled off, exhausted, into the clammy grip of the grass, she moved with him, caught in his arms. He stared over her shoulder into the sky. Her fingers played in his black curls.

But, gradually, the motion of her fingers slowed and stopped. "*Oh.*" Her voice was a warmth at his neck. He felt her stiffen suddenly, like an animal.

"Queen of Heaven, only now does it return," she said. She sat up. Her face was half-lost in shadows.

"Return?"

"All these years. So many men, just for this moment. I see them now. I see them all."

"I don't—"

"They fought here." She turned at the waist, unconsciously covering her chest with her arms. "My husband. Poor Saewin. Echoes. I think it was something I wanted. I might have stopped it. But now it goes on. I am an echo come to life."

She seemed to see Durand once more.

"You are not very like Saewin. Not really. There was cruelty in him. And Cerlac! The poor boy. He was so little like Eorcan. He did not deserve—"

She caught Durand's twitch. He thought of Cerlac, and of prophecies under the blackthorn.

"Every year it comes again, just like the first." Where there had been moonlight, now there were ashes.

"All this time." She looked out over the battleground. "It wasn't for sere fields and rotten flowers that our Spring Maid grieved, Durand. There were two men, and they were the best of friends.

"And as night closed round Creation, they met on the dying field: Bruna and Ilsander. She had teased them too far. Their war bands brawled for them from dawn to dusk among the gray stalks. And, as the Eye of Heaven sank in blood, Bruna slew his friend."

Bruna of the Broad Shoulders.

He heard the rotten gurgle deep in his memory: the voices of the blackthorn men, the adder girl. Bruna and Ilsander. The fingers of the blackthorn men had felt the blood of Bruna under Durand's own skin. They had named one of their own number Ilsander. This was what Heremund had spoken of.

"That was the cry they speak of when they tell the Maid's tale." She was huddled over him now.

"Who are you?" he asked, unable to think of an answer that he might endure.

"My duke was another Ilsander," she said. "I was so young. If I had told Saewin it was hopeless, they could have ridden off without a quarrel. Now, what has become of us? Poor Eorcan. I have damned us all with smiles."

She gazed at him, and he could see that just sitting close, he cut her raw. His every twitch of guilt and discomfort was broken glass. He could not believe that this child was the woman who had torn a land from Creation.

She reached out to touch the bruise on his chest.

"But I am not the one who suffers," she whispered. "The debt is mine, but I live on. I see now that I have lingered long in this otherworld place. There have been many Eorcans. Many Saewins. And there will come another and another until the end of days."

Durand opened his mouth. "It isn't right. We must fight." He would be more than some echo of the First Dawning. "One sin shouldn't echo forever. There must be some way to break this chain."

Her eyelids fluttered.

"I cannot think. My shame has bloodied your hands, but— but Durand, you live for me to grant you a boon." Durand tried to protest. "I am not powerless, even when the dreams descend upon me. Only Lost."

She found the green veil she had worn when first she arrived.

"Take this token, Durand. Take it with you from Hesperand. You have taken a life for me. In return, I shall grant you the life you wish. I will come for it when you call."

She pressed the wisp into his fist. Her eyes dimmed, becoming vague, as though her one act of defiance was all the curse would allow her. "The dream descends." Like a child, she curled against the torn green.

Durand blinked. "You cannot stay here," he said, thinking of the cold.

She shivered. "But I shall," she said.

"I will not leave you," he said.

"But you shall," she said.

He would do one thing. Putting conversation aside, Durand gathered the woman from the grass and crossed the broad green to the walls of the castle. Pale knights filed down to meet him, and the air smelled of beeswax. Scores gathered round him, candle-pale and awful in their breathless silence. Without surprise, Durand understood that the strange knights were dead men. He saw empty wounds. They took the Lady from his arms as gently as priests, and he knew she would be safe.

And as he turned, his eyes fell on one pale knight. Ashen

though he was, in the gray curves of his face, Durand saw the image of Cerlac.

The lead-dark gleam of his eyes was in Durand's mind until he returned to the camp and sleep claimed him; the Green Lady's token was in his fist.

🔯 16. Terns above the Glass

He awoke the next morning in his low tent, a light in his face.

It was not yet dawn.

Durand twisted among his blankets, groping for a blade. Then he saw Coensar's face and a lantern.

"First Twilight," the captain said. "I've waited long enough for life to hand me what I want. Now, I will act. Get up and pack your gear. I am not a young man any longer."

"I cannot go without—"

"Quick and quiet!"

Durand crawled out. Vaguely he saw that one of Guthred's boys was already tearing the tent off his back.

As he blinked into the predawn glow, he wondered where he was. Impossibilities crowded round. A thousand tons of dressed limestone had been snatched away like a page from a book. There was no castle, but there were leaves. Where the shining castle had stood, hulked a mountain of jumbled stones choked with black leaves.

Durand rolled, thick bushes catching at his tunic. He fetched up against a tree trunk. The knights' encampment was alone now, their tents stretched and tangled over a nest of bracken. Wild forest overhung the dripping place on every side.

Coensar, already moving off, said, "It was this way last time."

They were moving. Durand fell in step with the others as, dazed and silent, every man in the conroi stumbled off through the bracken and back into the gray-columned track. He could feel the castle ruin looming like some ogre in the dark. He thought of the woman inside. Though he knew this was Hesperand, he had not understood what that might mean.

Now, the woman he had touched—the woman whose wild-flower scent still lingered on his hands—was less than dust. He thought of the pale knights and the feast of the long tables. It was all gone.

All but the veil that tangled his fingers.

Soon, the River Glass churned in the mist. Lamoric's men stood as a band of shadows at the high arching bridge, now mossy green and bone gray. Though it seemed an age must have passed since they last stood by the span, every man of Lamoric's conroi had survived. Badan the toothless wolf was riding now. Berchard scratched himself even as he stared into the trees. Stepping onto the planks of the bridge, Durand looked into the swift water only to see fish waving like dark banners in the current behind each pier. They fought the cold flow that threatened to carry them off to the foggy Winter Sea.

Coensar stalked past Durand on the bridge and rounded on the men.

"We are safe enough," he began. "It may be Hesperand, but this is just as it happened seven winters past."

"Aye, well it's bloody strange," said Berchard.

Coensar nodded. "It is. But we're not likely to change it, so we might as well come to the business at hand." The captain cocked his head. "I've pulled you all from your blankets on a night you'd rather sleep than do most things. Yes?"

There was an equivocal grumble from among the men. Waking early was the least of their concerns. The river pounded under his feet. Droplets glistened in beards and cloaks.

"And I'd better have a bloody good reason for it, yes? Well, that you may judge for yourselves. I want old Cassonel," said Coensar. "All of you know that." Men nodded. "Well, I don't mean to wait another day, if I can help it." He drew Keening, the ancient blade sobbing once in the fog. "Cassonel barred a doorway. I will keep a bridge from him."

The conroi was still. To Durand, it seemed that this kind of thing belonged to the other world: the world of fey castles and green ladies that had left them in the night for this ordinary world of damp bracken and sore bones. Men would speak of this at noble hearths in all the Atthias. Coensar would block the bridge and fight above the Glass.

"We will hold Cassonel at the bridge," said Coensar. His eyes flashed like lanterns. He leaned forward. "We will hold Cassonel at this bridge, and we will do his old ballad one better!"

Big Ouen nodded to Berchard, and, even as their fierce grins spread through the conroi, Heremund spoke.

"*Oh Gods.*" He stood almost at Durand's elbow, and was looking out through a cage of his fingers.

"What?" the captain demanded.

Heremund said nothing. Coensar stepped down from the bridge, Keening still in his fist.

"What is the matter?"

The skald stepped from the others, his dark eyes moving. He clawed the cap from his head.

"Sir Coensar, I take no joy in saying it, but I think the Glass is bridged in two places."

"There's only *one* road," pressed the captain.

"I came round on the forest side. Not the main track, but some of them others might know. I came by a bridge at a town. They were calling it Sengreen. It can't be far."

Coensar looked into the mist, staring up the river. "A man is a fool to fight his doom."

Lamoric reached out. "It is a bad end to a good idea."

"The storm was fierce out here," Heremund offered. "Perhaps it has fallen."

"*This* bridge has not fallen," replied Coensar.

The stiffened lines of the captain's face threw Durand back to his own stupid heroism in the mêlée, and the lance that put Cassonel out of the captain's reach.

"Is it stone?" Durand breathed.

Heremund turned. "No. The bridge I crossed was wood. Rude, but solid."

"Durand, what's in your mind?" said Coensar.

Durand took a breath. "We'll take it down, Sir Coensar. Give me a couple of men, and we'll take axes to the thing."

Now Ouen spoke: "Never been a woodsman, have you? It's a cursed long job to hack out enough timber to bring down a bridge."

"There will be a way."

The captain snapped one flat hand between them, and Ouen's answer died on his lips.

"You will have your chance," Coensar said. "Durand, have your skald friend get you to the bridge, and bring it down." Excitement bared his teeth, and he pointed to Ouen. "And take our woodsman. Put that cursed thing in the river, or we're done for back here."

Durand would pay his debts. "We'll bring it down." Or it would prove to be impossible. Nodding to Coensar, he knotted the green veil in his belt.

"We are going to look like fools," Ouen said over the sound of the river. His hair was the greasy dun color of old rope. Each of them was peering up into the mist, hoping the forest was empty. Ouen swayed as his horse struggled on the narrow track. "They'll laugh at Coen, come up the river, and it'll be the three of us, chipping away at a forty-foot span with hatchets. They'll be lucky if they don't burst something."

Fog billowed. Ouen's grumbling wasn't enough to keep Durand's mind from storms and fallen castle and lost villages. They were still in Hesperand, and the Glass boiled down below the forest floor.

The trail clung to the high bank where the torn carpet of turf and roots threatened to slump into the gorge. Heremund led, followed by Ouen, with Durand bringing up the rear. Durand's latest carthorse nickered.

"If we can just weaken it enough to make it impassable . . ." Durand said, forcing his thoughts back to the job at hand.

"Aye. Baron Cassonel and his men come riding up, and there you'll be," Ouen said, "up to your neck in the river, whittling at the piers. Have you got a good sharp knife?"

"What else can we do?" Durand snapped.

"You're young yet. Someday you'll learn that most times there are no good choices. Says in the *Book of Moons*. You must take what's handed you with as good a grace as you can manage."

"*Gentlemen,*" interrupted Heremund, "the trail cuts down toward the river here."

"After you," said Ouen. They followed the track down

where the fog hung thick and the river rumbled. Ouen made a playful bow, though Durand saw a trace of his own unease in the big man's face.

Their horses slipped and stuttered down the muddy bank into the gorge, wallowing into a great stream of chill air that slithered down the river's course.

"Host of Heaven," said Ouen.

Ahead, something slapped the water. The sound leapt through the dripping ravine.

Heremund stopped, and then they could only hear the Glass.

Durand swallowed, and Heremund had just begun to turn—something cheerful forming on lips—when another wet slap sounded. And another. Each smack loud and unnerving in the mist, but Ouen had not drawn his sword, and Durand didn't want to be the first. He did, however, finger the handle of the hatchet. The thing would work as well on men as bridges.

Heremund nudged his horse into a cautious walk. Ouen glanced back, his face incredulous. The sound wasn't particularly threatening, but neither did it respond to any obvious explanation.

They approached a section of stream where the water turned around the shoulder of a hill. Beyond it, something twinkled for an instant in the mist. With the next slap, droplets glittered above the rise. Heremund hesitated, just perceptibly, then urged his horse around the corner.

"*Gods,*" he whispered, for the moment alone.

"What do you see?" asked Durand. Heremund was frozen there. Ouen hopped down from his mount, his big sword flickering from its scabbard. Then he, too, stopped as he turned the corner.

"What is it?" Durand pressed.

When he got no answer—no reaction of any kind from either of the men—he too dropped into the trail and approached the big earth prow. And saw it.

A heap of rags perched on a molarlike stone that erupted from the green gums of the bank. After a moment, the heap twitched into motion, and naked arms slapped a stained tunic across the stone. Durand made out the curve of a round face. It was a washerwoman. Or a girl. Under the glow of the smothered Heavens, he could make out a cheek like a blob of raw dough. She squatted amid a ring of soiled clothes. Her knees were against her chest under a simple green shift. He could not see her feet. The blue-gray tunic in her hands was stained with something dark. Cloudy tendrils streamed past in the water along the bank.

Abruptly, her squat face turned, and Durand was caught by black glistening eyes set in bruised circles. She had no more expression than a millpond trout.

Suddenly, Durand's sword seemed ridiculous. The mooncalf girl seemed about to run. He set the blade on the grass and turned empty palms to her. But she started up, round-shouldered and dwarfish. Her first, half-intentional start seemed about to tumble her into the water. "No!" Durand said. He heard Heremund gulp something, but was between the woman and the water—his impulse was to save her.

She shuffled backward. He was very close. Her forehead shone like a hard dome of wax above the doughy shapelessness of her cheeks. But all he could see were her eyes. They were darker than any he had ever seen. It was as though each pupil had dilated to swallow the whole bulging orb. The darkness seemed to stain the whites in viscid rings of brown—inhuman. Her slack lips parted to reveal a pike's white needle teeth.

"Durand!" Heremund hissed.

"Back," the girl-creature croaked.

"What?"

"Ba-a-ck."

"Durand, you must not bar her way!" Heremund whispered.

"Please." The creature wrung the blue-gray tunic between her hands. "Kings. Kings I see. I will tell everything. Ask what you will. I will tell all. Only let me back. Let me back."

"Everything?"

"Durand, no!" Heremund's fingers caught Durand's arm and pulled him hard, nearly throwing him into the water. The instant Durand was no longer between the washerwoman and the water, she snatched up the clothes around her boulder and leapt into the stony shallows at the bank. Somehow, she did not touch bottom, but tumbled in as if the edge film were a thousand fathoms deep.

"What in the name of every Power?" Durand whispered.

Heremund made the fist and splayed fingers sign of the Eye. "A Washerwoman."

"What?"

"A Washerwoman. We've been lucky." He eyed the high banks of the gorge.

"King of far Heaven! What are you talking about?"

"It is one of the Banished. Or they are."

"Why would something break its way into Creation just to wash its clothes?"

"Not its clothes. Look to your feet."

He stood on the woman's pale rock. The light was stronger now. Everything was red. He could see the marks of his soles smeared in fresh blood. The boulder was spattered. Its iron stink was up his nose.

"She washes the rags of those soon to die. Some say she's grieving, or playing at it."

Durand glanced around the group, searching for the blue-gray of the creature's tunic but found none.

"She might have told you." Heremund shook his head, still rattled. "She might have told you a lot more as well."

"What do you mean?"

"They say she knows whose clothes she's washing and how death will come. And they say she can tell you the day she'll beat the blood from your torn surcoat." He shook his head. "Who could live and know such things?"

Ouen stared out over the water, his sword of war in his hands. "Host of Heaven."

"Durand, they say to learn your doom, you need only bar her way to water."

Ouen was moving. "If we are to try this mad plan of the boy's, then we must get to the bridge. No matter what I say, we'll have to try. I, for one, am not wearing the tunic she was beating, and we'd look bloody stupid riding back without having clapped eyes on the bridge at all."

"Aye right," Heremund said. "If you get back in your saddle, I'll see if I can't get us to the bridge."

AROUND THE BEND, all three men stared up at a bridge as high and strong as a king's barn. "It's huge," Durand said.

Five fathoms over the water, the flat bed was buttressed with massive posts and trusses. Durand took a look at the kindling-splitter hatchets they had to work with.

"You know," said Ouen, "we could chop the *stone* bridge down and leave this one stand."

"I should have kept my mouth shut," Heremund muttered.

Ouen looked to Durand. "Your skald friend makes a good point."

Durand clambered up the bank. There must be something: a weak point. But the beams were thick as a warship's keel, and ten centuries of hooves and iron-shod cart wheels had pounded the deck solid.

Ouen strode out onto the bridge, pacing. Durand could not hear his grumbles, but crouched with the useless hatchet dangling from his hand. Coensar was done for.

Crouched as he was, he pawed hair from his eyes and caught a whiff of something sharp as his hand passed close: pitch where he had touched the braces. And suddenly he realized— they'd soaked the bridge with the stuff to keep it from rotting.

"No wonder . . ."

Ouen was pacing. "No wonder what?"

Durand didn't answer, but looked up craftily. "There's an easy way to get rid of a wooden bridge . . ."

"After the storm? The trails were full of mud. The trees are dripping. We'd be faster chopping."

Heremund climbed out of his saddle, and walked to the bridge beams, bending close, then scratching with a thumbnail.

"They've slathered the oak with pitch."

Ouen blinked at Heremund and Durand, and then the big gold smile dawned. "Coensar might have his chance after all!"

Heremund grimaced. "I guess they can build another when we're gone. They've got forever."

Durand turned to Heremund. "Try and get a spark. We'll get tinder."

Durand and Ouen split up, raking the trees along the bank for dry wood. Durand crouched—knees in the needles— under a big spruce, ripping rough handfuls of brittle, resinous branches from under the spreading boughs. The spruce twigs would burn, even if everything else in Hesperand was dripping. He carried the prickly mass back to the bridge.

Coensar would have his chance.

Heremund was crouched at the bridge, blowing at a bit of fluff in his hands. There was already smoke. "You'd best hurry."

"We'll set the kindling in place on Bower Mead's side of the Glass. We'll get the horses over the bridge, then we'll fire the tinder and bid the bridge farewell."

Durand shoved the dry branches under the bed of the bridge, and left Heremund to work out the details. Back and forth he went. He could hear Ouen working with his hatchet, gathering larger branches, but he kept at the spruce trees, wagering that the brief hot fire would be enough to get the old pitch to burn.

Soon they had packed the gap between the bed and bank with loose branches. Needle rays picked their way between the branches as the Eye of Heaven burnt away the veils of pink cloud that swathed the horizon. Ouen and Durand led the horses across the high span while Heremund labored under the bridge.

"I hope Cassonel and his boys're not riding too hard," Ouen said. "I'd hate to meet a squad of knights right now."

"They don't know there's any reason to hurry."

They tied the horses securely within the woods on the opposite bank. Though they would ride the animals back to Coensar the moment the bridge caught fire, if the horses weren't tied, the blaze would surely spook them before anyone could mount.

Heremund shouted from beyond the trees. "Whoa! I think that's got it!" Resinous smoke stung Durand's nostrils.

Forgetting Hesperand for a moment and smiling like boys, he and Ouen trotted out to the bridge. Yellow blades of fire stuttered over the edges of the bed.

Then someone was shouting. "Lord of Dooms, what do you think you're doing?" The stranger's face was leathery, and, though he was tall and straight for a plowman, there wasn't much to him. He stood just at the bridgehead, and he looked from the fire to the two strangers as though they were both mad.

"Bastards!" he swore, and, in a wavering instant, his expression changed from anger to fear. He started to run for help. There would be people enough in the village to stop them and douse the fire before it was properly started. Ouen stumbled through the ragged smoke to catch the man.

Durand jumped. The man had hardly made a step, but now he was bracketed between Durand and the fire.

The peasant's eyes snapped over the whole scene. He saw one chance: to dodge past the big lad on the village side of the bridge. He moved.

Durand lunged. His elbow hit the man high. It should have knocked the peasant flat; instead, the man struck the low railing of the bridge.

In an instant, he had cartwheeled over.

"God!" Durand said. His fingers batted an ankle, but he could not catch hold. A great hollow knock shook the bridge from a beam far below. There was a deep, sucking splash. Durand doubled over the rail, looking down. A red smear gleamed on the corner of a beam a fathom below, and the body tumbled bonelessly downstream.

The man's tunic was blue-gray.

Smoke burned Durand's eyes. Someone was pulling his sleeve, but he watched as the blue tunic tumbled and rolled to where the river rounded a bend—under a bank that rose like the prow of an upturned ship.

"Hells, lad," Ouen said. "Come on. Bad luck to stay behind when you're burning bridges."

Durand's finger touched the green veil's knot.

WHEN THEY RETURNED, it had already begun.

Coensar stood alone in the high center of the span, blue and silver against the shining mist. A spectral company had gathered on the Bower Mead side, their way barred. Horses huffed and thrashed their heads. The river spun.

For the moment, Durand and his comrades were trapped down below on the Bower side.

Coensar's voice echoed in the ravine. "No one crosses this bridge unless they come after His Lordship, Baron Cassonel of Damaryn. I've no quarrel with any man here but he, though you must all wait on the courage of Baron Damaryn."

Already, the acid bite of smoke had stained the air. Not a man of all those gathered rode for the upper bridge. Where Durand might have felt pride, now he curled his fists.

The Glass gurgled round the piers of the bridge, nearer to Durand than anyone. He thought of the dead man and wondered if he had already passed or if he had fetched up among the piers of the bridge and waited there even now. He had to force himself to look into the dark curls of the water.

There was no blue shirt.

Heremund and Ouen waited silently in the cool gloom beside him.

Cassonel did not make them wait long. Men moved aside, slipping out of view beyond the bank. Then, Cassonel's sable and silver standard appeared above the mist, a perfect rectangle. The baron had sent a standard bearer.

Coensar waited.

Finally, Cassonel himself rode out. His horse and surcoat were sable, but his limbs were sheathed in mail that might have been woven from the mist itself. Cassonel had taken the time to arm himself.

He stopped a few paces from the bridge, just in sight. "Sir Coensar," he began. "You mean to deny this bridge to me?"

"I wish the chance to return the favor you did me at Tern Gyre some years ago."

Cassonel nodded once: So be it.

Coensar spoke formally. "You, Cassonel, Baron of Damaryn, liegeman of Duke Ludegar of Beoran, will not pass this bridge without first besting me."

Cassonel sat erect. The top of his helm, clutched under his arm, flashed like a silver penny. "Sir Coensar, as you once fought to pass a door, I now fight to cross a bridge. So the rash acts of youth are never forgotten."

The man dropped from his horse in a rattle of armor audible over the Glass's rush. He set his battle helm on his head and raised his black shield, its two white diagonals like crossed swords. As he stepped onto the span, he drew his sword. The blade's weird hissing ring reminded Durand he was looking at the named weapon, Termagant.

Durand saw Coensar's hand dart up to turn his helm a notch, or seat it tighter, then the captain calmly settled into a fighting crouch. The terns and blue sky of his shield bobbed into view.

And for a moment the two swordsmen balanced there.

Water rushed below; horses coughed; Termagant and Keening whispered and moaned to one another; the Eye of Heaven gilded both mist and mail.

Durand could hardly see.

It was the baron who moved first.

Cassonel leapt into a deep lunge. The scuff of his soles on the bridge deck was like a startled gasp. Termagant glanced from the blue shield, and the baron narrowly evaded Coensar's fierce counter. Durand saw enough to guess: an undercut for the baron's shins. For a few heartbeats, the fight was on. Termagant shrieked like a high string. Shields blinded. Blades flashed at faces and shins. Few men could have kept pace.

Then the two combatants stepped apart, circling while the Glass poured into the sudden silence.

Coensar leapt this time, and Keening caught among the painted bars of Cassonel's saltire cross. The two men wrestled, grunting and straining, fighting to bring their blades to bear. For a time, Cassonel fought with Lamoric's men at his back. It didn't matter.

The two reeled apart, their blades tearing shrieks and whistles from the mist. One moment, Coensar was crouched under his shield. The next, Cassonel was staggering.

A rising cut flashed. It caught Cassonel's black helm, and chopped it into the sky.

And a heartbeat later, the tumbling thing struck the Glass only a pace from Durand, its gulping splash throwing water over the three under the bridge, and it sounded for all the world like a bucket down a well.

Overhead, Cassonel was reeling. Durand caught a glimpse of his face suddenly bare and crossed with dark threads of blood. The crowd hissed. Boots thudded on the deck as Coensar's stalking strides kept him a sword's length from his victim. Then the stricken man sank to his knees—twin thumps.

Durand imagined Keening's edge at Cassonel's throat.

"I—I—I yield, Sir Coensar," a ragged voice said. He must have spent a moment catching his breath, fighting for air.

Through the wooden deck, Durand could see a dark blot of shadow. And maybe a hand spread for support.

"My arms, my mount, and my person I surrender to you. Do with me as you will."

The captain might have done anything then. Nothing moved but the river.

There was a swish, then a snap as Keening shot home in its scabbard.

"Get up, Sir Cassonel," Coensar said, stepping back. "I want nothing more from you. It's not for arms or ransom I've fought, and I'll take neither. What I wanted, I have." He offered Cassonel his hand.

The Baron of Damaryn wavered to his feet. Over the bridge rail, the baron's bloody face was grim. "Though you will take nothing from me, there is something you must have."

"You've no need to—"

"Our king has put his crown at hazard."

Coensar narrowed an eye.

"This last loan he's had of the Great Council: shiploads of silver for the fighting in Heith when the Borogyn and his Marchers wouldn't come to heel."

"He has borrowed before," said Coensar.

"But not a penny has ever been returned, and this time the Council has demanded a surety. And he has pledged it all. Ragnal has pledged his crown."

Durand felt a shiver through his marrow, picturing a thing like the crown of Errest the Old pledged against a debt.

"Lord of Dooms," Coensar breathed.

"And there will be no coin."

"When must he repay it?" said the captain, not arguing.

"It does not matter. The marches have spent his silver for him. They say he could not have foreseen how long the fighting lasted."

"What are you telling me?" Coensar said, his tone flat.

"The Great Council will sit. It may be that the barons will be lenient. The king will come to Tern Gyre and meet them. I am not the only rider on the roads this moon."

The baron wavered a fraction then. Durand saw hands rise all round, as though to save the battered lord. But he caught himself and spoke.

"You say you lost that long-ago day at Tern Gyre, and you have lived with that. I won that day at Tern Gyre, but I have lived with what I've won. The Silent King knows all dooms."

The crowd joined Coensar, saying, "All praise to the King of Heaven."

LAMORIC'S MEN RALLIED at the bridgehead, including those who had waited under the bridge the whole while. As the retainers of other lords trooped across the bridge, some few were cheerful enough to jeer or shout congratulations. Everyone took his chance to slap their captain's shoulders. Though Cassonel's ominous tidings had unnerved them all, they had won a real victory.

Without thinking, Durand had stepped off a pace or two. The blue-shirted peasant wouldn't leave him. Lamoric watched as well, forced by the crowd to keep his Red Knight helm in place. The slotted eyes turned.

Guthred planted a hairy paw on Durand's shoulder. "Oh. You're just going to watch here, are you? There's plenty that's got to be packed up proper after our quick retreat this morning. What do you—"

"Guthred," said Lamoric. "Leave it."

The shield-bearer gaped for a moment. All the other serving men were busy, lugging packs and loading horses. But Guthred nodded. "Lordship." And got back to work.

Lamoric rubbed his neck. "That Heremund had a word. About this man on the bridge.

"You have had a bad string of luck, I think. It is a strange time. Unsettled." He paused. "A man cannot always see where a step will lead. Good beginnings have bad ends." He raised a hand. "This crossing of Hesperand—"

There was a shout from the bridge, louder than the normal jeers and congratulations. It seemed that Lord Moryn and his men were crossing. Moryn himself towered from a high saddle.

"Knight in Red," Moryn said, "I expect you in High Ashes."

Men of both camps jostled.

Moryn snarled at his men, "Stop!" And stilled them all. "You have missed nothing, Red Knight. The invitation—and the bargain—stand. I will take great pleasure in meeting you in the land of my ancestors."

"The pleasure will be mine, I think," said Lamoric. One of Moryn's lads gave Agryn a nudge, and the shoving match started with snarls on both sides.

But Coensar was moving. With the glamour of his victory still on him, he leapt between the two lords, setting his hand on Lamoric's chest.

"There's been enough brawling here already. Sir Moryn, His Lordship the Knight in Red bids you farewell on your journey. We will meet you again at High Ashes."

"High Ashes then," said Moryn, nodding a bow to Coensar. "These fools of mine will take their leave." The lean heir to Mornaway twitched his reins.

"And you lot, let him go," said Coensar to his men. "We'll see him again before we like. Get yourselves ready. They were the last to cross, and we're still in Hesperand."

As the other men turned to spur their shield-bearers or find their horses, Coensar caught Durand.

"Hold there, friend. Ouen was bragging about the bridge."

"Hells," muttered Durand.

"I'll make this plain," said Coensar. "Today could've gone bad. Because it didn't, folk'll forget." He narrowed an eye like a chipped bead of steel. "I made a mistake, and, if not for you on that bridge, I'd have suffered for it."

All of this was true.

"You hear me, Durand. I cannot tell you how many tourneys I've fought. I cannot count the times I've felt my teeth crack in my jaw, hoping all the while to have another chance at that man." He jerked a few inches of Keening from its scabbard. "This old sword could have hollowed a mountain by now. Every swing to fight my way back to the day I stepped into the sally port with that man Cassonel twenty years ago." He stopped.

"If Cassonel had left me standing over the Glass while he and the best knights in the land rode round to that upper bridge . . . There aren't years enough left to me; I would not have been a laughing stock for long." This was no light admission. "I am no Lord of Dooms to choose who lives and dies. I can only say that your fellow's life bought mine, and, as I reckon things, the debt's mine. You did what you must for the man who leads you. What else is there?

"So. There's something I must do." The captain stabbed his finger at the muck at his feet. "On your knees."

Durand looked down the few inches into the captain's face. Lamoric, nearby, had tipped his helmet off. There was no time to look.

"Kneel," ordered Coensar.

Mud clutched Durand's knees, water sopping up his leggings. The others—knights and shield-bearers—had set their tasks aside.

"Draw your blade."

Durand drew, and, when Coensar pointed, laid the polished blade across the slime.

"Old Hesperand must be your altar. You understand? It's time for orisons now. Right, then." The man wound up. Chain links smacked Durand's skull like a sack of nails—Coensar's mailed hand.

For a stung moment, Durand wondered if they were taunting him.

"There lad," the captain said.

Men in a ragged circle were smiling down at him—all but a disapproving Guthred.

"That's the last time you take one of those from me or anyone without giving one back. Right?" In one stiff gesture, the captain snatched up Durand's sword, squeezing mud from the blade. He took hold of the scabbard at Durand's waist and stabbed the blade home. "You're knighted."

The captain could not suppress a narrow grin. "Give me your hands."

Durand cocked his head.

"For God's sake, your hands, ox! Don't make me regret this." Coensar turned Durand toward Lord Lamoric.

"Stay on your knees."

Durand was beginning to lose track of where the jokes ended. Another smack and he might take his chances against the man.

But Lamoric smiled and opened his hands. In a rite as old as the Atthias, Coensar set Durand's hands between palms of his master.

"Sir Durand of the Col," Lamoric said, "on your soul, swear that you will be faithful, defending me against all creatures who can live and die, and I will be your lord and provider. By God and His Host of Heaven, swear it."

A real grin was spreading on Lamoric's face. Somewhere a horse spluttered.

"By the Lord of Dooms and his Heavenly Host, I swear it," Durand said.

The captain called to the men, "Have you witnessed?"

They bellowed their assent.

Coensar gave the joined hands one firm shake. "Good!" No sanctuary vigil, no sermon, no gentle dubbing with the sword. Durand remembered how he had begun: the trip home for coin and new linen. Here there was just fog, muck, and a clout on the jaw, but now he was knight and liegeman both.

The captain snapped him around.

"Now. If you're Lamoric's man, you're mine, no matter what you've done." The captain paused.

"And you're owed a share of our takings in this tournament. You'll need a decent horse at least. We've got that Cerlac's gear after yesterday. You'll have that."

With a vague nod, Durand accepted the belongings of the friend he had slain.

WHEN LAMORIC'S MEN turned to join the procession from Bower Mead, the fog closed around them. They could see no trace of the others. Lamoric's train was left alone in an uneasy dream of ancient trees. They saw no sky and heard no sound but the thud of hooves and rattle of tack.

Durand was a knight. But he rode a gray Germander rouncy that had belonged to Cerlac, with the dead man's packs and warhorse in the baggage train. What else should he do? He needed a horse. He needed all these things. But he could nearly hear the Host Below counting every stolen penny's worth.

Fog boiled and clotted.

Up front, Coensar dug his shield from his packs; most of the others needed no order to do likewise.

And the fog swallowed trees and armored men.

"Hells," Berchard said. "We need to catch the others and get free of this place."

Durand could not see the man's face when he spoke.

After what might have been an hour riding through the roiling void, the cart track dwindled away. Wet grass and bracken dragged at Durand's boots. He hoped that Coensar, up front, could see better than he could.

The trail was failing, and, worse, snatches of sound drifted beyond the hiss of grass and thud of hooves, as though something were moving out there.

Finally, the conroi wavered into a misty hollow of knotted grass where the trail gave up entirely.

"Aw, this is no trail," grumbled Berchard. "We're groping up some kind of deer run." And the man was right. Nothing bigger than pigs or deer could have tugged the kind of path they followed. He muttered, "Or rabbits, more like."

The captain stopped; they were lost.

Coensar climbed from his saddle, and the knights slid down to join him in the grass, grown men warily eyeing the forest like children. Durand joined their council only when Guthred and the skald had tramped out as well.

They spoke in hushed voices.

"Ain't going to let up," whined Badan, unable to stop searching the walls of mist. "And we've marched into the bloody heart of this wood."

"It's no good moaning about the weather," said Coensar. "We'll need to keep our wits. Agryn, where do you reckon we are?"

"Difficult," Agryn said. "I cannot say how far we've traveled. My dial is useless while the Eye is hidden."

"All right," said Lamoric. "We're meant to be riding East."

"Aye," said Coensar. The man's eyes glanced over the walls of mist. "East . . ." It was easily said.

"We've all hunted," Lamoric said. "We've all ridden forest tracks."

The men stared back at him.

He found the skald in the circle. "You. Heremund Crookshanks. What is the wise woman's story about moss?"

" Me, a wise woman? Surely no fog's as thick as that." He smiled at his own joke.

"You're a man who's traveled."

Heremund rolled his eyes. "*That* I'll confess." He lifted his hands. "And there are signs in the beasts and trees, though they're fickle things."

Guthred was nodding sternly. "The skald speaks the truth. There are signs. Moss shrinks from Heaven's Eye. Moist from hot. Birds and bees nest where the wind is weakest."

Heremund pitched in. "Pines, they lean *toward* the Eye. Most others, you'll get the best show of leaves to the south, unless you're right on a track."

"Ah," said Agryn, "and we can use the land as well. There's little enough written of the roads and rivers of Hesperand, but we know the Glass meets the Sanderling and Bercelet in Mornaway. Downhill may take us."

Badan grimaced. "Sailors steer by Hesperand hills along the shore of Silvermere, west. How'll we know we ain't riding down the Silvermere side, leagues the wrong way?"

"Then," said Lamoric, "we will have our birds and branches to lead us." He shook his head, half-laughing at it all. "Birds and branches. I suppose, we must take whatever help is offered if we are to reach High Ashes."

Durand and the others shared a smile then, suddenly men again, and ready to brave the elements.

THE WISE DO not sneer at the wilds.

Soon, thickets caught men and horses. The line rode up against tangles so dense they would have needed bulls and armor to pass them. More than once, knotted walls forced Coensar to backtrack and hunt for new ways forward.

Always there was fog.

Soon, from beyond their own thrashing and curses, other sounds reached them: snatches of voices far away. Between jolts and lashing branches, Durand would catch a yelp or ebbing moan that might be a goose or fox.

Berchard lifted his chin, reciting:
"Why does he ride, the Lord of the Lost ones?
Why does he ride, the duke, since his doom?
Who does he hunt, coursing the wild runs?
Why does he hunt, his hounds from the tomb?"

"It is a rhyme the Hellebore children say along the borders of this land," he explained.

"Hells, Berchard," Lamoric replied.

There was no mistaking the moan of hounds, baying somewhere beyond the smothering mist. Durand's fingers strayed to the green token he had knotted in his belt. Perhaps she would come as she had said.

Durand turned for some sign that the others had heard the howling, too, and found that some of the men had pulled swords, though no one spoke a warning.

At the tangled bottom of a shallow defile, they fought their way onward. The pack bayed through the fog, sometimes ahead and sometimes behind. Every man's head swung as the sound shifted, left and right. Durand could feel the brutes darting among the trees on silent feet, still a distance away.

Without orders, every man had urged his horse to greater speed, and, as they rode on, the walls of the defile opened and there was nothing to the world but mist and standing grasses lashing under their hooves. Durand heard other riders in the fog. He thought of the Host of Hesperand, trapped and riding after their liege lord, the cuckold Duke Eorcan. Durand heard hooves pounding the forest floor, and their own line sprawled wide until Durand found himself riding between Coensar and Lamoric, their horses now at a long canter.

Until they struck a sudden wall of vast trunks that loomed before them.

Cerlac's gray slid as the whole line balked. A man went spinning over his horse's neck.

Worse, between them and the trees was a wild-eyed gaggle of strangers. They shivered against the branches. Two bearded men-at-arms strained with battleaxes raised. There were women.

For a moment, both groups faced each other wide-eyed, blades hovering over the field. Then both sides seemed to absorb what stood before them. These were mortal men. Behind each of the bearded axemen was a woman, riding pillion. First of these was Durand's tiny Maid of the Stream.

The other, older woman spoke out. "What do you mean riding out of the fog at us?"

Coensar straightened, taking the lead as Lamoric withdrew, guarding his identity.

"An accident, Ladyship," said the captain. "We meant no harm to you or your people."

Durand couldn't take his eyes from the girl he'd met at Red Winding. They were not safe.

The flustered noblewoman seemed to recognize the captain. "Sir Coensar? I—I am Lady Bertana." She hesitated, eyes darting. "With me are my guards and my lady in waiting—as well as a party of knights and sergeants who've come from the tournament and with us by chance," she amended.

Some of the other men nodded bows. Durand watched the girl, thinking that she'd had a hard time, too. She glanced up at Durand, then looked to the now-hooded Lamoric.

Coensar was nodding slowly. "Once again, I apologize on—."

"—Sir Coensar," said Lady Bertana, "I feel I must confide in you. We have lost the others. There have been hounds and hoofbeats—though I suppose you may have been their authors."

"Ladyship, we've no dogs."

"No." She searched among the horses' ankles. "Perhaps, as the Powers have seen fit to draw us together, we would all be wiser to continue as a group."

Coensar scratched his neck. "Surely, Ladyship, but which way do you travel?"

Before the woman could frame a reply, something whooped deep in the forest, unnerving every breathing thing in the clearing. Her axemen tensed.

"*Out,* Sir Coensar," Bertana whispered. "We are going out. By the quickest route."

"Follow us, then. We will find the Glass."

🪢 17. The Hounds of Hesperand

Durand could not believe he had thought of geese or yapping foxes when he first heard these brute howls.

The party jostled westward through mist and trees while the pack coursed the forest, ranging invisibly like a shuttle on a loom. Durand kept close to his redheaded maid.

The ground fell away before them, but they stumbled on. Horns joined the baying of the dogs, bleating out, and the heavy rhythm of burdened horses boomed through the wood.

Shadows played at the edge of vision. There was no time to stop. Every man among them had drawn his sword by then, knowing in his bones that they were being driven.

Abruptly, the column skidded. Animals reared once more.

A fish-silver form had leapt into the roadway. Durand could see only flashes through the screen of startled horses. Urging Cerlac's gray wide, Durand saw the creature: an enormous hound. Though it did not have the heavy boar-hound shape, it stood taller than a calf. A pike-sleek head swung back and forth on its shoulders. Wrong.

Gray flesh bloomed and faded under Durand's gaze like embers at the bellows, baring the hooks of pale ribs one moment and shimmering coat the next. Gray bowels coiled. Veins pulsed like a multitude of worms.

The beast licked its lips and sprang back into the branches.

"Ride!" hissed Coensar into the silence. *"They're on us!"*

In a heartbeat, the forest hissed with the shredding passage of the entire pack. Uncanny horns bleated and shrieked, and Durand could feel the thunder of the charging host's hooves. Knights and shield-bearers and grooms all tore down the track, clinging low as racers.

Durand strained to keep sight of the flying haunches ahead of him, with the trail pitching and dodging like an animal between trees and leg-breaking hollows. The track forked and forked again. Each switch seemed to bat one rider or other from his saddle. But Durand rode on, resolved to keep near the young woman.

The surging thunder of the riders rolled nearer and nearer though they wove through fog and trees and hounds like will-o'-the-wisps. Someone screamed. Every switch in the track smacked another wedge in the face of their line.

Durand followed one rider. Abruptly, a great hound—with a salmon's leap—snatched the man into a silence as deep as the sea.

Cerlac's gray leapt the fallen mount.

As he rode on, the thunder of the chase seemed to drift off to his right hand, until, in moments, there was nothing but open forest to his left. He felt a thrill in his guts—here was freedom—but he was alone.

There was no sign of the maid, and no sign of the lord he'd sworn to serve. He could not leave them.

Hearing a snarl, Durand clenched his teeth, and spurred *toward* the sound.

He plunged into a river of clear air. Thirty paces away, a horse kicked from the earth, its legs in the air. Two great curls of shimmering greyhound rumbled, circling a bearded axeman. Before Durand could spur his gray, the first hound leapt, striking the axeman high and bearing him down. Blood flew from the lashing muzzle.

The Stream Maid stood behind. The second hound coiled. She threw up her arms.

Durand tore her from her feet—and from the jaws of the startled hound.

Down the clear seam they rode, and then back into the fog before the hounds could untangle themselves. The woman struggled, flung over the saddlebow like some raider's prize, but Durand could still hear the baying of hounds on their heels, and he would not stop.

"My guard!" she cried, but Durand didn't answer. "Let me up!"

They dropped into a roadway that cut like a canal through the forest. They had covered leagues since they first heard the Host, never circling.

Durand had only an instant to wonder which way he should go.

"Queen of Heaven," said the maid.

Ten knights waited in the road ahead, armed with shields and lances. Marsh light slithered over their gear and faces. The horses were hale and silver one moment, then pitted as a carcass in the field. He could see in and through men and horses both.

A tall man in a crown of silver falcons waited at the head of the conroi. There was a fringe of ash gray hair at his jaw, and a blade in his hand. A dark-rimmed hole gaped where his heart should be. He looked nothing like Cerlac.

"What is it? Why have you stopped?" said the maid, twisting to look up at him.

"The Host of Hesperand," said Durand.

Whatever the confused myth behind all this, there was no

doubt that this duke would not let him go on. "Here. Let's get you down."

"Down?"

Durand helped the young woman to the ground. She was warm in his hands where the air was not. He began to climb down himself. Though she was watching the strange riders, she turned when she realized he was dismounting.

"What do you mean to do?"

"Take my seat. I'll fight them."

"But you'll die."

He smiled. To him, she seemed as beautiful as anyone breathing. He was willing to take his chances. She looked up into his face, then her dark eyes widened.

"Oh no," she said, straightening. She took a half step back and shot a look down the roadway toward the blockade. "This is mad. All of it. I'm getting up behind you."

"There's no pillion," Durand said.

"Under the circumstances . . ." she answered. Stealing one stirrup for a moment, she climbed up behind the saddle. Durand found himself smiling still and doing as he was told. In a moment, her arms were tight around his waist. He could feel her chin digging under the blade of his shoulder.

"I saw you in the field at Bower Mead. I saw you at Red Winding. You're not leaving me here to play martyr."

Durand shook his head, still smiling, and unshipped both sword and shield. There were six riders, gray and centuries old, lined up across the road. Each man wore a conical helm and hauberk of gray mail. Long shields painted with curling animals guarded their sides, and every man held a lance in his fist. Cerlac's gray was quick and steady, but Durand wondered if he could make the animal charge such a line. And, if he passed them, he wondered how far they would get, two on one horse. He and the girl.

"Milady," said Durand. "I am Durand. Born at Col of the Blackroots. Will you give me your name?"

"Deorwen!" she said. "Deorwen."

He smiled.

"Ride," she said. "And Heaven have mercy on us both."

The Duke of Hesperand saluted Durand, sword to gray lips. Durand responded in kind, Cerlac's horse dancing awkwardly under its burden. The duke urged his shimmering stallion ahead of his men.

From the vantage of an irrationally good mood, Durand considered the puzzle in front of him with the mad feeling that he could crack it. He did have one advantage over the duke.

Limbering his shoulder, he shocked the jangled gray into motion. The spectral duke spurred his own mount forward.

With Deorwen holding tight and the gray running in a good open gallop beneath him, Durand's grin widened madly. The duke's lance was long; its bright point winked steady as the lodestar. The man would never miss. He wondered how many other men had seen the same blade in these woods.

Flickering horse and rider loomed, but, at the very last, Durand hauled Cerlac's gray for the trees. The duke twisted, his lance striking Durand's shield—not squarely enough to bite. The riders in the track twisted as well, fighting to turn from a standing start.

Durand's one advantage was that he did not give a damn about the old duke.

With a whoop, Durand dropped Cerlac's gray back into the roadbed. Now, with the duke's men tangled behind him and the duke himself charging the wrong way, Durand spurred onward with the fog whirling shut behind them.

As the poor gray galloped on—a hundred paces, two hundred paces—he felt its every stride checked by the awkward weight on its back. It was slowing, and the duke's men must overtake them soon.

They rode until, finally, the gray fell into a walk, then stood still, fighting to breathe in the mist.

Durand got his blade between himself and the roadway, knowing he couldn't see far enough to defend them. It had been a good run. But no swords flickered out of the fog to cut them down. Around him, it seemed the light had changed, and the world was a fraction more dim. The gray breathed between his knees as Durand listened. He could feel Deorwen's cheekbone and forehead against his back.

Water dripped, and they breathed.

"Queen of Heaven," said Deorwen. Her hands unlocked, retreating, for a moment, to linger on his hipbones. "We are alive."

Durand turned to look back at her. She was trying to look away, or so it seemed.

"Here. I'll get you down," he said. Durand put his hands on her waist and set her on the ground. For a moment, as he lifted her above the road, she looked into his eyes, surprised. And somewhere in the process, Durand missed a breath.

"I think we'll have to walk this poor brute awhile," he managed, climbing down.

She faced the road behind them. The tunnel of branches vanished fifty paces into the fog. It was hard not to imagine the duke and his men boiling out of the clouds. But, for as long as they stared, there was no sign. Nevertheless, Durand felt the weight of them poised there, ready to thunder down.

"We had best move on, I think," Deorwen said, finally. "Come on."

"Yes," said Durand, tearing his eyes away from the fog.

Deorwen touched him: his belt. She drew the long dagger from his hip. There was a smile. "The Banished don't like iron," she said.

Both of them glanced back into the mist. There was nothing ahead or behind them.

"Some things must be endured, because we have no choice," said Deorwen.

THEY PUSHED ON into the failing light. If someone had asked Durand where he was going, he would have said, "Away."

After an hour or more of walking, Deorwen spoke out.

"Do you know where this leads?"

He hadn't been thinking at all. "You'll be wanting to get back to her ladyship," he said, realizing. "Bertana. I didn't think. Did she—"

"I don't know what's become of her."

"You're right. We should try to find the others. I should get back to Sir Coensar and—" He nearly said Lamoric's name. "And the Knight in Red. And see you safe with your people." The only thing he could think was they should leave the road and ride north for a time. The bulk of the conroi had been off to his right before he turned back to get Deorwen.

"We could pass right by and never know it." She looked up into the low gray ceiling. "I think we may be losing the light."

There was no sign of Heaven's Eye, but the light did seem to be failing.

"You aren't saying we should make camp?"

"Well, we've found a road."

"Aye," said Durand. They would be mad to leave a good road behind with dark coming on. "Best to make camp now. There will be no moon, I think," he said, and they found a well-drained bit of ground a few paces from the road. Neither one of them had any way to make a fire.

When Durand gave Deorwen his cloak, she gave it back.

The sky was growing dark.

"You won't be much good frozen," she informed him.

"I'll keep warm walking."

She had sat down. There was a good thick carpet of turf, and it would make a better bed than Durand had known in the Painted Hall of Acconel.

"All night?" she asked.

Durand shrugged his cloak up around his ears. "I'll be happier keeping watch. You're the brave one if you can shut your eyes in this place."

"We'll take turns," she murmured, curling on her side.

"You first?" Durand offered.

"I would never have believed that this could happen to me," she said.

Durand laughed.

"When I was girl, I was the kind who wandered then. Gave my minders fits. Once, I lost myself in a wood on my father's land. I remember being very frightened. The wood was a wild place then. All of my nurse's stories, they made it sound as if every inch were thick with Lost knights, Strangers, and Banished spirits set to lure me. A child sees herself in such stories."

She stared off—seeing that other wood, Durand supposed.

"But as a grown woman . . . Those stories. Everyday things weigh them down. It's all the wise women do: whispers of the marriage bed, sour stomachs, and what to wash the babes and bodies in."

She stopped a moment.

"This is different. Like my dreams."

Standing under the trees with the wet straps of a shield in his fingers and a blade in his hand, Durand could only nod.

"That wood was like this," she concluded.

To his eyes, the woman looked like a toy, curled there: the small curve of her mouth, her blotched cheek, her hip.

"The wise women say the Lost work in circles," she said. "We all do. You can feel it here. Round and round, old things they can't set down."

Durand nodded, pulling his damp cloak tight. He had seen as much. They were all dancing in circles in Hesperand. The partners changed, but the steps were the same. He tried to pull together the bits and pieces he had seen. He remembered Heremund's talk of a great sorcery knocking the duchy free of Creation, and it was safe enough to guess that Saewin had killed his master. The Lady had nearly said as much. But what did it all mean?

As he looked at the soot and coal forest, the old spell rose before his mind's eye catching them up like a mill could drag a man in by his sleeves or fingers. As the big spell snapped tight round the dead man, all the oath-bound souls tumbled after their master.

And the whole mess was still here, Eorcan still groping after the author of his destruction, and Saewin still hunting for his Lady. It was mad. He thought back to Heremund's talk of echoes. They had broken a world.

Standing in the dark, he thought of the Bower's Lady, trapped in the midst of it all. His finger touched the green knot at his belt. He thought of Cerlac, now dwelling at the Bower Castle. Cerlac's horse tossed its tail, pale against the darkness.

And here he was with Deorwen—now sound asleep and curled like a pup in the grass. His eyes followed the curve of her hip, and found her lips, dark as her tresses against her pale skin. He wondered about her and tried to imagine what had brought her to this place. Had she been following him since Red Winding? A part of him wanted to believe it. But Lady Bertana's train had blundered into Hesperand on its way west from Red Winding, that was all. The place had drawn a great many in. He wondered where Lady Bertana's holdings actually lay.

He was tired, the air was cold, and the night was as dark as any he had seen, but pacing kept him awake.

———

HE WOKE TO find a hand on his arm, soft and insistent.

"Host of Heaven," said Deorwen. He could feel her breath against his jaw. *"Durand."*

Her face hovered an inch from his and upside down. Her eyes were wide. He had a sense there was something around them in the fog.

Baffled, Durand rolled to see.

"Queen of Heaven," Deorwen breathed, a new horror in her voice.

They were surrounded. In every direction, men were waking. Shabby, disheveled creatures levered themselves from the ground only to tip at once into huddled crouches or pitch onto their hands and knees. Scabbards jutted from hips—most empty. He saw madness. The men were shaking their heads and moving their lips, utterly silent. Mute tongues flickered against yellow teeth.

Though he could not have said why, it was like a graveyard had been tipped out and its denizens left to crawl upon the ground. The madmen stared about themselves in horror. Brown blood stained surcoats. Some of the men pawed disbelievingly at round wounds.

He counted dozens.

"King of Heaven," whispered Durand.

"You didn't wake me." Her face was close to his.

"I—" Durand hesitated. "I couldn't."

"They were just sleeping. All round. Till I woke you. Every eyelid snapped open as yours did." Despair shone from their faces like lamplight. The nearest was only a few feet away. His skin was wax against the blue of a rough surcoat, close enough to smell the old sweat caught in the weave—though there was nothing. Durand could see no way to move without stirring them all.

"The green is thick with them," Deorwen said.

"The green?" He remembered only a forest track.

"There's a whole village."

Like clods in a steaming cauldron, the sheds and hovels of a village rose from the fog at the limits of vision. Durand's graveyard was a village green. Deorwen and he lay in the rugged common ground near the road. Muckheaps, a tithe barn, and something that might have been a rough manor house loomed out there. More importantly, there was a ring of people: peasants by their small stature and hairy cloaks. Hands clutched a fence of woven hurdles, as the villagers squinted and whispered soundlessly to one another.

"The whole village has turned out. If I did not know I was awake—Queen of Heaven!" She pressed his arm.

The blue-coated man had reared to his feet, planting a boot by Durand's fingers, then staggering off through the others. Heads turned, though every face was confused. They were like men squinting at flies. The blue-coated man had his eyes squeezed shut and his fists locked in his hair. A bit of green cloth was knotted round his knuckles. Others followed, pitching onto their feet and stumbling through the crowd.

The faces twisted into silent rings—mute howls that set the peasants beyond the green running. The frenzy was building.

Durand thought of the green veil knotted through his own belt. "This is madness," he rasped. The things blundered near enough that he had to snatch his legs away, but there was no sound. The lips stretched and eyes rolled, but the breath in Durand's mouth was louder than the loudest scream among them. He must get Deorwen free of the place. He had to find the horse.

Deorwen tugged him to his feet.

He spotted Cerlac's animal—two dozen crowded paces off—but, somehow, he would rather touch a drowned corpse than one of these men.

There was motion in the crowd of villagers.

A fierce-looking man stalked up to the hurdle fence. His face was lean and starkly bearded, and he was wrestling himself into the embroidered robe of a priest-arbiter. Beyond them all, the black doors of a squat shrine hung wide.

The priest swung his arms open, and opened his mouth without a sound. He ranted. Spittle flew. A madman touched Durand, shooting a razor-edged tingle up Durand's forearm.

The priest was tugging his sleeves up his own forearms. He held a staff, and there was gold enough stitched through his robes to buy half the village.

Suddenly, he gave his arms a shaking jolt, and Durand's clothing flinched around his limbs.

Every one of the madmen jolted, too, cloaks and surcoats twitching as if in a sudden wind.

"Durand?" said Deorwen, her face ashen.

After another rambling silence, the priest stabbed his staff heavenward, and now Durand felt the push.

He fell. He dropped as though into a well, his ears filling. Everything was wrong. His face and fingers might have been knobs of root in a garden.

But, suddenly, he could hear.

"Saewin, Saewin, Saewin," the madmen's voices sloshed in his ears.

"I'm not Saewin," he gasped.

They echoed: "I am not Saewin! I am not he! A mistake. I'm not Saewin."

And Durand realized: They had been saying it all along. Every twitching mouth among the madmen was repeating the words until every beard was clotted with spittle. They had been with the Green Lady and Eorcan had ridden them down.

And, as he thought his mind would come adrift, he heard the dull thunder of hooves. All this, and now Eorcan was on their heels once more.

The men around him might have been ecstatic monks. "Traitor," they said, and "adulterer" and "oathbreaker." Then, always, "I am not he!"

Deorwen was speaking. He turned to look at her, seeing panic. Her lips were moving, at first with no sound, then her voice came on, all in a rush. His skin was caught in her fists.

"Durand!"

Creation pitched, and Durand reeled from the half-world of the babbling men.

The priest was still speaking, his eyes on the clouds, but now Durand knew that Eorcan was coming. He tried to reach for Deorwen, but found that his hands would hardly answer him. His face felt like so much cold flesh on a butcher's table.

The priest's ranting was some sort of ritual: casting out fiends. Durand's cloak rippled with the man's words. Between the priest and Eorcan they must leave.

"Come on!" Durand managed, fumbling at the woman's hand and hauling her into the crowd. They must get to the horse. Some of the madmen reeled out of their way. Some vanished like brown smoke.

The priest was turning. Up the road, the track crooked into the trees. They would get little warning before the duke was on top of them.

Without time for a saddle, he threw himself onto the horse's bare back and heaved the woman up behind. The priest's eyes glinted, tongue and teeth rattling another frantic abjuration, and Durand could see that his fit was building toward another great climax. God knew what would happen.

With the woman's arms clamped tight, he kicked the gray into a gallop so wild he could scarcely hold on to the terrified animal's back. He could feel the priest's words shaking Creation behind him, each syllable chopping a bite from the world, catching at his soul with frenzied claws.

The jolt, as it hit, was enough to throw his cloak forward into the wind.

They leapt the hurdle fence and swung into the road. The duke's armored squadron rumbled like a storm, their horns yowling out above the drumbeat of hooves. The woman screamed behind him. They hung on, and gained ground. They swerved between roadside banks. While a good rider could do clever tricks bareback, it took everything to stick to that animal as it careered through the fog, wild beyond controlling, and without bit or bridle. Trees swung down like a battalion of giants. They should have died.

After the better part of a league, the horse began to stagger, and, as it fell out of its cantering rhythm, the drumbeat of the duke's horsemen asserted itself on the road behind them. The duke would overtake them—nothing could prevent it—but a man would not face the Bright Gates of Heaven with a lance in his back.

Dropping into the trail, he hauled his sword free and turned to face his onetime comrades. He would die on his feet.

The woman was shouting at him, but somehow he could not make out what she said. She should run. He tried to make that clear. This had nothing to do with her. It was him they were after, not some woman they had never seen, but it was as though a thunderous wind were snatching the words from his lips.

Two hundred paces down the track, the Host of Hesperand rumbled into sight. He knew them all. He could see lances by the score flickering under the canopy of branches, and hard men on big horses with Eorcan of Hesperand and his tall Peregrine Crown at the forefront. His onetime liege lord would not stop for parley. He had betrayed them all and deserved no reprieve. On Eorcan's dark lance, where there might have been a duke's banner, trailed knots of green rag, some clotted black.

Duke Eorcan raised his lance high and swept its green rags down in the ancient command to bring the charge home.

The woman was tugging at his sleeve, and again her wind-snatched voice was in his ears, vague and desperate. She would be killed, but he had no time. If she must stay, she must stand behind him. At most, he would get one swing. At best, he would sell their lives dearly. Eorcan's deadly lance was coming on.

The woman took hold of his arm. There was something strange about her touch, almost as though she were a creature of cold water. What could she have to tell him?

In a glance, he took in leaves tumbling down and a whole track full of leaves behind her: a world of brown leaves. Red. There was something wrong with that.

Before him, green leaves stormed down the track.

The woman was looking desperately into his eyes.

In an instant, lances would pitch him into the air like a sheaf of wheat. She was saying something, her lips moving.

Durand.

He blinked.

"Durand!" she said again, and, this time, he heard.

The scent of autumn filled his head.

The wall of lancers struck then—a crumbling cloud billowing round—as Durand looked into the depths of Deorwen's eyes, and she said once more, "Durand."

Eorcan and his riders were the dust of crumbled leaves and Durand clung to Deorwen, hanging on as the spent force tumbled past them in clouds. He stared down into those dark, dark eyes, now trembling with tears. They had pulled him from that black dream.

For a long time, and with the force of a convulsion, he

kissed her—standing there among the autumn leaves once more, on a straggling trail where autumn Mornaway met Lost Hesperand. The Blood Moon hung pale against a blue Heaven.

The Green Lady's favor had left Hesperand.

18. Mornaway Welcome

Deorwen saw it without turning, just as they finally parted, half-wondering, half-sheepish.

"The bridge!" she said.

Durand wavered as the weight of their strange flight left him. He had been someone else.

"No wonder the forest seemed so familiar," she murmured.

Durand blinked. "I don't understand."

"There," she said and pointed.

Durand turned and saw a glint through the trees: a bit of white masonry half a league across the tawny countryside. It was all so bright. So free.

"It's the Forest Bridge," Deorwen said. One hand rested idly on Durand's hip. "It's right by—"

She hesitated, her face oddly empty. She had turned half away. "It goes nowhere anymore. Parties will ride out through the forest just to see it. High Ashes isn't far, I think."

They must already be on the Duke of Mornaway's land. There was a scent of river mud in the autumn damp. "Is it the Glass?" Durand asked.

"Aye. The Glass. They might have come this way. They'd have to cross at the bridge."

"All right," Durand said, nodding. It was possible. He touched her arm, a reassurance.

With the bright Eye of Heaven steaming the Otherworld damp from their cloaks, they led Cerlac's horse down the track. This was open country. Light blazed upon shocks of yellow grass between the trees. The country fell gently toward the river, and the two wanderers quickly lost sight of the bridge as they left the high ground. Long cords of bracken played snare. They startled a flight of pheasants. A red squirrel, inverted, watched them from the bark of a rowan tree. The earth under their feet was stiff and cool.

Durand turned his mind to the others: those they had left in Hesperand. He had seen a man mauled. He remembered another running full-force into a tree. There had been more. If Lamoric did not find his way from the trees, Durand was lost once more with a hard winter coming. And now he must think about Deorwen as well.

"The bridge is the only crossing for leagues," she said. "And if worse comes to worst, there may be help for us."

They heard the Glass pounding away, hidden down a gorge somewhere beyond tawny banks of fern. The air grew damper, and the white bridge hove into view, matched towers of ivy-wrapped stone guarding either end. It looked more like Hesperand than Hesperand.

"No wonder," Deorwen breathed.

Then Durand heard cursing.

At first, he could see nothing beyond the round towers. With a cautioning hand raised to Deorwen, he trotted up to the nearest of the great stone drums, and stole a look under the gates.

There, in the midst of the span, stood Sirs Ouen, Berchard, and Badan, all fighting with a gray warhorse. The animal, its ears spinning, balanced on planks slapped over a gap in the bridge deck. Heremund the skald perched on a railing, urging them on.

Durand stepped out.

For a moment, no one noticed him, then Heremund happened to glance up. His mouth opened.

"Durand!" he said, after a moment. He seemed more astonished than pleased.

Durand grinned.

All four men looked up, gape-jawed as cattle, then recognition flickered over the whole lot. Everyone dropped what they were doing and tottered over the broken bridge to catch Durand in their arms and pound his back.

"We thought you were dead for sure," said Berchard.

Ouen winked. "When we thought of it at all."

"Off rescuing damsels," Durand said, indicating Deorwen with a sweeping gesture through the bridge gates.

Turning, he saw that Deorwen had hung back from the old gates and only now appeared, a hood pulled up over her head.

"Hells!"

The howl was Badan, left behind. As he shouted, the planks detonated. Everyone turned in time to see Badan, forgotten at the warhorse's bridle, plunge through the deck of the bridge.

"Badan!" shouted Berchard.

Everyone dropped the welcome and slid into place around the hole, sprawling on hands and knees. The big horse hit in an explosion of water that shot spray ten fathoms high and over the bridge on both sides.

"*Badan,*" Berchard gasped. It seemed a ridiculous way to die.

A hand flashed from the hole, catching the one-eyed campaigner by the collar. "I'm right here, you daft, blind, stinking whoreson." The fuming knight climbed Berchard's back hand-over-hand out of the ravine and onto the deck. It took every man to keep Berchard from following the horse.

Badan's face was splotched with rage. "What do you mean leaving me with that harebrained monster? Did you reckon it was just going to stand there while you kissed half-wit here hello?"

Berchard tried to throw an arm around Badan, but Badan shrugged him off. "Next one you can take across yourself. I'm done."

The others stood watching him go, until, finally, Ouen dusted his hands.

"Shouldn't we get the horse?" Durand said.

Big Ouen smiled, quirking an eyebrow. "One of Badan's, and he's been rubbing me raw since daybreak."

With the sudden appearance of these four, Durand had forgotten all the others. He caught the big man's arm. "What of all the rest?"

"All waiting, almost. Coensar. Lamoric. The lads you saw here. Agryn. Some, we saw go down. There are only a few missing, and we've been waiting on them most of the day. You're among the last."

"And Lady Bertana?" Durand glanced back to Deorwen, now a hooded, downcast shape.

"She'll be cursed glad to see your friend there. Been driving us mad with questions. Have we seen her? Are we looking? A maid with red hair? But enough of that." Ouen glanced over Durand to Deorwen.

"Come along," Ouen said, "we're waiting on news from High Ashes. If Moryn's really managed to get the Herald, His Lordship's got a fight on his hands."

DURAND FOLLOWED THE others across the river. Deorwen would not take his arm. Tugging her close for a moment, Durand pressed her: "What is the matter? Have I done something?"

She shook him free.

"Durand."

Under his feet, the old bridge was falling to pieces. Great gaps had opened in the bed, and, even for men to pass, sections had to be bridged with planks.

At midstream, Berchard pointed downriver. Badan's scalp flashed as he herded a flock of grooms along the riverbank, chasing the "harebrained" gray. The Eye of Heaven sparkled from the water.

Deorwen would not even walk with him.

"I was sure," said Heremund. "I felt something. Something in the forest." There was dread in his face. "But here you are, alive." He shook his head.

Durand opened his mouth at this, but could think of no reply.

Meanwhile, Deorwen had slipped behind him with her head ducked low, as if she were ashamed of him or herself or something.

The survivors crowded the far side of the bridge like refugees from a war. Bedraggled people huddled around the last of the supply barrels.

"Nearly all of us have come through. But I felt something out there," Heremund continued, half-whispering. "But there's been nothing to do but wait. Waiting for survivors. Waiting for news."

The skald tried something like a grin. "Lamoric's been pacing himself a ditch up there, thinking maybe that the Herald's moved on. They've sent for word."

They tightroped the last few planks.

Friends and strangers looked up as Durand set foot on the

bank, every eye dull. A man wiped his nose along his sleeve. Half of these men had likely lost someone out there, and Durand wasn't the man they hoped to see.

But the Knight in Red tramped toward him, battle helm in place.

For several heartbeats, he just stood there. Coensar stalked up after him.

"My Lord," said Durand, dropping to his knee.

Lamoric neither moved nor spoke. He might have been a wooden figure. Durand could just hear hard breathing.

Finally, the red helm dipped.

"Durand," Lamoric said.

"I'm glad that—" Durand began.

"Good. Good," said Lamoric. The young lord seemed to glance among the staring faces, then mumbled something that might have been, "Check with Guthred for your things," and left them standing there. He had not seemed angry.

Heremund was rubbing his jaw.

"There's something in the wind, mark me." Again, he put on a smile. "Let's see about getting your things. You had that Cerlac's horse?"

As Heremund spoke, Durand realized that Deorwen had started away, leaving without a word. He darted the few steps to catch her.

"Whatever it is I've done, I'm sorry for it."

She wouldn't stop, and he was left watching her back, the cloak clasped around her shoulders.

Among the survivors, Lady Bertana had spotted her handmaiden. The woman wept.

Distracted Heremund caught Durand's sleeve. "You'd best leave her be, I think." He stopped. "Ah. What's this now?"

A troop of mounted horsemen broke into the clearing: peers and sunburnt huntsmen both. At the head of the company rode a grim-faced captain with shoulders as square as if he had a roof beam under his tunic.

"What is this?" the skald muttered.

Every man in Lamoric's conroi had his eyes on this man, and, for a moment, Durand forgot both Deorwen and the skald.

Without a word, the big stranger hurled himself down from his saddle and stalked up to Lord Moryn.

"My Lord," he said, dropping to one knee.

"On your feet, Sir Waer."

Waer stood, taking in the scratches and green bruises that marked Lord Moryn's face. "You should not have left me back," he concluded grimly.

In the abruptly silent crowd, no one missed a syllable.

"How is the shoulder?" asked Moryn.

"Mended before the Blood Moon rose."

"Good. Good."

Waer looked none too pleased.

"I have brought with me the Knight in Red," Moryn added.

The big man's dark eyes swiveled, unimpressed. Across the camp, Lamoric bowed.

"We got your message, Lordship," Waer reported.

"We fought at Red Winding," said Moryn.

"Aye, Lordship."

"I intend to fight him once more at High Ashes."

Waer nodded. "If the man wants a fight, Lordship, I'm sure we can oblige him."

All the men in Lamoric's retinue were listening now. Ouen licked his lips, for an instant like a lizard. They might still have crossed Hesperand for nothing but the long road home.

"The Herald's come," Waer finished.

While corsair-grins spread through Lamoric's camp, the big man only stuck his foot back in the stirrup iron and swung into his seat.

Heremund was shaking his head.

DURAND SAW NO chance to get Deorwen alone on the ride for High Ashes. The track was narrow and the company large.

He fingered the green veil and waited.

The skald kept up his muttering.

Finally, the company broke from the forest into a great bowl of turned earth and open pasture where the Glass slithered into the evening shadows of a proper valley. Commanding the Glass was High Ashes itself, a fort of wooden palisades cunningly locked in the river's elbow. He remembered Lord Moryn calling this his father's "hunting lodge." Though it was no stone castle, the tower-topped hill and river site made the place a fortress. To pry Duke Severin from the place might require a thousand men.

A thousand men or the arrival of his son.

In a robe of supple wool and sable, the duke tottered from High Ashes, trailing an entourage of wellborn liegemen. A man of seventy winters, the duke was no longer as tall as his son, though he had something of the same stiff posture. But where fierce Moryn was lean and quick as a greyhound, Severin was brittle as a sack of branches.

He smiled.

"My son, I am very happy to see you."

Moryn knelt, setting his clasped hands between his aged father's palms in the ancient gesture of homage. "I am only sorry that I was forced to delay my arrival."

The old man touched his son's shoulder. "Word of your trials has reached me." His smile faltered. "You are the first man of our line to travel Duke Eorcan's lands since they fell."

"But I am here now."

"Yes." Force returned to the frail smile. "Yes, and I am greatly pleased." He trembled as he turned. "Now, you must rise, and tell me of these gentlemen whom you have brought with you. I do not recognize these arms."

He peered toward Lamoric.

"Father," Moryn answered, "these men belong to this knight in red. He has hidden his own face and colors to fight in the tournaments. They call him 'The Knight in Red.' "

"Knight in Red! I am pleased to welcome you to our gathering," said the duke. "It has been our custom to keep this a small tournament, principally of our own followers, but I think our men will welcome the opportunity to pit themselves against such outlandish foes. And before the ancient Herald of Errest himself! You will, no doubt, require good food and warm beds."

Taking the duke's lead, Lord Moryn turned to the company. "Red Knight, sleep within our walls, and join the feast in—"

"I am sorry," said Lamoric. His horse was dancing. "I am sorry, but it is impossible."

Duke Severin was confused. Moryn raised his chin.

"In any case," Lamoric continued, "we would happily make our camp in the pasture here."

"The *pasture*," Moryn managed.

Waer looked ready to tramp over and knock Lamoric down. But the old duke spoke up: "You may pitch your tents where you will, I am sure. If that is what you wish."

"It is, Your Grace."

"Then so be it."

Durand's mouth opened. He felt a mad impulse to flatten Lamoric himself. How was he to find a chance to speak with Deorwen now, with all the guests in the feasting hall and him bedded down in a pasture?

"SET UP CAMP," Coensar said, and the same fools who had dropped the warhorse went to oversee the establishment of their encampment below High Ashes, Guthred looking on with a skeptical eye.

Durand trailed in their wake, feeling trapped.

Berchard led their straggling line past wrestling peasants, men lifting great round stones, and a group casting spears to arrive at a space of empty pasture. High Ashes was a fairground sort of place that day.

"Well," Berchard said, finally, "this looks as good a place as any. Few stones, thick turf." He hopped up and down on his toes. "It's likely a better bed than they'll have up in the castle."

It could not have mattered less to Durand, and none of the others bothered to argue. Guthred tramped past, squinting at the ground, getting set to issue orders. With all the fairground activity, none of them had noticed the strange gang of workmen digging nearby. Abruptly, one rangy villager in a dark cap hopped off his riverside seat and strolled over. He left a half-dozen of his fellows standing with shovels and mattocks on some sort of ridge.

"I wouldn't pitch that here, Your Lordships, not if I were you."

Berchard thrust out his bearded chin. "Would you not?"

"I would not, and that's a fact," the rangy villager affirmed.

Berchard nodded: *fair enough.* Somewhere wrestlers were shouting. Or the men heaving the great stones.

"And why would you avoid this spot, then, if you were we?"

"Well. All through here? It's about to go under."

Berchard paused. "Under?"

"Aye."

Ouen lowered a long arm across Badan's chest; the bald knight had already started to snarl.

"For the big tussle in the morning," the raw-boned villager explained.

"Friend," said Berchard. "I'm afraid I've lost you."

"We're setting the river back. Shifting it off the old island."

Now, Ouen had a firm hold of Badan.

Berchard patted the air. "Wait a moment now, I think I'm starting to see. Darkly, mind you, so go slow."

"The river," said the villager. "The Glass?" Berchard nodded helpfully. "It's meant to run round this way." The man, turning to face the castle hill, waved his arms, showing a channel swinging around the old fort on the north side. "But they dammed it off so it cuts this way, back down an old oxbow."

"An oxbow. I see." Berchard nodded. "So. Where, then, would you establish your encampment, were you all of us?"

"I'm sure it ain't my place to say, Lordship."

"Of course not," Berchard agreed. "Foolish of me. We'll find our own patch. Just you make sure to tell us if you plan to dump a river down it, right?"

"As you wish, Lordship."

"As I wish," Berchard said and turned to the others. "What about up there, then?" he suggested, gesturing vaguely, and they were off to high ground on the castle's flank.

Heremund was sitting there already, scratching his neck and muttering.

DURAND THREW HIMSELF into the numbing work of heaping barrels and unrolling tents, using his back like a mute beast. All the while, he was conscious of the castle's stockade wall.

Shouts drew Durand's attention to the dam. While the peasants must have been digging for long hours to cut their black notch in the berm, the river had suddenly outdone them. Durand glanced in time to see the peasants high-stepping like herons as the water lipped over the dam and poured into the deep pasture where Lamoric's men might have pitched their tents.

Finally, when the last stake was driven and the last pole raised, Durand joined the others where they gathered round a fire. Beyond, the dark water poured into the turf, filling the earth to send a gleaming edge spreading across the lawn, clear as the glass for which the river was named.

The cooks of High Ashes were roasting meat in the castle yard, and an agony of crackling odors boiled over the wall to torment the men.

Badan shook his head as if to dislodge the smell. "Where's this fight to be?" he asked. "What did he say?"

"In the river by the sounds of it," Berchard said.

Heremund was nodding. He had the look of a man working on some riddle. "This business with the island. I wonder."

"*What* do you wonder, skald?" Badan griped.

"Islands under rivers. There was a king, once. One of the Atthians; one of the Voyager's get. They turned a river over his bones."

"Ach. Whatever it is," said Badan, "it had better be a dry and windy night if they expect us to ride horses on this island of theirs in the morning."

"I expect we'll fight on foot," said Berchard.

Ouen grimaced. "Or the island's stone. I got in a scrape once. Argued with a man. He had us run out into the yard and do it right there."

There were lewd groans.

"You're a bunch of sick whoresons, you are. We lined up right in the courtyard. Horses on the cobblestones." The man thumbed his gilded teeth. "Lotht these whed the little bathtard knocked me off."

Lamoric and Coensar joined them, Lamoric's face still hidden by his helm.

"Gentlemen," said Lamoric.

"You still wearing that thing, Lordship?" asked Ouen. Lamoric tipped the heavy bucket back far enough that he could grimace out from under the lip.

"Blast that Moryn calling us in. How was I to manage that? It's all family in there, nearly. Half of Duke Severin's men stood by me in Evensands for my wedding. That's only the Weaning Moon. They're not deaf, and they're not daft."

Durand nodded along with the others.

"The man wanted me to sit at the table like a fool, my head in this bucket all night while his father's court jabbers and stares and dines on heron and pheasant, and I'm stuck there like some leering madman. May the Eye turn from him, the bugger knew I had to turn him down. And turn his Grace down. He knew it."

There was nothing for a man to do but nod and look at the ground between his feet. Up near the gates, a wrestler was thrown hard. They heard the grunt, and the hollering of the crowd.

"Well," said Lamoric. "It'll all be over soon, one way or the other." Reseating his helm, he started for the tents.

"Evening gentlemen," said Coensar, and the company was left alone.

"Well, call me simple, but I don't understand," said Berchard.

"Ah," said Ouen. "He's got to hide his face. There's family and strangers about. Maybe after dark—"

"Host of Heaven," sighed Berchard, "not the Red Knight business here and now; the Red Knight business altogether—what's it mean?"

Suddenly, Ouen looked as though he had something caught between his back teeth.

"And what's this between Moryn and Lamoric?" Berchard pressed.

Heremund was worrying at whatever plagued him, but it was he who answered. "Could it be that? It couldn't, surely."

Berchard rounded on the little man. "How about you tell me and I'll decide."

"Huh. Gireth and Mornaway. They're loyal men. Mornaway has a daughter. Gireth's got a son. It's an alliance. Lamoric's been a might high-spirited. Better known in alehouses than court or sanctuary."

"Good lad," sneered Badan.

Heremund waved a hand, like a man batting at a fly. "But it's to be an alliance. And it's the Weaning Moon and the flowers are blowing. And so old Duke Abravanal—he'd been poorly, I reckon." The little man winced into the sky a moment, unsatisfied.

The whole lot of them had leaned forward by now, Durand

included, and they watched as the little man grimaced and dug a finger in his ear.

"Skald!" Berchard prompted, and Heremund blinked back at his circle of listeners.

"Ah. So Abravanal casts his net out wide and hauls his boy in from wherever he's haring, and they all troop down to Mornaway for a high sanctuary wedding in Evensands.

"Now, as they're polishing the plate and stringing up flowers at the high sanctuary, there's dark news on the roads."

"That'll be Borogyn," ventured Berchard.

"Mad Borogyn's got them rising up in the Heithan Marches."

"I see you're listening," chided Berchard, but Heremund only rattled on.

"The old Prince of the Marches, his sons have thrown their lot in with Borogyn. King Ragnal's calling up the war host of Errest the Old. Every duke's bound to bring his men."

"Aye . . ." agreed Berchard.

"Duke Abravanal was too ill to march, and he reckoned his eldest must stick by his side, so he gives the host of Gireth to Lamoric. An honor."

"Now, back to the wedding," Berchard prompted.

"Hmm," Heremund said. "So, riders tore home through Mornaway and Yrlac to bang on the door of every Baron of Gireth. But the wedding's underway. There's a little feast. Husband and wife-to-be and their families. What with wedding and war on the morrow, there's butterflies in the guts of young and old. But all go to bed safe."

"It's a harrowing tale so far, skald," Berchard said.

"Ah. All . . . but our Lamoric. I reckon some of his cronies must've made the trek to Evensands, but what happened that night's all a bit clouded." There were brothels and alehouses enough in most towns to shine a light in those clouds. "I do know, though, that there was trouble at the sanctuary the next morning. At First Twilight, there was no sign of him for the vigil, and that sent big brother hunting."

Berchard was shaking his head. "I hope he hasn't got in-laws like mine."

"Guthred could tell a sight more, I'd wager, but it all ended with bride and family and half of Evensands sat in the sanctuary as the Eye of Heaven peered down the river without a groom. But then there's raised voices outside, and Lamoric's there. His brother's found him. They've brushed most of the straw from his surcoat.

"After that, Abravanal gave Gireth's war host to one of his barons—Swanskin, I think—and not his son."

"Redemption," declared Berchard. Durand looked up at the stockade walls of High Ashes, almost marveling. All the lords of Mornaway were inside. "A summer of hard fighting, and now he's up against it. All them ghosts and butterflies. Now's the test. All the in-laws staring on. I wonder how—"

"Hang on," rumbled Ouen. "His Lordship hired me on for a simple trick: We're bound for Tern Gyre, if we can get there. We'll fight before the prince and the barons. They all think they know our man up there. His shield's been on the tournament roll since he mumbled his first word." The big man did not mention Lamoric's reputation as a wastrel and a fool. "But we're going to ride through like heroes, and, when we've bested every whoreson who rides out against us and they're looking to name our Red Knight commander first of equals and hero of heroes, and every green eye is on him, he'll pop off that red helm, and show them who he really is." He poked Berchard once in the surcoat, giving them a great slanted flash of his golden teeth. "It'll be the greatest trick played in a hundred years. His Lordship will be marked out for great things, and we'll all be there with him, finished with grubbing for pennies forever."

"And so here we are, starving in a cow field," Badan sneered.

"Better than the river," Berchard offered.

Heremund was back to shaking his head and muttering.

"I wonder what went on as the boy's brother dragged him to the sanctuary," pondered Berchard. "I might pry a word or two from Guthred after—"

Just then, Guthred appeared at their fireside.

"If you're through with this philosophizing, I've got tidings for you. Coensar's taking mercy on us lot with the feast on upstairs. Any who want can go."

Men grinned and backs straightened. Durand started to lean onto his feet, pleased to have a chance to get inside.

"Anyone who wants to leave his betters out here in the weather can head right in." Guthred grinned. "That's the word you'll get from me."

Badan was on his feet before Berchard caught his cloak.

"You're a cruel man, Guthred, my boy," said Berchard. "Plain cruel."

Guthred paused to give them a grimace, then continued on his way.

WITH EVENING COMING on, Durand glanced up to find Heremund staring at him.

He looked away.

Cool shadows had filled the valley by then, but the murderous scents boiling over the stockade seemed to fill the whole world. Pork and mutton and beef and goose and venison curled in the air.

To Durand, the smell was only a reminder of Deorwen caught out of reach. He eyed the timber wall.

Berchard, however, was drooling. "King of far Heaven, what are they doing up there?" he demanded.

Heremund shook his head. "Blood Moon."

"Ah right," said Berchard. "They'll be salting, smoking, and pickling, and stewing, and roasting everything they can't feed through winter."

"King of Heaven," groaned Badan. Some of the others, though, wore a more somber expression, suddenly thinking hard about surplus throats cut for winter. If Lamoric's trick failed, they would likely all be on the road.

"And they'll have beer and cider and—"

Durand stood up. It was no use. The others could talk about glory and food and death as long as they liked, but, like a steady wind, thoughts of Deorwen drove his mind. Had he done something? Was she ashamed? All his doubts were foolish, and worrying did no good. He must get her alone and settle things. If he asked, she would tell him.

One of the bunch said, "See, now you've driven Durand away." But Durand didn't respond. He marched over the shadowed pasture, skirting the wrestling match for the castle gates. He didn't plan to eat inside, but he would have to barge in if he were going to get near Deorwen. A single drawbridge spanned the ditch at the wall's foot.

He had just stepped out onto the boards when a throng of pages and serving men burst past him. He got a glimpse of the bottom, five fathoms down, then caught hold of the nearest boy.

"Here," said Durand carefully. "I've got a question for you. Can you tell me where I might find Lady Bertana?"

The boy had a platter in his hands, full of pies. He managed to stammer, "What?"

Durand glanced to Heaven. "A woman. Arrived with us. With the Red Knight. Past forty. Not large. She had a maidservant and bodyguard." He tried to think of things a boy might remember. "The man would have had an axe."

"No, Sir. And I'd remember, Sir. We've been doing up rooms. I'd have been there."

That stood Durand up. If the boy were right, Bertana hadn't gone inside at all. He could not think why she should spurn the duke's hospitality.

Durand looked across the dusky fields, thinking that he might even have set up the woman's pavilion and not known it.

"Thank you, boy," he said, ready to let the child go, but then the smell of the pies asserted itself.

"Who is all this for?" Durand asked.

"You. The Knight in Red's men. Duke's orders. We were to carry the feast out."

Snatching one of the little pies, Durand nodded. "Go on. And make sure your master knows we were grateful." She was somewhere out there. He could remember nothing of Bertana's tents, but now he knew to look.

The boy was already gone when he looked back.

He tramped back. Most of the company had gathered along the new watercourse, watching the river lay the grass flat and circle High Ashes in a moat of running water, but Durand steered clear of them. If he were to retain any dignity at all, he could not be asking every passing shield-bearer where his woman had gone. He would have to see what he could find on his own.

Between the stockade and the new moat, there were only

two dozen tents. Unless Bertana had run off to live with the peasants, she and her maidservant must be there somewhere.

Durand walked through the camp, seeing no sign. On the far side, where the old river's elbow still curled, something was rising from the water, broad-backed and shining in the sunset. He thought of some dead leviathan, all scales and slime. This must be the river island where they would fight.

As he turned back, his eyes fell on a gray-bearded man with an axe in his fists. The axeman stood outside the flap of a good-sized pavilion.

Durand grinned.

"Evening," he said, slipping between the tents toward the man.

The guard only stared.

"You were with Lady Bertana in the forest, yes?"

Blue eyes stared from among lines and creases. The beard was stiff as old thatch.

"May I speak with her? Is she inside?"

The axeman made no move.

Durand stepped forward, thinking to knock at the tent flap, but the guard intercepted him. He wore a byrnie of iron mail and carried his bearded axe in both hands.

"I only wish to speak with her," Durand said. He didn't like being treated like a stranger.

Then Lady Bertana ducked through the tent flap and stepped out.

"I am sorry, Coelgrim, but I thought I heard voices," she said. Looking up, she added, "Ah," as though, somehow, she had not known Durand's voice.

"Ladyship," Durand said.

The woman nodded acknowledgment, though she seemed uneasy. Looking closely, Durand decided that he should have told the boy that Bertana was past fifty, maybe sixty. Her skin was soft as a kid purse.

A smile twitched, and she looked toward the growing stream below the camp.

"The water is running on both sides?"

"Aye."

Avoiding his eyes, she added, "The Glass will soon ring us right around."

"I want to see her."

"She is not here," the old woman said, but Durand knew: Deorwen was inside, three paces from him, through a canvas wall. If he wanted, there was nothing anyone could do to stop him.

The water was rising.

"You are certain," Durand said.

"I am certain, Sir Durand," Bertana breathed. "She is not here."

Durand nodded and turned his back.

He felt like taking something in his hands and breaking it. He made for open ground, tripping over guy ropes and tent stakes. He wanted to feed the old man his axe. He wanted to tear through that thin skin of canvas and pull Deorwen out. It was like the whole of Creation was laughing at him. How many times had he met the woman before they had kissed? How many times had he let her pass?

He heard someone draw steel, like a breath on his neck.

"I want the whoreson! I'm calling him out," a voice shouted. It was Moryn's big retainer, Waer.

Lamoric's men were scrambling up from around their fire. Sparks boiled in the air with Waer standing practically in the flames. Durand darted through the tents.

"Now I've had the whole story," Waer snarled. "I've heard of the slipping and the dodging. Waiting on this and waiting on that." Waer jabbed the air with his fingers. "Riding men through Hesperand, swapping sides. I—"

Lamoric emerged from his pavilion, settling the red helm on his head.

"Here!" said Waer, stepping forward. "I'll twist your—"

And Durand stepped into the man's path.

"What the hell's this?" Waer said.

"You want to fight someone, try me."

Waer looked Durand up and down. Though Durand had a few inches on the man, Waer looked like he could wring a bull's neck.

"I suggest you not speak to His Lordship that way," Durand said.

Waer just nodded. "You'll do to start."

Durand sucked a big breath and began to haul out his blade.

"The King's Peace!" Berchard said. "The King's Peace! No private duels outside the lists!"

Both men hesitated.

The faces of Lamoric's retainers were frozen in alarm.

"This is no royal tournament," Waer growled, not moving.

"Then we're here as guests of Duke Severin," declared Berchard. "Your *master's* guests." Waer would call the wrath of the Traveler down on his lord, drawing blood from an invited guest.

Durand noticed a couple of the men glance up the bank toward the wrestlers.

Waer caught this as well. The mob watching the wrestling was all watching him now.

He nodded. "Right. Come on then."

They walked up.

Wrestling in the Atthias was an ancient thing, and they used the Errest style in Mornaway. Men wore their fighting gambesons and didn't scramble on the ground. There were dozens of trips and throws, and Durand had fought a hundred tiltyard bouts. He was soon surrounded by urgent hands, snatching off his sword belt and surcoat, then helping him into a stinking gambeson coat of stuffed canvas. Lamoric's men murmured advice, telling him to use his reach or watch his legs.

In an airless moment, he was thrust out in front of the furious Mornaway man.

It suited Durand well.

"Take hold then," Waer said, and Durand did, one fist in the man's collar, the other in the man's belt. He felt Waer's knuckles turn against his hip and ear as the big man took hold as well, breathing garlic and sour wine into Durand's face.

They jostled while some village reeve or bailiff waited to shout the word.

Then it began.

The Host Below had made Waer of ship's cables and bridge timbers. Durand's first heaves left the man rooted to Creation.

"Moryn's told me the games you've been playing," Waer growled.

Even as the man spoke, he was twisting.

Durand crooked his leg to hold him, and they staggered together.

"Bastards," Waer grunted.

Suddenly, he pivoted, and Durand found himself whipped against the earth. Only a desperate twist saved him from the kind of flat fall, hips and shoulders, which would lose him the match.

As it was, he had lost a point.

The bailiff told them, "go."

Now, it was all straining. Durand tried to wrench the Mornaway man one way and then the other, but the man might have been an oak.

They bridged against each other, straining.

Waer shot kicks at Durand's legs.

Each boot gave Durand a bruise and a chance to throw.

Somehow, Waer reversed him. Durand could hardly breathe as he got to his feet.

The bailiff was shaking his head, "Just shoulders. Just shoulders."

Now, rage had hold of Durand. There was nothing like coming to a fight in a blind fury and getting tossed around like a fool.

He opened his hands and beckoned Waer in.

Now, Durand scrambled for any advantage, breathing in the knot of the man's jaw like a forge and bellows. For an instant, Durand felt he had his man.

Then Waer dropped: a tricky maneuver.

Like a pickaxe, the man's shoulder chopped Durand in the guts. Waer drove harder, lifting. With sheer main strength, he wrenched Durand free of the ground.

In that reeling instant, with the air rammed from his lungs, Durand decided that he would not go easy. He locked himself onto Waer's shoulders. He drove his knee into the man's ribs. He pitched Waer off balance.

Together, they went down—Durand first—Durand losing.

But, as the ground knocked the wind through Durand's teeth, he held on to Waer's neck, whipping the big man over.

It was an awkward fall: head and neck and shoulder caught.

As Durand opened his hands, Waer did not move.

Durand struggled loose amidst the suddenly silent ring of onlookers. He got up.

Waer was still.

In the hush, the bailiff stepped into the circle, bending low over the sprawl of knees and elbows.

Durand wavered, slapping at the dirt marring the old coat. He could feel whatever impetus that rage had given him dying as his friends closed in, silently helping him from the stinking coat.

The man lying in the dirt was a lord's companion and liege-man to the duke.

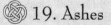 19. Ashes

Waer did not move. No one looked from the wellborn wrestler—maybe corpse—face down and arms sprawled.

No one spoke.

Finally, there was the smallest motion: His arm shifted, crooking at its elbow. The whole gathered crowd took their first breath.

Then Lamoric's lads were slapping Durand's back.

Ouen squeezed his shoulder. "Lad, I thought the lot of us were going to have to run for it."

"Hard head and stiff neck," Badan muttered, clucking his tongue.

The others either cursed the downed man or thanked Heaven he hadn't snapped his neck. Durand strained to find Lamoric where he stood with Coensar beyond the circle. A great deal depended on how Lamoric reacted.

But, as Durand looked, every face was turning toward the castle gates.

It was Lord Moryn.

He and many of the duke's liegemen were rumbling over the drawbridge. The lean lord's mantle flapped after him. At the edge of the circle, Moryn stopped, surveying the spectacle. His man, Waer, was awake, if not on his feet. Some of the crowd glanced to Durand; Moryn gave him a hard look.

Then the Knight in Red stepped forward.

"You have interrupted your feast?" Lamoric asked.

"My man, Waer, had no business interfering."

"I am surprised to hear *you* say it."

Moryn closed his eyes for an instant. "Waer is rash. He left without a word. I came when I learned."

"Not in time, however," Lamoric said.

"What do you say?" said Moryn.

"You have chosen your moment well, my Lord. This fellow of yours had ample opportunity to reach me before you could arrive. If Sir Durand here had not been so quick, he would have done."

Durand wondered. Around him, the other retainers were fidgeting like pageboys.

Fire glittered in the slits of Moryn's eyes.

"Do you say you had no intention of loosing a thug to lame your enemy? Of hobbling your opponent before you must meet him in the field? Of finding an accident to preserve your reputation among your father's men?"

Moryn snapped his blade into the chill air. It glittered with his eyes. "To face a creature such as you, a man needs no such tricks."

Lamoric left his own blade lie in its scabbard. "I commend your cleverness, Lord Moryn. Waer is a loyal man. He is rash. He would not need an order, just a well-chosen word. And you can sleep, an innocent."

Moryn's blade twitched. Lamoric's hand drifted toward his own. There was a sound at the High Ashes gate.

A second delegation of wellborn soldiers stepped into the autumn night. This time, Durand found himself looking at half the barons of Mornaway, with Duke Severin stalking at their head.

"Gentlemen!" the old duke said, showing some sign of the warrior he must once have been. "Peace. There is bad blood, but I will not see it spilt. You are guests. I am told that a time and place has been agreed, and I believe that time will come soon enough to satisfy anyone's honor."

Lord Moryn was nodding. He sheathed his sword.

"I have agreed that we will fight before the Herald of Errest," Moryn said.

Lamoric hooked his thumbs in his belt.

"Good, good," Severin said. "Now. There is food prepared and waiting. Men have labored. Beasts have died to fill our stomachs. It is not fitting that we should ignore their sacrifice."

Moryn nodded, and, with his men gathering up the disoriented Waer, withdrew beyond the stockade.

Durand left.

It was all too much. Lamoric was half mad, but Durand was no better himself. Serving men stared up at him. He walked toward the walls. Unless he wanted to swim the new moat, there was nowhere to go but to the open ground above the castle ditch.

Yet again, he had survived a mistake. The fight with Waer had been stupid and dangerous, and it had done nothing to untie the knot of his frustration. He understood nothing. In the space of a heartbeat, he had lost Deorwen.

Everything had gone wrong so quickly.

"Durand!" A voice behind him.

Heremund bandied down the grassy ringwork. Durand remembered an ape once at a fair.

"I reckoned Waer was it," the skald gasped. "But there is something else."

Durand knotted his fists for a moment, then turned. Anger was stupid.

"What made you blunder in like that?" Heremund demanded. "What made you bolt?"

Heremund's avid brown eyes looked closely into Durand's face, then it seemed that realization dawned.

"*Ah.* A mistake, yes? Nothing to do with Lamoric."

Durand exhaled through his nostrils, eyes shut.

"I see," Heremund said.

"Then let me be a while."

Heremund nodded deeply, but, as Durand turned to continue his walk, the skald trotted alongside. "First there's old Traveler," he said. "Then you in the hills over that horse's neck. And that stag by the hut."

"*Heremund,*" Durand said.

"The Traveler don't turn up for everyone, boy. Some hear a rapping. There's a staff-heel click as they choose to murder or not—a wife, a child—to cheat or not, to pick up or set aside.

There's only the tapping, and a prickling on the neck to say that someone's there."

Durand remembered the forest at Gravenholm and the rapping in the dark.

"You, though," said Heremund. "You meet the man himself."

Heremund looked round them both. "I see you crashing through a dance, hooking dancers with your arms, changing the spin of the whole thing."

Durand remembered the news after Traveler's Night that sent him careering down the road to Red Winding and Bower Mead and High Ashes and God knew where.

"Little good it's done me," said Durand.

"Don't know," Heremund muttered. "Maybe it ain't done. Maybe it's hardly got started." He was shaking his head. "Your talk has the ring of doom about it. I—"

Just then, a tremor passed through the whole of Creation. A footfall. Durand steadied himself. Very faintly, bells moaned on the air. The throb spoke from some shrine in the castle and another somewhere beyond the valley rim. Durand stood facing the Glass and the strange island. Rings spread across the surface.

"*Hells,*" Heremund breathed, casting about.

In the midst of the river, something—a black pane of shale—slid from the broad back of the isle. A cold wind tossed Durand's cloak and rustled in the skeleton branches of the trees above the valley. The weather was changing.

"Hells," said Heremund. He gaped at the dim sky. "Hells, hells."

Durand caught hold of the little man. He could hear shouts now. Animals screamed. "What does it mean?" he demanded. He felt as though Creation had changed. The world's horizon seemed like the prow of some vast ship on a vaster ocean.

He shook his head.

"Someone's being a fool," Heremund gasped.

As he turned under the black valley rim, waiting for God knew what, someone moved in the camp. Durand would have known the walk from seven leagues. Only twenty paces from him, Deorwen stood before Bertana's pavilion, looking into the vault of Heaven.

"This dance of yours," Durand said. "I'll tell you this for nothing: I'm not the one swinging partners round." With this, he freed the skald and darted for Deorwen's back, once again dodging the web of guy lines between the knights' pavilions. She stared up until he had come close enough to touch her.

"Deorwen," he said.

Her eyes were still wide from the sky.

"Oh, Durand. No."

He caught her elbow. For an instant, she looked at his hand as though it was some foreign creature, then she pulled free and darted back into Bertana's pavilion.

Durand pushed after her, ducking into a crowded space of red walls and strewn herbs. There were chests and trunks. Lady Bertana stood, and bearded Coelgrim crossed to meet him. After a bewildered instant, Durand spotted a bright slit of twilight where a second flap had just closed.

He found no sign of Deorwen back under the eerie Heavens. Shadowy people stared up among the tents, holding the Eye of Heaven between themselves and the whole of Creation.

The girl had vanished as completely as if she had never been.

Durand held his hands loose and eyes tight shut. Every dark thought shot through his skull. It was an effort to breathe. Tents and ropes webbed him round, walls and ditches and moats and rivers blocked and barred him. He turned his eyes to Heaven, where the Eye beyond the valley rim touched strange ripples in the clouds, as though someone had pitched a stone into the firmament.

He heard Coelgrim step into the space behind him, the cool weight of an axe now in his hands, but Durand did not even bother to turn.

"Your lady is safe," he breathed. "You needn't worry on my account."

Without waiting for the man's answer, Durand stalked away, tripping over stakes and ropes and tethers. Again, he went for open ground.

He had to get free.

Water brimmed in the ditches. Another push, and he would swim for it, spending the night in the freezing forest wastes. He teetered along the fathoms-deep castle ditch. He would get himself beyond the sight of men, alone for once beyond the curve of the castle's wall.

Finally, he stumbled round the far side where the split Glass poured back into its channel.

There, he found a silent figure, pale against the river dark.

For a death-cold instant, Durand thought of Cerlac and the Glass that brimmed with spirits. He thought of the washerwoman. He thought of the blue-shirted peasant and the Traveler himself.

The figure was turning, a long, pale face coming into view. But it was not Cerlac or any of these others; instead, the man was Agryn. A Holy Ghost, perhaps, but not the dead from Hesperand.

The knight's dark eyes narrowed.

"What was all that?" Durand asked.

"I don't know." The strange dial dangled from the knight's fingers.

"What did it mean?" With the river and the gloom and Agryn being so still and the shadows of his past with the Septarim, such a man might know anything.

"I cannot say," answered Agryn. He stared at Durand for a moment. "I was never one of the Septarim. Nearly, once. The Heavens are a looking glass, they say. Or a pool, more like."

Durand had heard stories of bare monasteries and long rows of knights waiting still as corpses upon their biers, cool as wax and old as foundation stones.

"You have been in an accident," the knight said.

Durand did not know where to begin, but Sir Agryn raised a knuckle toward Durand's face and fists. There were scrapes. Mud. "Waer came for Lamoric. I was lucky."

"Let us hope Lamoric has your luck tomorrow."

Durand stopped for a moment, then had to nod. Lamoric could lose. The whole surge of events that had carried Durand here could ebb away.

"If Lamoric fails, we will be turned out, penniless, scattered before the wind," said Agryn. "Winter will be hard when taxes have emptied every strongbox." He turned his eye on Durand. "It is a hard road for a knight without lord or land."

His long face studied the dimming horizon. Suddenly, Durand wondered how many winters this man had seen, alone on the road.

"Why did you leave them?" Durand wondered.

"My Holy Ghosts?" He paused. "For my wife."

Now, Durand was surprised. "I didn't know you were—"

"Dead of fever, when Carondas was king."

Old King Carondas had been buried in Ferangore sixty winters.

Again, there was the dry laugh. "She was among the wise women who came to cleanse me of this life. I lay down on the bier. She carried dead man's balsam. I left my brethren and God and the king. I left with her, so heartsore was I at the thought of letting her go."

"God," said Durand.

"I was meant to serve the kings of Errest. The Powers called. In turning from that calling," said Agryn, "I turned the Eye of Heaven from me. A man cannot slip the doom allotted him. We will see what becomes of Lamoric, and all of us whose fates are bound to his."

Durand nodded. They had not lost yet. Nothing was finished. "If the Herald's fair, we've got a—"

The man fixed Durand with a dark eye. "The Herald of Errest stood with Einred's sons at Lost Princes; walked the Halls of Heaven; rode before the grieving king at the Plain of the Skull and the Waste of Fettered Bones; winded the Crusader Horn at the black gates of the Burning City. Servant to ten kings. He keeps the Roll of Errest and the fame of all peers living and dead. His ruling will be the mandate of Heaven."

Durand rubbed the back of his neck, eyes on the turf.

"I am sorry," said Agryn.

"No." The man was right.

Durand closed his eyes, his mind spinning. Deorwen returned to his thoughts.

"But the Powers, I feel them, nearly, in this," Agryn confessed. "As I did in those days long ago. Perhaps there is cause to . . . to hope in this."

Durand heard anxious ages in the man's voice: battles enough to make Coen's striving seem the trial of a moment.

When he looked again on Agryn, the austere warrior's eyes were fixed on the valley wall.

"The Eye of Heaven has left us," he said. "Night has fallen."

On the riverbank, he sank to his knees.

Durand left the man to pray.

The Glass filled with stars.

He would not wait forever. He would find Deorwen and learn what was in her mind. If it must be done in secret, he would allow her that.

Among the camp's canvas alleys, he passed grooms currying horses. Some tents were dark, but when he came upon Bertana's, it smoldered like a banked fire. He read the shadows thrown against its red skin, picking out Coelgrim's shape and the softer form of Bertana. He saw the shadows stop, as if they had heard him. There was no sign of Deorwen.

Reasoning that the grooms were nearby enough to have seen where she had gone, he walked into the warm fetor of the tethered horses.

"Have you seen a girl?" he asked.

The nearest boy looked at him across a mare's back, his face like an apple. He held a rough blanket.

"Here," Durand said, hauling the blanket over the mare's back. "Have you seen a girl? From the Lady's tent."

"The red hair?" the boy asked.

Durand stared into the boy's face. "Aye."

The boy nodded quick and stuck a finger across the camp toward a tall pavilion glowing like a horn lantern among the dark peaks of its neighbors. "That one," he said.

Durand looked at the pale glow and took a deep breath. "Thank you," he said, then, with a nod to the boy, he walked toward the illuminated pavilion.

He would set it straight. She might be afraid for her honor. Women were. There was always a woman or two among the camp followers who would whore for pennies, and here he had come tramping out of the woods with her alone and she was no whore. A woman might take pains to make it clear.

The dark tents at the heart of the camp made his going hard, and he was sure there was more rope in a camp like this than in all the ships at Acconel quay. He skirted a quagmire where some fool had penned his mounts among the tent stakes.

The lit tent swung nearer. For once, he would not charge in roaring like a fool. He would keep his temper.

Finally, he reached the rear of the glowing pavilion. A murmured conversation was taking place beyond the canvas.

Berchard and big Ouen turned as he stepped out. Both had their eyes wide, more curious than surprised.

"Durand?" Berchard asked.

Durand could only stare. This was the tent. It was the only lit tent. There was movement inside.

"You all right?" asked Berchard. "That Waer's inside now. Fit, by all accounts."

Durand could not nod and pretend with Berchard. He could only stare. The boy might have pointed to any of a dozen tents, but he had not. Here Berchard stood on guard.

Durand's hand went for the tent flap.

"Boy," Berchard said, raising his eyebrows. "They say he's with his wife."

With a twist that surprised the one-eyed knight, Durand slipped past and shoved himself into the pavilion of his liege lord.

Lamoric perched on an oak chest, a surprised look on his face.

Deorwen sat in the young lord's cross-framed chair, her face frozen. Lamoric seemed ready to forgive a necessary intrusion, and they had been doing nothing more than talking. But Durand could no more breathe than fly.

"Durand?" Lamoric said.

Durand managed to take his eyes from Deorwen.

"Well," said Lamoric gamely. "This is a happy chance. You have met my wife? She has told me of your courage in Hesperand."

Durand stood in the doorway. Lamoric knew nothing.

"Since our wedding day, we have been made to creep like adulterers," Lamoric said. "Now, in her father's domain, it is madness."

Deorwen—Lady Deorwen, daughter of Duke Severin of Mornaway—forced her eyes to her husband's.

"It was at our wedding that all this Red Knight business began," Lamoric explained. "My father's fault. My friends had insisted on celebrating on the eve of the great day. There was a great deal of drinking. There were women there, from an alehouse in the town. And though it was not my father whom I wronged—" He bowed to Deorwen. "—he was greatly angered."

Lamoric looked to Durand.

"I thought I would prove him wrong."

"Yes, Lordship," Durand managed. His finger fell on the knotted veil at his belt. The Lady of Hesperand would grant him a life.

"But there's little mystery to the Knight in Red with Lord Lamoric's wife at his side. Guthred's bad enough. Still, my lady has followed again—and through Lost Hesperand."

Durand understood that they had been arguing. Lamoric would have left her behind if she had let him.

When Lamoric looked away, Deorwen's eyes met Durand's, strained and edging on frantic. She thought he might say something: rail against her, or confess. Durand forced himself to croak a few words.

"Wanted to wish you good fortune, Lordship," he said. "For the morning."

"Ah, well, I—"

Durand could wait no longer; he ducked from the tent.

He left Berchard and big Ouen with their mouths open, reeling away to find his own tent—another thing stolen from Cerlac's belongings—and stumbled among his few possessions until he had cleared a space where he could lie down.

She should have told him. Even if she could not tell him whose wife she was, knowing she was married might have been enough. His hand brushed the green veil knotted in his belt. He remembered Saewin and the Lost duke. He had stumbled into the same sin.

In all the time of their slow falling, she should have said something.

Perhaps an hour later, there was a voice at his tent flap, whispering *"Durand."* It could have been the girl, but he did not answer, and she did not come in.

He wondered if this was what Heremund had foreseen.

20. Beneath the Ripples' Gleam

The time had come.

A hush fell over three hundred souls as Lamoric's retainers stepped out. Music faltered and gossip stumbled. Banners switched in the wind. There was hardly room between the riverbank and the castle wall for another living thing. Above the stockade walls, Heaven was a heavy gray, laden with the threat of rain.

Faced with the sudden stillness, Lamoric nodded a shallow bow to the gawkers and led his men through the mob to the bank of the old Glass channel.

Durand shuffled along with the others as the silent throng allowed them to reach the riverbank. The first rank of peasants had their toes in the slime.

"Where are the lists?" muttered Coensar.

"The island," Lamoric said, jostled as Guthred jerked at straps and buckles, cinching him in.

"There's hardly room to stand a horse, let alone ride," grunted Guthred.

"No horses," Lamoric answered. "Just a punt and boatman to get you there."

Guthred's nod was tense. The mounted pass gave every decent rider a chance, but foot combat had a way of squeezing luck and accident from a tussle.

"You'll be fine," Guthred lied.

Durand pawed hair from his eyes, not thinking of Moryn's suffocating speed and anger. Not thinking that this was their last chance to reach Tern Gyre. Deorwen must be out there among those teeming faces. She would be looking at him, and he could do nothing about it. As Lamoric's sworn man, he could never do anything about it.

Firmly, he fixed his eyes on the thin gleam of the severed channel. With the Glass racing down its ancient course once more, the water around the humpbacked islet lay murky and slack. Peasants had supplied a weathered punt for Lamoric's use.

As Durand was wondering whether the thing could hold an armored man's weight, something stirred the crowd.

"That'll be them," growled Guthred.

Duke Severin tramped out in the midst of his barons. A heap of moss-green cloak balanced on his shoulders as he chattered at a stranger: the Herald of Errest, a man who had seen three centuries and walked the Halls of Heaven.

Like a figure of alabaster, Kandemar the Herald stood over six feet tall. His hair hung pale as ash over a bloodless brow. But, at his hip, Durand spotted the slender chased-ivory trumpet that had sounded before the walls of the Burning City. Ancient sigils traced its mouth in silver.

Mornaway's household guard opened an aisle through the crowd, conducting the procession to a reviewing stand at the stockade.

"I have kept it just as it was," the duke was saying. "Although the keep itself is perhaps small for our needs, there is adequate accommodation in the yard, and the few good beds provide something for my liegemen to squabble over." To Durand, the man seemed distracted, his eyes darting across the cut while he spoke.

The Herald, like some Power in a sanctuary frieze, hardly noticed. As the duke spoke, the ancient man's attention slid to the island and then—to Durand's horror—to Durand's face.

His guilt was scrawled as plainly as black letters on parchment. To be held in the ancient eyes of the Herald was almost to face the Throne of Heaven.

Before Durand could suffocate, a sturdy priest stood in the reviewing stand, shooting a pointed glance at Severin.

"I see it is time to begin," the duke apologized.

The murmurs of the crowd dwindled away under the rumbling Heavens.

The duke tried a smile.

"We are gathered once more, here on the banks of the Glass." He hesitated. "We have come to remember. In the Atthian Chronicle, is written the history of this place. Or so the priests explain." He looked to the sturdy priest, but found little encouragement.

"In this time of whispers and strange tidings, it is wise to remember that it was the king, Ceodan, son of Saerdan the Voyager, who commanded that the founder of Mornaway, Mircol the Hunter, travel to the Valley of High Ashes."

Ouen grunted, muttering, "And here I'd forgotten."

"Mircol came to put down the king's enemies. He pursued them with iron and fire until they turned at bay, on a meadow thereafter called the Barrow Isle, and met their doom at his hand." The old man raised his own hand, upturned.

"It was on this land Mircol fought. And, for his victory, the Voyager's son granted him this place. The Glass, it is said, was turned by his word to cover the remains of slaughter."

As the duke spoke, the wind rose, but Durand hardly noticed. Instead, he searched the crowd for any sign of Deorwen—the Herald be damned. He only wanted to look. Beyond it all, great volumes of cloud rolled against each other, churning like a summer storm.

"And now my own son, Lord Moryn, my heir and heir to ancient Mircol's domain, has come to High Ashes under the Blood Moon as once I did, and my father, and his father, knights and lords back to old Mircol's day. Here he will set his life at hazard in memory of the deeds of that first king's man to hold this land."

A sharp gust caught the duke's robe, causing an avalanche of green cloak from his shoulders.

Duke Severin raised his voice over the wind. "Most here will know the customs of this combat. Knight in Red, you fight on the Barrow Isle. You must go armed with sword and shield and fight on foot. If you—or Lord Moryn—should be too sorely wounded to continue, you may yield without loss of honor. There are no spoils to be taken. The vanquished man must cast his arms into the Glass: sword and shield." Some of Lamoric's men grunted at this. A good sword was nothing to throw away.

The wind lashed around the old man. His cloak struggled like an animal.

"Make your peace with the King of Heaven both of you," the old man said. "The time is upon us."

Durand had not found her face.

Heralds blasted a fanfare against the wind, and it struck Durand that he had not seen Lord Moryn either. Just then, like a fiend summoned by his thoughts, a shape slid from beyond the island, standing in the bows of a low boat: Lord Moryn, tall and straight as an icon in procession. Waer worked a heavy pole to thrust his master from the far bank.

Blade drawn, Lamoric stalked into the prow of the gray punt, almost as if he meant to walk to the island. Hands caught the gunnels. And the Host Below fanned a black hope in Durand's heart: What would become of Deorwen if Lamoric were to die?

Just then, the young lord turned, and, raising his sword, picked Durand from all the people crowded round. The sword's point winked at Durand's breast.

"If he's bringing that Waer, I'll have you, Durand," Lamoric said and grinned.

And there were hands slapping Durand's shoulders and muscling him into the teetering stern. Ouen set a pole in his hands. He caught sight of a blade glinting at one end. Then, with a shock like lightning, his glance fell on Deorwen—her face a pale oval in a dark hood.

"Steady, Durand," Lamoric said.

Durand felt a crawling chill. He wanted to swat the Knight in Red off the prow—the pole had the weight. Instead, he clamped his jaws, stabbed the pole down, and shoved the shore away.

Lamoric had to catch his balance.

As Durand dug the pole in, he eyed the gray Heavens as if the Silent King were leering down. He was in no mood to play Lamoric's shield-bearer now. And, with the wind kicking up, poling the boat was no easy feat. The pole stuck and slid under the river's skin, sliding over hard surfaces in the bottom slime.

Lord Moryn had alighted. Waer sneered from the back of his lord's boat while Durand wrestled to keep his own punt straight. A last shove rammed the bow against the island's scales for Lamoric to leap ashore.

The Red Knight's hop sent the punt bucking like a headstrong pony, but Durand poled off as Waer had done.

On the island, Lord Moryn and the Red Knight sank into guard positions, waiting while Severin stood on the shore. It took both Durand's fists to hold the boat steady in the wind. He wondered if, next time, they would fight on stilts. Or up in trees. The Herald watched. This was the end of a hundred leagues' wandering.

At the duke's nod, trumpets brayed over the water, and the two knights were in motion.

Lamoric started a crab-wise circle of the island, his boots slithering on the stones of what looked like a treacherous battlefield.

Lamoric leapt and swung. Lord Moryn countered. Back and forth they went. Moryn had the better footing, but both knights scrambled. Each stop or start pitched one man or the other to his knees. Quickly, great fingers of mud spread over Moryn's diamonds and Lamoric's crimson. Cross-guards smacked the rock. Shields clopped in rolling dodges. Everything had a desperate edge.

And Lamoric was getting the worst of it. Moryn moved with savage economy, throwing tight, shearing swings. A bad lunge cost Lamoric a blow across the back. A slip brought the iron down over his head. Moryn's blade punished every mistake.

Durand winced, hunkered in the boat. High overhead, the clouds were rolling now like mountains, while iron lightning flashed on the Barrow Isle.

Moryn's sword whipped down. Durand's liege lord was fighting for his life. For his every probe to claw a mailed shoulder, Lamoric caught a thunderbolt of steel over collarbone or forearm. Moryn's sword—even blunted by iron rings—fell like an axe. Lamoric lived, he was even brave, but bones could break or red helms fold. Any slip could be the end, and the hopes of many would end with their lord.

Lamoric fought.

Then Moryn caught him. A blow flashed down, nearly dashing Lamoric against the earth. He reeled, and, as he staggered, Moryn stalked him.

Lamoric tried to keep his shield in play, but Moryn swung, and a second great blow landed.

With the crowd hissing, Durand found himself crouched in the boat as if he would rush over the water.

Again, Lamoric pitched across the island, barely able to keep his feet. The watching mob was so silent, every brush and slide could be heard under the wind.

Lord Moryn waited for Lamoric to catch his balance, then

hauled back and sent a third blow shuddering down on his stricken victim.

Lamoric dangled like a hanged man, skin torn under steel like flesh from a stewed apple. Yet still, he stood. To save his life, he must yield; the Red Knight game was over. They had lost, and it would be back to the road for all his men. Everyone on the river saw it, but some mad will held Lamoric upright. His knees would not buckle, and Lord Moryn hesitated in the face of it.

As Moryn watched in horror, Lamoric dragged back his sword, low and two-handed like a reaper with his scythe. Durand wondered how much blood the red knight garb hid. Lamoric wavered there, half-slumped for a moment. A good shove would have knocked him down, but Moryn held off. Then, with all his might, Lamoric heaved his blade into one great oafish swing, sure to miss.

And it would never have landed. Moryn would have slipped it. He would have twitched his shield. He would have done a hundred other things more clever than Durand could conceive of. But, just then, Creation shuddered.

In the instant of that swing, the bells bawled out, sobbing. The roiling sky flashed flat, as vast rings swung from horizon to horizon like a pond swallowing a great stone.

The punt shuddered under Durand's hipbones, and the black scales of the island slumped, pitching into gray water. And, back on the island, there was something moving: bowel-slick flesh, pale and gleaming, bulged under the Barrow Isle.

And, in the midst of all this, the arc of Lamoric's wild swing came down: one iron bite behind the ear that knocked Moryn sprawling.

Durand had an instant's stab of elation. Lamoric had won.

But Lamoric reeled after the weight of his swing, and the bowel-and-bellies gleam under the island erupted in his path.

Durand saw a livid face, broader than a shield, and a vast taloned hand, and then the boat flipped.

He was under in an instant, snatched by the weight of his armor. He scrabbled at a boat that spun like a barrel under his nails. Water shouldered every other thought from his skull. No man can swim buckled into fifty pounds of iron. Each firm hold he got on the punt seemed to pull it under. Then, like a living thing, the boat popped loose, and he was down. It was all he could do not to haul in a breath.

He hit the bottom, his skull fit to explode.

Through the quicksilver flinch of water overhead, Durand could still hear the madness of the Heavens. It roared in his ears.

He fought to master himself. He was drowning. His fingers curled in the slime. He made himself understand: The water could not be deep. He had not fallen in the sea. He'd been poling. He could fight.

With that resolve, Durand thrashed, kicking and dragging himself, trying to get his feet under him and fighting in the direction of the island. He slid on rounded forms, slick as grease. Some were shields. His fingers caught on knobbed shapes: skulls, long bones, rusting blades. He understood then that he crawled through an upturned grave. More importantly, he knew that he had found the island's flank.

He tore into the air, sliding and splashing onto a shore that pitched like a living thing under his hands. Half-erupted from the heaping shields and helms and bones, an abomination thrashed: an ogress, a troll, a giant mockery of woman. Even caught and pinned by the weight of the barrow, the Banished fiend was larger than horses. And it screamed in spasms that convulsed the barrel-hoops of its ribs fit to burst its blue vellum skin. Creation itself seemed to shudder with its screams.

And Lamoric flailed in the talons of the thing's free hand.

As the water poured from Durand, he spotted Waer. Moryn's comrade, too, stood on the pitching island, but he had already seized his master by the collar and was pulling Lord Moryn to their boat.

With time and space for a heartbeat in the thunder, Durand knew he should strip off his armor and swim for it. He should lunge past Waer into Moryn's boat. He looked to the screaming masses, and—right off—saw Deorwen and the two wide circles of her eyes.

He turned to Lamoric. A knight-at-arms did not leave his lord to die. The ogress was wrenching itself loose. A second hand slammed down, free to push. Long breasts swung. With a roll of black eyes and a twitch of her livid face, the hag bared teeth and lifted Lamoric.

Durand charged.

In all her ages under the muck, it must never have crossed the brute's mind that anyone would try such a thing. She hardly twitched. Durand struck knees or shins, and, in a pitching instant, a weight like drowned bulls crashed down on him. The monster had just pulled its bulk onto one taloned foot, and now she pitched onto face and forearms.

Flashes burst in Durand's eyes.

Crushed and fighting for air, he prayed Lamoric was free. Then the hag was in motion.

A weight like a boulder tramped Durand's shoulder. He scrambled, gulping for air. He managed to yank his half-crushed feet from under the monster's shins, and twisted.

A full fathom over his head, the hag's face snarled under a thatch like a root ball. He read outrage there, but Durand could not get free. She smiled.

The monster shadowed the world until nothing remained but the glinting points of her teeth and a chill like deep clay. He could hear the hag haul in air like a rotten bellows. She smelled of the bottom.

Durand understood that he must die.

As the monster began its fatal leer, a jolt shook her frame. The hag froze, her mouth jutting like a clay funnel. Durand looked for an explanation and found a strange glint in the dark near his knees.

The glint was a blade. He recognized the long shaft of the pole. The thing had plunged through the monster's back to split a shield by Durand's knee. He heard a high wheezing sound.

"Durand? Get out," Lamoric commanded. "For God's sake."

Durand blinked. The creature was braced on trembling arms, her face stiff as retching. Then her eyelids twitched.

In an eruption like the hundred warhorses at Red Winding, Durand and the monster both burst into motion. Durand sprang, twisting and scrambling for freedom, while a scream ripped from the hag's body. He lunged out of reach. She was nailed to the island. And thrashing now. Every blow stamped debris into the air. Lamoric perched high on her shoulders. The fiend groped at its back, but the slim lance held the brute, like one needle holding a forest boar. No barbs or spines armed the blade, but the earth or the island held her.

Lamoric rode the hag until one sudden buck threw him wide, and he crashed down in the water beyond the fiend's talons. The river swallowed him whole.

Durand tried to crawl, but then saw motion all around him: boats. Boats of all kinds hit the water, the whole crowd jumping into the cut. As peasants and peers hauled him to his knees, he looked at the flailing hag. Rotten shields splattered as she lashed and twisted. The lance couldn't hold long. In his mind's eye, the hag was already loose and ravening through the crowds, then he remembered the duke's speech: Mircol had turned the river.

The strangers were hustling him from the island, desperate and wide-eyed.

"The dam!" Durand shouted. A few of the harrowed men stole glances at him, but not one of them stopped. He jerked in their hands.

"They've got to close the dam! Send in the river!"

Bearded elders and young boys looked down.

Someone said, "Right!" and the call went up.

IN THE LEATHER bottom of some peasant's boat, Durand got his breath back and soon found himself on his elbows in the grass. Lamoric sprawled beside him, alive. The red iron mask was gone, but another mask of muck and blood served just as well.

"Durand? Are you all right?"

Durand pawed at his own face with the shaking heel of his hand.

"I am," he answered.

"I thought it had you," said Lamoric—Lamoric, his lord, who had saved him. "Ah," Lamoric added, "here are the lads."

With curt glances, first Guthred, then Agryn, and then the rest crouched around their lord, swords in their fists. The fiend was still howling out in the water. Berchard shoved dry blankets into Lamoric's hands and Durand's.

Only Coensar did not stoop. Like a ship's master, he stood above them all, first looking across to the island, then, in a glance, taking stock of Lamoric's condition. Without a word, he strode up the bank for the duke's box.

"Host of Heaven," said Lamoric. "I thought I was dead. She

held me tighter than iron, and I could do nothing but hang there waiting for her. My head. It could have been a grape in her fist."

The wary knights shifted, giving Durand a glimpse of the hag down a narrow alley of knees and shinbones. Already, a clear tide poured into the channel, clean water rising on the flanks of the island. A swing of the hag's fist clipped a spray into the air. She flailed as the water rolled over her prison once more. And soon, a last reaching talon was all that could break the surface. The Glass swallowed the Isle and its prisoner as if they had never been.

Lamoric was looking him straight in the eye.

"Durand, you could have stayed in that boat," he said.

"No, Lordship," Durand said. He could not.

Lamoric looked into the Heavens and saw the marred clouds. "God. What does it mean?"

Durand had no answer.

Sir Agryn spoke. "The Blood of Kings, Lordship." He seemed uneasy. "It is the image of the day that King Carlomund left this world, five years past. You had to be near Windhover to see it so plainly." A vague memory of the day rose in Durand's mind: Acconel, a hundred-fifty leagues away, rocking as if it were a ship under a dark sky. When its king died of violence, the kingdom shuddered.

"I don't understand," Lamoric said. "Has someone died?"

Coensar reappeared, stepping through the circle to kneel at Lamoric's side. "I think we shall see that for ourselves soon enough, Lordship."

"What are you saying?"

"The Herald. He's put the Red Knight on the Tern Gyre roll." He grinned for a moment, with a glint of hard humor. "You'll be there to ask the king yourself."

21. The Seal of the Patriarchs

They made three leagues before Durand's boots had a chance to dry, riding the Hesperand borders for Tern Gyre. The Knight in Red did not tarry to eat the hero's portion, instead ordering his stunned retainers to strike their tents and take to the road.

They traveled in a silence that suited Durand to the ground, and they left Deorwen and her mistress-servant behind.

Suddenly, a gang of riders jounced past on the narrow forest track. Though not one would look Durand's way, they were not strangers: big Ouen, Badan the Wolf, one-eyed Berchard, and more. The whole retinue balled up around their lord where he rode at the head of their cavalcade.

When Lamoric noticed, Badan bellowed "Right!" and the whole conroi caught hold of their startled lord, heaving him up and out of his saddle.

"And this one!" shouted a voice at Durand's shoulder, and Durand found himself grabbed as well.

Then the branches over the track were swinging. Knights huffed and waddled between him and the sky, lugging him somewhere. He heard the river: the Glass.

Ahead, the first gang was already shouting. "One, two—" then, "Wait! He's still in his bloody mail coat," and "Shuck him! Peel him!" Lamoric had never taken the time to strip off his Red Knight gear. Durand, however, had got free of his own hauberk as soon as he could get the thing off. There were whoops and shouts of laughter.

One of the bearded thugs carrying Durand shouted helpfully, "Wait now, *this* one's ready!" Feet slithered in the riverbank clay, and then the bastards were swinging him: "One, two—"

"*—Gods!*" Berchard gasped, his voice shot through with real horror.

Durand's assailants checked their swing, tumbling Durand into the shallows before he could see what had happened.

When he spluttered to the surface, there wasn't a noise in Creation but for the river. In the midst of the mob, Lamoric sprawled shirtless in the track, looking for all the world like someone just cut from the gallows. Red wounds and bruises spread over his chest and shoulders, stark against his pale skin.

For a single heartbeat, Lamoric did not move.

Then he winced a wry smile, looking on the livid evidence of his beating for the first time, smeared, mashed, split, and grinning feebly at Coensar and the others.

"Worth every one."

Some nodded. It was plain to see there had been nothing holding their lord in his saddle but will.

"Aye, Lordship, maybe," murmured Berchard.

"All right," Coensar said, quietly. "We stop here."

"*Captain,*" Lamoric began, firmly.

"No, Lordship. Guthred? Agryn? Let's see what we can do about this. He'll be no good to anyone as he is."

An empty glade above the road would make a decent camp. "Durand," said Agryn, "lend us a hand." And Lamoric hissed as they took his weight.

"We've got leagues to cover before the Eye leaves us," Lamoric protested. Despite years in a castle yard, Durand had never seen a living man more badly beaten. Puckered grins of ragged flesh crowned the worst bruises.

"We'll need bear gall," breathed Berchard.

Guthred hissed, "You've *got* bear gall?"

Berchard shrugged. "You have it, you don't need it. You need it, you don't have it."

"Where's Coen?" Lamoric looked from face to face among his bearers. His eyes met Durand's. "Tell him—" he stopped, gasping as they shifted. "Tell him we'll stop here an hour. An hour, then we go on."

"Comfrey," said Guthred. "Yarrow. Bloodstone. Self-heal, maybe."

"Marsh mallow," offered Berchard.

"You've got it?" said Guthred.

"I think I've got some in my gear."

"Fresh?"

"We must press on," Lamoric said.

"I've bear grease in a salve," said Berchard. "And coral, blessed by the patriarch at Wave's Ending."

Lamoric twisted. "We haven't time to stop. We should—we should try for Hellebore by nightfall."

Agryn marshaled others to gather blankets, and they sought out a level spot. "What do you say, Guthred?" he asked.

"Plasters anyway. Poultice. Warm. Something to dull the pain. Something to draw the evil from the wounds. I've got all we need in my gear. We'll have to get the wounds clean first."

"This spot will serve as well as any," said Agryn, "though it might have been better to get further from the Glass and Hesperand. I will light a fire. Someone bring Guthred's things."

Gingerly, they lowered Lamoric onto a space of flat turf. By the look on his face, though, they might have been tossing him across a harrow. Durand found himself wincing.

He went pale, his head lolling, then reared up. "What day is it?"

"By my count, there are seven days until the tournament at Tern Gyre," Agryn said evenly.

"Agh. It's a hundred leagues."

"Nearer fifty, Lordship," Agryn said. "Most on the king's roads."

One of the boys handed Durand Guthred's bag. He remembered an earthenware flask the man used on the more battered knights, and found it quickly enough. The shield-bearer took it with a nod.

"A few things in wine," he told Lamoric, feeding the man a long swig.

Lamoric grimaced. "God, I hope it wasn't good wine."

It was all he could do to keep his head up.

THE SHOCK OF Lamoric's wounds receded a little from their minds as the men worked. Within the hour, the company had pitched tents and built a bonfire—at first to boil the various concoctions the muttering barber-surgeons devised, then to roast venison it seemed old Mornaway had sent along with them. Berchard and the old man's steward had also managed to smuggle a keg of decent claret into the baggage.

The whole company crouched round Lamoric, not willing to let him from their sight.

"Well, I for one thought our friend here was gone," said Berchard. "Then up *he* pops." The man thrust his bearded chin Durand's way. "Thrashing like a crocodile and straight after her. And she doesn't know what's hit her. Wakes up after God knows how long in the muck, and suddenly iron-shirted goats are crashing about on their hind legs."

"What else could I do?" Durand said. They were trying to make a hero out of him. It was just as well they hadn't seen what was in his mind.

"Berchard," said Agryn, "the lad cannot be goat and croco-dile both."

"And then—" Berchard continued, too loud with Lamoric asleep at his elbow. Catching himself, he continued in rough whisper, examining a poultice plastering Lamoric's shoulder. "And then His Lordship with that pole! It's no wonder our Herald wrote him in. Host of Heaven! If we'd known it was so easy, we could have skipped Mornaway's boy altogether and gone fishing for river monsters."

Big Ouen leaned back, knotting his fingers in back of his blond mane, gold teeth winking. "It all seemed so far away before now, this Red Knight scheme."

"And harebrained," added Badan.

"Badan. God's sake," snapped Berchard. He was just peel-ing the vile-looking poultice from Lamoric's shoulder as Badan spoke. If Lamoric's eyes were open, he would have heard.

"With a gross of good silver pennies for the season," Badan added.

Ouen held a big hand up flat, his straw-bearded face still thoughtful.

"Maybe that," he said. "But somehow I don't know if I ever reckoned we'd see Tern Gyre. Now, I can see us there in my mind's eye. All of us, with the pennons flying. The Herald and the prince looking on. All the best men of the kingdom won-dering who our Red Knight is, with their tongues wagging over everything we do. There's not one of us has had a chance like that."

"And if we win, eh?" Berchard said.

"Aye," Ouen said, and the whole company was nodding, firelight in their eyes. "No more roads. No more rain. Happy days for sure."

Cool as an eel, a breeze chose that moment to coil through the little campsite. The Eye of Heaven guttered in the damp boughs of Mornaway.

Despite the fire and blankets, Lamoric shuddered. Every man twitched a look his way, noting the drowned pallor and cadaver features—a specter looking very little like a hero who might lead them to a victory.

"We'll get him under cover," Agryn said, ordering Durand, Badan, and Ouen into action. The three shuffled their lord into his pavilion. The man's skin was hot as candle wax as Durand closed his hands round the lordling's ankles. Badan and Ouen then played nursemaid, hauling out rough blankets. Durand stood back against the canvas walls. Lamoric groaned. The group's physicians muttered over dressings and hissed orders.

Heremund popped through the tent flap, in a breath of smoke and without a word, kindling a lamp.

None of the others had noticed quite how dark it had become, but now the flame glowed over every stark bruise. And Durand remembered standing on the Barrow Isle with his heart divided, needing to save this man and wanting him crushed from Creation. Here, the living man lay like a vision of the dead one Durand had wished for.

He forced himself not to turn from what he had wanted.

Lamoric had caused him no harm—had saved his life, in truth. But Deorwen filled his mind's eye. He could hardly breathe for it.

Heremund was watching.

Turning from the others, Durand shoved through the tent flap and outside.

Three cloaked riders looming in the High Ashes track. The first had an axe at his hip. Frozen, Durand made out Lady Bertana's shape beyond the axeman, and Deorwen beyond them both.

Coensar and the others at the fire stood to meet the new arrivals, and Durand took his chance to slip into the cool gloom of the riverbank.

Deorwen swung down into the firelight, her face blooming in its glow. Durand retreated further into the shadows. It seemed to him that she might be searching from face to face.

Coensar put one knee in the mud.

"Lady Deorwen," he said.

"Sir Coensar."

"Your husband rests in his pavilion."

Her lips parted for a long moment before she spoke.

"I would see him," she said.

"Yes, Ladyship," Coensar said and conducted her from the

light—or almost. At the very edge of the firelight, Durand imagined another searching glance.

He stood then, his heart kicking in his throat. In a tent hardly ten paces away, Lord Lamoric lay shattered in his blankets—the same man who had pinned the hag to the earth when he could have fled—real and sick and alive. What was Durand doing?

A shovel bit into the ground.

Confused, Durand took a moment to spot Berchard in the brush. He must have bustled out of the tent right on Durand's heels. The old campaigner tossed his shovel aside and gingerly held a clotted mass of barley-meal over a hole.

"*Go,*" he said. "By the Powers of Heaven, go! Go and take the evil you carry from our lord. By the Champion, by the Warders, go!" With that, he let the foul poultice fall from his hands and into the earth.

Durand blinked. He must have taken another step backward. His heel sank into silt and pebbles, and, just as he felt the water grip his ankle, he heard a wet slap behind him, then another: *slap-hiss, slap-hiss.*

He turned and looked out over the Glass.

There, among the shadowed hulks of trees, pale figures swayed, like banners of worn linen. Sounds murmured above the gurgle of the river. The gray shapes moved along the far bank, half-invisible, though he could hear their voices—women's voices speaking and the slap of laundry on the stones. He had forgotten how near Hesperand was. The sharp tang of lye burned in his nostrils. He stumbled—just a half step to catch himself—and every pale shape froze.

Dark rents opened: mouths and hollow eyes all staring.

Somewhere beyond the fringe of trees, gray hounds bayed. He thought he heard someone murmur "Saewin."

"Durand."

Durand felt a hand on his arm. An ugly little man looked up at him, beady eyes blinking on either side of a mashed nose. Concern worked a crease between those eyes, and Durand knew the skald.

"Come away from the water," he said, and gave his arm a tug.

"Heremund," Durand said, stupidly. It seemed a long time since he had spoken with the little man.

The skald cast a shrewd look across the river.

"I would have seen us push through to Hellebore before we stopped. We are too near. Especially now," said Heremund. "The blow that shook that old hag free. That was no little thing. There's been nothing like it since the old king."

Beyond Heremund, Deorwen would be alone with her husband, crouching by him where he lay. But this was not the whole world. One man's heart was not the end of Creation.

He remembered the Heavens.

"Carlomund," said Durand.

Heremund made the fist and fingers at the dead king's name. "And before that God knows."

Durand nodded. "The Blood of Kings." It had been five winters since the old king died a-hunting. "In Windhover, old Carlomund went riding . . ." the ballad went. All his sons were there. They said Prince Biedin warned him to be careful, and that Prince Eodan and Ragnal rode with him. "Too many princes" was the general conclusion, but even a king can die in a fall.

"Someone's being a fool," said Heremund. "Kings and the land. The Patriarchs used to take better care."

"And that thing in the river," Durand added, probing.

"The old knots still hold old Errest together. Nobles sworn to kings: oaths for land, oaths for swords. Ties and bindings. And all the thousand thousand Banished spirits knotted to the land and bound since the *Cradle*. And there's the king smack at the heart of it all, keeper of oaths, crowned heart of the realm. Seal of seals. Three days under stone, and the whole realm is tied."

"Like the oaths that tore Hesperand from the world," Durand breathed.

"Even when the old fools've got it right, you can hear the air alive while the old king dies and the marked heir waits his turn to head down into the crypt of his fathers. Like the whole realm is thrown in the Heavens, but neither caught nor fallen."

"And a thing like that hag slips free," Durand concluded.

But who had died? He remembered Baron Cassonel on the bridge at Bower Mead, with all his grim talk of royal debts coming due.

"You heard Cassonel?" he asked.

"Aye. Could be that. Poor Ragnal. There ain't nothing's gone right for that one. Ever since his father fell off that horse—the old fool—there's been something. Now, it's the marches splitting. One year a drought, next a blight, then a famine. And always more taxes and more taxes, and there ain't been a penny in his strong room since they crowned him. Now, the Great Council has him, if they want him."

"Heremund, what if they put a usurper on the throne?"

"'As the king goes, so goes the kingdom.' So the wise women say. They are tied. That is the point."

"And a usurper would suffer with his stolen kingdom."

"Perhaps. What if the old rite doesn't hold? All those knots the Masters and the Patriarchs have woven. What if it all flies apart?"

People moved in the firelight.

"That explains why they've been sniffing around Radomor," Durand realized. "At least he's got the right blood."

"Beoran and the others have been skulking behind the scenes," Heremund whispered. "There's been a thousand men like Cassonel on the roads these last moons, racing over the realm, testing knots. Just this summer, Yrlac and Gireth were bound. What's become of that? It'll be a near thing, but it takes a cold heart to vote down Heaven's anointed."

Durand was lost. "Have they killed him, then?"

"That's the question. But I ask you, where was the middle of that mess?" Heremund pointed into the sky. "Did you see them ripples spread?"

Durand nodded. "From the south. Somewhere across the Glass from High Ashes." He could hardly forget.

"South or southeast, aye. Maybe the Plain of Yrlac? Maybe south Gireth toward the Blackroots?"

Durand didn't like to think of his father's Col right in the middle of that thing.

Mostly to himself, he said, "But the king's in the Mount of Eagles at Eldinor. They're saying Ragnal must be in Tern Gyre in a week's time. All fifty leagues north, and nowhere near Yrlac or Gireth or the mountains."

Gray-bearded Ailnor, Radomor, Radomor's child—

Alwen's son. All were the children of Carondas, who set aside the crown. There was as much royal blood in Yrlac as flowed in the halls of Eldinor. Had Radomor done it, then?

"Durand?" The skald peered darkly into Durand's face. "I should ask you about Radomor now, shouldn't I?"

"Aye."

A man on a mountaintop might have seen all of Heremund's messengers riding back and forth, but, from this riverbank, Durand was blind. The duke might have slain his son, or Radomor his father. Or both might have gone. Or the child. Forces were moving, and a man couldn't tell where.

For a time, he had known.

"Blood's been spilt in Yrlac," he concluded.

"That's all you will say?" asked Heremund.

"It's all I *can* say, for certain."

The skald put a hand on Durand's arm. "Let's get away from the water."

LAMORIC LIVED OUT the night and woke resolved to carry on. He would not cast aside what had cost them so much.

They set off once more, riding north along the borders of Hesperand, leaving the forests of Mornaway as Agryn said his Noontide Lauds.

Deorwen stole urgent glances Durand's way, but Durand quickly learned that crowds and the Eye of Heaven kept her off him.

He did not wish to speak.

All night and all morning, he'd heard the trees creaking in Hesperand, moaning and sobbing like voices. He was in no mood to tangle with Deorwen. He couldn't trust himself.

Just as the forest gave way, Lamoric cut his rouncy from the line. The sudden halt nearly pitched Durand from his saddle. He would have landed right on Heremund's back.

Lamoric sat leaning over his saddlebow, though he managed a grin.

"All right, lads," he said. "Here's the game." He twisted, squinting a look across the wide plain of Hellebore behind him. "I am informed that somewhere out there is the Lawerin Way. The Lawerin Way will carry us through the city of Lawerin to Eldinor and Tern Gyre beyond. But that—" He twisted once more, pointing across the plain where Durand could just make out a gray lump on the northern horizon. "*That* is Cop Alder, the first good lodging we'll hit for ten leagues, and it's on the Lawerin Way. Heremund tells me it's maybe five or seven leagues, but I say we don't camp before then. It means we'll be riding in late, but I say we try it. I say we ride until we get a hot supper, beds, and a roof over our heads."

Where once the men might have shouted "hoorah!" they only nodded. Murmurs passed among them.

Lamoric tried for a rakish smile. "All right. Cop Alder then. For a warm bed."

Durand gave Heremund a poke. "What's this Cop Alder?"

"Healers. And a good place to be with all these strange happenings. Coensar's put him up to it, and Agryn."

The cavalcade snaked north between the hamlets and hedges of southern Hellebore until it struck the Lawerin Way, a royal road some ten paces wide and clad in grooved stone. The racket of iron hooves on stone spooked some of the horses: Few had set foot on a proper paved road in their memory.

By dusk, Guthred was riding double with Lamoric, just to keep the man in the saddle. And, by that time, they had been within sight of the hilltop town for half the hours of daylight.

Now, looming over the Lawerin Way, the place seemed strangely still. Durand looked up at tall sandstone walls and steep roofs. From the sheer-sided look of the hill, he guessed that it had once been some chieftain's stronghold. Now, though, was anyone's guess.

"Here's your Cop Alder," said Heremund.

Beyond a forgotten ringwork, the town walls were oddly angular under their pitched roofs. No dogs barked. No children cried. Strange bastions jutted at the corners. Huge and squat and grim, Cop Alder looked all too regular and too strange.

And there were bells ringing.

"There," said Heremund. "There's your answer."

A cowled line shuffled from the town's high gate. A few of the knights around him made the fist and spread-fingered Eye of Heaven. Feet slipped and stumbled on the track under the weight of four biers. The muffled shapes of dead men hung draped in pale linen. Durand spotted a hummocked graveyard under yew trees at the bottom of the hill.

The dead men would pass close.

Strangely then, the procession veered their way. The elderly monk at the head of the company tramped right up—sending uneasy horses shying back—and stopped before Coensar and Lamoric, halting the others with a thud of the heavy staff in his fist. There was a broad smear of yellow ochre on each man's forehead.

The leader glanced up—despite the crowd and distance between them—at Durand. Then he turned his water blue gaze upon Lamoric, who sat like a dead man bound in his saddle.

The captain interposed himself. "Father, I'm called Coensar, a retainer in the service of His Lordship, Sir Lamoric of Gireth." There was no sense playing Red Knight games here.

"And I'm abbot here." Durand caught a trace of the south in his accent.

"My apologies, Father Abbot. Had I known your path, I would not have—"

"—But you have." The old man seemed to be wincing, twisting his head as he listened. Spindles of white stubble stood on his jaw, and there were scratches—some like the stroke of a pen's nib, but a few welted gouges as well.

Coensar nodded. "My men need beds, Father."

"Fair enough," said the old man. "I've men must find their beds yet this evening as well." He shoved his staff toward the biers. "And we'll see them tucked in before Last Twilight. Take your horses up and wait."

Coensar nodded sharply, and they wheeled from the procession to climb the flank of Cop Alder's hill.

As they crested the green earthwork, Durand took a look back across the plain toward Hesperand and Mornaway, retracing the whole long afternoon in an instant. Then his eye stopped.

Hard by the forest, he saw pavilions spread out against the darkness of the trees.

"That'll be Moryn," said Heremund. Durand hissed an oath, though Heremund ignored him. "I reckon we're not done with him yet."

Durand shook his head, and they rode through the open western gates of Cop Alder.

IT WAS, OF course, a monastery.

The men waited in the close chill of a narrow courtyard between inner and outer walls, their breath steaming in their hoods. Every man was uneasy, but, as Durand peered about himself, he saw traces of a pattern in the strange walls and tall roofs. The whole structure had been built in one piece, all of the same storm blue slate, layer on layer. A rich man's prayer book of carvings coiled over every doorpost and lintel.

"We pushed all day to reach this?" Badan was griping. "This frigid bloody maze will make—"

The nearest door squawked—loud as a crow—and the abbot stalked in with his somber brethren.

The old man slapped his broad hands like a workman returning from the fields. Berchard raised the fist and fingers. "What are you lot doing standing here?" the abbot demanded.

"Waiting," said Coensar. "Beds, and a meal if you have it."

"The meal, you've missed. It'll soon be Last Twilight now, so beds will have to do you. Have your serving men follow my lads to the stables. The rest of you had better follow me to the lay dormitory."

The abbot tramped off, for an instant setting a hand on Durand's chest to get past. The wide, water pale eyes met Durand's. Then he was gone, his staff ringing from the slate and off around a corner as the knights looked from man to man. Durand played crutch to his lord as they set off, following the echo of that knocking staff. Durand's memory returned to the forests of Gireth, as they wound their way through the strange building.

Bertana and Deorwen, following, were uncomfortably near.

The locking angles of rooftops turned above them as they walked what turned out to be a crabbed circle of narrow corridors taking them fully around the entire monastery before they could turn inward. Lamoric's pace allowed the others to move well ahead.

Finally, Durand and his lord turned the corner onto an empty passageway and silence—alone. Durand spotted a low door standing open. As he ducked under, the abbot faced him. The scratches marking the old man's face and knuckles stood starkly against his skin.

"This is where you'll be. And don't think I don't know what you are, you lot. You're no pilgrims, and you're no honest household guard. The Patriarchs don't hold with these orgies of extortion and butchery your kind has fallen into, and I don't care what you call them. You will mind where you go while you're here, and you'll keep silent."

The abbot winced tightly, noticing Lamoric.

"And him to the infirmary; two of you can take his arms. And those two." He gestured with the head of his staff to Deorwen and Bertana. "They'll go to the women's—"

Deorwen protested, just a heartbeat late, "I must stay with my—"

"*They* will go to the women's quarters and keep quiet." Two monks appeared to take the women out. Deorwen's eyes caught Durand's for the first time that day, and then she was gone.

There was silence in the gloom while the abbot waited. The men had been caught off guard.

The captain stood in the center of their group.

"Agryn?" Coensar said. "You'll give Durand a hand with His Lordship?"

Agryn nodded—after the briefest hesitation.

"Come," said the abbot.

"All right," said Coensar. "Everyone get comfortable. There are alcoves in here somewhere. And likely a candle."

"Rushlight," the abbot corrected from the corridor.

Durand and Agryn followed the old man into the passage, Lamoric between them.

"Wait," the abbot said.

Astonished, Durand watched as the old man pulled a black ring of keys from his belt, rattled the door shut, and turned the key on an armed conroi. Sigils had been painted over the door.

"Right. Follow me," the old man said and tramped off between the sheer, dark walls at a pace that curled Durand's lip.

THEIR SMALL PARTY walked another hitched circle round the maze, then turned inward once more where a vast well gaped at the heart of the monastery.

Durand hesitated on the threshold of the shaft. It might have been a keep hollowed from the storerooms to the open Heavens, or a mine, opened to the air. They were at the bottom of an emptiness, thirty paces wide and nearly twenty fathoms deep.

Beyond a screen of pillars, he heard shovels.

Monks, bent in prayer, shuffled in an open square. None looked up. As Durand wavered, he understood what he was seeing: They had locked a turf maze at the bottom of the stone one, the scuff of countless sandals wearing knee-deep tracks in the earth.

Lamoric's weight hung on Durand's shoulder. Agryn shot a look over the lord's neck: *come on.* They were losing the ancient abbot, and Lamoric could not last much longer on his feet. As it was, he hardly moved his legs.

Durand held his questions, and they passed two more shrouded bodies as they slipped through the deep garth. Fresh earth lay strewn on the flagstones.

The abbot with his yellow-smeared forehead stood, his arms crossed round his staff like some Banished thing from a mountain cave.

"Here," he said. "Bring him this way."

And, with a nod, they did, hauling Lamoric into another dim chamber. This one, however, was not empty. Wounded men—the abbot's brother monks by their garb—occupied several pallets.

Durand looked to Agryn. "What's happened?"

But the abbot silenced him with a raised hand: *Wait.*

"Leave him and go," the abbot said. "He'll be right again in no time. The warder will let you back." He gave Agryn another of his pointed looks. "I expect you can find your way, brother."

"Yes, Father Abbot," said Agryn, and caught Durand by the arm and rushed him out to retrace their steps through the stone maze.

"What's going on?" Durand demanded. He heard the bite of spades once more around some distant corner.

"It is difficult to be sure," Agryn hedged.

"He seems to know you."

"Aye, he knows. A man must be hard to live this way. They are watchers here. Pacing the maze since the *Cradle*. I do not know the story of this hill, but some wild chieftain will have called up some fiend here. And, whatever it was, seventy generations have not tramped it down. The people of this land were desperate when Saerdan and his Sons of Atthi first came. Your Heremund will not tell you that, I fear, but here you can feel it, even under this sacred weight of masonry."

The slap and rattle of their boots and scabbards followed them down the passageways.

Durand suddenly had a glimpse of the hill in his mind's eye: packed with clawed things. He imagined the solemn men in the cloisters, overwhelmed in a moment, buried or hauled under.

Agryn had truly begun to hurry.

"And they've lost men just as we nearly lost His Lordship on the Barrow Isle. All across the kingdom, it will be the same. It is a dangerous business to spill the blood of kings. People do not understand."

"That old man's stare," Durand said. "It's like a razor."

"He's blind, Durand. Cataracts."

Durand missed a step, but Agryn's pace was insistent.

"We must move," he said. "From what I can see of the Heavens, we are nearly at Last Twilight. I would not be abroad in this place after."

He was almost running, taking turning after turning with speed enough that Durand's flat soles caught and slid to keep up. Finally, Sir Agryn pelted into a corridor Durand recognized. A monk waited by a low and painted door, a ring of keys rattling in his shaking fist.

As the door shut them in darkness, the bells of the monastery's sanctuary rolled in their high towers, tolling for the last light of day.

The rushlights fluttered on a dozen amber faces against the dark.

"We're locked in," whispered Berchard, "but there's a half a wheel of sharp cheese, and a few pints of claret to wash it down."

It was the only time Durand ever heard old Agryn laugh.

A RUSHLIGHT'S RANCID flame is short-lived, and the old abbot had spared no more than they needed, so soon the men subsided into their stony niches. Beyond their dormitory, chilling sounds bounded down the dark passageways of Cop Alder. Monks chanted. Distant screams shot through the dark. Agryn muttered; the click of his tongue and teeth matched the monkish rumble. Durand could feel the air shivering in his clothing like a living thing.

"Ah," said Berchard. "It's nights like this I see things with my Lost eye, you know."

"For God's sake," hissed Badan from the blackness, *"keep them to yourself. Talk of something else."*

"What of Moryn then? What do you think of him tracking us north, eh?" said Berchard.

"Aye," Badan said. "What's that whoreson want now?"

Coensar answered, "He's bound for Tern Gyre, just like us." There were oaths and groans. "He'll be carrying his father's vote to the Great Council. They must all be there."

A yowl leapt through the passages beyond the door, the shock so strong the hinges clicked.

Shadows twirled the thread of light under the door, while knights and shield-bearers stared, mute.

Someone hissed, *"Gods."*

"Sleep all of you," said Coensar. "I promised you beds, and you have them. Now sleep."

In his alcove of hard-edged slates, Durand rolled onto his shoulder, listening to Agryn's mutter and the thready sounds beyond the door. He wondered what had gone on in Yrlac. Nearly, he prayed that it was Radomor who'd been hounded to his death: a death at the hands of that grim-faced cadre of knights who surrounded Duke Ailnor. It would mean that this was the worst, and that the shock would pass and the kingdom emerge whole and sound. But he had seen Radomor, with his bald skull hot as a cauldron, glowering from his father's throne.

He must know. It was good they were going to Tern Gyre. The magnates were gathering: Beoran and Yrlac and Hellebore and Windhover and Gireth and all the others. Lying there in the dark, Durand knew that he needed to see what storm had struck the realm.

As exhaustion pulled him down into sleep, he heard many men threading their whispers with Agryn's muttered prayer.

———

WITHOUT WARNING, THE door rattled open, spilling watery daylight across the room. The abbot stooped in the gap, twisted and black as some hieratic sign.

"First Twilight, Milords. Time you were gone." He paused a mad instant. Then the bells tolled for the daylight. He grinned, saying, "There. I wouldn't lie to you," and was gone.

Durand rolled painfully from his stone cot, planting booted feet on the flagstones and scratching fleabites on his neck. "Bricks and beds," said Berchard.

"Wha?" Badan was grimacing.

"Two things you shouldn't make without straw," was Berchard's answer.

Others groaned and brayed like a barnyard.

"I'll check on His Lordship," said Coensar, hands on his knees. His breath steamed in the chill air. "The rest of you see if you can pry something warm to eat out of these tight buggers. Remember, we'll see Tern Gyre in a few days, right?"

Durand's first need, however, was the privy. First on his feet, he ducked into the passageway and got directions from the warder monk—too many twists and turns—and set off.

It was strange seeing the place under the pale twilight after the wild sounds of the night before. Like memory, a mist swirled around his ankles and beaded the carved Powers and beasts round the doors. Whatever Lost souls had been racketing through the place, they were sleeping now that the Eye had returned to the vault of Heaven.

Meanwhile, Durand's quest was getting urgent. Twice, he doubled back, certain that he must have gone the wrong direction. Finally, he ducked into a narrow room he had never seen. A stone bench along the wall sported six holes.

The blind abbot stepped out in front of him.

"You, is it? Wandering off?"

Durand wasn't about to explain.

The man grunted. "You're not at the center yet, but you will be, yes?"

"Father, that's not where I'm going."

"What? What're you going on about?" He grinned in the pale light, showing gaps between wide yellow teeth. "You'll find your way to the center yet, mark me. But there'll be trials: fire and water and faith and blood."

All Durand wanted was to be left alone with the privy bench; he'd had enough of prophecy.

"*Ah*," the abbot said. "They've already been at you, haven't they? Have they called you Bruna?"

Durand took a half step backward.

"Bruna of the Broad Shoulders. It's a wise woman's game. They'd see Bruna in you, and say nothing—or warn you that honor and treachery are two sides of the same door. Hags. You're a big stone. You'll make ripples. That's all they see. They love to natter about the big stones, the wise women."

A white brow twitched over one bright, blind eye. There was still a cracked smear of ochre.

"Don't worry," said the old man, leaning close as a conspirator. "What I see is mine to know. I keep secrets." He was tapping his nose. "All of this business. Oaths and fear. Just remember what we're fighting here."

"Fighting?"

"The Son of Morning. His Host. The Banished. This is a kingdom that'll fall hard when it tumbles. It's like a net stretched tight over all those things—a net of knotted oaths. Creation is packed with Lost souls and creeping fiends, and, the Patriarchs of old, they stuck the king in like a finger holding all the knots. You think we're not all fear-mad in this place? That we would not run away if we could? Cop Alder's shaking like a fat man's buckles. But we've sworn oaths fit to curdle the blood, and, if we ran, who would hold the door behind us?"

The man's pale head nodded. "It is the same with you: hemmed in with oaths and fear and dreams and women."

Durand ducked past the man's leer, stalking down the narrow room. He could wait no longer, and, when he looked up, he saw that the ancient abbot had not left.

"Remember what is at stake," the blind man said. "Remember it is everything!"

No one waited in the refectory when he found it; everyone was crammed in Cop Alder's tall kitchen. He heard Lamoric's voice before he saw him. Durand took the last steps to the doorway warily.

"As soon as we're able, we must go. It was clear as—" he hesitated, staring from startled knight to startled knight before snatching up a knife. "As this blade, I tell you. Every bit of it.

"The banners rippling over the headland like fresh blood. Blades and helmets flashing. Knights and warhorses storming the lists by the hundred. Wooden stands steep as a thousand siege ladders thrown against the walls all around. And everyone was there."

Pale as a candle, Lamoric stood in the midst of his retainers, eyes shining like a pair of fat pearls. He still held the knife.

"You were wrapped up in it, Badan. And Coensar." He spotted Durand hesitating in the entrance. "And you, Durand, you were there. Powers of Heaven . . ." He goggled like a fish, while Berchard and Heremund and even Deorwen shot Durand looks from apologetic to pleading. "Walking on the horses, by my oath. Walking on the horses with that old sword flashing. And Agryn." He wheeled to face Agryn. "I saw you. You were riding. Riding all wrapped in your yellow gear. I saw yellow everywhere."

Deorwen's face was stricken.

Durand tried to make sense of what he was hearing. "Was it a dream?" asked Durand. "Have you had a dream?"

"Aye," said Lamoric. "While I lay in that infirmary. I've had one of Deorwen's dreams! They were cheering us, Durand. Cheering us! The whole kingdom was looking on and cheering us! I should tell the wise women.

"We must thank these holy men for their hospitality, and then make all haste to Tern Gyre! Come on!"

Lamoric tottered past Durand and out of the kitchen. A dumbfounded troop of knights and serving men churned in the room, then snatched up loaves and cheese, and followed their lord. Durand felt the first stirrings of something like a crusader's frenzy in his heart and was carried along on the tide.

He caught hold of Heremund in the press.

"Did he really have the dream, Heremund?" A man could

fall from Creation with his eyes shut. He might have glimpsed Tern Gyre.

"*I reckon so,*" hissed Heremund with a glance around, "But Deorwen, she went to the infirmary door for him. The monks said there was screaming. All night, he was wild with fever and screaming."

"*Heaven's King,*" breathed Durand.

"Aye," said Heremund. "We are not finished yet, friend."

🪢 22. Wings of Memory

A day's ride from Cop Alder, the Lawerin Way sank into a coppiced wood near Medlar. There, between little Medlar and a nameless hamlet, the party pitched wet tents and gathered around a double campfire to fight the chill. The skald plucked the first notes of a hollow tune from his mandora. He had hardly played in days.

Pulling a blanket up around his ears, Ouen let the firelight flash in his gold teeth. "I'm going to get me a wife and hall somewhere. Settle down before I catch one the monks can't patch. What's fame for if not land and women? And not just anyone, either. Only the fairest widows for Sir Ouen. He was with the Knight in Red at the Gyre, eh?"

Beside him, Lamoric laughed out loud. It was hard not to believe in the young lord's dream, gleaming over the dark of bruises and omen. Every man had caught his ardor.

"That's the way, isn't it?" said Badan, leering. He grappled with his belt and jingled the pennies in his pouch. "Gets them every time."

Across the fire, Lady Bertana clucked her tongue. Glancing up, Durand caught a look from Deorwen.

He had not allowed himself one word with her since he had learned the truth. He wanted to forget everything that had happened between them and simply be the man the others thought he was. But she took his breath. With the smallest of gestures, she let him know that she wanted to step away.

He would not leave.

"What about you, Heremund?" asked Lamoric. "Will you fight beside us?"

"Me?" The skald smiled. "I'll be singing 'the Red Knight of Tern Gyre.' " He startled a chord from the gut strings of his mandora.

Deorwen had begun to stand, her eyes on Durand. He felt the pressure to join her.

Just then, a sharp knock among the trees turned every head back toward Cop Alder. No one moved.

Coensar was still as a hawk, watching.

Another knock followed, then a pop sharper than anything coming from the campfires.

Durand got to his feet.

"*Right*," said Coensar. "See what's out there. And take Agryn." Agryn nodded, standing. "Any trouble, come right back."

Without a word, the two men stepped from the firelight and into the gloomy damp. Durand had left Deorwen, and, even facing God-knew-what in the dark, there was relief in walking away.

After thirty paces, the gloom and the noises beyond pushed Deorwen from his head. The roads teemed with madmen and thieves; he had seen as much with his own eyes.

Another dull report echoed down the road. Durand touched the worn pommel of his sword.

"How far?" he whispered.

Agryn rubbed his jaw. "They are some way off still, I think."

"I suppose we ought to get a look at them," Durand said. Neither of them wore armor.

"Aye."

"Now I could use that blind old man and his second sight," Durand joked.

Agryn took a moment to peer into Durand's face.

"He had things to say," Durand admitted.

"Such folk do not always realize that we are not all like them."

Something in the man's look hinted. "He spoke to you as well, didn't he . . ."

After a moment's stillness, Agryn let out a long breath. Just then, something moved up the track. They heard murmured voices.

"Let us come upon them from the forest," Agryn whispered, and led Durand silently up the roadside bank and into the trees.

Within twenty paces, Durand could see firelight. The wet tang of stables reached his nostrils. Men were laughing.

Durand spotted a screened approach, and, hooking a finger toward Agryn, wormed himself behind a knot of blackthorn right at the camp's edge. Agryn pointed to the canvas of one tent wall: Lord Moryn's blue and yellow diamonds.

In the branches, something scrabbled to life right over Durand's head.

A maze of oak branches stretched against the Heavens. Half-lost among the crabbed lines moved black and shaggy forms: rooks.

One brute flapped its wings, dropping a rain of debris into Durand's eyes: loud.

"What's that?" said a voice from the camp. Durand knew the bullying tone from his wrestling match.

"Spirits in the bushes, you reckon? Should we go have a look?"

Durand grabbed his sword, but saw that Agryn seemed ready to come out of hiding. His hand was nowhere near his blade.

Recognizing their difference of opinion, Agryn nodded toward the trees, and the two faded back into the woods—a sensible compromise.

THE NEXT DAY, an oxcart was all it took to catch two companies of mounted knights-at-arms.

As Lamoric's men wound their way north, the Lawerin Way sank between steep banks until only a mounted man might see the mills and towers of passing villages from the road. The ancient way narrowed, trees crowded close, and a vast oxcart lumbered in the track ahead of them.

There was no way around, and soon Lord Moryn's party was right on their heels.

Durand found himself at the head of the party, driven nearly into the back of the tall cart.

A ragged black shape alighted on a branch overhead.

"I suppose my father will have sent Landast," Lamoric was saying, voice muffled in the red helm he must wear with so many of Moryn's men right behind them. "I don't imagine he'll stir himself to travel as far as Tern Gyre this time of year."

As the cart lumbered on, Durand saw more of the black birds. They hopped and chortled among themselves.

"Your father's not a young man," Coensar answered.

"And my brother will carry his vote to the council with great care. Landast does everything with great care."

Coensar smiled indulgently.

All around now, black mockers lurched and chuckled in the canopy of branches. Others had begun to notice. There were scores, thick as the leaves of a black summer.

"Durand," inquired Lamoric, "Coen was meant to say, 'He must be a comfort to your father' just then, was he not?"

Durand blinked. "Yes, Lordship."

"You see?" Lamoric said.

Two of the ragged black birds swung in to squat on the roof of the cart. Jet eyes glittered.

As Durand's mouth opened, someone at the tail of the party began to cause a commotion. Durand twisted to see Waer, the wrestler, arguing with some of Guthred's men. Horses and men jostled in the narrow roadway.

In the commotion, the huge cart jerked out of the ruts to crash in a bawl of oxen. The rooks croaked into the air, abandoning their roost and chuckling at some private joke.

Durand twisted, a warning on his lips, just in time to catch a furtive stranger scrambling in the back of the cart.

They were ambushed.

"Down, Lordship!" he hissed, as armed men scrambled into view on every side. Only two paces from Lamoric's throat, a brown hand yanked the cart's cover wide and thrust a crossbow forward.

Durand was already leaping. He got his hand out. With a finger-numbing clank, the heavy weapon snapped its bolt into the Heavens. A second man inside was just raising his bow, and Durand could see no way but to hurl the first attacker into the second. In an instant, a bloody steel point stood from the hapless assassin's ribs.

Then there was someone scrambling in front of the cart. Durand leapt over the driver's bench and out among the hobbled oxen. One of the brutes screamed and kicked from the ground. Beyond it, stood a figure from another world: Gol Lazaridge, with his glass-chip eyes flashing and his head cocked in surprise.

"Bloody Durand, I don't believe it," he sneered and, with a smooth gesture, drew his sword.

Hopelessly, Durand noted that the man—a better swordsman than Durand already—wore a coat of mail rings. Durand had only his surcoat and tunic between him and the man's blade.

"Gol," he said, as coldly as he could manage.

"You cost me a plum spot, lad." The captain grinned to show the black slot where most of his upper teeth should have been. "But I'm working everything out now with this little surprise." He nodded toward the fighting, then paused. "A gift for my master, eh? And now here you are, a gift for me as well. The Lord of Dooms can surprise one."

Durand got his hand on his own sword just in time. With a sudden lunge, Gol's blade shot the distance between them. Only Durand's mad dodge and the half-freed blade of his sword saved him.

Gol was smiling.

Durand got his sword up between them, feeling as though any breeze could cut him. His blade was shaking. He needed a mail coat. Meanwhile, Gol settled in behind his shield, leaving Durand with nothing but shins and glinting eyes to swing at.

The old captain moved again, blinding Durand with his shield and whipping cuts at his shins and ankles. Durand blundered back into the legs of the kicking ox.

Then Gol stepped away.

Already, blood pounded lights in Durand's eyes. He could hardly breathe. The whole world had dwindled to five paces of cart track. He heard cloven hooves scrabble against the cobbles. All the dreams and fears in Creation wouldn't help him now, if he didn't find a way to beat the man in front of him.

When Gol lunged, Durand attacked.

A lad in the Acconel yard once told him you could beat a dog by ramming your arm down his mouth, and that's what Durand tried. Beating Gol's blade aside, he leapt down the man's sword arm.

In the collision, Durand caught Gol around the neck. The man snarled. Shield and mail and swords caught the man's hands like shackles. He scrabbled backward. Durand twisted. They were bound together, sword and sword, and arms straining.

Durand could not let go.

Then the old captain dropped. Though Durand held on, he lost his grip on Gol's sword. He could feel the wet shock of the man's blade—too close for a proper swing. Both men sucked at the air and strained. All Gol needed was an instant to leap off, and Durand was done. The captain smashed back, using his skull to crack Durand's nose. Durand could feel his fingernails slide and tear against chain links. An elbow rammed the last air from his lungs. There were only heartbeats left.

Gol had a knife at his belt.

In a scrabbling instant, Durand's fingers caught the weapon. Gol must have realized, but Durand was on the man's back and already ripping the blade free. The captain's hands locked in Durand's face and hair, but Durand drove the dagger's point upward, scrabbling over mail-shirt and collar. He could feel the man's nails screwing into his eye, then, finally, the dagger slipped from iron links and shot home, deep in the captain's throat.

Durand lay half-pinned in the road. It was as though someone had overturned a cauldron of blood. As the gore ebbed among the cobblestones, he heard the rooks laughing.

🔘 23. The Broken Crown

The rooks spun and tumbled down the Lawerin Way, a cackling cloud of rags. Beyond the cart, the sounds of fighting were finished.

Numb, Durand stepped past the crippled ox—still gulping convulsive breaths—and shuffled to where he was sure to find a killing ground. He remembered crossbows and figures moving on the banks, too close and too many. Some—or all—would be dead.

But familiar faces glanced up.

Between the two ditches, knights and animals sprawled in clumps. Shield-bearers picked through the wreckage, clearing the road. In the midst of it all, a knot of men crouched round Lamoric's prone form. Durand could not see whether their lord lived or died.

Faces popped up to look at him: Heremund, Berchard, Agryn. Coensar's face was stern. Each man wore his own version of shock. Finally, he saw Deorwen. Bent very low, she looked up into his face as though she was looking at a dead man.

Abruptly, Lamoric craned his neck. A sword wound had split the sleeve over his shoulder. *"Hells,"* he breathed. *"What have they done to you?"*

Durand blinked. He went to brush at his cloak, and saw his hands—shaking and bloody as a butcher's. A sticky mask covered his face, and his cloak stuck and clung with the stuff.

"No no," he said. "I met the captain on the road. It's his, or most of it."

There was sick, gusty laughter.

"Gods, Durand, wash up. We'll all be sick," Lamoric managed.

Deorwen was raising a hand, shaking, to her face.

Through luck or the intervention of the Powers, Lamoric's company had lost only three horses and two men, though a few had taken crossbow bolts.

"We're lucky," said Coensar. "You don't walk out of a trap like this, let alone drive the bastards off. They hadn't the men for it, and I think we got more warning than they intended."

A commotion turned their heads.

Stalking through the wreckage came Waer the wrestler at the vanguard of half-a-dozen knights, including Lord Moryn himself. Durand and a few of the others stood up to intercept him as Lamoric shoved his helmet back on, grumbling an oath.

"Very pretty," said Waer. He set big fists on his hips.

"You should watch what you say," Ouen warned, but Waer only laughed.

"Very pretty indeed. We all get bottled up behind your lot, and then they're on us. What did you pay?"

Lamoric forced himself into the thick of the confrontation. "I lost men!"

Waer sneered. "Or did they threaten you? Was that it? You had another half league behind them than we did. Did they have you at the point of a sword, telling you to shut up and let us come on? Was that it? A coward's bargain?"

"Waer!" said Moryn.

"It's easy to call off your dog after he's bitten, isn't it, Milord?" said Lamoric. Durand could hear a hitch of pain in his voice. "Why don't you just say what you wish and have done with it? This man and his temper are a bloody thin excuse."

Waer lunged forward, caught short by his friends even as his fingers hooked the air at Lamoric's throat.

"You are enough to make a man ill, Moryn," said Lamoric. "You needn't worry about us getting under your feet any longer. There is more than one way to Tern Gyre, and I won't be on the same road with you any longer. Coensar?"

Coensar nodded stiffly.

"And Guthred?" Lamoric said. The aging shield-bearer looked up from his work in the blood and torn flesh. "Get that lot ready to travel. We'll find a sanctuary to take the dead. And get a party forward to butcher those oxen and heave them out of the road."

THEY LEFT THEIR dead in a town called Lanes Hall and rode north down back roads as a ship tacks into the wind. Where the Lawerin Way would have been straight and clear, now they navigated a maze of hamlets, following Heremund the skald. The little man knew every well and standing stone in Errest, but mysterious strangers stalked the countryside, and black shapes flapped from felons swinging at every crossroad.

They chose to make for Port Stairs. The men judged that from its cliffside perch above the Broken Crown, the city was no more than twenty leagues across the bay from Tern Gyre.

Berchard swore that coasters and fishermen crossed the Crown every day.

Outriders questing ahead of the party reported lone horsemen and slinking strangers among the hedgerows, though none would stand when challenged. Once, they heard hoofbeats over a rise—a fleeing rider. Durand could feel eyes on them from every side. He shot a glance at Deorwen and kept his hand near his blade.

Out ahead, Badan and two of Guthred's shield-bearers were hunting for a refuge.

"You can feel the buggers, closer and closer," muttered Ouen. "A hand's closing about us. We'll wind up missing Lord Moryn's party yet."

"Mind what you say," cautioned Berchard. The Sons of Atthi did not name a doom they hoped to avoid.

"I've never seen an outlaw band who'd attack so many swords," said Ouen. "It's madness, or it's not finished."

Abruptly, Agryn spoke. "I'd be happier if we had shelter."

They were losing the light of Heaven.

Coensar stood high in his stirrup irons, twisting to look out over the gloomy fields. "There!"

Badan and his shield-bearers appeared from the gloom ahead, their horses puffing clouds.

"What news?" demanded Coensar.

"There really are men on these roads, Coen," Badan said, eyeing the hills and hedges. "Luring us into some hard corner or waiting for a chance, I can't say. Quick to ride and slow to answer, anyway. But we've found a place. The plowman we rousted called it 'Attorfall.' Big enough to get inside and bolt the door."

"Let us hurry," commanded Lamoric.

DURAND JUDGED IT a miracle that Badan had found the place at all.

In the dusk, a deep curve of shadow swallowed the village entirely. Badan and his shield-bearers pointed at what seemed a lonely, oak-scabbed hump of hill, and no one believed them. Then they saw it. The whole village—two dozen barns and cottages—huddled where the hill's old flank had slumped into the road. Shingles, thatch, and walls were green with moss and black with damp. A dog barked.

"Hells, Badan," said Berchard, "there's a wellborn man living in this warren?"

"Some vassal knight of Hellebore's," Badan answered.

"Heaven help him."

Ouen winced. "Aye. Look there. A stone house."

"It's green as old pork," was Berchard's dubious answer.

Now, the dog was yowling.

"Let us get inside," prompted Agryn.

They rode on into the cramped alleys of the village and under the staring eyes of long-haired cattle. Durand watched Deorwen and Bertana moving through the damp as faces peered from between the green boards of their shutters.

All of the men went armed.

Berchard pointed at an ox. "I can actually see mold growing on this one. They're more than half vegetable, these brutes. I—"

"—Keep your eyes open, all of you, and your mouths shut," directed Coensar. "No more surprises."

At the next corner, a stooped manservant met them. This was no knight-at-arms.

"Sir," said Lamoric. "I am Lamoric of Gireth and these are my retainers and traveling companions. We have encountered trouble on the road and crave the hospitality of your master. There are womenfolk among us."

The servant regarded them wordlessly, slack and gray as a mushroom.

"We mean no harm," said Lamoric.

Another moment of silence passed. Durand heard leather straps creak around him—belts and gauntlets. No one wanted to turn back into the shadows on the road.

Without a word, the servant turned, and the company followed him through a crowd of sheds and coops and into the gloomy entry stair of the greenish manor house.

Durand kept an eye on arrow slits and upper windows, and kept his fist on his blade.

Stepping through an open door, the whole party crowded into the stair—a place damper than tombs—and a door rattled open above them. Durand followed the others shuffling into a cavernous darkness, conscious of keeping himself between Deorwen and the unknown.

But they found only the lank servant bowing in the gloom. "Sir Warin of Attorfall," he announced.

And no host answered.

The room was dark as a pool and nothing twitched. A dog was growling. Two dogs. Badan was already grumbling when a vague shape finally shifted in the murk.

Lamoric cleared his throat. "Sir Warin? I am Lord Lamoric, second son of Abravanal, Duke of Gireth. These are my retainers and traveling companions."

Durand thought he made out the long shape of a table.

"You come armed into my hall," grunted a voice.

"We met trouble on the road." He lifted his hand, triggering a booming bark from one of the dogs. "We mean no harm."

Eerily, flames appeared in the dark silence, bobbing in the empty air. They could have been candles borne by Lost souls. The lamps clunked down on the tabletop with a whiff of fish oil.

"Dinner and a roof?" said the reluctant shape that must be Warin.

"Aye," said Lamoric. "For a night. My men and I are bound to Port Stairs on my father's business."

It was a simple lie.

Warin grunted again, and the manservant ushered the men silently to his master's table where smoky lamplight gave the party a better look at their host: a sour old man, his thin hair bristled over the pale bladder of his face. He sat between two simperingly uneasy women, each like toadstools. Flustered, they were almost too late to usher Deorwen and Lady Bertana to sit by them.

As the men settled uneasily upon the benches, new servants appeared from the dark, thudding trenchers down and leaving the party with flat loaves and a wheel of what looked like yellow wax. Men like Badan and Ouen made faces, though Lamoric held his pleasant smile and picked up a bit of bread.

From the strain in his neck, he might as well have tried to bite an old woolen stocking.

In the candlelight, Durand could make out two monstrous mastiffs, bone-gray and looking as big as steers.

"You've a lot of men with you," their host grunted.

"I have, and I'm sure we're grateful for whatever you can spare. Have you had many guests of late?"

"No. No guests. It's lean times."

The servants returned, setting down tumblers and slopping out beer. One of the simpering mushrooms pulled at her lord's sleeve.

"These two are my daughters," Warin said, an introduction that provoked nodding bows from the pair.

In silence then, the men took their second bites of coarse bread or scrabbled at what they hoped was cheese.

Durand shifted on the bench, and his hand touched something on the seat: a pair of men's gloves. Well made, but too new for Warin, and he had never seen them before.

"So, Sir Warin," Lamoric ventured. "You will have seen the signs in the Heavens?"

"I've seen. Turned the milk sour in half my kine."

As the man scratched his wattles, his servant slipped in at Durand's elbow. The gloves were gone when Durand looked.

"And there are men on the roads. Messengers, maybe. Spies. I wondered if you might have heard something."

"There's always strangers on the road. More when times are uncertain. If you're asking after the king and his kin," Warin said, "we've heard naught, though I wouldn't be surprised with tax on tax and fines and levies. And now this great loan. No one much liked the story of Carlomund riding out with those two elder boys of his and coming back with a busted neck."

"Sir Warin," Lamoric warned.

"No one's ever much liked King Ragnal."

"And what of His Grace of Hellebore? Has your duke sent you warnings of his plans? I'm told the Great Council will sit at Tern Gyre."

"He'll do as sees fit."

"He's sworn his allegiance at the high sanctuary in Eldinor."

"Many oaths were sworn to old Carlomund."

"Some might call that treason."

"And some might call it late!" The old knight stood and snapped his fingers for dogs and daughters both; the whole lot got to their feet. "Finish as you like. You will not stay long, I trust."

Attorfall and his kin left for the wooden stair that led to rooms on the upper floor.

"My father would have hanged that man, I think," muttered Lamoric. He seemed tired. Deorwen cast her eyes down.

"I'd hang him for this wheel of cheese." Ouen gestured to the waxy block.

Lamoric nodded toward the upstairs rooms and asked his captain, "Are we in danger, do you think?"

"Attorfall does not seem a man of action, Lordship," Coensar whispered carefully. Servants still prowled the gloom.

"And no one could have known we'd stop here," Berchard added.

"We should be on our guard," Coensar concluded. "Men at the windows. A man on the door."

"Who are the bastards?" said Ouen. "Those weren't common outlaw brigands this morning, were they Badan?"

"You'd never go for a company of knights," he admitted. "There's plenty better game on the roads. Priests. Traders."

"You heard what Moryn's man said," Lamoric replied. "He said we arranged this trap. What if it's him? Is it so hard to believe Moryn might have been behind the whole thing? What better way to hide their complicity than to point a finger at us?"

Durand did not believe it. Gol had not expected to meet him. There had been more than the Red Knight's men on that road.

"Which way will the Duke of Mornaway vote?" Durand murmured, surprised to hear his voice aloud.

Men turned.

Agryn spoke, choosing his words. "Duke Severin is a faithful vassal." Lamoric shot a sharp glance at the long-faced knight, but Agryn continued. "There is honor in his house. He would never vote to cast his king down, not if it cost him his last acre."

Agryn looked Durand full in the face, waiting.

Durand swallowed as Deorwen's stare joined the others.

"That captain," he said. "The man I killed. I knew him from Yrlac. I worked for him. He was called Gol."

Some nodded, maybe having heard Gol's name or having met the man. Some were puzzled. He wondered how many now knew he had served Radomor. He wondered what Deorwen understood.

"Radomor's man?" Coensar pressed.

"He made it sound as though he was on the outs with Lord Radomor. My fault, getting away, I think. He meant the ambush as a present for Radomor somehow."

There was a lot of shifting around the table while Durand schooled his features. He dared not look to Deorwen. Finally, Ouen thrashed his head, astonished.

"But Radomor, he fought in the Marches. He led his father's host under the king's banner."

Agryn nodded. "He was gravely wounded leading the vanguard on the second day. A fine career nearly blighted."

"But *I've* had nothing to do with Radomor," protested Lamoric. "He was my brother-in-law. I don't understand."

Durand struggled. This brother-in-law had sealed his wife in a tower. In all of Durand's confessing, he had never quite said as much. Now, he had delayed too long.

But Coensar was nodding.

"Lord Moryn carries his father's proxy," he observed.

"And this was to be Gol's little gift for his erstwhile master?" Lamoric said. "I wonder. How would he have taken it? I remember once my sister's cat left an adder in her bed. Dead, though."

"Gol was a hard man," Durand said, a coward still.

"The man was a savage," Berchard amended. Agryn shot a disapproving look across the table; a wise man did not speak ill of the newly dead. Berchard finished timidly: "I saw him in Pendur."

"So he might well have gone further than anyone asked him," Lamoric reasoned. "A lord must be careful whom he takes as his liegeman."

Coensar spoke, eyeing the shadowy corners of the feasting hall. "Maybe Gol was hunting Moryn. Maybe he never meant to find two strong parties in that road. Maybe he thought he had help. We can't know. The roads beyond this hall are still thick with strangers. Lamoric, taken, might make a lever to change his father's vote. Maybe Moryn's not quite the man his forefathers were. Eat. Watch. We don't have far to go."

They finished their lean meal and bullied the stooped manservant for some old straw pallets. The women and the wounded got the good ones, though Deorwen complained. The rest—those not on watch—stretched blankets over damp straw, silverfish, and earwigs, muttering charms against vermin.

Durand lay on one shoulder, listening to the farts and grumbles of the men and to the rustle of things alive in the dank Attorfall straw.

Deorwen was breathing somewhere in the dark. He tried to put it from his mind.

He pictured Radomor boiling in that furnace hall down in Ferangore, and all the magnates riding to the Council at Tern Gyre. There were too many men too angry with Ragnal, and there were too many Cassonels stitching them together.

Durand wondered how many votes the magnates had. If the fools meant to overthrow their king, they would need to win at the Great Council, and they would need someone to stand in the king's place. But Radomor had not answered when Cassonel asked, and he was not heir while his father lived.

But someone had died in Yrlac.

Whatever Radomor once had been, Alwen's betrayal and the nagging doom of a skald must have changed all that. He might do anything.

If you set aside Lost Hesperand and the Marches, there were thirteen duchies. Cassonel's Duke of Beoran would vote to throw the king down. Mornaway would never, and old Abravanal of Gireth would no more rebel than he would sprout wings. Cassonel had spoken of some angry heir coming to power. Durand tried to remember the duchy. Was it Cape Earne? And what of Hellebore? And the widow who held Saerdana and Germander. How would she cast her vote?

Something chose that moment to scamper across his ankles on tiny needle claws.

Durand mashed his palms over his eyes. War at the heart of the realm would sweep up every man, woman, and child in Errest, catching them all by their countless oaths and tearing the land to pieces. What did a king's man do when his own sworn lord declared for a usurper? What oaths did a man keep?

When Durand opened his eyes, a tiny flame stirred at the top of the stair. It winked in the first floor passage where old Warin's room was. After an instant, the light swelled. In its wobbling circle, Durand made out Warin's sour face.

But there was a stranger in that circle as well. Durand remembered the gloves.

"Durand?" one of the watchmen asked.

In a moment, Durand had crossed to the stairs. Fumbling at first, he caught hold of the wooden steps and vaulted up.

Though they had only seen one door into Attorfall—as the hall backed on the hill—there were plenty of windows in the master's rooms on the upper story. A trapped man could escape that way.

At the far end of the high passage, a door pinched out the light. Durand charged. In a heartbeat, he was down the passage and throwing his weight against the door.

Warin spun, half-dousing his candle. Durand had seen what must be Warin's bedchamber; a cloaked shape bent in the window frame.

Huge dogs bounded for him.

"Stop!" Durand roared, but then the dogs were on him. Paws struck his chest, and muzzles fought for purchase against his jaw and shoulders. The snarls filled the castle. Boots thundered on the stairs.

BADAN, OUEN, AND half of Lamoric's men chased the stranger until the darkness and bad roads turned them back. They found no trace.

At Attorfall, they barred the doors and sat their host at his own table, his daughters wailing upstairs—over the dogs, Durand suspected. The brutes had been stubborn.

"What is this?" Warin demanded.

Coensar leaned close, while Durand stood guard. "Attorfall, I'm afraid you told a little lie when you said you hadn't seen any guests."

Warin answered in a strained whisper.

"I don't see what business that is of—"

Durand squeezed the man's shoulder.

"*Warin,*" prompted Coensar.

"I may've seen something. There have been men. Mostly just stopping to spend the night. Men from Beoran. Cape Erne. Heronleas. Highshields."

"And your lord?"

"I've given bloody *oaths.*"

Durand moved Warin's arm into a painful position.

"His Grace has warned us all," said Warin, "that there may be trouble after Tern Gyre, and he's been talking about this leech of a king we're lumbered with and how there might be better men for the Hazel Throne. Is that what you're so desperate to hear?"

"Who're these better men?" demanded Coensar. "And don't think you can play clever with me now."

"I don't know. Maybe he fancies himself for the job, I don't know."

"Right," Coensar said, and Durand let the man loose.

"Get out of my house," Warin gasped.

"You've left something out, Warin. You've had a very recent houseguest."

"One of Hellebore's men. A messenger only. He's the one told me there might be trouble after Tern Gyre. To be ready if there's a call."

"Now he's seen us here, what does he intend to do?" prompted Coensar.

"I don't know. He may plan to catch the duke up in Tern Gyre. Or warn his people there are men from Gireth on the move in his lands. Maybe they won't take it so kindly."

THEY SET OUT in the dark, taking whatever shepherd's tracks Heremund could scare up for them. When light returned, they passed scowling swineherds and poachers on forest tracks.

Knights and shield-bearers all kept their swords handy. Coensar made certain that outriders patrolled in strength and kept a rearguard trailing them in case of ambush.

Finally, they crossed Hellebore and Saerdana to reach the chalk cliffs above the Broken Crown and the harbor city of Port Stairs.

———

"DURAND, WE MUST speak," Deorwen said.

For a moment, the party jostling around them was out of earshot. At every turn for the last fifty leagues, she had been trying to corner him. Now, as the party packed the switch-backing streets of Port Stairs, Deorwen slipped in alongside.

"You've avoided me long enough," she said.

Durand kept his silence.

The town tumbled down a chalk cliff, heaped on the terraces that had given Port Stairs its name. The street to the quayside zigzagged like a weaver's shuttle, and, at each bend, the Port Stair burghers had thrown up a sanctuary idol: the Warders, the Champion, the Maid, the Queen.

She caught him under the twin Warders with their shields and their coats of nails as the street reversed itself for the next "stair."

"You must give me a chance to explain."

"There's no need," Durand said. He spurred his gelding into the next street, and into the crowd again. *"Damn you,"* she hissed, but the old rule bound her: Secrets could not stand the Eye of Heaven. For Durand, the press of the crowd meant safety though he could feel her eyes on his back as riders moved between them.

He drew a deep breath of sea air. Port Stairs was a strange place. Shops and houses crowded so close on every side that, even though the town was one street deep, a man could only catch the glint of the waves in quick alley glimpses.

Another sanctuary idol hove near: the Maid, free and tall, almost as though she could see the waves. The baggage train balled up around her skirts.

"Durand, we have to speak. It does us no good to pretend," Deorwen said. But this was not the time, and a time would never come. He must be like the tooth-puller and snatch the rotten thing out with one twist. It would be a mercy to them both.

"For God's sake," she said, but Durand spurred his horse into the next street once again. This time he wound up knee to knee with Lamoric at the head of their crowd.

Just then, Berchard rode up from the quay to the head of their column.

"Lordship," he said, drawing in beside Lamoric. "There are some few deepwater freighters stuck up here until the storm season's past. There's a cog name of *Solan*. I spoke with her master. She's got a deck that should hold horses, and they're set to cast off."

Lamoric flashed a wide grin. "He'll ferry us?"

"He's ferrying breeding stock to Biding," Berchard said. "Says he'll press on to Tern Gyre if we pay him."

Lamoric nodded as they rode into the press at the next bend. Here, a tall figure in pale limestone and a traveler's hood clutched its tall staff in bony hands. Someone had jammed real pennies in its eyes.

"I told you," said Lamoric, "we are fated to reach Tern Gyre. The Powers have swept all obstacles from our path."

Berchard winced at this, risking a quick glance at the idol. "Perhaps, Lordship, if Heaven wills."

"In any case, it sounds as though we had better hurry," said Lamoric.

Their train clattered onto the quayside.

Sailors and longshoremen swarmed over a broad-beamed ship. Half the deck was already full of horses, and there were men already on the mooring lines.

Berchard pointed.

"That's her. That's the *Solan*."

Durand led his mount straight onto the deck, hurrying with all the others to get their gear aboard before the *Solan*'s master cast her off. Deorwen could not get near. Guthred tramped back and forth, hissing orders and getting the skittish animals blindfolded and across the gangplanks. In the end, every horse would need a man standing by.

"*How* much?" Berchard shouted.

Durand spun to see men like Coensar and Agryn standing with Lamoric as the young lord spoke with the ship's master. A round, bowlegged man, the ship's master stood firm.

"It's a fair price for short notice and an empty return," he said.

Berchard looked ready to take them off the ship, when Lamoric drew a purse from his saddle.

"Here," he said, grinning. "I've paid the men, we're on our

way to Tern Gyre, and this is the last of it." Right before the master's nose, he shook the bag of pennies for weight. "You want one pound of silver, and you shall have it."

Dubiously, the master took the bag.

Lamoric smiled, slapping the dust from his hands.

"I'm imagining you'll have a few pennies more than I owe, but I'll not worry," he said, grinning to his friends. "I've wagered my whole fortune on this venture."

Not a few men blinked at this. Old campaigners caught at their hats and cloaks. They were still a long way from anything like victory. Now, they knew there was no going back, at least not for the young man who led them.

"Right, then. Cast off!" shouted the ship's master, shaking the sack of pennies by way of punctuation. "Signal the pilot." Sailors scurried over the deck.

"Let's get where we can see where we're going," Lamoric said, and his companions followed him up to the forecastle. The harbor boatmen were tying on, ready to row the big ship out into the bay.

Durand intended to stay aft with his horses, his fingers curled in the gray's bridle, but then he saw her. Deorwen made her way between the animals. Durand nodded to one of Guthred's boys, *take him,* and climbed the steps into the ship's open forecastle.

He didn't look to see her scowl. He could feel it.

From the crowd at the forecastle, Durand looked back toward towering Port Stairs and the shining cliffs of Saerdana looming twenty fathoms above their masthead. He wondered, even seeing it bright and clean as new silver, whether its lady stood with the king or against him. She held two duchies on her own. If she had been swayed, then the vote could go badly. Durand knew nothing about her, except she had managed to hold two duchies.

Above the deck, sailors freed the long yard and prepared to hoist the sail, while oarsmen under the bow hauled away, dragging the *Solan* into open water.

Two duchies—or was it three?—looked out over the Broken Crown. He couldn't remember. No wonder there were so many messengers riding the roads. With fourteen duchies represented at the council, each duke must be testing the others, sniffing the breezes and taking care not to land on the wrong side. Any king would kill the men who voted against him.

Deorwen stared up from the deck, dark eyes accusing, though Durand was safely surrounded and in plain sight. At her side, Lady Bertana practically writhed with disapproval, twisting toward the sea and back, but Deorwen kept her eyes on Durand. Sailors walked between them. Grooms and shield-bearers scratched their necks and looked around, bored and stuck holding bridles. Someone would notice.

Durand turned away.

"Well," Berchard was saying. "*I* had land once. The priests assessed it at nearly two thousand acres."

Ouen, beside him, raised his blond eyebrows.

"That would do me."

"But I couldn't hold it. There were debts and debts, with one thing and another, and sickness among the peasants, and blights, and there was no hanging on." There were sheepish looks around Lamoric's circle. "It's a long time ago now," he said, then caught a breath.

"So . . . I've been a hired soldier most of these past twenty years, guarding this and that. Fighting. From here down to Mankyria without ever getting enough coin together in one place to buy back half what I lost as a young man, but that's the way of things. You'll meet one or two who've done well but not many. And now I'm starting to creak a little. It takes longer to get out of bed, and I don't like sleeping on the ground.

"Feather beds," said Ouen, nodding. The gold teeth glinted.

"Hot food," said Berchard.

Badan sneered at the pair of them.

"It's all right when you're young," said Berchard, "but I've put these bones through about as much as they'll stand. It's one reason I've come back north after so long away."

"And yourself, Agryn?" Berchard asked. "What do you plan to do when we're great men and famous?"

"I will rest," he said. "If the King of Heaven grants me leave."

"Aye," said Berchard. "That's it, isn't it? When a man's on the road he's always moving. There's no sitting down when he don't know where his next penny's coming from. He's always on the scrounge, thinking: What if I catch one this time? Where will I be this winter? He can't ever really rest."

"It has been a long time." said Agryn.

The ship's master bandied across the forecastle, and bent to look down over the bows.

"All right, you lot. That's enough. Cast off the towlines! We've sea room enough to set sail."

As the crew hauled away, Durand got a last glimpse of the terraces and gleaming cliffs before the crew raised the broad rectangle of *Solan*'s sail and blocked it all.

Deorwen stepped forward, making sure she caught his eye.

THEIR WHOLE SHORT voyage passed that way, though the chatting did not last. Lamoric's men paced the forecastle, peering northward or heading down to the deck where they could examine their animals or riffle through their gear. If they had not been wrapped in their own cares, not one could have missed Deorwen's stare. As it was, knights of a hundred battles sat on the deck, worrying at their swords with whet-stones. Eventually, out of sheer frustration, Guthred dug out his grinding wheel and did every man's blade properly.

Durand felt the pressure of seasickness in his skull— seasickness wrapped in the tight bands of Deorwen's stare. What was he meant to do? He did not want silence. He wanted to stand close, breathing in snatches, mouth to mouth. He haunted the bow, as far forward as he could manage. They said it helped the seasickness to look forward.

A few hours after Agryn prayed Noontide Lauds, Durand spotted a break in the even white cliffs, far off to the south-east. With a needle of shock, he realized that he was looking on the Gates of Eldinor, the strait that led to the Gulf of El-dinor. Squinting, he could make out white towers bristling like needles above the waves. This was the capital of Errest the Old—once capital of all the Atthias—standing in splendor, a round isle moated in leagues of seawater, clad in white stone. As he watched, he realized that some of the towers moved—the masts and sails of many ships. Somewhere among it all would be the Mount of Eagles and its Hazel Throne, carried from the Shattered Isle and fashioned from the chest in which Queen Aellaryth set her Young Princes upon the waves. Somewhere was the high sanctuary where kings spent their three nights in the crypt of their fathers and awoke hearing the whispers of the kingdom.

Once, the whole of Creation had turned around that spot, and, even now, Errest the Old looked to Eldinor. Kings beyond counting. Heroes beyond number. Powers of Heaven walking Creation. Durand marveled that it could all come to rest on bad debts.

He glanced back and found Deorwen's dark eyes.

🪢 24. The Wreck of Dreams

God," said Lamoric. "There it is." The knights stared out. The cliffs of Tern Gyre glowed above them, red as a towering wall of embers. Men punched each other in the arms, acting like boys.

"We have come to Tern Gyre," Agryn said, with curious solemnity, and a few of the others took a moment to make the Eye of Heaven.

The *Solan* had dropped half her load at Biding, and swung northwest, tacking into a stubborn wind. Now, with her bow pointed straight into the open sea beyond Tern Gyre's head, the fortress crept into sight.

But Durand had a glimpse of the brute cunning behind its design. The whole castle stood at one end of a chalk arch, some forty fathoms above the breakers. All the miners and engineers in the world could not reach it. He imagined an enemy trying to get at the place. The arch was narrow and open. A whole war would have to be fought two men at a time, and, if Durand knew the builders, there would be a fearsome gate at the castle end.

Now, though, it was packed with all the barons of the realm.

"I never thought we'd see it," Lamoric said. "You've all done better than I could ever have hoped."

As the *Solan* struggled her way toward the headland, Durand made out another feature of the castle's defenses: a landing and a stair on the sea. It was the cunning finish to a shrewd design. Even if an enemy squatted at the bridgehead for a thousand years, that enemy must watch as supply ships docked out of reach, passing the garrison food and freshwater every day.

The deck shifted as the bow swung about.

Lamoric said, "What's that fool doing?"

They were near the Barbican Strait, where the Crown broke and the Westering Sea stretched out of the world. With the wind and waves and twilight, Durand hadn't noticed the sailors scrambling. Now, though, his ears picked out a desperate edge to the voice of *Solan*'s master. The little man stood in the aftercastle, alternately shouting to a bull-necked sailor on the steering oar or to the crew handling the broad sail's sheets and braces. Between roars, he muttered a charm against drowning.

A look into the rollers told Durand why: A great current bulled through the strait, driving them toward the cliffs. This was where the tide filled the Broken Crown. Durand peered about, suddenly uneasy. He knew a little about boats from his years by Silvermere. The wind followed the tide through the Barbican. *Solan* had to tack wildly across it just to keep from falling into the cliffs. The sailors called it clawing off a lee shore, and, with tide compounding wind, it was likely to be a grim business.

They sheered north across the face of the wind, cutting sharply toward rocks that boomed and thundered nearer in the surf. Even men like Badan opened their eyes. Agryn abandoned his prayers of thanksgiving, setting one hand down for balance. Any moment, the master would swing the *Solan* round and dart back to steal sea room from the wind.

Just as the ship's master opened his mouth, Durand saw a vast shape flicker in the blazing light: A black swell had shouldered its way into the strait.

Sailors on the sheets looked up. The master shouted his order. The wave hit.

The forecastle flipped like a catapult. Men sprawled. Durand slid—even having seen it coming—tumbling across the deck until he fetched up hard against a bulwark. There were screams from the deck. In an instant, Durand was on his hands and knees. He saw a kicking mass of men and horses, black and red under a full sail.

The master roared from the aftercastle. "Come about! Bring her about! Get the sheet! I need a man on that damned brace!"

In an instant, Durand understood. *Solan* was still driving toward the breakers, and the toppled crowd in the ship's waist must have crushed anyone working by the rail. As long as the sail was taut and full, they could never make the tack. Someone had to free the sail. With the deck a shambles, there was no one.

The deck pitched.

Durand leapt down into the waist and bounded over men and beasts with his eyes on the line that held the sail. If he could free it, they stood a chance. A screaming tangle of thrashing limbs blocked his way.

The starboard rail sketched a dark trace toward the line, and he jumped. His soles slid, but he threw himself forward, catching at shrouds and stiff canvas to keep his balance over the waves.

Solan ran another fifty yards. There was no time.

Durand pitched from the rail, leaping bodily into the sail and its straining sheet line. In a moment of cracked knees and bruises, he got his hands on the knot and fumbled the whole thing free.

The ship's master was roaring. "Hard on the steering oar! Bring that yard round!"

And *Solan* wallowed, stalling in her headlong drive for the rocks. Bleeding sailors hauled the sail round, and Durand tied off his line.

Solan bobbed once, coming about as the sail snapped tight once more, throwing the whole weight of the wind behind the master's will and snatching the bow round in a titanic jerk.

Durand struggled from the deck. Thirty or forty men looked back at him with one rattled expression. He searched the faces for Deorwen.

Then he felt a shadow moving in the storm.

They had been saved from falling backward into the cliff, but now, on her new tack, *Solan* shot along the foot of the vast wall.

They had no room.

The cliff wall rippled by, thundering full of jagged stone and breakers only yards away.

There was no room, and they could not claw off. While a square-rigger was handy—quick and easy to switch tacks—no square-rigged vessel could turn back into the wind now. They skimmed the exploding breakers, screaming toward the landing. The stone wharf loomed in a sliver of cliff-sheltered water.

They were coming on fast.

"Reef the sail, lads!" the master shouted. "For your lives!"

Solan shot past the rocks at the cliff's foot, heeling so hard the yardarm scrabbled over the cliff face like a blind man's stick. Then they were free. Free and gliding across the slender shelter of the cove.

"Hells . . ." the master said, but it wasn't relief. The little man clutched the rail at the front of the aftercastle; his eyes were on the quay.

"Lean into it, steersman," he growled. "We've got too much speed." The wharf was coming on fast. "Get the fenders over. Anything you can find." Men scrambled to get bundled cordage between ship and bare stone. Durand caught hold of the rail.

Solan struck.

The whole vessel groaned like a beast, splintering planks through the forward quarter. The drag of rending timber bled off speed. Within a few heartbeats, *Solan* stopped, and the men were leaping ashore to loop lines over bollards and make the ship fast to the wharf, vowing the ropes would hold her even if she should sink where she lay.

Knights and sailors scrambled to their feet. Horses flipped and kicked, righting themselves. Durand found himself face-to-face with a sailor—maybe the man who should have been on the sheet—and the man shook his head.

"The Lord of the Deeps is great," he said, pawing lank hair from his face. "The wind switched. Just at the last. Veered straight off the sea." His voice hitched as he started to make the Eye of Heaven. Something had gone badly wrong with his shoulder.

"I have to find—" Durand began. He was about to say Deorwen. "—Someone. Did you see a woman?"

But the sailor was lost in the constricted world of unset bones. Durand started to pick his way through the tangle, hooking people to their feet and helping others calm horses. Finally, he let go one bridle and turned face-to-face with Deorwen, six inches from his nose. She had to look up.

He said nothing, but caught his breath like he'd been punched.

"I am glad to see you well," she said.

Durand nodded, staring down into her eyes. "I must—the others. They'll need help," Durand said. Somehow, he managed not to catch hold of her, not to lift her from the deck—not even to touch her.

ON THE LANDING, the company took stock and began the difficult task of leading the horses up the long stair to the cliff top. They had lost one boy—a quiet one Durand did not particularly remember—and three others were badly hurt. Several took minor wounds to ribs and wrists and shoulders. None of the knights was even hurt as badly as that. And of the animals, two warhorses and four packhorses had to be put down—their life's blood given to the sea. A few of the men took the chance to punch Durand in the shoulder.

AT THE TOP of the winding stair, they came to a postern door with the Eye of Heaven in full red flood around them. Durand had been lugging a bag of someone's gear. Coensar took the last few steps alone. He lifted his hand to knock, then hesitated with his fist hanging, a long shadow on the door, and only then did Durand's memory come awake: Cassonel and the twenty-seven men. The Duke of Beoran. Coen at a postern door. He never imagined stairs or men with their backs to a forty-fathom fall.

Long before Durand could have steeled himself, Coensar knocked.

They slipped out of the light through a narrow passage and blinked into a stone courtyard. The storm had gone completely. As Durand's eyes adjusted, he realized they stood in the midst of a crowd. Light winked and slithered over a hundred jewels, darting in and out of the supple darkness of fur cuffs and linings. Durand had never seen so many nobles in one place.

"*Durand, the helm!*" Lamoric hissed, and, in a heartbeat,

Durand had the bag from his shoulder and Lamoric's five-pound iron bucket looping through the air.

A man stalked forth, wearing an expression of sympathy.

"My Lords, we see fallen men on the quay; don't we?"

Lamoric stepped from his men, his red helm magically in place, and put one knee in the sod before an active-looking man, clothed himself in rich but simple black.

"Your Highness."

Your Highness. Durand felt a stab of awe. Here, once more, the age-old blood of Atthian kings flowed in a living man. Durand joined the others in taking to their knees, and tried to determine which of the great men stood before them. A trim, dark beard marked out the blade of the man's jaw where the king's was fair—and more sturdy. The Prince of Windhover was meant to be a blond man and larger again. This one must be the youngest brother: Prince Biedin, Lord of Tern Gyre.

"We watched your vessel's arrival with considerable trepidation," Biedin confessed. "There was quite a crowd of us on the walls. Her master is to be commended."

"Yes, Highness."

"We will have men attend the injured at once. Now," said Biedin. "I am correct in concluding that you are the 'Knight in Red' they have all been talking of."

"I am, Highness."

"Please," Biedin said, "stand. Many were surprised, I think, that the Herald did not extend an invitation to you after your performance at Red Winding, and whispers have already reached us about High Ashes. A man might have thought such heroism a thing of another age."

"Your Highness."

"Sir Knight, you and your retinue are most welcome to Tern Gyre." He hesitated, lifting a hand to the walls confining the courtyard. "Sadly, space is in short supply at Tern Gyre on the eve of the great event. If you agree, my seneschal will see that you and your pavilions are happily installed in the main encampment beyond the bridge." He set his hand on Lamoric's shoulder.

"That would suit us admirably, Your Highness."

"Good. I will make certain that my priest helps see to the

unfortunate. And my man will send along a cask of wine to fortify your spirits."

"Thank you, Highness."

"And we all look forward to great things on the morrow," said Bieden.

Lamoric and his men bowed low and followed the seneschal as the prince returned to the warmth of his hall.

Heremund ducked close to Durand.

"I'll see if there ain't room for one soul, anyway. I must see how the magnates are disposed." With a pointed strum on his mandora, the skald tramped off. Durand wished him good fortune.

While most of the entourage trailed after the prince, a part of the crowd detached itself to follow Lamoric's retainers. Waer was first among them.

He called to their backs: "That ship's master looked like a damned fool to me. What kind of madman lands his boat on a lee shore, eh? You might all have drowned, with the whole court, nearly, looking down as you wave your arms. But I suppose a ship was the only way."

A few of Lamoric's retainers turned as they walked.

Big Ouen glinted a few metal teeth at the man. "You're right clever behind the King's Peace, friend, but I wonder what you'll say when we're in the lists, eh?"

"It only gets worse," Waer sneered.

Berchard grinned at Ouen. "I had squirrels once at my old house. Chatter, chatter, chatter. Little buggers always on about their nuts."

As the two parties bantered, they walked under the gatehouse and stepped out onto the bridge: a natural stone arch forty fathoms over the surf. The back of the span was just broad enough to admit a single cart.

With the Eye gone beyond the Broken Crown, they might nearly have been walking in the empty sky.

The horses hated it.

The seneschal led them to a patch of open ground under the wheeling gulls, and Waer left them. A pavilion in Mornaway diamonds stood ahead of him.

LAMORIC'S MEN SUBSIDED around a bonfire of borrowed branches and huddled in the glow, getting something cold to eat, and doing a poor job of drinking the prince's wine.

Berchard was yawning, though his good eye glittered.

"The Marshal here. Whoever leads the company that wins the day. He's meant to get a boon, just like the old days. He asks a boon of the Marshal that's lost. It can be anything. Horses. Some fine tract for hunting. An heirloom blade. All the fish from his weirs for a season. Favors. Gerfalcons."

"I'd settle for a joint of beef in the hall," Badan groused. "Cold fare is right hard after chasing across Hellebore and Saerdana and sea voyages and a shipwreck." He tore off a hank of tough bread. "What I want is a joint roasted till the meat slides off the bone."

"Your teeth still giving you grief?" Berchard needled dryly.

Durand did not laugh. His skull was packed to the eyeballs with treasonous dukes and crashing ships and rooks and Deorwen and Tern Gyre. He left the others and went to look for his tent, but, beyond the firelight, Lamoric caught him by the shoulder.

"Durand," he said. "I want you to know. The hag. This business on the ship with that line. Even the damned helmet this evening. You've been a lucky stroke." The man glanced toward the gleaming slit windows of Tern Gyre. "And now we are here." He was smiling.

Durand nodded, feeling false as an adder. "Aye, Lordship."

"Whatever happens," Lamoric said, "I will not forget." The man's face shone.

"No, Lordship."

"No." He nodded. "Now go. You'll need rest. We all need rest." He jerked his chin toward a kneeling Sir Agryn. "That's Last Twilight, I think. The Eye is gone. The man's better than a bell."

"Good night, Lordship," Durand said, and left them all for the shelter of his tent. The canvas walls glowed and flickered with fires and passing shadows. As he lay down, music pressed in around him. He hadn't noticed it when he was outside. Someone was playing a fiddle. Drums thumped and rumbled. He heard tabor-pipes swirling. Women shrilled like birds. Men roared.

He pressed his head against the ground. Lamoric had bought the best men he could, and here was the chance he'd paid for. Now, everything was down to two days' work. Every man in Lamoric's fighting conroi gambled with him. He could hear it in Berchard's talk about coming home. About old bones. He could see it when Coensar's knuckles stopped before the postern door, or when big Ouen dreamed at the campfire.

But they could lose.

Again, the music asserted itself. People brayed and lowed and shrieked, flickering against the canvas. He wondered how many of the tournament knights—brawling second sons and country sergeants—knew about the High Council and the vote. How many guessed that this might be the place that un-did the kingdom and set the Banished howling and blood against blood.

Somewhere he heard a voice: Waer or a man like him bellowing a laugh.

As he lay with his head spinning, the campfires slowly burned down all across the headland. Mumbling souls close by found their beds.

Durand thought of Lamoric, taking him aside, talking debts and honor.

Abruptly, something touched his tent. Nails scrabbled at the canvas and a stubborn shadow spread over the wall, and, when he made no answer, a hand flapped, knocking.

"*Durand.*" Deorwen.

"Host of Heaven," he said, but she slipped inside.

"God's sake. You can't come here." Suddenly angry.

"We must speak," she said.

Durand wrestled himself to his feet.

"There's nothing to say," he hissed. "You're his *wife*." The others could be anywhere. They could be right outside.

"Yes."

"You could have told me," he protested.

"He was playing Knight in Red and I was playing lady's maid and then it was too late. I tried to keep away."

"Aye," Durand said and fought for a heartbeat to check his momentum. He remembered her ducking away at Red Wind-ing and after. "You did.

"—But no," he said, as memory warmed. "No. You had chances. You had chance after chance. You could have said something. Any time we met."

"Durand—"

"Sure, you had to keep quiet when I pulled you out of that river. Then you had your secret, but, afterward, why hold your tongue? Why?"

"I—"

"I knew about the Red Knight game that first night on the bluffs. Why didn't you put me off all those other times?" He couldn't look at her. His hands clenched and unclenched.

"It was a mistake, Durand. A mistake."

"Why didn't you just tell me?"

"All of it," she said.

"If you'd said you were married to *anyone*."

"I couldn't. I just couldn't." She caught hold of him.

He felt her heart beating. He tasted her breath. She was too close. They were right in the middle of her husband's camp—Lamoric's camp. But she was too close. They kissed—like drowning. And he felt her hands over him, pressing and darting under wool, under linen, soft as doves. Her body was hot and smooth under his fingers. He hadn't realized how cold he was. Cold through his bones.

People said that mad sailors lost at sea would slake their thirsts with great gulps of salt water. It was like that as they struggled together in that dark tent.

Afterward, they were alone and still.

Somehow, the tent's center pole had come between them. They curled around it, face-to-face, lying like shipwrecked travelers on a midnight sea.

"The marriage," she said. "My father. We had just come through so much, he and I. And I remembered Lamoric. We met once before. He had an easy smile. He had dark eyes, I thought. And so I listened to the wise women. 'Women weave peace with their bodies,' they say. I went and we swore our oaths under the Eye of Heaven and the Weaning Moon. And then he was off—that same moon. He was so wounded when his father sent Gireth to war without him. This Red Knight dream of his. So I took the road on his heels. I was his wife.

All of those vows I'd sworn. The wise women said as much. I had to go."

Lamoric had left her the same month they were married. She reached out, brushing black curls from Durand's forehead. Her pale cheeks blotched.

"Everything is in this, Durand," she said. "All the lands his father gave him. The quarries and quarrymen. The peasants and mills. Everything." Durand remembered the last pound of silver.

"He's a fool," Durand murmured.

"He—" She paused, her hand sliding to his shoulder. "All his life, he has lived on his father's gifts and his brother's leavings. Nothing earned. I think he gambles all of these things to prove whether he deserves any of it."

Even in the dark, Durand closed his eyes. He wanted to reach down and find rage. He wanted to despise Lamoric the fool. But his father's gifts and his brother's leavings. Durand remembered his own brother and his own father and all the leagues he had traveled. He could feel her breath stirring against his lips. His lidded eyes.

"And then there was you, charging from the reeds like a bull when he'd forgotten me. And you seeing me and knowing when my eyes were on you."

"This cannot be," Durand said.

"I know," she said.

"He does not deserve this."

She gathered herself up, curling her feet and skirts under her. He felt her hands slide from him.

"What can we do?" he said.

"Nothing. We can do nothing. This is the way they talk, the wise women. There are things that must be done, it doesn't matter how. Hardships must be borne. The Queen of Heaven, She is never where Her husband is. The Eye and the moons. Because She came late to Creation, She lives not where She loves. Sometimes nothing is all there can be."

Durand climbed to his feet. She had stepped toward the door. He kissed her.

"God be with you," she said and slipped away.

Durand stood where she left him. He stood still as a hanged

man after the kicking's stopped. Beyond his thin walls, living people moved. Low voices. Fires. Laughter.

God.

DURAND FELT LIKE a ghost.

The lonely Eye of Heaven returned with a storm of ragged gulls that swung over the headland and plunged from its cliffs, shrieking in the cool sea wind. Heremund flapped his hat to keep the things off as he tramped across the bridge from Tern Gyre.

"Durand!" he said, showing the gap between his teeth. The birds were all over him, swooping and pecking. Someone must have fed the things. "I'll end up like Berchard before long." The skald closed one eye, still grinning.

"What've you learnt?" asked Durand. The two men hovered at the edge of the camp.

Heremund sobered. "They're having their Great Council right after the fighting, and runners have come already, saying King Ragnal's camped near Biding and will be here by noontide."

Durand looked around, as though he might see the battle shaping up in the pastures down the long Eldinor road south.

"As far as the rest is concerned, it's damned hard to read. I mean, there are some you can tell right off. They'll vote as a pack if there's any sign the Council will go against Ragnal. The boy from Cape Erne spends his time either sour as a man with a bug in his beer or gloating like he's just won a fat prize; Hellebore is a pig of a man who'd stick a knife in your back if you so much as filched a pigeon's leg from his platter; Beoran looks like a mad ship's master, daring the storm down upon him. And there are others I wouldn't trust: that Highshields couldn't walk a straight path if he shut one eye and bit his tongue, and old Maud of Saerdana. There ain't a man alive has a blind clue what she'll do next. Oh, and she's relishing every moment of it, trailing about like a merchantman in bunting and bows with half the magnates in the kingdom hanging off her gunnels."

Durand tried to understand it all. "And Radomor?"

"He ain't here, and there's no word from Yrlac yet. And it's not so much that no one knows his mind. Seems like *every*one knows what's in that man's head, somehow. Only it's never the same thing twice. Sometimes he's alive. Sometimes he's dead. Or he'll be one of the Powers of Heaven when he passes the Bright Gates. I heard the Duke of Garelyn explain it to old Maud. He's a hero, is Lord Radomor. He fought for the king only this summer. Won't believe Radomor wants the crown. It was the Reaper's Moon before he rode home from the fighting.

"But there are others. And I saw something in Maud's face. She was rolling something on her tongue when Garelyn stood there singing Radomor's praises. Plumped up like a hen." Heremund made a face. "Maybe he is dead. There was certainly talk about poor Alwen."

This was what mattered. This was where the kingdom balanced.

"Is Lamoric's brother here?" Durand asked.

"Aye," said Heremund. "Got here early. He'll cast Gireth's vote for the king, that much we know for certain. There's a lot of shifting and shuffling going on, but I think the vote is close."

"I don't like the silence."

"No one does," said Heremund. "You can see them all buzzing at each other behind their hands. Rumors like wasps. Some were even thinking our Knight in Red might be old Radomor, till they saw the size of him. Radomor could eat two Red Knights at dinner."

Durand rubbed his neck. "Well," he said, "Ailnor or his son must come soon."

"By tomorrow eve, we'll—"

Over Durand's shoulder, something caught Heremund's eye. Durand glanced around.

Waer had come to the edge of Lamoric's camp, and Agryn, Berchard, and Ouen had gone to meet him.

"You're a nervous lot," Waer said.

"You can be on your way," Ouen said.

"A man can't walk by?"

"Depends on the man," Ouen answered.

"You should take a good look at yourselves," Waer said. "It's not only me who's watching you. Where does a man's honor lie when he's hiding a coward? Slinking behind tricks, making off with cheap victories. What do you think they're saying about you out here?"

"Oh," said Ouen. "And what are you hiding behind? Gabbling on under the King's Peace. Are you trying to get our master banned from the fighting—or maybe just your master, eh? Save Moryn from facing the Knight in Red a third time?"

Durand began walking to join his comrades, the skald behind him.

"You won't have to worry about Lord Moryn," Waer barked. "Come dawn tomorrow, you'll find him riding at the head of the whole bloody North Company. Marshal of the North. If your man can't see him from where he's hid, tell him Moryn's fighting before half the peers of Errest against the South and whatever lord drags himself here to lead them. I don't know whether your lad will be able to see from the—"

"You really do need the Peace," Ouen growled.

Durand had stepped into line with the others.

"Now who's hiding?" said Waer. "Eh? You're clever. That's twice now you've thrown that in my face. But, somehow, I don't think they'd be banning anyone if I bashed a few of those whore's-bangle teeth down your throat."

Durand saw an uneasy look on Agryn's face.

"Hold on," Durand said. "There're bigger things at Tern Gyre than us, and we'll be at sword's point tomorrow. I don't think—"

Waer rounded on him, big jaw jutting.

"And what makes you so wise suddenly, boy? You shut your mouth and maybe I won't say anything about what I saw last night."

The blood stopped in Durand's heart, black as tar. Creation sagged away.

Waer kept talking.

"You think that Lady Bertana would be happy to hear what you've been up to with her lady's—"

"—Shut up," Durand said.

"Oh. Now I've—"

"Shut up!"

Durand must have put his hand on his sword. He heard someone saying his name.

"Put that toy away before I teach you a lesson," Waer said.

Durand's sword balanced in his fist while Waer slithered his own blade into the cool sea air.

"Looks like I've pricked a sore spot," Waer said.

Durand tried to bury the point of his blade in the man's face. The wrestler ducked back.

"He drew," Waer said, recovering. "You saw him." But the sneer was gone. They had seen Durand draw. No man would contest a peer's right to answer.

They had no armor. It hardly registered.

With a tight swirl, Waer caught his cloak in his free hand— a buckler of wool.

Durand lunged to jam his blade in Waer's face, but this time he felt a sickening tug in his thigh.

Waer had got him.

Durand hopped back, switching a headsman's blow at his foe's neck, covering himself, but, somehow, Waer caught the blade and scissored a bloody ribbon down Durand's forearm.

Durand wove. Gulls screamed. He could see people running. They might be shouting. Blood looped down his arm and filled his fist. Something squashed in his boot.

Waer was a Coensar. A Gol. A Cassonel. Every move bristled with snares, and a touch of the man's long blade flayed Durand's arm like a glove.

He wasn't going to stand it.

Durand took a high line and another slithering gash. But then he saw something. Something about Waer's arm as the man countered the downward stroke. Durand didn't think but simply launched another downward slash. And now it blazed clear: While the smallest shift of his shoulder would have pulled him free, Waer threw an awkward slapping parry instead.

His shoulder was wrong.

Half the knights in Errest had sprung a shoulder. For all that Waer looked like a block of gristle, he couldn't hoist his right arm above his own neck.

Durand attacked. Blood flew when he swung his sword, first low, then scything back and forth. Blood mashed in his boot. Waer jolted backward.

Then Durand raised his blade for the high cut. The high cut

Waer could never reach. He could even see the man's eyes flash, the square blank of his face almost wincing. Then the man vanished.

Durand's blade flashed a few inches short of Waer's crown. He didn't understand. Hands caught him. Gulls were screaming, storming past him all around. Diving. He felt someone peeling his sword away, but he bulled forward. In a sobering moment, he understood. They were forty fathoms above the sea. Waer had stepped off.

"He comes! He comes!" A shout.

Durand was ill.

All the peers of Lamoric's retinue gathered around him. Lamoric had rushed up, dropping his red bucket over his face.

"King of Heaven, what have you done?" he hissed, but Durand could not see his eyes. The helm twitched toward Tern Gyre, where men were already crossing the bridge. At their head rode Prince Biedin himself, clad only in his tunic. Without a word, Lamoric's men moved to screen the site.

"What is this?" he demanded.

"A dispute," Berchard said. "An accident."

"Who are you?"

Berchard nodded with as much respect as haste could allow. "Sir Berchard," he said. "A knight."

"A knight in whose retinue?"

"An accident, Highness. The man, Waer, he fell from the cliff's edge."

"Swords were drawn . . ." said the prince.

"An argument. He wasn't careful of the edge."

Durand could see Biedin in his saddle, a long black mantle swung across an undershirt. Berchard was brave to put him off, but Bieden knew. Durand had broken the King's Peace. He had killed a man at a tournament under king's license, and he had done it outside the lists. He could neither take it back nor mend it.

A rider pelted across the bridge, drawing up in a hail of stones.

"Highness!" the man said, leaping from his horse and dropping into a low bow.

"You have been to the quay?" Biedin demanded.

"Yes, Highness. He is dead. The men on the quay. They saw him fall."

Biedin swiveled back.

"Whose man is he?"

"Moryn Mornaway's, Highness," Berchard tried, putting him off.

Biedin's eyes flashed with real fury this time. "Whose man is *he*?" Now he pointed.

Durand felt Lamoric stepping away from him. He saw hands catch at the young lord's crimson mantle.

"Mine, Highness," said Lord Lamoric, the Knight in Red. "He is mine."

"Red Knight. You acknowledge the fault?"

"I do, Highness. It was a matter of honor between peers."

"Let the dead man's kin see to it, if they must. But the King's Peace is broken. One of your men has broken it. Do you agree?"

The wind caught at Lamoric's scarlet mantle, and Durand thought he saw a tremor in the man's legs. He stood his ground. He nodded.

"We will depart at once."

Durand thought he would be ill.

And abruptly, there were birds.

Huge birds descended from the Heavens, wheeling on wings longer than a man might reach. Biedin glanced around himself. Witnesses and accused twitched and turned as talons spread big as hag's fists and beaks gaped wide enough to pluck highland lambs. Slate and spray-white, sea eagles settled.

Then the eagles stood silent; Creation had gone mad.

From the Eldinor Road, great drums thundered. And, as one, the wild eagles turned.

A murmur moved over the crowd, and the hundred peers gathered on the headland looked from the end of the world toward the Eldinor Road. Peers of the realm sank to one knee as every commoner for a league prostrated himself on the flesh of the world.

Durand, Biedin, and the Knight in Red were the only figures standing on the headland when Lamoric, too, sank to his knee. Durand dangled where he stood, unconscious of blood and wounds. Something smelled of beeswax. He thought he saw some manner of procession. Berchard tugged Durand's good sleeve, and he managed to gather wit enough to follow the rest to the ground. Every knight dropped his head.

First came riders, clad in bright robes. These men rode out to flank Prince Biedin, then wheeled to face the oncoming procession. Biedin pulled his cloak shut. Drums big as feasting cauldrons shook the air. Next, two files of chanting priests swayed forward under jeweled robes, swinging censors to bless their master's way.

On tall horses, the Septarim arrived: fearsome warriors to a man, cool as death, and armed in silver mail. These were the men Agryn had left behind.

The Septarim parted around Prince Biedin, finally revealing the man at the heart of it all: a mounted warrior like a hero chieftain from some ancient saga. Lean and broad-shouldered, his gauntlets and mantle and belt and boots were all as jewel-laden as a *Book of Moons* at the high altar. A thousand stones shone in a thousand knots of gold, while on his brow rode a darkly flashing crown of red gold and the fat, black sapphire that had been worn by every king since Saerdan Voyager: the Evenstar.

Ragnal, King of Errest the Old, had arrived.

The monarch scowled from his finery like a lion in bows. Every baron on the promontory turned his eyes to the earth.

Lesser men followed: a knot of black-robed functionaries scuttling on his heels, half on donkeys, half on foot, peering about like starlings and noting what they saw on parchment.

Every man bowed lower as Ragnal stopped before his brother.

Durand could only make out embroidered boots as the king dropped from his saddle and stalked up to Prince Biedin, now kneeling in the road before his own fortress clad only in a mantle and the shirt he woke in. A curt wave of the jeweled gauntlet stilled the chanting priests.

"Biedin," said the king.

Biedin bowed deeply, setting his hands between his brother's.

"Great King. My liege. Your Steward of the castle and lands at Tern Gyre welcomes you. My land is your land. My hall is your hall. I welcome you to this, your tournament and Great Council upon the rock at Tern Gyre and thank the Host of Heaven for delivering you safely to us this day."

The gauntlets opened. Ragnal scratched the wet-straw mane at the back of his neck with leather fingers.

" 'My Great Council,' " Ragnal quoted wryly. "Let's get inside; I've been riding hours."

Biedin stood.

"Yes. Of course, brother," he said. "Follow me. There should be room enough for your retainers." The prince twitched his cloak close against the chill.

"Something wrong?" the king asked.

"An accident, they are telling me. Someone has got himself killed. The Gyre is a precarious place."

Ragnal grunted. "Let's get inside, brother."

Biedin led his king across the high bridge.

25. The Woven Rings

The mob pulled away, the monks took up their chant, the cool riders of the Septarim led their mounts, and the eagles of the sea took wing.

Barons, knights, and servants followed the king and his brother through the gates of Tern Gyre. Every one of them stepped away from the Red Knight and his men, until only they remained standing in the wind.

Lamoric turned and left, trudging stiff-legged for the tents. The others followed. For a moment, Badan broke the numb silence, leaping for Durand and roaring oaths fit to scald the air. A few of the others kept him from pitching Durand after Waer. Some of the last courtiers looked their way, eyebrows raised as they stepped under the gates.

As Badan subsided into sobs, Berchard glanced to Durand. Durand did not move.

Then there was only the skald and the wind over the sea.

"Come on." Heremund pulled his cloak tight. "You'll have to get your things."

Durand looked toward the retreating backs of his comrades,

heading off toward the huddle of tents. He looked toward the gates of Tern Gyre. It was done.

"Come on," Heremund said. "You can't afford to leave them now." The bowlegged skald waved him on, walking backward toward the tents. "Gods, and we'll have to look after some of those cuts. The blood. He nearly took that arm with him, looks like. And your leg."

The skald spoke to himself. But Durand followed, reaching the abandoned tents where the others now stood, faces empty and fumbling at the air with their hands.

"Over," Ouen said to Berchard. "It's over."

"Where will you go?" asked Berchard.

Ouen stopped when he caught sight of Durand, meeting his eyes with surprise. Heremund caught Durand's elbow, leading him toward his own tent.

Lamoric stood with Deorwen. Guthred knelt in front of the man. "Tear it down. Tear it all down," Lamoric said. Deorwen looked to Durand, baffled but pale with premonition. Durand stumbled to his own tent.

He crouched on the threshold. His head spun like a crust in a soup bowl. His fingers touched the earth. He must go. He began to fumble with packs and pegs and guy ropes.

Guthred and a few of the boys stumped in around him, plucking things from the grass and pulling up stakes as Guthred directed them with silent gestures. Another two boys led his horses, while the rest churned and folded all of Durand's belongings into rolls and saddlebags. It could have been magic.

Finally, it all stopped.

"There you are, boy," said Guthred, not rushing. "Get up." The heavy features of the man's face said more about shouldering burdens than gloating at failures. He plucked up the reins and mashed them into Durand's hand.

"Check your bags before you put your head down tonight," Guthred said. He nodded his chin toward the scabbing blood. "Get that cleaned up."

Durand nodded, then turned from the camp and stumbled off, passing faces that stared but never spoke.

FOR A TIME, he rode, not thinking but simply traveling down and down wherever paths ran, like a slow tumble. Finally, he came to the sea, just as old Waer must have done.

It struck Durand that he remembered no scream but the birds.

The precipice did not fall directly into the water, as it seemed to from the heights. Instead, rubble lay over the feet of the old cliffs, smashed by the waves or the long drop so that a man might walk below. Still, the going was rough and he had to lead the horses.

In the hours since the scene on the headland, the Lord of the Deep had grown restive once more. A strong wind howled through the Barbican Strait, driving mountainous waves against the cliffs. The rocks boomed and hissed. Spray lashed the sky like rain.

Durand staggered. It was over. All those men. He shot a despairing glance through the columns of spray, high up the cliffs. They were hard, most of Lamoric's men, but this wild chance had drawn them all in. Wishes: fame, women, land, safe haven. Every man on that ship had been as full of dreams as a boy. And then it all fell off the cliff with Waer.

Another gray mountain exploded. Durand staggered, his thigh stabbing tight as Cerlac's gray gelding lashed its head.

It wasn't a hundred men with steel-bladed lances. It wasn't a squad of fierce soldiers. It was one fool undid them all. His lie. His temper. He had not noticed the fiends as they set the girl in his path. He thought of the blackness under the glowing walls of his tent, making love silently while the men brayed outside. That was madness. He should have turned her around. He had meant to send her away. It was meant to be good-bye.

Waer need not have seen her.

His thoughts fell on the Green Lady's veil. She had said she'd give him a life for the life he'd taken, but how many had he taken now? He snatched at the rag belted round his waist. It could not save him if it could not save the others.

Durand flung the green veil into the wind.

As he brought his head up, though, he saw something through the sheets of spray: a tall figure also struggling with the broken path. He saw a staff like a single gray stroke of a monk's brush. He could not believe that anyone else would be walking on a day like this. The figure stopped, turning—tall and gaunt under the onslaught. Somehow, the man had seen Durand. In a moment, however, winds and rain pulled a hundred veils over the figure.

Durand staggered on, half-realizing he was walking through a full gale. One wave scrambled over the rocks to catch at his boots. The gelding shrieked.

Despite it all, he heard a shout, this time from behind.

Another murky shape—smaller—was picking its way down a rubble slope a few dozen paces behind him. Durand reeled forward, jerking on the lead reins. A man could not be alone in this world. Not even a madman on a storming beach.

"Durand!"

In what felt like an instant, Heremund the skald was at his elbow. How slow had he been walking?

"Hells, boy. You're killing these horses of yours." He had to shout. "Durand? Is that what you want? Ah. Screw it, I'm getting you under shelter." He peered ahead, one hand locked in Durand's cloak. "There's a cave ahead. Can't be far. Here!" Suddenly, the little man was moving, bowed legs pumping almost faster than Durand could follow.

They came under the shadow of the vast chalk wall. Durand pitched against the stone, having trouble getting his breath.

"Oh, for God's sake," said Heremund. Under the little man's feet, the rubble had been ground into a narrow trail.

"It's just ahead here," he said. He patted a tall upright blade of stone. "Ah. I thought those were the Gatekeepers. Here it is."

The man turned a hand, revealing the mouth of a cavern half-choked with ferns. The little man waddled inside, turning to say, "There'll *just* be room enough for horses."

He stepped in.

A thousand white figures, kings and the Host of Hell, stared from every surface with empty eyes. For an instant he could see. Some knifepoint had cut them into the walls. Then the rump of Cerlac's rouncy blotted out the light. In the sudden dark, he did not know where to put his hands.

"What is this place?"

"Here, I'll try to light a fire." Durand heard the man scuffling around. "Now, if there's a bit of driftwood up here, we're in luck."

"What is this place?"

"Ah." He stopped a moment. "Sure you want to hear it?"

Durand could think of nothing the man might say that could do more harm.

"Well, it's got to do with the festival back on the cliff top. Were you ever there?"

Durand shook his head. He could hear the horses stamping behind him.

"Tern Gyre's royal land, yes? Since Saerdan shot the Barbican Strait. King Einred the Crusader took two of his boys with him. The Battle of Lost Princes. The Herald. Einred left only the youngest at home. Up there," Heremund pointed beyond the ceiling to the fortress on the headland.

Durand made out more and more of the walls as the skald spoke. A thousand tiny figures with gash mouths and splayed limbs covered the walls and ceilings of a long cave. Durand could only barely make out Heremund's finger as it pointed up to the Gyre.

"And the priests, they were prophesying victory. Victory, victory, victory, every one of them, goading the men into the boats and down to the Dark Sea. All but one." He scrambled up from his haunches, and began grubbing around in the dark.

"Maybe we can find it here somewhere. You heard of Blind Willan?"

Heremund tramped deeper into the cave, and Durand followed, empty and rattling as an old cart. Something like a stone bench or tiny altar stood in the dark.

"Here it is." Heremund was reaching down. Durand heard something like a metal clink. "Here," he prompted. "Can you feel it?"

Durand bent low, ignoring distant agonies. In the middle of the floor, someone had fixed a cold metal ring.

"This is where they chained him."

"Who, Heremund?" Durand breathed. "This Willan?"

"No. Well, yes and no. Willan was the king's son. The youngest who stayed at home. As youngest, he was Steward of Tern Gyre—like our Biedin back upstairs. And this prophet of doom, the one voice not chanting victory, he was Willan's own chaplain. A foreigner, they say, name of Hugelin. An honest man."

Durand found himself wavering where he stood. He held his right arm close, the long slashes stiffening at their dried edges like parchment. He still couldn't get his breath.

"Oh, for God's sake," said Heremund. He caught hold of Durand's arm for an instant. Durand wanted nothing more than to fall. "Sit down, before you fall on your head. What *did* that Guthred pack you?"

Heremund riffled Durand's saddlebags.

"These poor horses. You know better." There was a pause. "Ah. Here we go. I knew it." Durand heard a slosh. "Get some of this down you. And some water." The little man thrust a wineskin into Durand's hands. The stuff tasted foul.

"Drink it. You've lost blood."

The little man continued digging in the packs.

"Anyway, this Hugelin, the other priests all up and down the country said the king and his sons would come home safe. Hugelin carped that he would never see the day. The Crusade might scatter the Sons of Heshtar like ashes, but the king should leave his sons home. The Patriarchs barked at him, but he wouldn't relent and, despite his grumbling, the armada of Errest sailed. And no one liked to hear Hugelin after."

Durand took another long pull on Guthred's skin. It was thin stuff, watered. As the horses shifted in the entrance, the half-light under the storm glowed into the cave.

"And when the news came back, they liked him even less, constantly grumbling and muttering and talking of dead men on the Plains of the Skull or the Waste of Fettered Bones. Seeing it all. Demanding they pray. Forcing death rites on them all.

"Finally, Willan had his fill of it. You can't imagine how angry he was. His men seized old Hugelin. They remembered what he said about never seeing the day, and curled their thumbs in his eyes. And he was no man to go quiet. They hoisted him by the armpits and dragged him. But, now as then, it was bad luck to touch a priest. They could feel the Eye of Heaven on their backs, watching every move. And they didn't cut his throat. He was lucky. They took him down the cliffs. But they didn't drown him. They dragged him to a narrow cave: a wormhole in the rock. They shackled him. One of the men hauled out a mallet and hammered a ring into the floor, and they chained him there without thought of food or water and they trekked back up the cliff to their beds. He was his Creator's to keep or kill, they reckoned, and the great hall was quiet."

Heremund chuckled. "But the bastard lived."

The light shifted over the thousand tiny faces, but then it was stranger, almost as though the shadows were alive upon those almond faces and hollow eyes.

"And the Lost Princes didn't. Einred sent his flagship, *Eagle,* with its wide sail black and the Eye of Heaven ember red. The Lost Princes were gone."

Durand found his gaze playing over the shadowed carvings. He saw a ship there. Its sail marked with Heaven's Eye. His mouth opened.

"They rowed *Eagle* straight for Tern Gyre, those men, because Willan was heir now: crowned prince. What's it, seven hundred leagues? He saw the black sail. He saw the grim faces of the oarsmen. He saw it all and he knew, right? His brothers were dead. He was heir or *Eagle* wouldn't be sliding under his cliffs. His mind went right to the man in the cave."

Durand could see the narrow scratches of shipped oars around the little warship: a galley. He saw the prince and the fortress on the rock.

"And so he came down, past the men hailing him on the pier and on to the cave where he'd shackled old Hugelin. And he let the old man free. He'd been living on God knows what, drinking from the rock and eating whatever crawled into the cave. The prince's men were watching. Some of them, the lads who had hauled Hugelin down in the first place. He made them put out his eyes, did Willan. The Crown Prince of Errest. Grown men, soldiers, they were sobbing like boys as they did as he bid them, and he made them shackle him to the floor.

"Hugelin only nodded, then he pointed to the walls. 'I have written it all down,' he said, 'so a blind man might read it.' "

Heremund shrugged.

"How long?" Durand asked.

"Well, it had been fully two years before word of the princes set Hugelin free. Willan stayed that long. He drank from cracks in the rock, and fed on crawling things that reached the cave. And they've been doing it ever since, with a few exceptions, the Prince-Stewards of Tern Gyre. Popping down for a night's vigil before the tournament. I don't see Biedin down here, though he may come. That's this tourney. The anniversary of those tidings. It's meant to remind.

"They say the future of princes is carved on these walls."

Durand exhaled. Heremund crouched in the middle of the room. Suddenly, a flame bloomed in his hands, and all the eerie figures were dancing.

"Here we go," he announced. "Who'd have thought horses' arses would make a good windbreak, eh? We'll warm you up yet, if the place can stand the smoke." He had the saddlebags heaped around him. He laughed, something striking him. "They used to call our *Biedin* 'The Lost Prince.' He was a quiet lad. Those two big brothers always harrying him. One day he wandered. When anyone bothered to notice, they couldn't find a trace. King Carlomund's men swept every road for a hundred leagues. Three nights passed. They halfway thought he was dead. But then the lad turned up, wandering like a ghost in the high sanctuary. Three nights lost, right in the king's own high sanctuary."

Heremund groped in one saddlebag. "I think Guthred's stuck some of his wound salve in here as well. I suppose the weather's washed most of those cuts out by now. We'll see if you can stand putting this stuff on them. If I were someone else, I'd look at stitching that arm, too. You're going to have some scars to scare the grandchildren, that's certain."

Durand laughed, a wry puff through his nose.

The little man crabbed over, peeling back Durand's sleeve and setting to work with an apologetic wince and a finger full of pork grease.

"Host of Heaven," he muttered. "I'd say it wasn't going to hurt, but you know that's lying."

Durand closed his eyes. A few cuts wouldn't kill him, if he watched them. As Heremund worked, he opened and closed his stiffening hand. He could feel the ache setting in to fuse his bones.

"The fingers move, anyway," Heremund said.

Durand looked the man in the face.

"You know that I heard. I was near enough to hear why Waer died, I mean."

Durand swallowed. He closed his eyes; then, as steadily as he could, asked, "Does Lamoric know?"

"I don't think so. I don't know if everyone caught it, and then Waer was dead and there was the prince and the king. I don't know."

"Good. She doesn't deserve . . ." He faltered. She had watched her husband and her lover lose everything for her: house and lands and all. She didn't deserve any of it. Lamoric shouldn't be heaping anything more on her because Durand was a fool. He didn't want that.

"They never do, you know?" said Heremund.

"No. They never do." He thought of Lamoric's sister up in that tower, with him outside standing guard, and it pulled him in. Lamoric, Alwen, Radomor, Deorwen, the men on the cliffs packing everything they had left to stagger out on the roads in time to meet the snow. He saw Alwen drifting down the Banderol, curls tumbling over the rail. He had visions of frozen shoulders at the roadside, humps in the snow. He saw Deorwen, shocked and watching him leave.

"Something else," managed Durand. If they must talk, it must be about something else.

"Right. Right. Get that legging off, and I'll see to that jab Waer gave you. I don't suppose it matters. Gods, you'll never save these woolens."

The battered leggings were tied at his waist cord, but, with the skald's help and some salt water, he managed to peel the bloody sticking thing from wounds and hair.

"Now I get a look at it," Heremund said, "it doesn't look so bad." The little man spat, muttering some formula. Durand winced down to see him opening the wound like a red mouth. "I'll give it a good stiff washing out though and tempt the spirits with a bit of strong wine. I don't think you've done anything serious. You're meant to let it seep a while and just keep an eye out."

None of it mattered. He'd told Deorwen good-bye only to get them both caught—maybe. And here he was, fully across the realm from where he had begun. If he sold everything he had, he could just manage to make his way home to grovel at his father's gates.

He stopped himself. He had cost the others far more than he

had cost himself. His whole great, fearsome, desperate quest to cut himself a place in the realm—it was a child's thing. But he had done more harm than any child could manage.

"I wonder what's going on up there now," Heremund said, even as his fingers fumbled the leg wound open to take a jot of wine. He mumbled a charm and spat once sharply on the floor.

"Old Hugelin's done with this place, I reckon," he muttered. "It's them upstairs. All those magnates in one hall. You should have seen it. Some never meant to ride out for this one. Garelyn looked like he'd combed his mustache in a briar patch. Some of the others were just sopping it all up, preening and strutting. They'll be feasting by now, I reckon. Oxen turning over the hearth fires. Swans. Peacock. Eel. Dolphin."

Durand tried to imagine.

"How will the vote be?" he wondered. Everything was very far away.

"Well, I don't know. You ever seen a man balance? A rope-walker? You're either up or you're down. There'll be some on either side now, but if they feel it going, I count seven who'll vote the king down."

"Seven?" Durand hauled himself to his feet, he took a limping step toward the cavern mouth. He needed air. "How many are there?"

"Fourteen places at the Great Council since Hesperand." Fourteen duchies.

"Heremund, what happens if they tie it?"

"Even in times dark as these, you don't throw down the King of Errest with a tie vote round a council table. Of course, it's all a question for the priests if Radomor doesn't put his nose in."

But Radomor was coming. The rebel barons would never have shown their faces here if they thought Radomor was dead. Durand's hand fell on the gray gelding's flank. If the rebels thought they were going to lose, there would be no one in Tern Gyre but lackeys. And if they smelled a tie vote on the wind, they would turn it. Durand remembered Gol and that muddy road in Hellebore. He remembered the marshal's boon: anything asked.

Moryn was marshal.

His eyes were drawn to the hand he'd spread against the carvings. The shadows jittered. He peeled his fingers apart and found two tiny figures sharp and curved: a child's painted birds. Black notches.

He turned from the cavern gloom to the bright storm outside, and, plain as day, two dark shapes tumbled across the crashing waves: black, ragged birds.

"Durand!" called the skald.

Durand was already outside, barefoot and barelegged. The birds circled each other, gamboling like drunks and pinwheeling in the wind. He could hear the things laughing. Not gulls or terns or even eagles, but rooks. Two rooks beating the air for Tern Gyre.

"Help me get this back on the horses!" Durand said.

WITH HEREMUND ON his heels, Durand took a slashing course back up the cliffs and onto the trail from Tern Gyre. Blood seeped into the rain running slick over his skin.

He hardly noticed.

"Durand, for God's sake, you're going to kill yourself!" Heremund shouted. The little man clung to the withers of dead Cerlac's bay warhorse. "Hells, you're going to kill *me*."

Durand dropped from the gelding's back and limped a tight circle, beating the ache in his leg as he searched the ground for signs. He couldn't listen to Heremund. If he slowed down, he would turn back. The thought of standing in front of Lamoric and his men again sat like a weight on his chest. But he had to go on. Pride and shame could push a man hard, but he would not stand by. He would walk up in front of every last man, and he would tell them whatever he must, and somehow he would turn them back.

Durand's reeling path had struck a metaled road that looked like the one for the South.

"They'll have taken the Eldinor road, yes?" he called back.

"Lamoric? Aye." The rain lashed down fit to shove him down. "Hells, Durand. What are you thinking of?"

He looked up and down the road. With the rain battering the muck, there was no sign of which way they'd gone or how far. Lamoric could still be lurking around Tern Gyre or he could be halfway to the inland duchies. Durand covered his face for a heartbeat, then chose south. If he were Lamoric, he would be riding hard to put Tern Gyre behind him.

With time passing unknowably in the gray Heavens, the road finally broke the line of a natural bank, dropping through a gap down a four-fathom ridge. Durand was soaked and shaking with it. He couldn't still his hands; even locking them tight in the waterlogged reins did no good. He fought to keep his head from sagging.

"What in the Hells are *you* doing here?" demanded a voice.

In the middle of the road stood Badan, having appeared like some nursery-story troll. His bald head gleamed with the red fringe round the back of his skull dripping as if someone had scalped him. A chained flail dangled from his fist. "I asked what you're doing here, and I expect an answer," he snarled. The chain rattled.

Durand stared down on Badan. Under the ridgeline, curious faces huddled as men and boys crowded under tarpaulins to take shelter from the rain. He saw Guthred with his hands loose at his sides. Ouen's face was frozen.

Coensar climbed out of his makeshift shelter.

"Durand, you are passing through on your way south?" the captain offered—suggested.

"No," said Durand. His tongue was stiff in his mouth, and his heart beat in his throat. "I've come to speak with His Lordship."

Water streamed off the captain. "Durand," he explained. "There's no talking left."

But Lamoric was already on his feet, stalking into the track. Coensar stopped him, too late.

"You must go back," Durand said. His clenched teeth chattered.

Lamoric's eyes flashed. For an instant, his head was rising out his cloak like a turtle from its shell.

"You must go back," Durand said, his jaws tight. "You've got to go back."

Lamoric stared a moment, then looked past him. "Skald, has he gone mad? Was he not there this morning?"

Heremund, crouched on the back of the big bay like a child, simply shook his head.

"Durand," said Lamoric, "you woke the prince himself. He came out to bid us a good bloody morning. It was only by God's grace that he did not hang you. And you're cursed lucky some of these men didn't cut your throat."

"You've got to go back," Durand managed.

Lamoric stared, then shook his head.

"It's over now. It's done." He spread his arms at the line of huddled men. "You only found us together like this, because there's but one road off the headland. There's no Red Knight anymore. There's no one to go back." He blinked like a twitch. "His retinue is disbanded. He has no companions. You must wake up. I tell you, because you did me service. It was finished the moment you sent that bastard Waer off that cliff."

Some of the others had stood up now, ranging around their onetime lord. If he could, Durand would have run. He ducked his head, pawing his face with stiff fingers.

"Radomor's coming," he said. "He's coming for Moryn." He couldn't get a good breath. "He's coming to swing the Council. It'll be war if we don't stop it."

"Radomor?"

"They've been at him. I saw the Rooks. I heard Cassonel bring word from . . ." Names swam. "From the Duke of Beoran. They wanted him."

"This is madness," said Lamoric. He looked to Coensar, and Durand, too, checked the pale man's eyes. He saw no sneering there. "Radomor, he's my brother-in-law."

"I was there," said Durand.

"He wouldn't do it. All this madness with his father. He's an honorable man. He's led men for the king. Just this summer." He looked for support. "The man took a wound in the Marches."

"He was so angry," Durand said. His face was hot.

"He stood up for her, Durand. Poor Alwen. He shut that man Sitric Gowl up when he called her snipe."

"He's not the same man, Lordship. I know it. I was there. Pure fury. He drowned the man who'd done it. Drowned him where everyone could hear, just sitting there. His friend. And he shut your sister up in the tower and her boy with her." There were many eyes on him, but he could not stop now. The whole thing must come out. "They hung a strong door, and there was to be no food. No water. Not for either of them. He was so angry."

"It was suicide," Lamoric said. "I can understand. The shame of it. She never meant——" But Durand wouldn't let him go.

"We held her up in that tower, Lordship. I caught her by the arm! We kept her there days, the babe starving. I stood guard, Lordship, till I bolted for Ailnor. And I found the old man praying, Lordship. Praying to shake his nightmares when I came. No one saw Alwen after. No one. Radomor was leading us through the wilds with his men playing that she had been moved. That she was at some country manor. But I saw him, Lordship, sitting in his father's throne with his skull hot as a cauldron. I was there."

It was almost as though Lamoric had crumpled under his cloak. The rain came down.

"He cannot be king, Lordship," Durand said. "We must go back. The Red Knight is lost, but you've got your *own* name. You can ride back under your father's colors. They're deadlocked up there. Those traitors can't pry the king loose, but Radomor of Yrlac is coming and he'll lead the South Company against Lord Moryn." They all knew Moryn. Even Lamoric knew him, no matter how he talked. Moryn would do as his honor demanded. He would lose, and he would know, but he would kneel and offer the victor his boon. He'd be honor-bound and Radomor would use those bonds to twist one knife-slim favor from his bones. There was only one thing Radomor wanted. "You have to stop him."

Durand could see Lamoric struggling with the air, his sopping cloak moving with his shoulders. He could feel the water sliding down his face, pooling in his boots.

"God, Durand," Lamoric said. He shook his head. A long silence passed. Durand had asked him to march back to Tern Gyre with all his dreams wrecked. He asked him to throw his lot in with a man he hated. There was no sound but rain.

"If I go, we must all go," Lamoric snarled at last.

Durand blinked back at him a moment. Without a word, the others had all risen by now, wrapped in shrouds of tarp and rain-cape, silent and staring.

"If I must go," said Lamoric grimly, "you must ride with

me and fight beside these men—these men who remember. You must join me when I join Lord Moryn and his companions after they've set old Waer in the boneyard."

Durand stared down at the young lord, eye to eye.

"Yes, Lordship," he said. "So long as we ride for Tern Gyre."

It was then that Agryn spoke, looking north beyond them all to where Tern Gyre must stand beyond the rain.

"To Tern Gyre," he said.

🔗 26. The Eve of Battle

Even from the bridge, Durand could see they'd shut the gates.

"Could it be dusk?" Heremund wondered. He squinted up into the rain. "I don't know how they could tell."

Rain dropped past the men down the forty-fathom gulf on either side of the bridge.

"Hmm," said Heremund, remembering. "They'll be up on the watchtower now, all crowded with the priests, squinting off toward the Barbican Strait, just like old Willan did, the night he gave up his eyes. I'll wager the rain's likely thrown a chill over it. The poor things'll be damp right through their silks. Maybe someone will have brought a few cups of hot malmsey." He shivered.

Up at the head of the column, Durand picked out Lamoric side-by-side with Deorwen, his lady wife. They were just coming under the ship's-bow arch of the gatehouse. Rather than hiding back among the baggage, now Deorwen rode pillion right where everyone could see her. Her idea. Where before she'd been a liability to Lamoric's Red Knight pose, now she made a perfect blind. The man on the palfrey was no Knight in Red. *This* was Lamoric and *that* his new wife, the poor thing dragged along in the rain.

The rest of the train waited on the bridge. Durand could hear Badan muttering just loud enough to make himself plain.

"Whoreson boy's mad. Changing a few cloaks and hopping on each other's ponies ain't going to fool nobody. Bastards'll know us right off."

"It ain't got to fool them long." Durand glanced to see Guthred speaking for him. The man's eyes were on the gatehouse. "It's just to grease us under the gate. If they press him, His Lordship can say whatever he likes. We're a bunch of thugs he met on the road, saying we'd left the service of some strange knight or other. Whatever he likes. He's son to the Duke of Gireth, and there's little enough light anyway."

"The whole thing's daft," Badan concluded. "Riding back for something that ain't even happened."

At the head of the line, one of Guthred's boys was shouting up through the drizzle to the gatekeepers. Only tension kept Durand's head from falling against the gelding's neck.

"Then they'll head down to the docks," Heremund was saying. It took Durand a moment to remember. He had an image of the nobles crowded atop the round watchtower. "The whole wellborn mob and a dozen gilded priests all tramping down the cliff stairs, dragging their fur hems behind them. I think it's wine they pour then. Every man in the company."

A face appeared among the battlements.

Guthred's man shouted something like: "Lord Lamoric, son of Abravanal, Duke of Gireth."

Durand kept his eyes on the guards: two now. It should have been easy. Durand could make out little more than the curve of their wide-brimmed kettle-hats. Wind and rain snatched words away. Abruptly, the helmets switched. It looked like the two guards had turned around, putting their backs to the bridge.

It made no sense.

Just then, a shiver ran down the spine of the stone bridge under their feet. Someone inside had started winching up the old gate.

No one moved.

For several heartbeats, they just sat there, every man wondering what would come next, but no sign came from the gatehouse. Finally, Lamoric spurred his palfrey forward and the whole company marched under the gates.

Durand made his way under, muddy rain dripping from the teeth of the portcullis to slither down his neck, but then the head of their line seemed to ball up. Men in the gatehouse jostled, their horses spooked by the sudden stop in the cellar dark of the place. They might nearly have been underwater.

Durand slipped the gray through and into the courtyard where every one of Lamoric's retainers stared up at a tower on the seaside wall. Half the magnates of old Errest stood there, still as stone or tapestry. It was hard to make them out. Everyone had rushed to the parapet, crowding close. Every mouth gaped and every eye bulged, staring out on the Broken Crown.

Up the inner wall to that tower swung a stair.

Though no word passed between Lamoric's men, each one slid from his saddle and crossed to the stair. Durand found himself a step behind Ouen up the wall, but then, suddenly, the big man stopped, as frozen as all the others who had reached the battlements before him. Durand ducked behind him and slipped into a place at the parapet where he could see out over the Crown.

It came like a pond skater: a warship shimmering over the black Broken Crown. Two banks of long oars pulsed down its sides while every silver-pale plank and spar glimmered. A ram reached over the waves. A sail black as caverns hung against the night, the Eye of Heaven picked out on its midnight surface. Just as Durand understood that the warship was aiming to land at *Solan*'s quay, an unheard order twitched her sweeps up: four standing rows.

She was coasting in now, and she must be *Eagle*.

Through fathoms of rain and spray, a shape was plain on *Eagle*'s jutting forecastle: the figure of a tall man standing. The people around Durand were moving now, but Durand could not go. He leaned into the embrasure, narrowing his eyes. A long mantle swung round the man's shoulders, and, on his head, Durand thought he made out a metal glint.

He must get closer.

"Ah," said Heremund, tugging on Durand's cloak, "Now look here."

Heremund smirked. Around them, the crowd was draining away. Some flapped down the stair, making their way to the quay. He picked out another line darting across the courtyard and the safety of shrines and stone walls. King Ragnal had gone.

"Something's coming, that's certain," said Heremund, shoving his nose back through the parapet. "And not only the ship."

Durand launched himself for the stairs. Here was *Eagle* slipping through a fissure in the world, an apparition before the magnates of the kingdom. She might be gone at any time. Somehow, Durand knew the vision to be as fragile as a tinder flame in the palm. He had to know what it meant.

Only as he dodged past Heremund did something cause him to look back. Behind the skald, Prince Biedin stood alone, the last man on the watchtower. He stared down on *Eagle*'s decks, his bearded chin caught in a curl of gloved fingers. The uncanny radiance of the Lost ship was in his face.

Durand hit the wet cliff stairs so quickly his smooth-soled boots nearly pitched him into space, but it was worth the stab of panic when he caught sight of *Eagle* once more. She had not blown out or flickered away. Durand thought of the long voyage to this shore from the Throne of Heaven. Creation had been turning more than two centuries since the Lost Princes set sail, and only through this narrow crack, this anniversary day as it swung round, had light slipped through from beyond.

He ran, slapping down the open stairs as the great warship slid into the sheltered blackness below, its hull and sweeps throwing cold light mirroring deep. He saw bearded fighting men standing at their oars, colorless as lead and quicksilver.

Just a few paces separated *Eagle* and the quay.

Durand charged. He leapt around slow-footed courtiers. He plunged ten steps at a time. Then, just as his feet slapped the quay, *Eagle* touched the shore, and, in an instant, the eerie light winked out.

In the sudden gloom, sound stretched. The waves hissed and rolled. The wind moved under the cliffs. Finally, Durand heard the shuffle of other feet: soft boots from the stairs behind him. The last he or anyone had seen of the great warship and its crew was the face of the man on the forecastle. Its image swam in Durand's eyes: long, all jaw blade and cheekbones. On the brow, a chill crown, and two black pits where the shadows swallowed the eyes. He could almost see the man stepping ashore, but the gap between earth and sea had been too far.

A prodigy.

As THE WIND lashed the headland, every man among Lamoric's retainers mucked in to pitch the tents. Hammers pounded stakes into the sod. Callused hands held centerpoles. Despite cuts and gashes from his fight with Waer, Durand caught hold of the heaviest rolls of canvas, lugging them like corpses, and burying himself in hard work like a penitent. When the carts were empty, he tramped toward Guthred by the heap of trunks and barrels. The old shield-bearer stood with one of Biedin's men: a serving man sent along when Biedin's seneschal gave them the patch of ground the Knight in Red left behind.

"Truth be told," the seneschal's man said, "I thought we was going to lose half of them when I saw them running for the shrine."

"The shrine?" Guthred asked.

"It's all in pieces. His Highness has the lads tearing it up. It's in with the new, and everything's out: icons, altar, tiles, and floor. All these high lords and ladies they come rushing in, the ones running from the watchtower. We don't have light in there. And the floor's all up. Nothing but pits. The young Duke of Cape Ernes, I think he's got his wing in a sling for it now."

Guthred nodded, but, as the pair saw Durand, the stranger shut up. Durand picked up a trunk. The thing felt like they'd packed it with anvils.

"There," Guthred said, pointing, "Berchard's tent." Durand passed other conversations, killing most with a step into earshot. Badan, though, was chasing off anyone who got close, and he found Durand almost right away.

"I've just been talking with the boys next door, Durand," he said, breathless. "You know what they tell me? Our Moryn's Marshal of the North, sure, but Baron Brudei Hearkenwald is South Marshal. The man's got sixty winters on his roof."

Badan stabbed ten stiff fingers into Durand's chest, knocking him back a step under the weight of Berchard's trunk.

"Brudei Hearkenwald, ox. You reckon His Lordship's going to grin when he wakes up and it's old Brudei he's come back for? And all with his last horse and mail coat wagered on the end of it? And half the peers knowing he's the Knight in

Red, likely, and knowing him for a bad loser who can't play his own game by his own rules?"

Durand dropped the trunk and raised his hand. He wanted to roar back at the fool, to snap a fist into his toothless jaw. But his hand was full of blood. Waer's long cut had opened.

Durand bent and hoisted up Berchard's trunk, turning from Badan with the man's scorn blazing on the back of his neck.

SLEEP WOULD NOT COME.

Was Lamoric's Red Knight game one of these open secrets? After five moons riding, someone must have caught on, hearing the man's voice or catching loose talk. Men drank, and the peers of Errest were, half of them, family. Durand had betrayed Lamoric, and now Lamoric looked a fool, crawling back on his father's name where his own would not take him.

But now they were back in the same mud waiting for the same battle.

Only it wasn't the same battle at all. This was no game. If they won, they'd keep Moryn off his knees and Radomor off the throne.

Durand rolled onto his shoulder.

Under this storm of strategy and politics, worse things slid in the deeps of Durand's soul. He tried to conjure up the faces around him as Waer spat those words on the headland. He saw sneering Waer and Agryn looking on, and Berchard. He remembered Ouen arguing. All of them would know.

He wondered how many others. He wondered about Lamoric.

Durand mumbled a profanity, and forced it all back down long enough for other doubts to rise.

What if the whole treason plot was madness? What if he dragged these men here for nothing? What would become of them then? With a long winter swinging down and their lord destitute and finished, the last thing they wanted was to lame a horse or lose their arms to some rich lord. Every man's fist was tight around his last few pennies now there might be no more. Who knew what might happen when the last was gone?

Once, he had seen the Heavens when a king died. He had seen the Banished stir in their chains when royal blood was spilt. With the king cast down and a usurper on the Hazelwood Throne, only Heaven's King knew what Hells would be loosed in the land. It would be better if Durand Col were a fool, his friends starving, and the people safe.

⊛ 27. Leopard on the Green

He must have slept, for now he woke in the dark.

Breathing rose and fell from two hundred sleeping men beyond the tent walls. The air was still as caverns, but he heard the horses: anxious stamps and snorts. Animals saw the spirits, and smelled them. Cats were always watching *something* move through a room when no human eye could see.

Something was coming.

Rolling silently to his forearms, Durand moved to the tent flap and looked into the cool stillness. Horses, tents, palings—everything seemed to be in its place. The Blood Moon hung above Tern Gyre.

Durand set his palms flat on the ground.

And flinched back. It was alive.

Worms and grubs and maggots stood, wavering like a second crop of grass. They were beads and fingers and phalluses—white veins meshing the sod.

One spasm had Durand on his haunches, sword in hand.

As the worms crawled over sleeping men and bedclothes, he forced himself to stay in the doorway with his eyes wide even as his mind wrestled with memories. This was why he had dragged them all back.

He forced himself out under the moon, feeling the slime under his soles. The serving men too poor for tents lay under slithering cauls. He walked in widening circles through tents and cold fires, certain beyond reason that the worms were the first breath of the coming storm.

He could feel eyes on him.

Back toward Lamoric's tents, one horse whinnied.

Only a few paces from the spot where Sir Waer fell stood a gathering of tall men and dark horses. Durand was suddenly conscious of the headland's height above the sea and the fields south. He was standing alone on the top of the world with these strangers.

A profanity slipped out on Durand's breath. They had stepped from the Otherworld, and the Blood Moon's glow did little but sink shadows deeper into their mantles.

Plain under the moonlight, Durand stiffened but held his ground.

They were knights, all mantled and all still. A pair of low shapes stole from shadow to shadow with the sleeves of their black robes dangling like the wings of carrion birds. Some manner of hunchbacked brute knelt before the lord of the company. And the stooped figure of a new Duke of Yrlac hulked at the center of it all, his skull gleaming like a shield boss.

Durand remembered poor Duke Ailnor at Fetch Hollow. They had both known the doom that waited him. It had been a fool's hope to think the old duke might live.

He felt the heat of Radomor's stare, and knew that the hot silence back in that Ferangore hall had had nothing to do with uncertainty; it was the sneer of a man who had bartered his soul and been offered a crown.

Abruptly, a figure stumbled from the tents only a few paces from Durand: Heremund Skald. If he had appeared but a foot closer, he would have caught three feet of Durand's blade.

"Something's come." The little man's tongue worked against the roof of his mouth. He stared into the air, his eyes rolling like a sleepwalker's as he squelched among the glistening worms. *"Something moves."*

Durand grabbed the startled skald in both fists, and spun him toward the figures at the bridgehead. The little man's mysteries were finished.

DURAND GOT A short keg to sit on and took to working his sword as he kept his eye on Radomor. Heremund hovered anxiously, speechless.

As Durand watched the night through, the writhing carpet finally sank below the turf. The sky paled to a cool blue. Agryn appeared among the tents already clad in his war gear and yellow surcoat, and with no more than a glance at Radomor and his companions took himself off to the eastern cliff. The man knelt to wait the Eye of Heaven.

For all the others on the hilltop, the arrival of Radomor's crew was a bigger surprise. As each bleary soul stumbled out of bed, they saw the strange company and stopped to stare. Many drifted into line around Durand's barrel. Some seized weapons. Others simply stood, half-dressed and staring, as Durand honed the notches from his blade.

Dawn changed the strangers. Drop by drop, dawn poured crimson into the hooks and finials of mane and talon on their chests. It was Yrlac's rampant leopard, red on green. Soon the fanciful creatures seemed almost to glow.

Heremund scratched his head with his hat mashed over his skullcap. "Everything you ever do will come to nothing," he whispered. "Gods. Gods."

After hours of silence, this is what came from the man's mouth. Durand felt the hair on his neck rise, but answered flatly, "Let us hope you were right."

"Gods," Heremund muttered. "What's the man done?" He shook his head. "I can't breathe. The reek of it's boiling in my throat."

Durand left off polishing his sword. There was nothing in the air but the sea wind.

"What do you mean? What is it you smell?" he asked.

Again, the little man's tongue was working in his mouth. "I met a wise woman once. She said she felt the spirits on her like cold fingers. Said a room full of people was like a fist rolling knuckles over her. Me? It's a thing I taste. Or smell maybe. Same thing." Again, he licked compulsively at the roof of his mouth. "All I taste now is lead. Hot lead crackling in the air."

"You're telling me you've got second scent?" Durand asked.

The skald suddenly began slapping at himself, purse and belt. He stopped, and reached for his throat.

"Here," he said, drawing a dark-stained rag from his collar. "You'd better have this back."

Durand took the offered rag. Only as it touched his hand did he realize. It was the Green Lady's veil.

Before he could wonder, Ouen appeared at his side, rapping his arm with big knuckles. Soon, Berchard joined them, setting his hand on Durand's shoulder, while Badan grumbled something about Durand and luck. Finally, Lamoric and his captain joined the line.

Men from the castle—Durand recognized Biedin's steward—crossed from the gatehouse to speak with Radomor and his preening Rooks. He couldn't hear what passed between them.

"Those are Yrlac's colors Radomor's wearing," Berchard said.

"If Radomor lives, he is the Duke of Yrlac," Lamoric said. "I cannot believe . . . He has slain his father. He has come to take the throne."

"And he ranks Baron Brudei Hearkenwald," Coensar added. "He'll be Marshal of the South."

AND, IN THE south, Radomor waited with his armored champion still kneeling obeisance. He had spent hours on his knee.

With his eye always on the Lord of Yrlac, Durand took lances, his roll of armor, and the rest of his gear to the north end of the courtyard. He curried his stolen bay. He checked the nails on his shield straps, the wrap of his sword hilt, and the leather of girths and reins, all the while watching down the canyon of stone walls.

This was a day that mattered.

Under wheeling gulls, the castle yard filled with knights and serving men of all descriptions. Durand watched the knights, guessing at who might cause them trouble when the fight started. From time to time, a Mornaway knight would stop for a moment and stare, but Durand said nothing. There was nothing to say. When he had nearly finished, a trio of heralds passed him carrying stakes and hammers. Berchard and some of the older men made a point of finding out what wood they used. Apparently, there was some augury in the choice. Berchard and Agryn consulted with a wary eye on the heralds.

"It's hazel in the north," said Berchard. The throne of Errest was hazel from the chest of the Young Princes.

"The king is here," ventured Agryn, carefully.

"I suppose we're north of Eldinor," Berchard allowed.

Across the narrow yard, the heralds swung a hammer to drive the northeast corner stake into the turf. It sank in three blows.

"Did he crack it?" Berchard asked.

"I heard no crack. We fight in the North Company. Hazel is well favored," Agryn concluded. He sounded like a man reading words he'd written long ago.

Durand checked his armor, knotting knots and cinching straps. Meanwhile, the squad of heralds stalked down the narrow yard, choosing another stake.

"East?" asked Agryn. Something about the man's tone caught Durand's attention: He chose the word as a money-lender might choose a key.

"Hawthorn against the Banished," said Berchard. "Wind-fallen, the lad said."

"Good."

Durand buckled the garter under his right knee, but watched as the lips of both old campaigners silently counted the hammer blows. This time five. Their eyes twitched narrow.

"South?" murmured Agryn.

"Elder" was his answer.

Agryn nodded, and now Durand joined them in watching the heralds cross the yard, passing under the watchtower. Duke Radomor turned as they stepped close. His Rooks looked up, bent as hounds.

"Evil in the elder," whispered Berchard. The herald's lad took the stake. One rook cocked his head. The other grinned like a fox yawning. The boy steadied the stake, while the older man hauled back. *Crack, crack, crack* and the thing was firm.

"Now, what is west, Sir Berchard?" spoke Agryn.

"Blackthorn," Berchard murmured. "For fate."

Durand rubbed his neck: memories of withered blackthorn men stirring. Fate.

Agryn nodded, and the heralds were coming. They had turned their backs on Radomor and his Rooks to head straight for Durand and Agryn and Berchard and the whole gaggle of Lamoric's men drawn to the campaigners' whispers. Lamoric himself watched as, right at Agryn's feet, the herald's lad ducked low, one knee in the turf. The senior herald wiped his forehead and raised the big hammer.

With one swing, he struck the blackthorn stake deep.

Disbelieving, his boy gave the thing a firm tug with both hands, but the stake held fast—one blow.

Agryn's eyes were leagues away. Across the yard, the Rooks were still looking on.

"*Sir Lamoric,*" said a voice, half-choked. Lord Moryn stalked up to the one-time Knight in Red.

Lamoric almost stammered. "Moryn?"

"I am . . . *surprised* . . . to see you here." The man had only his padded coat on. A gang of shield-bearers had chased him, lugging the rest of his gear. A good dozen Mornaway knights stalked up behind.

"You will find my name on the roll," Lamoric said.

"Waer was my father's man twenty winters."

Durand held his ground.

"And yet," said Lamoric, "you've said nothing."

Durand watched the sinews in Moryn's frame cinch tighter. His men set hands on blades. The whole reason Lamoric's company had turned round and marched back to Tern Gyre hung in the scales. Moryn could turn them out.

"I expected to find you in the Southern Company. I thought you meant to face me. Now, I find you here in the midst of my own company."

Balanced between two gangs of fighting men, the young lord closed his eyes tight, then spoke quietly.

"Lord Moryn, you are my wife's brother, a man of honor, and scion of an ancient house."

No one spoke.

"I have wronged you and taken your name lightly, but I now confess that I know you for what you are: a masterful swordsman and true knight. I swear that I mean no slight to you in offering my service."

Lamoric had his battle helm tucked under one arm. He seemed to discover it. "You said you would make a trophy of my helm. I give it to you freely. On my honor, your family is my family, and your life is my own."

The lean Lord of Mornaway stood, wary. Every man could see him taking stock, and, in the long silence, no man breathed. If Moryn cast them out, Durand could not see how they would continue. He tried to picture them fighting *with* Radomor, standing up with those green knights—the preening Rooks. If Durand was to defend Moryn, he must be in the fight.

Finally, Lord Moryn lifted his chin.

"Keep your helm. You will need it if you are to fight for me."

Men on both sides spat or hissed or swore then.

"As you are now my comrade in arms," Moryn continued, "I must tell you what I have told the others of our company. Though I am prepared to fight, I do so without a full conroi behind me. I came to bring my father's vote to the Great Council, but Prince Biedin has invited me to take up the reins of the North Company."

"Radomor will try to take you," Lamoric said.

"He may try. I do not fear it."

"No," answered Lamoric. As he bowed, Lamoric's glance met Durand's, then a fanfare brayed from the keep.

Gulls leapt from the parapets.

Moryn grinned.

"We have made our peace just in time. Take your place in the lines and soon we will see how great a warlord this Radomor is when true Sons of Atthi face him."

With a curt flourish, Moryn departed, chased by his flock of shield-bearers and serving men.

"You heard him!" said Coensar. "Send your shield-bearers to the rear. Get your horses to the line. Those trumpets were the king."

They were in.

In a few darting strides, Durand had his bay warhorse to the line between the hazel and blackthorn stakes. Among the others, he saw eyes and teeth flashing—grim mirrors of his mood. Some others took their chance to mutter prayers or make the Eye of Heaven. But Durand felt the Silent King's hand in setting the table and clearing his way. Now, he was sure, that king would lean back and let them hash it out.

As the ranks formed, Durand searched to find the king they fought for. The stands were hard to see from the mill of men and horses, but, between rumps and noses, Durand caught a flash of antique gold. Under a stiff weight of embroidery, Ragnal prowled the stands, arm in arm with his black-clad brother. King Ragnal had shed his chain of priests, leaving only his flock of black-clad functionaries to follow him, pale as mushrooms as they peered about. A knight who saw a priest on the way to a tilt knew to make his peace with the King of Heaven. It seemed the King of Errest knew the hearts of fighting men.

"Come on. In line, Lordships," Coensar was saying.

Over the bay's back, Durand noted big Ouen clopping his bone-white carthorse into line at his side. The thing was seventeen hands if it was an inch, and would be good to have close by.

High above now, Ouen squinted across the lists. "I do not like the look of that man."

The sellswords in Yrlac green were slipping their horses into line as well. The hunchbacked duke climbed into the saddle of a monstrous black stallion. His new bodyguard or champion climbed onto the warhorse beside him. Durand saw that they must be separated. Of the Rooks, Durand saw no sign.

Beyond Ouen, Berchard popped up, now high astride the brown stallion from the joust at Bower Mead. He winced. "Rado don't look so good now, does he? I suppose that's this wound he's meant to have got at the Downs."

"Aye," said Ouen. "Looks like a busted collarbone. Maybe some ribs. You say he took it when?"

"When was Hallow Down? Summertide, anyway. When Ragnal rode into the Heithan Marches. And I'd say a man would need to mash his backbone to end up that pinched over."

"But he's here now," Ouen said. "And I don't like the look of him. Maybe we can arrange for someone else to face him."

Berchard grinned. "Maybe."

Battle could be like the *Solan* on the waves. Decide what you liked, but battle had its tides. He would have to watch and read the thing. In the end, Moryn must win and Yrlac must not, but nothing else mattered. For all the blackthorn stakes and wise women, no one knew his doom. Durand jabbed his boot in the stirrup iron, and made to swing up.

But fingers caught his elbow.

Agryn faced him, alone in the shadows between two great animals. "Durand."

"We are about to ride."

Agryn jerked Durand's arm. "Listen to me. When I began, I

set out to serve the king, and I told you that I turned away at the last, and long years have passed since," he said. "Longer than most would believe."

Durand felt the lines around them forming up. Everyone was in the saddle. The knight's grip tightened on his arm.

"We know what happened. Berchard, Ouen, and I."

Durand wavered.

"I know what it took to ride back. To see what must be done and turn us all back to this place. We know. . . ." Agryn hesitated. "We know he has not treated the girl as well as he might. And he will not know. He will hear nothing from any of us. We give your secret back to you."

Staggered, Durand made to ask—something, anything. But a practiced twist propelled Agryn high in his saddle. Durand saw him for an instant, gold against the sky.

"Come on," Coensar was saying. "The stands are full."

Now, Durand climbed up. Ouen, Berchard, and Agryn waited at his sides. Not looking his way particularly.

"Here we go," Ouen said.

The white figure of Kandemar, the ageless Herald of Errest, stalked onto the turf below the king's box. Nodding horses half-obscured the man for an instant, and then he opened his statue's gash of a mouth.

"Hear me, you who have gathered on this rock." His voice, unheard except when the king commanded, croaked deep and dry in their ears. "For His Majesty, Ragnal, and His Highness Biedin, I bid you welcome." The Herald bowed slow to the onlookers and each rank of combatants, a man who had walked the Halls of Heaven.

Durand knotted his stuffed cap tight under his chin, and hauled the iron hood over. His hands shook as he lifted Cerlac's helmet from the saddlebow.

The Herald moved like a slow dancer.

"We come to this ground to honor the dead and pay homage to the living blood. Here, long years past, calamity fell. In the seventeenth year of Einred's reign, while the Crusade raged beyond the Sea of Darkness, two royal princes fell, valorous but beset by many foes. Since tidings of that day first touched these shores, the Sons of Atthi have shed their blood and proven their valor. On this very height of land they have done this."

The pale Herald lifted his chin a fraction; his water blue eyes flashed.

"Those who fight affirm that valor still lives in the hearts of Errest the Old. Here, where a third son became heir and grief first set foot on the soil of Errest, you men rebuke the vile Host Below and confirm that the blood of kings endures."

Now he raised the chased horn, holding it like a rod over the companies.

"Each man who fights here this day, I charge you: Remember the valor of your house and the honor of your name. Cast defiance in the face of cowardice, despair, and treachery."

The Herald stared over them all as the wind tugged at his garments.

He lowered the horn.

As he turned, the nodding heads of the horses entirely obscured him from view. Durand crunched his helm down and yanked the last flap of mail tight under his jaw. A hundred horses in the long trappers of a hundred families hunkered down across the yard, muzzle after muzzle snorting and nodding in anticipation. A hundred knights stared through masks—a long gleaming row of slot-eyed iron. In the heart of the Southern line, Radomor pitched his helm down. Durand's eye flicked to Prince Biedin. His Highness stood, alone now of all those in the reviewing stands. His arm was raised. The man wore black. Every man and beast quivered like a bolt on the bow-cord. Biedin's hand twitched an inch higher, then, with a slashing down stroke—

They were thunder.

Two hundred heavy horses launched themselves under the walls of Tern Gyre. Durand rode at the crest of the thundering wave, hunting the juddering line of the South for a target. Radomor was out of reach, but one slot-eyed iron face twitched his way: a man in black checkers. Durand saw eyes glint. Rivets. Stubble. And there was hardly time to wrench the point down.

His lance struck first of the two hundred on the field. He was three lengths ahead.

The lance-head bit hard, shoving Durand in a fierce twist even as the enemy's lance caromed off shield and shoulder and mailed jaw. Durand felt the dry detonation of a hundred lances behind him, while the checkered knight tumbled from his saddle. Men cartwheeled. Durand could hear whoops and roars among the knights over screaming horses. The others caught him. Already, Coensar and the other captains were howling: "Hold ranks! Hold ranks!"

Durand felt blood slick in his ear. Under his boots, the shield-bearers and serving men of the Southern camp looked up. As a courtesy, the shield-bearers rushed lances to the extended hands of men whose weapons were shattered. It seemed strange.

"Durand!" Coensar barked. "Watch yourself. It's no horse-race. Now, boys, take what these lads will give you. If you want your own, you'll have to get past Radomor and his company."

Twice more, the two companies cantered across the yard to exchange passing blows at midfield. Durand rode the third one nearly twisted backward, incredulous at his own line. Men shouted laughing jeers at each other. Finally, the two lines linked together and began a taunting kind of mêlée.

For an hour, Durand ducked through the rush and shudder of this mock battle. When he could snatch his eyes away from the laughing swings of the knights around him, he hunted for a chance at Radomor or one of his men, but the green knot around the duke bristled with dark lances. Yrlac made no move.

Baffled, Durand fought on as the Eye of Heaven rose, straining to stay alert, while the knights around him kept up their jeers and laughter as though this was nothing more dire than a country dance. Knights trotted off the field when their crests came loose. One man surrendered rather than fighting on when his shield straps tore. There were village ball games bloodier.

He felt like the only sane man in Creation. Most of the riders on the field had no idea that, behind the day's sport, a narrow vote and the ancient crown of Errest hung in the scales.

Radomor would make his move.

As NOONTIDE EMPTIED the lists, Durand followed Lamoric from the field—close enough to hear the scornful chuckles of the other knights. He scowled.

Lamoric's men formed a grim pocket in the Northern Company. As the young lord climbed down among his retainers, Durand finally saw what the crowd must have seen: There hadn't been time to send for Lamoric's proper gear; he had no coin for new. And so Lamoric of Gireth rode that day in the panoply of the Red Knight. His red shield bore no Acconel Bull; his trapper, surcoat, and pennons flapped in empty crimson. Plain for all to see was the game that Lamoric had played, that he'd lost, and that he'd slunk back with his father's name to protect him.

He was a laughingstock.

Even as Durand dropped from the saddle, Badan was on him, sneering and jabbing with two fingers.

"All right then, Durand. If this fight's so bloody desperate, why're we the only ones who know it? These greenies? They don't even want to play. I don't think they've hauled one man down yet. Where's your bloody war gone?"

Badan eyed a snickering passerby.

"I cannot say," Durand confessed. With all the signs he'd followed, he could not believe he'd made a mistake.

"We'll be famous for this trick," Badan spat. "Here we've got the prince and the herald and the king himself looking on. All the best men of the kingdom snickering in their fists, with their tongues wagging over everything we do."

He made to swing for Durand's jaw, but a couple of the others caught him. Durand was conscious of the crowd around, watching them. Outsiders laughed; those nearby were sullen.

Badan shrugged his warders off, tugging his surcoat down over iron links. "The Red Knight'll be red all right," he muttered. "They'll be singing this one till next Traveler's Night."

"All right, Badan," Coensar growled.

Every knight felt the needle glint of the captain's eyes. Any who looked saw that he had yet to put old Keening away. The mob around was still watching, and Badan shut his mouth.

"Well," said Berchard with a conversational air, "anyone get close enough to hear these greenies? I reckon Radomor's gone and bought himself a lot of Southerners."

Ouen nodded. "I rode near enough to hear one swearing. Sounded like a Mankyrian, I thought. You know, like a dog barking? They're all wearing Northern gear though."

"Wherever he's got them," grumbled Badan, "they've got no ballocks if they go about in his colors. You wouldn't catch me letting my lord throw his colors over my back like I was his damned horse. The lot of them should be whipped bloody."

Ouen shook his head. "I'd have wagered heavy that Yrlac wasn't sticking his neck on the block just for a bit of fun."

For a moment, none of them spoke. Durand felt blood burning in his face but paid it no heed.

Sullen Badan twitched a sneer. "Maybe he's heard these same wild tales our Durand has, and he's thumbing his nose at the lot of us just to teach folk not to wag their tongues. Maybe it's a game to him."

Agryn shook his head. "If it is a game at all, it is another sort."

"You see shadows everywhere, monk. If fight bothered him, he'd be winning it." The wolf turned on Durand. "This boy's led us back here for nothing, and now here we are: a pack of fools."

It was Coensar who answered. "Radomor is here. He's taken his father's titles. Maybe killed him. I don't call that joking." The captain looked across the field where Radomor sat among his men like a wild leopard among the pigeons. "Look at him. Think on where he is now, and what he's likely done. His father dead. His wife. This man must make his move in earnest, or the king will throw him down."

DURAND HAD NEARLY gone the whole day without taking a serious injury, when a sudden shadow flickered up and he was blind. It was all he could do to ride from the lists.

"Lance shaft," Guthred said, as Durand slid down from his saddle, blinking and gulping for air. From the pain he'd have expected to find a bolt between his eyes, but he knew a broken nose for what it was.

His eyes were full of water.

"It's a mess," said Guthred. "The boys're bringing yarrow, a hammer, and a pair of pliers. Everybody's in playing with tack and gear and—"

"*Thumbs*'ll do a broken nose," Durand protested.

"Sit down. You bent your bloody helmet. I'll have to twist

the nasal back if you're going to get it on. Ah, hold still." He was getting up. "I've got Berchard *and* Badan to deal with as well."

Durand groped for the battered helmet, and found the thing swinging at the nape of his neck, tangled by its straps. The blow had knocked it clean off his head.

In the hours since noon, the mêlée had loosened up as tired men lingered beyond the lists, taking longer and longer to find their way back to the hard work on the inside. At the far camp, even Radomor loitered on the sidelines, out of reach. Moryn led his scattered company from the front.

Durand only needed to stop the bleeding and stuff his helmet back on. If he could breathe, he could fight. He tried to untangle the helmet, thinking he could likely stamp it straight with his heel.

Armor jingled behind him—someone dropping from a horse. Durand blinked his eyes clear enough to recognize the captain's sweating face.

"Where's Guthred?" the man demanded.

"Badan and Berchard came off again with—"

The captain grabbed a fistful Durand's surcoat. "Get them back on the field."

"What do you want me to—"

Coensar pointed. Across the lists, green knights were cinching up their mail coats and snugging their battle helms.

"Tell them Radomor's been pacing those bastards of his."

Releasing his grip, Coensar swung back into the saddle. "Get them out there! He's going for Moryn now."

Durand lurched to his feet.

It was true. Before Durand could turn a single man round, Yrlac's conroi rumbled into the field—an iron wedge with Radomor at its head. The mêlée had dissolved into individual contests with Moryn's company caught up in scattered private duels.

All alone, the lean heir of Mornaway wheeled his warhorse on open ground.

Coensar pelted across the field for him—too far—but Agryn was there, turning just as Moryn did. There were only a few knights in Coensar's command. Durand pitched himself against his bay, heaving himself up. Hopeless, Coensar galloped to intercept the Yrlac scythe.

But Agryn was already there.

"To Moryn!" Durand roared. Berchard and Ouen scrambled after him. They could see it happening.

Understanding in an instant, Agryn stabbed his warhorse into motion, gold and silver panoply leaping like fire. He was like a bolt from a great crossbow. His warhorse took three pounding leaps toward Radomor and the center of the iron wedge. Agryn's lance-head dropped, and, with one blow at the perfect place and the perfect time, the conroi exploded.

To save Radomor, one knight—his Champion—had swerved. The desperate move threw all three men and their horses into a headlong collision. Green and gold tumbled. The rest sheered off, some stumbling.

And every rider on the field was in motion then, tearing circles across the churned ground. Coensar's command swung tight around Sir Moryn. Lamoric and some of the others rode down any fool still dueling. They had no time for honor.

As the chaos unraveled, Radomor's champion rose from the earth, swelled lungs great as foundry bellows, and lifted the new Duke of Yrlac from the wreckage.

DURAND WAS FIRST to the tangle of horses, with Guthred and others pelting after. The three maimed and shrieking animals lashed at the ground. For a time, no one could see Agryn at all, then Durand spotted a shimmer of gray mail in the broad sheets of his horse's trapper. But the animal kicked and screamed, its heaving flank thrashing over Agryn's hips and legs. It did not matter. Anyone could see. Agryn lay face down, the iron bucket of his helm mashed into the turf.

Half the men of Mornaway's North Company had gathered. Guthred turned to the skittish lads in his charge. "We need a bow!" And when they didn't move. *"Now!"*

When a crossbow, massive as an anchor, was slapped into Guthred's hands, he flipped the thing right over and *thwocked* a bolt into the horse's skull. Three times, moving with no more emotion than the cogwheels of a mill, he set the stirrup of the heavy bow on the turf and wrenched the string back.

Bolts jutted from the horse's temple like an eruption of brown, bloody teeth.

Durand walked forward then, as bolts thudded into the second animal—in Yrlac green.

Hooves swished past him as he stepped among gold sheets and silver, yellow and white. The pinned knight was still. The skirts of the man's surcoat were flipped over his back, dropping into impossible voids. Durand remembered Agryn's strange gratitude in the moments before the first charge. This faceless shape in the muck was not him.

Durand didn't hear a last bolt thud into the jaw of the horse in green.

Agryn was dead, but it seemed important to free him. Durand set his hands against the man's horse, and shoved, nearly horizontal above the mud. He pushed, feeling the warm bulk yield under his hands.

Soon the others joined him, and Agryn was free.

REPORTS FROM THE Yrlac camp said Radomor lived.

As the Eye of Heaven bled into the sea, Lamoric's men said muddled prayers for Agryn and one other man dead on that day. They were standing on the bare headland, far from sacred ground. There were no wise women to cleanse and dress the dead, though Deorwen anointed their foreheads. There were no priests. Guthred stitched the long shapes of both men into their own bright trappers, and the conroi made sure that both fallen comrades had the spurs and belt and sword of a knight-at-arms so they might be known at the Gates of Heaven. Durand didn't know the second knight at all, and he found himself wondering how well he knew Agryn. As they stood over Agryn and the other man, he studied the ground between his boots, keeping his swollen eyes from the living and the dead.

Another day of fighting loomed before them. When the sun rose, Radomor of Yrlac would ride out. Unless Agryn had smashed every bone in the man's body, Durand knew that Radomor would come. The whole thing no longer seemed like some grand task, but a simple act of endurance.

A shadow fell over his boots. "Can you write?" asked Berchard.

"What?"

"Can you write?" Berchard repeated.

"No."

"Ah. blast. I just thought. We hadn't asked. Curse it all," Berchard muttered, absently clawing at his beard.

After a moment, Berchard punched Durand's shoulder in absentminded reassurance. Walking away, he stopped at Guthred's shoulder and whispered something in the man's ear that made Guthred wince.

The man turned.

"All right," said Guthred. "You and I'll fill the graves."

"Here?" Durand asked.

"Aye."

Guthred passed Durand an iron-shod shovel, and Durand stabbed the blade into the heap of loose earth. Abruptly, he realized there wasn't enough of the stuff, and, for the first time, looked down into the grave. Agryn's yellow shroud was hardly a foot below the turf.

"Guthred?"

The man looked, his expression heavy with a dull sorrow that stopped Durand's tongue.

"All right," was all Durand said.

HE AWOKE TO torchlight and the sound of shovels.

In an instant, he was on his feet and stealing closer, with a vision of the Rooks in his mind's eye. All he found, at first, was a torch struggling in the night wind over the graves. Then he made out hunched figures, working low. He jerked his blade free of its scabbard.

And he stopped, astonished at what he saw.

In a momentary bloom of the guttering torch flame, Badan the wolf appeared, working low over one grave, stabbing the earth with a shovel. His red hair hung in tendrils. Then everything vanished as a stubborn gust fought with the torch.

Durand blinked into the sudden blackness for a moment. He heard the shovel bite. The next lull in the wind freed the torch fire to splash over the face of Coensar. He was standing back. The man whose fist held the torch high was one-eyed Berchard.

"What in the name of Heaven's Host . . ." Durand spoke before he could stop himself.

Berchard glanced up, his face touched with regret. Coensar simply looked.

"We're doing what must be done," Coensar said.

"Agryn was the one who wrote," Berchard added, as though this was excuse enough.

Durand blinked. They were mad.

"No one's died, have they?" Coensar murmured, half-wondering. "Since you've come. We haven't lost anyone. Not in the tourneys."

Abruptly, Durand understood. "There's only been one real tourney. The Glass was something else."

"We're unclean," Coensar said.

Durand saw them hovering over the open grave. He remembered Agryn, fighting for his king. He felt the weight of his sword in his fist. "You bloody well are! What in the name of—"

"Killing a man's plain murder," Berchard said. "Ransom's theft. Honor's pride, or vanity." He rubbed the socket of his living eye where fatigue or pitch-smoke needled.

"The wise women hate us, and the Patriarchs won't have us in holy ground," Coensar continued. He sounded tired. "The graybeards put a ban on the tournaments and see no reason to help the fools who die fighting them. Sometimes we find a wandering friar who knows the rites."

"We are unrepentant and likely to draw the attention of Them Below," Berchard said.

Badan grunted agreement.

Yellow cloth flashed in the shovel wounds. He wondered why he should be surprised that the Host of Hell had its eye on them.

"So what is this?" he asked, finally.

"He's not in hallowed ground," Berchard said, and, glancing around the bare headland, made the Eye of Heaven. "Don't think we do this lightly. A man buried in the open is free for anything that might pass. Bad business. And worse, sudden death! It's like sounding a hunting horn to the Banished, the Lost, and their kin. Creation's full of things that won't let a corpse lie. And what if the man's soul wants vengeance? You've seen the gibbets at the crossroads."

Durand did not deny it.

"You don't want the whoresons finding their way back to

the ones who strung them up . . . or dragging themselves home, pining for their kin."

Durand gave in.

In solemn silence, then, Badan slit the yellow shroud, baring a flash of bloodless skin.

"Hands and feet, Badan," Berchard said, stiffly. "We'll dig some proper graves."

Badan had a hatchet. He lifted the thing as the others flinched away.

Durand took up a shovel.

They worked deep into the night, digging black graves. Durand worked under the earth, quietly certain that they were *all* mad, but that every bit of madness was real. Finally, hands drew him from the darkness, and he helped take up the shrouded bundles, passing the bodies down. Each was rigid under its parti-colored shroud as though some dark terror gripped a body robbed of its soul.

Badan swarmed down each hole, looking every bit a werewolf ghoul. They passed him down a mallet and long iron nails.

Tock. Tock. Tock. The mallet fell.

Durand, Berchard, and Coensar hunkered down by the heaped soil, the sea wind playing. Berchard took a quick pull from a wineskin. There was black sea on either side. "You'll find a lot of burials that start shallow, then get dug deeper overnight. Murders, suicides. Some do it with childbirth mums. And the little ones, too, if they pass before their naming day. The Lost look through those like ragpickers through old clothes."

Badan worked, and, as he moved in the narrow grave, his weight, for a moment, must have rested on Agryn's chest. The corpse moaned.

Durand's throat locked.

"Host of Heaven," he hissed.

"It's lungs. Like bellows," Berchard said, but he repeated the Creator's sign, and downed another swig of wine. "Just lungs. I heard one naming the Powers that way."

"Hells."

Berchard handed Durand the skin. The wine tasted of hickory and acorn. He passed it on to Coensar.

Badan kept working, either fearless or soulless.

When he finished, and the graves were mounded with earth, all four men stumbled away and collapsed.

Berchard pawed muddy sweat from his high forehead, sighing, "It's a shame you never learned to write, lad. It's a far cleaner way than this," Berchard answered. "We scratch a few lines from the *Book of Moons*. Our old friend—"

"—Agryn?"

"*No names at the graveside*. Our friend there, trained to join the Holy Ghosts way back. He'd have been the one."

"Aye."

Berchard nodded. "Was up at House Loegern or Pennons Gate—don't remember which—for years ready to serve the king. There was a girl or something."

"That's why he could quote so well," said Berchard. "*The Book of Moons* and all that. No matter what else they get up to behind their walls, those Holy Ghosts teach their lads properly. A few lines on a bit of copper—or lead if there's no copper at hand—and past the dead man's teeth. Best chance; the Banished can't get past it. Worst, they can't get out."

"Good thing we had Badan around. Bloody awful work. A soldier I knew in Aubairn once, he confessed it to a priest. Priest made the poor bastard march to the Shrine of the *Cradle*'s Landing in Wave's Ending. And the priest was right." He shook his head. "You can't do a thing like that without it marking you."

The one-eyed campaigner almost grinned. "But Badan's a whoreson bastard."

28. Upon the Rock of Tern Gyre

In the profound sleep that followed, Durand dreamed of movement through the darkness. A thousand thousand shapes flitted like the shadows of every bird that flew under Heaven. Sketchily visible, one detached itself. Like a creature of deep seas, the thing rippled between the tents: a shape of claws and smooth muscle, flat skull, and eyes like blue coals. It had nothing to do with Radomor or Lamoric or Ragnal or even Durand. The wild thing slithered with the haste of an eddying wind between the canvas walls of the encampment. Durand felt himself tugged along behind, floating and watching.

Suddenly the hulking, scurrying monster came upon two long rectangles in the grass. Durand remembered the graves. The thing seemed to stare in an intent pause, then it passed its talons through the earth, which rippled and flowed around its hands. Durand recognized the mud he had tamped with his own shovel.

The thing plunged. It sank as it had flown, treating earth and air like water. With the sinuous power of a reptile, it churned downward, and Durand was tugged along for the ride. He caught the glint of needle-teeth. After a moment, through the thick slurry of earth, came a flash of yellow. A winding sheet. Durand saw crude stitches, then earth, then the stiff white curls of cold lips and nostrils.

Invisible fingers worked at rigid lips, darting in for a look at the smooth blue-gray passages beyond. Then it pulled back to tug. Its talons caught in the winding sheet and it jerked and pulled as it coiled upward through the earth. The corpse of Agryn rolled out of the straining cloth as the creature pulled and pulled, jerking the shroud away. The body itself was snagged on the nails Badan had driven through, and it hung like a drowned man caught on the way to the bottom. The greedy fiend heaved and tugged, frantic. Finally, it burst into the air yet again to tug on a corner of canvas—the only bit of Agryn that had made it to the surface.

IN THE YELLOW and green half-light of Cerlac's old tent, Durand winced a little air through his broken nose and blinked thick eyelids. He smoothed out his bedroll and checked his few possessions. His fighting surcoat was stiff as a butcher's apron, cold, and more brown than green. Slashes scored the face of his shield. Here and there, popped links scabbed his hauberk. The long leaf blade of his razor was powdered with rust.

They must not only survive another day; they must win. The wait was like an itch in his joints.

A ruby slit of light shot into the tent gloom as a woolly head appeared through the tent flap, bobbing a few feet above the floor. It was one of the shield-bearers. "Sir? I'm shield-bearer to Sir Berchard. Guthred sent me after your surcoat. He says he'll be cursed if he lets you ride into the lists in soiled gear and make Lamoric look a fool. He's told me your horse had no trapper, sir?"

"What?" started Durand. The boy's floating head blinked up at him in complete innocence. "No. There's no cursed trapper."

The young man nodded and stepped inside, unself-consciously ignoring explanations that didn't concern him to tromp after Durand's muddy, bloody surcoat. "There's been no time," Durand said at the top of the shield-bearer's head. The boy balled the mess up and backed out, grinning politely without listening.

"There's breakfast," the boy said.

Again, Durand stood in the empty tent. The acid scent of lye bit his eyes. It had carried in with Berchard's boy—likely up to his armpits in it for hours. Honest work, but no longer his to do.

He pulled on his cloak and went after his breakfast.

As he stepped into the dawn, he shot a glance down a chance aisle between the tents. The churned earth of Agryn's mound lay dark against the east and the cliff's edge, and he thought of his dream. Uneasy, he walked the canvas alleyway toward it.

As he stepped squinting from the lane, two silhouettes ceased speaking. Durand was already too close to step away. Lamoric and Deorwen turned to face him. He could only bow.

"Durand," Lamoric said.

"Lordship; Ladyship," Durand said. Deorwen was playing her part, appearing mild and easy even after all that had happened.

"Did you see my brother yesterday?" Lamoric asked.

"I don't—" Durand faltered.

"My brother. Father sent him. With our vote. Gireth. So he's come. I saw him up there."

"No. I didn't think—"

"No. But that's him. Landast the heir. Too wise to go haring off to tournaments and rebellions with duties at home." He gave his wife an apologetic glance. "But that's how it's always been. Him at home, and me off riding. Him taking up burdens, and me playing games." He waved to the others and the Red Knight gear he still wore. "But it doesn't matter, does it?"

Durand thought of a thousand things that he should tell this man. Deorwen was right there. Even now, he was tempted, but he looked the man square in the face.

"This is the grave?" said a voice from the brightness.

Across the mounded earth stood a socket in the bright dawn: the Lord of Mornaway. No one answered.

"Lord Lamoric, after what has happened, I must—"

"Moryn, I have not always been the sort of man a brother would wish his sister to marry," Lamoric said. His hand crossed to Deorwen's arm, and she allowed him to take her hand.

After a moment's silent consideration, Lord Moryn abandoned much of what he must have planned to say, asking simply, "Why have you come to me now? Why"—his empty hand then faltered over the gray mounds—"this?"

"We had good reason."

"Radomor."

"He thinks he will be king."

Moryn did not argue, instead nodded slowly. "Many might follow such a man."

"*If* Ragnal loses the crown, some might suffer a man like Radomor of Yrlac to pluck it up, but when we are victorious today none of this will matter."

"Why only then?"

"He will take your vote from you."

Moryn made to protest.

"He will have the victor's boon," said Lamoric, "if he can best us."

Moryn stopped a long time, then. The shadowed face turned Durand's way, needled through with dawn's rays. "It would be his right."

"He will snare you with your honor."

"I have sworn," Moryn murmured. "As commander of the North Company, I've vowed to keep the customs of this place under the eyes of the prince and the king. Kandemar the Herald stood by. By their word are half-a-thousand knights bound to my house, and we to them. Trees and fields and mills and rivers beyond counting. I must serve as the king's justice in a thousand cases." He paused. "There is no recanting."

"There will be no need," Lamoric vowed. "We will see to it, brother. Return to your people. Arm yourself and speak to any who will listen. On this day, it is in our power to keep war from our doorstep."

Lord Moryn faced this oration in silence. The grave was between them.

"He was close to you," he said.

"Agryn kept his own counsel, but I have known no wiser man," Lamoric allowed.

"He spoke to me," Durand said.

Moryn nodded, then straightened his surcoat. "Let us make certain that his life has bought more than one day," he said and left them standing around the grave.

"The others are nearly prepared to go in," Deorwen prompted.

Lamoric nodded, touching Durand's shoulder. "I am glad that you turned us back," he said. Then Deorwen and Lamoric left as well.

Durand settled to his knees, facing the dawn as Agryn had only a day before. His fingers closing in the chalky earth scraped a tatter of cloth: a yellow triangle of winding sheet jutted from the turned earth. It could have been some strange flower. He took the canvas between two fingers, letting the fabric slide as he looked into the earth.

In an hour, the rain returned.

DURAND WATCHED THE king and his train of black-clad toadies take their places. Despite the black sapphire crown on his brow, Ragnal looked like he should be in the battlefield breaking armies, not perched among traitors and cowards and fools.

Rain slithered through steel links.

The lines waited under the low Heavens. Iron-mailed hands scratched collars, slapped the necks of horses, and juggled battle helms. There were no pretenses. Agryn's ride had turned the mood. If anyone felt he wasn't part of a real battle, he was mad. Some had even changed sides: rats leaving the Mornaway ship.

Heremund stood among the shield-bearers, his shoulders up around his ears as the rain pattered down. "Radomor's got as many men today as yesterday. Not one fell. No one so much as wrenched his ankle."

Though the drizzle darkened their shoulders, Yrlac's green men stood straight as ever. Yrlac himself scowled fit to steam the rain from his skull. Before him the monstrous Champion knelt, his helmed head on the earth. Neither man seemed much the worse for a fall that had killed a strong man and three horses only the day before.

Today, the Rooks flapped through the lines, stirring up the animals.

"I don't like it," said Heremund. "Yrlac and that Champion of his should've gone for a start. Radomor and his friend never so much as popped a shoulder. They had to *drag* Radomor off. He shouldn't be there."

Guthred grunted, rain trailing down his stolid face.

"And your company's down quite a few as well, I see," Heremund ventured. A score had gone. "Looks like the square after market day."

"Men are what they are," Guthred said. "More'll leave for fear than join for conscience."

The skald nodded. "A shame."

Guthred shrugged. "Worse shame, we're down four ourselves. Agryn and the young one, Cadarn, yesterday, and two more've come up lame 'smorning. That bastard Musgered's found himself a torn shoulder—didn't notice till this morning. And Badan's got fever." A superstitious quarter of Durand's mind recalled Agryn's moan and Berchard's words about desecration marking a man. It was just as likely to be cowardice.

"Bad luck," Durand mumbled.

He looked back to the bedraggled lines. It was bad. There were too many men in Radomor's host, and Moryn's company stretched very thin to line up against them. Surveying the grim line, Durand tried to conjure up some strategy that might counter Radomor's numbers. What he needed was something like Radomor's ploy on the first day. By letting the conrois think they were out for a day's sport, Radomor kept the fighting light and his men safe. And hitting hard right at the day's end gave everyone the same message: A real battle was com-

ing on—just in time for Moryn's North Company to stew in
their tents all night.

"Clever," Durand grumbled.

"Radomor? He spends a day playing with us, then picks up
twenty of your men for the rough going today."

"We're better without them," Guthred said.

Durand wondered if this were true.

"I spent some time watching the stands while you lads were
busy," said Heremund. "You can see which way the wind
blows, that's certain."

Durand peered down on the skald. "There must have been
some people sitting up when Radomor rode after Moryn's
head."

"Aye, though they sat down again when your Agryn stopped
him," Heremund said. "You could see them tensing up. Noble
arses coming up off the benches. All these dog-feral gleams in
their eyes. And then nothing." Heremund grinned his black-
socket grin. "Beoran was near swearing over it."

In all this thinking about battlefields and strategy, a man
might forget their real business: the Great Council and its vote.

"How do they stand?" Durand asked.

"Same as ever. There were as many ready to get up as not.
As many grinned as cursed. Radomor's still got to win this,
I'd say. And it's still ours to lose."

Durand nodded, filling his chest with sea air. "Right. Let's
get to it then," he said and climbed into the saddle.

As Durand swung aboard his nameless bay, Coensar cut his
stallion from the line, riding out before Lamoric's retainers.
He looked over them all.

"Yrlac will come for Moryn Mornaway—that's certain—
so we won't have to go looking for a fight today."

Ouen laughed. The rest smiled cutthroat grins.

"You're all going to keep your damned heads up, your eyes
open, and watch for each other. You know this, but I'll tell you
anyway: We're bigger together, and we're going to stay together, or it'll be me you've got to worry about and not some
mad Duke of Yrlac. Got it?"

Half the men, smiling at this none-so-grand speech, hoisted
swords or lances in wry salute. Coensar flashed a grin back,

every inch a bandit captain. "Right. Watch for it, and let's see if we can't take this Radomor's head."

Horses stamped and nodded down both lines. Kandemar the Herald spoke again, holding the ivory battle horn like a scepter over them all. Durand pulled cords and cinched straps tight to creaking. The hardwood lance in his fist felt light as a reed.

Coensar was right: Radomor would come for them, and that would be their chance. They would fight and they would win. Again, Prince Biedin's black gauntlet was high in the rain. Durand's mouth was dry to his neck bones. The bay underneath him bobbed, its ears twitching. Then Biedin's hand chopped down, and two hundred horses surged into motion.

The hard men who'd stayed behind in Moryn's Company drove their horses with glinting eyes and clenched teeth—no cantering pass. Radomor's turncoats, meanwhile, howled like Writhen Man savages, some with their lances cocked overhand. A man could lose his mind. The whole rumbling arc of Moryn's line might have been falling toward a mirrored earth of flaring nostrils, feral eyes, and iron glints.

There was a heartbeat.

And Durand struck a man under a dog's-head crest. Dog Head's lance swatted Durand's shield. His own splayed point stamped shield and fist into his victim's snapping ribs, the shaft exploding into white blades and ribbons. Then they were past.

Durand cantered on, sucking mud and air through his teeth. The girth on his saddle had held. The hit to his shield had not been a square one. He was alive. He threw the lance butt from his stinging hand and wheeled. Dog Head's mount cantered riderless. The man himself rolled in flying skirts.

"In line!"

More than just Lamoric's conroi, the captain called the whole company together. Durand focused beyond Dog Head's writhing to see Radomor's line thundering in a great wheel. Never slowing, they swung back through the rain. A hundred horses rounded like death.

The others were too slow.

Coensar clawed his helm back and swung his sword in the air, shouting "Wheel! Wheel! Back at them! Back at them!" But already the enemy ranks were rolling into their charge, shaking the earth under the hooves of their scattered adversaries.

On Moryn's side, lone riders wheeled, men slapped helms over bare heads, and warhorses pawed the air. There was no hope of turning the whole line in time.

Coensar's eyes flashed hollow, shouting only at the men near him: Lamoric's retainers. "At them!" And, alone, Coensar and the arrow of Lamoric's men sprang for the heart of the South Company.

Scattered allies flickered past, then, long before the stricken could leave the field, the conroi broke into the open ground before the enemy. It was mad and wild. Durand tore his sword free and thrust it high over his head, then the iron arrow and the thundering wave exploded over the fallen horses in the middle of the yard.

Men and horses screamed.

Lamoric's conroi struck deep, tearing, as the giant South Company spasmed tight around them. Durand's shield leapt under a storm of swords, maces, and beaked hammers. All he could do was spur the bay mindlessly onward hoping no one could take aim. Fallen horses pulled eddies around themselves. Durand ripped himself free and lurched into one such pocket. For an instant, he knew that a living man lay in the tangle under his horse's hooves.

As soon as he found this refuge, the storm of blades flashed down on him. Barefaced, Durand found he could see and act where men in full helms were blind. Almost before he realized this, the surge threw a knight against him: a savage who shuddered blows against Durand's shield while Durand fought to get his blade around. Razor edges sparked through the thin shell of planks. Durand jabbed his spurs, and, in an instant, his massive bay had launched itself forward, its half-ton bulk bulling a gap between the two horses ahead. The landing ripped a scream and a leg from Durand's attacker.

"Durand! This way."

Coensar, barefaced, but in his blue and white, screamed from a clot of fighting men round Mornaway. There might have been a league between them.

"Watch Lamoric!" he roared.

Radomor's men had pried Lamoric from the rest of his conroi. Twenty paces separated Durand from his lord, with every step of that distance seething with soldiers. Already, it looked as though someone in the South Company had figured out that Lamoric—and the ransom of a duke's son—was ripe to be plucked. The old Red Knight helm bobbed and tumbled in the cataract of Radomor's killers.

Clamping his jaws, Durand spurred the bay into that mob. Blades flashed. He could have been plunging down a river. The bay lunged and wallowed. He found that the only way forward was to cock his feet over the brute's shoulders. Blows clattered over his shield and mailed knee. A thunderbolt fell over his back, turned by iron and padding. He lashed at anything that came close.

There was no room.

Each lunge covered less and less ground. A dead man could not have fallen in the crush. Stealing a glance through the storm, Durand made out Berchard pinned at his master's side, laying about with an ugly spiked hammer. Half the paint had scabbed from the man's helm. He couldn't last.

In one motion, Durand planted his feet on the bay's withers and reared up over the mob. A grin jagged across his face as he looked over the blind tops of helmets. Suddenly, Lamoric was only a few steps away. Durand pitched himself toward his comrades, stilting a wild path across the battle with his boots slamming down on cantles and groins and withers and thighs. Friendly knights swore. Enemies swung too late. Berchard, his now-naked head gleaming, spotted Durand at the last moment. Berchard's opponent glanced up, too, just in time to catch a three-foot steel blade through the eye-slit of his helm.

Heaving the dead man by belt and collar, Durand dropped into his place.

While he fought for Lamoric then, one vain quarter of his mind could not stop thinking of the spectacle he had just made.

THAT STALEMATE GRIND outlasted the rain. Soon, even Radomor's company had had enough. The heralds, optimistic men, called a halt to the fighting. It was noontide and time for dinner.

Despite the muck and gore, Durand felt a grim satisfaction as he watched the enemy host withdraw, the men weaving their way back across the rutted, littered mire. A few men were still tussling. The two companies had been like pit-dogs locked at each other's throats. As they disentangled themselves, Durand could almost feel each long fang withdraw, one by one, leaving scattered, bloody knots behind.

His eyes hardly registered the dead.

LAMORIC'S RETINUE DREW itself together and led its horses out of the lists. Shield-bearers ran skins of wine to their knights.

Durand felt someone jerk the reins from his hand. It was only as one of Lamoric's shield-bearers led the animal away that he noted the blue and green trapper hanging from it, and remembered that it wasn't really his. He would have to call it a trophy.

The boys had erected a pavilion within the walls, and soon they were through the flap and out of the weather. Guthred's crew of shield-bearers inspected men and gear, and each group ignored the conversations of the other.

A shield-bearer screwed a beaker of claret into Durand's hand.

"That's the worst morning I've had since before my wife died," Berchard rumbled—a joke, but forced. He sat down heavily.

"A bad one," Coensar agreed.

The labored breathing of the knights filled the silence for a time. Around the circle were broken noses, smashed teeth, snapped fingers, and sprung shoulders. Lamoric wasn't the only battered one. Wind over the walls lashed a patter of rain over the tent's roof.

"How many'd we lose, do you think?" Lamoric said.

"It's hard to say. One we had from Garelyn. A handful of the others didn't make it back," Berchard said. Something had him wincing.

"Three," said Coensar.

"I don't suppose there's any chance we could withdraw," Berchard quipped.

A few of the men snorted.

"Ah well," said Berchard. "If we don't fight him now, I suppose we'll only be fighting him later."

"He likely won't forget us," Coensar murmured.

"You're right. We'd best get him now." Berchard flashed a grin. "It's the only safe thing to do."

While the bearded campaigner chuckled, a scowling Guthred probed broken rings over his knee. Berchard winced.

"I'm taking a look," said Guthred, levelly. "Get the legging off."

"Ugh. I'll have to do it all over again!" Berchard griped, and Guthred fished high under the man's hauberk, reaching—Durand guessed—for the cord that knotted chain leggings to his belt. Berchard caught his wrist.

"What do you think you're doing? Get your hand out! If you've got to take the legging off then the whole thing comes off. I'm not going in to fight this bastard all crossed up."

Lamoric smirked through the rusty smears on his face. "You put them on right once today already—"

"And that's why I'm still here to complain."

The whole conroi was fighting with grins.

But Guthred would not be put off, and soon Sir Berchard sat perched on a barrel in nothing but a pair of gray breeches. Everything came off: surcoat, hauberk, gambeson, tunic, cap, and leggings—all to uncover a wound, in the end, that was nothing but a purple smear of bruise. There was nothing Guthred could do. Undeterred, however, he hauled out a bacon-stinking salve and rubbed it deep. Berchard swore that the man was punishing him.

Finally, Berchard stood in the middle of the tent, all pasty skin and plastered rings of hair. "All right," he said. "All of it. Right back on."

Lamoric's knights were weeping with laughter.

Berchard ignored the whole lot, gesturing to his woolly-headed shield-bearer. The boy picked up the gambeson.

"No no. The leggings first. No, always the left first." As the knight sat, the boy pulled the quilted leggings over Berchard's big white feet. "Right, now I'll tie them up. The gambeson's next."

The boy picked up the sodden coat and struggled to get it over the knight's head. Berchard slithered into the heavy thing, bouncing to shake the kinks out.

The dome of his skull gleamed like a fresh bun as it bulged

from the collar. Berchard did not smile. "Next it's the hauberk, boy." The shield-bearer bent over the heap of what looked like disarticulated iron links, and pawed with increasing agitation under the scrutiny of the knights until signs of the collar and shoulders allowed him to see which way was up. Soon, though, a smiling Berchard had the hauberk, and was struggling half-in and half-out to reach the sleeves and get the long coat over his shoulders. The shield-bearer's help saved him.

"Well done, boy." Briskly, Berchard tied a red coat-of-plates around his trunk. It looked, except for long rows of rivet-heads, like a regular surcoat right down to his blazon: three yellow songbirds. "Saved my life a hundred times," he said, rapping himself on the chest. Finally, he plucked up his white linen arming cap, and tied it under his beard. The shield-bearer handed him his chain hood. "Well guessed," the knight said, dropping the thing over his cap. "Leave the gauntlets. I won't put them on till I'm ready to leave.

"Gods, though," Berchard said, pressing the palm of his hand to his side. His good eye blinked. "Do you think I've got time for the privy?"

They nearly threw the tent down on him.

When he finally shook off the last laughing attacker, Berchard brushed off his surcoat.

"Oh." He looked up at the shield-bearer. "I've lost my helm." He turned to Coensar. "I threw it off during the fighting, but it looks as though the chain snapped." There was a roundel on his coat of plates from which a finger's length of chain dangled. "I shouldn't be surprised." He looked to the boy. "Do you think you can find the thing? It's got my birds here on the crest. Or it did have. I suppose we'll see."

Durand watched the young man duck through the tent flap, excited by the attention and responsibility. Then Durand remembered just where the boy was running and the blood and dead men who had been trampled into the mud by two hundred horses. He had never seen anything like that at the boy's age. Some pale corner of his mind realized that he'd never seen anything like that himself until that day. He stared into the swirls of the carpet, forgetting the wine in his hand.

Before an hour had passed, a herald's boy ran past the tents announcing that the last mêlée was about to resume.

THERE WERE CARRION birds over the field. No one had had the wits to shoo them away. The men shuffled to a halt. The creatures hopped among the bodies, plucking and tearing with the black daggers of their beaks.

"Never seen anything like it," Berchard said.

"Nowhere but a battlefield," Coensar said.

As they spoke, Berchard's young shield-bearer reappeared. He had the helm clutched to his chest. A syrupy filigree of blood, muck, and rain streaked it. Its crest was mangled.

At a glance, Berchard stopped—the boy's eyes stared from gray-bruise circles. Berchard took the helm gingerly. "Good boy."

THE GREAT MEN of the kingdom slid their way back onto the long benches of the reviewing stand. Durand read the gray pages of their faces. He saw Lady Maud with her chin high, moving like Heremund's ship in bunting. He saw an active-looking lord with an iron beard and sycophants trailing from his sleeves: Beoran. He saw Prince Biedin set his black-gloved hand on his brother's arm. He saw the king, loaded down with gems, but grim and watchful as a lion in a snare. Rain poured down.

Coensar was speaking.

"I'll say it once more. We're to fight as a conroi. No one wanders off. No one lets another man get separated. We'll shove ourselves into Radomor's face and stay there till he can't stand the stink of us. We'll do all that 'cause breaking up nearly cost us this morning."

He looked to Durand, then back to his men.

"And before we go, I'll tell you where I screwed up," the captain said. "I reckoned they'd all go for Moryn. I reckoned they'd come for him and knock down whatever got in their way. It never struck me how many would see our Lamoric and still be looking out for their own purses. This, now, is Rado's last chance. You know what that means by now."

Then they waited in the saddle. Men sucked last, shaking

pulls from skins of blood-colored wine. Warhorses stamped and tossed their heads.

The trumpets brayed, and they drowned the sound with howling as they exploded across the field. Lance-points stormed past Durand like iron birds. The two hosts hurtled into each other, and then caught, locking in a long, knotted convulsion.

Durand spotted gaps, setting his bay leaping and spinning through the crowd, hunting for every twitch in the throng. A hundred blows battered him, but he saw: after the first pell-mell collision, some part of the enemy had sagged away. Spinning in his seat, he fixed on the reason: There was no Yrlac green. Radomor's uniformed foreigners had gone, leaving their allies to fight a mismatch.

There was nothing to do. Durand fought on and on while bands of agony clamped his ribs and shoulders. If he lowered his guard for the briefest instant, a sword or mace would whistle over. The thousand agonies of each moment drove every thought from his skull; he forgot the missing soldiers in green.

Then the captain shouted a warning, and Durand flinched from a flash of motion and a sheet of mud and iron. Green horsemen crashed through the line. The soldier beside Durand jolted into flight, batted from his seat like a doll. Horses tore through on all sides.

The men of Yrlac could have been the leopards of their blazons as they clawed their way into Moryn's men, slashing with the energy of fresh arms and clear heads.

Coensar screamed Lamoric's conroi close, "To Mornaway!" And, catching each other by arm and bridle, they bulled their way toward the diamonds of Lord Moryn's surcoat, hoping only to outride the green men who rode the same course.

Flashes burst in Durand's skull as they finally battered their way through, then, with disorienting speed, the green horsemen tore free of the battle. Durand's bay actually stumbled as the shoring weight of the green horsemen whirled off into the rain.

Though he was exhausted, Durand and a half dozen threw themselves after the retreating knights, jouncing to a halt in the open yard only when Coensar shouted them down.

Curtains of rain swung shut behind the retreating horse-men. The free men of Radomor's company looked baffled as any of Moryn's knights, as the whole Yrlac conroi fled.

Someone whooped in victory.

Coensar raised a cautioning hand to his own men. "They're coming back. Wait for them." He stood in his stirrup irons, scanning the rain for shadows.

A few knights began to shout to one another. Somewhere, a duel clattered back to life.

When even Durand doubted that Radomor would ever re-turn, hoofbeats shuddered in the air: very close. His eyes swept the gray void. For one breath, he would have sworn that Radomor was already through—invisible. The ground throbbed in a hundred directions. He gaped, and then heard the screams explode behind him.

They had circled.

Blades sleeted through men and horses.

Only a few paces from Durand, Radomor's Champion tore through the crowd, batting men down like scarecrows, nearer and nearer. With mace and fists and fingers ripping through armored knights, the Champion looked like a beast scaled in iron. As the brute took the last man in his fist and threw him from his seat, Durand found himself caught between the Champion and the son of Mornaway.

Durand clenched his teeth. "Hells!"

The Champion loomed high, whipping his thorny mace down for Durand's head. Three spikes jutted from the inner face of Durand's shield. The Champion reared back, wrench-ing his mace free with a force that nearly tore the shield away. There could have been a bear in the man's hauberk. The mace whistled down, a single spine flickering through Durand's gauntlet and knuckles as he threw a parry high.

Durand jabbed his spurs home, the bay leaping clear as iron thorns swept past yet again. But, setting his teeth against ter-ror, he knew that he must not run. He turned back against the monster. The thing must not get by.

The Champion had already made to move on when Durand pitched back into its path. He was like a dog at a bull's ankles. Durand barged into the Champion; a disembodied throb roared from the man. He vibrated like his skin had been packed with bees. An obscene reek and a gray beard gushed from under the monster's helm.

Durand swung, but his hesitation cost him. The Champion's mace struck first: a claw of spikes tearing Durand's shield. The big man muscled the mace into a swing Durand could do nothing about. Hardwood thundered over his shoulder. Iron tines darted between the bones of his back.

For an instant, Durand was nowhere.

Lolling.

He was drowning, gulping for air, doubling over against his will. He heard a whining, high, and the beehive roar. Some quarter of his mind waited like a falling man waits for the earth. Another part knew that a killing blow would fall in an instant, and he would be driven from Creation.

But he lived: long enough to wrench a glimpse from the chaos. A wedge of Radomor's men had driven through to Moryn. Knights of all sides surrounded the lean son of Mornaway. And Durand could see, in that instant, that the two sides were balanced. Radomor's Champion had turned his head. All at once, Durand saw that the man would hurl himself against this stalemate like a thunderbolt.

It would all be over.

Durand lashed out. The wild blow scrabbled from the Champion's shoulder. The monster twisted, unable to reach back, as Durand's second swing clipped his helm, catching and wrenching it round. The Champion flailed. Now, Durand reeled free. He swung again and again with blacksmith blows.

The thing would never reach Moryn.

A last strike clanged, and Durand rose in the stirrups, reversing his blade and, with the force of both fists, drove the point down into the brute's chest.

He meant to throw his weight behind the driving point, but the blade slipped deeper than he could understand, plunging like a fork into straw. A torrent of flies battered Durand's lips and eyelids. No blood erupted.

They were falling.

Durand landed hard in a belch of corruption: a tanner's midden, a putrid grave. Flies stormed around him, curling in his eyes, clotting his mouth and nostrils. Under his hands, the man was like rotten branches. Impossible. Durand scrambled, remembering only at the last instant to snatch his sword free. The blade came away dry.

Now, Durand was crawling at the bottom of a maelstrom of horses and flying muck. No one had time to look down, but Durand hardly noticed. He scrambled.

Then a great shape whirled high above him. Durand heard a roar, and a hail of iron-shod hooves stabbed down. He had to forget horror. He had to roll. He caught glimpses of green as hooves hammered from warding arms. Above it all, the red leopard of his attacker's crest seemed ready to leap over its master's shoulders. This was the duke himself.

The hideous will of the man bore down on Durand alone.

Suddenly, the hunchbacked duke was gone—a mighty storm sucked back into the clear blue Heaven. But the duke was only gathering himself. When his horse was clear, Radomor spun, a razor-edged axe flashing in his hand, and charged. Durand couldn't move for mud. The duke rode a hail of flying muck, and his axe flashed high.

Then a spray from another horse slashed across the duke's path. Hooves stamped down. Coensar's blue and white flashed. Durand tumbled and tore himself to his feet. There were limbs and men in that mud. He could be crushed as easily by friends as foes.

The duke and captain turned round each other, Radomor suddenly without a helm. The duke's beard jutted from a tight chain hood, his eyes flashing like spear-points. Coensar had cornered the hunter. Durand staggered from the tight gyre of the circling horses. If Coensar struck swiftly, the day was over.

Duke and captain circled shield to shield. Blows flickered through the rain with the snap and flash of lightning.

They swung apart, forcing Durand to pitch himself another few paces off just to keep clear. Their circle trampled the carcass of Radomor's champion. Durand saw what looked to be masses of crawling, muddy rags as a hoof *shlupped* from the corpse.

It was no even battle. Radomor needed only to delay his attacker. Any moment, some green bastard would spring from the crowd and spot his paymaster in trouble. But the duke was not waiting. His shining blade flashed out, biting deep into Coensar's shield. It could have had his arm. But, just for an instant, the face of the axe was trapped in the wood. Durand had a sudden flash of Cerlac's blade caught just the same in Hesperand.

Coensar seized his chance, ripping at the breaking shield, pitching the duke into Keening's arc: a flash with the bite of a siege engine. The blade skipped from ear to bad shoulder.

Even Durand stumbled with it.

In the instant that followed, Radomor managed to jam his spurs home, and his warhorse lurched out of the tight circle of the warriors' dance. Radomor's leopard shield tumbled from his fingers. He lolled; any other man would have fallen.

Silence and rain flooded into the churned space between them.

Men looked to Coensar as though asking permission, but he only huddled over his saddlebow, watching.

Radomor turned from the lists. He should have been in the mud. Keening had struck like a thunderclap. The blow would have split an oak tree. Durand could hardly believe the duke was alive, but here he was—awake. He had lost, that much was certain, but he should have fallen.

There were scattered cheers.

As the duke rode, Durand saw his face: stiff with fury enough to keep his seat if every limb had been torn from him. He would never fall. And the Rooks were flapping into motion among the man's tents.

On the field, Yrlac's shocked host sagged away from the fight, and Moryn's men bounded close to Coensar, tipping their helms back and clapping his shoulders. Moryn himself, a few yards away, looked around like a man doubting his deliverance. Horses reared and knights, thrust their lances in the air. Only a neat step kept Durand from being trampled under by heedless comrades.

Durand glanced back through the rain toward the rebel duke. The Rooks had reached up to their master's hands, and a faint, clotted blackness poured from their lips. As Durand stared, he felt their strange sorcery tugging at the breath in his lungs.

Durand looked on, alone in horror. While the others slapped Coensar's shoulders, shadows came alive over the Duke of Yrlac, brimming—as he turned back toward the celebrating fools in the lists—in the sockets of his eyes. A snarl of bare teeth glinted in his beard. As Durand howled a warning, Radomor pitched his wild-eyed mount into a turf-shredding rush straight for Coensar.

Knights—shields loose, faces bare—began to turn. In a heartbeat, the duke would crash down on Coensar and his crowd of well-wishers. The duke stood in his stirrups, the bloody axe high.

At the very last, Coensar wrestled Keening around—hopeless.

But Radomor did not swing. A twitch sent him past Coensar and careering on to the Lord of Mornaway.

Moryn was just turning round.

Too late, his men understood. Too slow, they sprang to close ranks. The duke's tall horse tore a gap. Moryn's mouth was a black hole in a white frame. Swords slapped Yrlac's armor. The wheeling axe met Mornaway's shoulder and chopped him down.

Yrlac rode through as Moryn cartwheeled to the mire.

Durand swayed where he stood. Killing the heir was pointless. Where was the boon? What was to gain? Rain poured down like misery. Ouen and Berchard jounced close and reached to hook him under the arms. Durand swore, shaking off their nursemaid hands. Radomor's green knights were whooping as they left the field. Durand looked for the spot where Lord Moryn lay and saw a crowd of his people. As Durand slogged toward them, he caught a glimpse through the screen of henchmen: Lord Moryn was pulling himself up from the mud.

"Great is the Lord of Dooms." A grin twitched across Durand's smeared face. Yrlac had not succeeded. Moryn had survived. They had won. The crown was safe, war averted, and all of them were free. Ouen and Berchard trotted into the celebration.

It was then, as they left him momentarily alone, that he heard something: a slender whistle.

He was alone for yards in every direction, and the thin shrieking sound rose from nearby.

Someone moaned, *"No-o-o."*

The mangled form of the Champion lay only a few paces

distant. The sounds piped from the carcass. Or somehow beyond it. "It is enough. It should be enough," he heard. The dry shriek whistled on, arising from some deep place as though the flattened corpse lay over the gate of some vast catacomb.

Abruptly something slithered, real and palpable in the rain. Something moved among the clay rents and craters. Blackened tongues of linen retreated into the mouths cut by hoof and blade in the Champion's mail. Gray hair poured long and brittle as spider's webs from the iron cask of its helm.

All at once, the Champion levered itself from the mud. Durand was alone with the thing.

Its twin voices moaned, lost in their dark passages below Creation.

Durand's hands jerked into the sign of the Creator. He couldn't turn away. "Hells."

The creature turned. Its mount lurched onto the field beside it—though its eyes flashed. For a moment, the man's tall carcass stood in the muck, dripping. The last long rags drew themselves in. The iron cask turned. Durand could see glints where his blade had struck it. For a moment, he felt himself under the eye of the man. He knew he could not fight this thing. Not now. But the towering Champion turned from him, finally, and swung onto its tall horse.

🧿 29. The Lion Snared

Your feet! The king, the king is standing!" said a voice. As the Champion rode from the field, Durand must have sagged. He found his hands in the mud. A wind had blown in from the sea, gusting strong enough to lift the trappers of fallen horses.

Berchard caught him under the arm.

First, Durand saw Kandemar the Herald. The man was up, with his long trumpet in his hands and his tabard lashing. In the stands, Ragnal stood on wide-set legs. He had startled his oily flock of servitors. Around him, baffled lords and ladies—for and against the king—got to their feet as well, catching at hats and wimples. Prince Biedin looked from his place at his brother's elbow with a mollifying half-smile on his face, for the king himself wore a scowl.

With stiff fingers, Ragnal gestured to Kandemar, and, with one note of his slender trumpet, the pale Herald lanced the gale. Every man in Errest stopped silent and listened.

"Right," said the king into the empty wind. "It's done. Now we'll see the rest finished and know where we stand."

With this, the great man caught his flying cloak, and stalked from the box with starlings, lords and ladies following in his wake. The feast was set to begin as soon as the company could gather.

Now they would learn the result of all their labors.

CREATION FELL INTO darkness, tossing like a fevered giant. From the vast waste of the Westering Sea, came the greatest in a litany of storms.

Durand tore a clean tunic from his packs as the gale snatched and tugged at his tent. Beyond the loose-skinned drum of the tent, he heard the bark of laughter.

Durand knew the men's minds: Despite all the cunning games Radomor had played, he had lost. Radomor's tricks had left him with nothing, and few men would see valor in that last wild charge for Lord Moryn. Petulance. A man's honor demanded more: A fighting man accepted his doom.

And so they chuckled among the tents as they brushed their best surcoats and gossiped about the king's haste. They played games with the wind.

But Durand had seen the fury stamped on Radomor's features. He had seen the dead man climb from the muck and knew that nothing was over. Radomor would not rest.

He buckled on his sword, setting teeth at the protests of mace-torn shoulder, weeping cuts, and black bruises. Radomor and his creatures would not stop. No one was safe from the Col to the sea. And they all stood on the balancing point: a kingdom teetering on the stormy rock of Tern Gyre. The canvas round him slammed and thundered. His eye fell on the Green Lady's token, black in the shuddering dark.

He could not leave it behind.

The voices were gone. Other knights, with shield-bearers and servants to sponge and brush and comb, had moved more quickly. Whatever happened, he must be there. He must keep his eyes open and be ready.

Taking a deep breath, he stepped into an empty courtyard and was rocked by the wind. Some tents had blown down. One rolled and bounded through the gloomy yard. He was momentarily alone. Above the salt grass yard towered the keep of Tern Gyre. In the wind, Durand saw things: eye-corner shadows that vanished when he turned. Firelight shivered in the narrow windows of the fortress. The Rooks would be slinking through the keep. Radomor's Champion would be poised above the high table. In his mind's eye, Durand saw Radomor sitting on that Ferangore throne. Creation rolled and thundered, full of rain.

A mouth of stone yawned in the keep's flank. Beyond was a stair. Durand pitched himself through the wind and slammed the great door behind him.

Beyond the whistles of the muzzled storm, Durand now heard Biedin's feast upstairs. But, as he listened to their blithe laughter, he flinched from something much closer at hand. The shadows around him seemed to be rustling—small living movements—like moths' wings.

He caught hold of his blade, thinking that, even after all that had happened, he must be mad to be in this place where the rage of Duke Radomor and the schemes of his Rooks had Creation itself boiling like a cauldron.

"I'll see where they've put us." It was Lamoric, his voice hammered flat by the length of a staircase. "Wait a moment."

Deorwen waited alone on the threshold of Radomor's Great Council.

Durand cursed himself. She should not be in this place. He mounted the stair. Some of the lads could get her out and safe. There might still be time.

"Deorwen—" he began, reaching out.

But a great hand caught him, and Ouen was smiling down, gold teeth winking.

"Durand, lad. Come inside, why don't you?" He was grinning, but his grip was tight enough to pop seams. "There's a place with us. Lamoric's just stepped inside to see where the Marshal of the Hall plans to sit them."

Durand glanced to Deorwen.

"For God's sake, Ouen," he said, "it's not—"

"Come on. The lads were wondering. The Prince sets a fair table. There's wine."

Durand left Deorwen there, staring after him with wide, shocked eyes. He couldn't explain to her. He couldn't fight Ouen now, and there was no shaking the big man's grip.

DURAND PITCHED INTO a hall full of men who laughed and gloated while the wind wailed at the arrow loops above them. Tern Gyre's feasting hall was a tall, smoky room where a coat of smooth plaster hid the keep's dark fabric. On a dais at the head of the hall stood the high table, white as an altar. There were chairs for the whole of the Great Council: Biedin, the king, and every Duke of Errest—even the old ghost of Hesperand—but the only man seated was Radomor of Yrlac, hunkered like a dead man's curse at some fairy-tale feast. Mud and blood blackened his surcoat. Rust stained his scalp.

This was the man Durand had seen on the throne in Ferangore.

Ouen half-shoved Durand on.

Below the dais, serving men had set benches and tables around the great blaze at the center of the hall. There, Durand sat under the pressure of Ouen's hand while the wind moaned outside.

"There you are lad, sat down and safe." He snatched a cup of wine from one of the other's hands. "Here. A shot of this will do you good."

Durand set the cup aside. Green knights leaned on their elbows and talked with their knives. The massive Champion sat hard by the dais, his notched helm hanging over the table. The Rooks preened.

Berchard, snug at Durand's side, spoke as Ouen threw his leg over the bench. "Thought you'd got lost," he said. "How's the shoulder?"

Durand hardly remembered. "Fine."

Straight across Biedin's hearthfire, the king's black gaggle of functionaries wrestled with a jug. Though they were bald and soft with years, these men—treasurers, clerks, cofferers, and chroniclers—plucked at each other, slopping wine back and forth and gabbling like children.

Berchard was eyeing Durand's back, seeing God-knew-what.

"You'll need a new surcoat, I think," he decided.

A glance showed a dark stain, but, with Radomor hunkered at the high table like something risen from the Hells, he did not care. He could not believe the others were laughing.

The heavy notes of great drums boomed and rolled, summoning all eyes to the high table for the somber procession of the dukes of Ragnal's Great Council. A stooped man, some prelate by his beard and jeweled robe, took the lead. He carried a gilded sunburst high over his head.

Each lord to step out behind him wore a city's ransom in stones and stiff brocade. Weapons glinted at their hips and crowns winked on their brows. A snapped collarbone had not kept Lord Moryn away. When the procession reached the high table, each magnate stood behind his own tall chair, noting, with varying humor, Radomor's presence there, already sitting.

A thread of the gale outside curled through a window to bludgeon the candles down. Radomor got to his feet. The hearty Duke of Beoran gripped Radomor by the elbow, squeezing his reassurance and muttering through a lopsided smile.

Kandemar, in the meantime, had appeared.

"My lords, ladies, and gentlemen," spoke the Herald, "His Royal Highness, Ragnal, by the Grace of far Heaven, King of Errest: the Elder Kingdom of the Atthias, and realm of the *Cradle*'s Landing."

The drums called every man and woman to their feet. Only Radomor did not heed them.

The priests swayed forward, incense swinging. They parted around the table. In their wake, the Holy Ghosts filed in, forming a rank behind the dukes, as cold as ancient Kandemar.

Candlelight was golden. Incense bloomed.

Finally, into the stillness of the feasting hall, prowled Ragnal, King of Errest. An heirloom blade glinted at his hip, and, on his brow, the kingdom's black sapphire, the Evenstar, winked in its knotted band of red gold.

"Let us begin this foolishness," Ragnal rumbled, and at his word, the feast began. Ragnal's priest-arbiter said wise words over courses of heron and porpoise and ox, and lords passed tokens among the brave. All the while, the gale built beyond the walls. Lightning snapped at the arrow loops with force enough to make the warriors flinch. Durand's hand hardly left the blade at his hip.

Through it all, Radomor neither spoke nor moved. According to every word Heremund had uttered, there were not enough votes to unseat the king. But here was Radomor in his fury. Soon every man at the tables had one eye on the dais, reading the smug looks among those who meant to vote the king down. Even the fools heard the storm. It was all about to fall in.

And, right in the heart of it, was Deorwen. She sat a few places up the table, but was nearer to the Rooks and the Champion and the dukes of Errest. She lifted a cup to her lips, and caught what must have been Durand's wild-eyed stare.

"What was it you called those black fellows?" asked Berchard abruptly.

Durand found Ouen squeezing his arm.

"—'Rooks' wasn't it?" Berchard said.

"I think it was, Berchard," said Ouen.

"You know. I met these two lads, engineers, taking a barge up the Green Road. I'm on this barge—caravan guardlike what with there being word of bandits on the Gray Downs south of Wood's End—"

"When *ain't* there?" said Ouen. "Good pickings down that way. Half the trade from Errest runs up and down the Green Road. Or so I hear."

One of the Rooks glanced up, transfixing Durand in a hollow instant between heartbeats.

"Now," said Berchard, "I'm standing there with a crossbow in one hand, scratching fly bites with the other. These two lads are staring down at the river, and it's thick as fish oil in the heat, and the flies are hanging in clouds over us, and I'm mopping my forehead, stifling in the mail coat I'd got on, when I mumbled something about how bloody hot it was. And these two lads, they just took up laughing, saying they'd just got back from the South and how a man didn't know hot until he'd spent time choking on the dust in Totarra."

Now both Rooks had turned from the plucked carcasses on

the shared trencher before them, and were looking across to Durand, eyebrows raised. He could hardly breathe.

Somehow, Berchard kept talking. "They'd just got back from working the siege of Pontiam. The one in the song?" He set a hand flat on his chest and sang out loud. *"In Pontiam nine towers stood, though Barris stood alone. For Waldemar, old Barris would, though many more had flown."* He smiled into Durand's face. "Over the Weasand from Vuranna?"

Transfixed by the attention of the Rooks, Durand held his tongue.

"Anyway, they got talking about King Waldemar down there—a hard man they said—and the rebellion, of course. These Rooks of yours sound like a pair in the rebel camp, what with the black robes and all. Worked in a noble's court. Used to be priests. Or so they said."

Across the hall, the Rooks were playing with him now, smug grins splitting their waxy faces.

"Priests?" breathed Durand, incredulous.

"So these lads said," said Berchard. "Scribes or arbiters at some court or other. Anyway, our friends must've got greedy cringing around the high table, tugging their master's brocade sleeves, crawling over silk carpets, sleeping in dank cells, sucking stale water while the nobles slosh their gilded mazers of Vuranna's best all around."

As Berchard spoke, the two Rooks poured claret dark as blood. One licked his lips. Durand felt something strange under his hand, but he couldn't look away. Lightning flashed with the crack of thunder hard upon it.

"Seems their rivals had a habit of bowing out. After one feast, the castellan and three bailiffs got so ill that all died but the castellan. Said he lost every hair on his head."

Ouen laughed. "A lucky escape."

"—And a month later slipped on a stone staircase. Fell so hard they could hardly tell who he had been. It wasn't too long before our pair were the only ones left—where once there was a whole choir whispering in the rebel's ear.

"And they'd had their beaks in the wrong books: moldering tomes, scrolls. Things left in cellars from the Heshtarian days before the Crusade cleared the bastards out. They fell to spending nights upon the wastelands, crawling among the catacombs and altar stones rotting beyond the eyes of Heaven and living men."

Under Durand's palms, the tablecloth seemed to tingle.

"If it's the same pair, they came to nothing."

Durand wrenched his eyes from the Rooks. *"What?"* He could not look further than Berchard's face.

"Backed the wrong horse. Their pet rebel was too faithless for the faithless. With the Rooks in his ears he'd swear anything to anybody and break his word just as easy. Our villains, they slipped away just before Waldemar caught up with the rebel. What they did to that man . . ."

"Thorough?" Ouen laughed.

"So they said," Berchard allowed. "And thorough with the Rooks, as well, what they could find of them."

Back across the fire, the Rooks grinned. With a tiny ripple of his fingers, one roused the picked dove on his trencher. For an instant, it might have been some sleight of hand, but then the creature's walnut skull twitched up as if conscious of the pain of being cooked and picked to pieces. The Rooks smiled at Durand, as though they were sharing a joke.

"This is where my engineers came in, you see. Priests came down to deal with the Rooks' rooms, including two of the Patriarchs themselves. Laid each chamber open to the Eye of Heaven and razed the rebel's castle. But that weren't enough! No. They turned a river over the place. *That* was what these engineer lads had been doing last. They hired on with the Conclave after they lost their contracts with the rebel. They wouldn't speak about what they saw when the Rooks' rooms came down or when they took the floors up."

The tablecloth sensation—as though he had his hands in something damp—nagged him till he looked down. Like a spreading stain, the whole of the cloth around him had turned black. As he lifted his hands, he saw their silhouettes, pale as the Lost but filling in.

"God in Heaven," Berchard said. Ouen grimaced, twitching his hands into the air.

Table, wall, bench, and food were all scabbed over. A half-finished leg of goose had sunk in on itself, putrid with mold. Maggots teemed. Behind the leering Rooks, a similar broad fan of mildew had bloomed over the plaster. Insects scrabbled

down the table. One of Ragnal's own black functionaries
plucked one of the running things—cat-quick—and popped it
in his mouth.

The lads on Durand's bench leapt back. Durand could see
the Rooks chuckling between themselves. Each man of the
Holy Ghosts turned, half to Durand, panting with his hand on
a sword, and half to the Rooks.

He saw Deorwen's eyes on him, flashing deep and dark.

"Enough of this farce!" roared a voice from the head of
the hall.

The warrior King of Errest stood poised over the high table.
From the straw, Durand watched, feeling living things swarm
under his boots.

"Let's have done with it," said the king. "We're all here; I
see no reason to dance round this business all night. Beoran?
Yrlac? What say you?"

Creation boomed outside as the bearded Duke of Beoran
leaned on his elbow to savor Ragnal's show of temper.

Radomor, however, swiveled slowly. "Now, my cousin. Let
it be now."

Ragnal regarded his opponent then: a man who had fought
for him under the summer moons, a man who shared his
blood. At the center of this wreck, Durand saw real hatred.

"*A fearsome thing is the wrath of princes,*" said a voice.

Durand nearly emptied his guts, for this was no whisper in
his ear. It writhed in his skull like a fistful of worms locked
tight behind his jaws.

The Rooks were looking his way from the midst of Radomor's green thugs. And, if they had been smiling before, now
what fun the bastards were having.

"*These jackals. Hardly fit for conversation, whatever their
virtues elsewhere. Far more pleasant to chat with old friends.
Have you told your dashing lord how you watched over his
sister? Hours and hours. She and that poor baby. Do you suppose she took comfort, knowing there was a kinsman standing
nearby?*"

"So be it, *cousin,*" Ragnal was saying, "and as I am still
ruler of this land, I call the Great Council to begin, and,
though I am the subject of its debate, I claim my right to pre-

side." He turned his glare on the assembled company. "Be you ruled by ancient custom, the judgments of the kings and the word of our patriarchs. No man speak false or bare steel till we've done with this business, on pain of damnation."

Durand thought he heard a murmur of assent bubble up from the throng around him, but his head was taut with the seething malice of the voice.

"And now we shall hear it," the voice said.

Ragnal loomed over the table, almost sneering as he spoke. "Here is the matter: To furnish this realm with an army to pacify the marches, I borrowed coin from this council. As surety for the sum, I have pledged"—he plucked the Evenstar Crown from his head—"this bauble and all the trouble it has brought me. Now that the term of this loan is concluded, I am informed by my treasurers that there can be no repayment." There was an apologetic ruffle from the black functionaries. "Therefore, I must petition this, my Great Council, to forgive the debt."

Leaning there, with his mane and beard of copper gold, the King of Errest looked up and down the high table.

"Who," he rumbled, "will speak for forgiveness?"

For a moment, no one could move.

Someone nearby was saying, "Durand. Durand what is the matter with you, boy?" Then it was Deorwen's voice, and someone telling her, "For God's sake, go."

"Who will the brave one be?" said a whisper grinding and slithering in his brains.

Durand closed his eyes, gulping for air and clenching his fists.

At the high table, he saw a tall lord stand: the Duke of Garelyn, neighbor of Duke Abravanal. They had bound their duchies through the marriage of their children. He looked like a wild Marcher, with his long mustaches, or some arcane lord from the deep of Fetch Hollow. The duke smoothed his long surcoat and knelt before the king.

"I would have the honor, my King, if it pleases you to grant it."

"He is well-spoken for a country lord, do you agree? Like a dog trained to walk on its hind legs."

Durand clasped his head in both hands. He could feel his friends close around him, but he could do nothing to answer them.

"Have we given you our thanks for old Gol? That plan was all his own—his ambush—though he may have made certain assumptions. It is strange how like children grown men can be. In the end, he only wanted back into Radomor's good graces. But we had no need of him any longer. All that blood, and his own knife. He would have held it a thousand times, and then for it to grate among the bones of his neck . . ."

Durand could taste blood. He could feel the veins and tendons in his throat. He could feel the catching edges of razor steel. The words writhed and twisted. People were trying to drag him from the hall. He shook himself free.

"You have fought by our side, Garelyn," Ragnal said, "and been our staunch ally. We can think of no man better."

Garelyn nodded deeply and stalked into the space before the high table as the gale churned and wailed like Lost souls at the arrow loops. The man had to pitch his voice loud over the storm.

"Your Majesty, your Highness, and honored lords of the Council. I will speak plainly. Our silver was not squandered. It was not spent on horses and hunting lodges. It has not bought mansions in Eldinor or wine from Vuranna. In short, it wasn't spent as I might have spent it." Some of the gathered nobles laughed. "The silver was spent where we were told it would be: on putting down Mad Borogyn and his Marchers. It went to knights and marshals. It went to stablemen and common soldiers. It bought remounts and victuals. It bought these things, and, with them, it bought peace and security on our eastern marches. We have not fattened our king's purse with this money; we have bought safety and freedom for our merchants and tradesmen and our brothers in the marches. Were we mistaken in rendering this money to the king? Was His Majesty mistaken in calling upon us? Should we send back our hard-bought peace for the return of cold silver? I say we should not. My king has bought my peace with my money. I, for one, will not—"

As he spoke, the whole castle shook.

A bolt crashed against the rock of Tern Gyre itself, sending the tall lord staggering. Durand pictured turrets sliding into the sea. He felt the jolt through straw and hands and knees.

"He had been doing quite well. Let us hope the storm has not disturbed his pretty speech."

The duke, eyes darting at the high row of arrow loops, made to continue.

"We are forced," he said. "We are forced to speak in base terms—terms of commerce—when the very security of this realm is at issue. Only because this council would not grant its king the aid his cause required is this payment called 'loan' at all. Only because this council would not take up the duty its honor demanded was our king forced to hazard his crown. Where a soldier in the field risks his life to defend his home and honor, our liege lord risks his crown to defend *our* homes and *our* honor. This debt is not his shame, but our duty. Only by taking up our duty will we be free to lift our heads."

The tall duke stood a moment, grim-faced with his long mustaches. The storm flickered. He really might have been a Fetch Hollow man.

"So says Garelyn," he concluded. "Let him who wishes deny it."

The Rooks were clapping their hands, laughing, while Durand's head crawled with their whispers.

On the dais, Ragnal turned to fat Hellebore, smug Beoran, and the Duke of Yrlac.

"Who among you would speak against forgiveness?"

"Great King," said Beoran, "if it pleases you."

"Another performer! And we had thought to entertain with our little puppet show. We might have saved our efforts."

Durand pressed the heels of his hands into his eyes. Beoran took Ragnal's snort as permission to stand and bowed from the waist—looking every bit a cocksure ship's master. "Your Majesty, your Highness, members of the Great Council."

Durand looked up to see Beoran smiling, splitting his iron beard in a genial grin full of teeth. "If the storm will allow me, I'm afraid that I have been left to pose the obvious question: Is the king not to be held to the same standard of honor as even the meanest of his subjects?"

Durand heard snarls around him.

"My!" exclaimed the writhing voice. *"He is a daring trai-*

tor, is Ludegar of Beoran. Ware pride, Your Grace! Ware pride!"

Durand could barely breathe.

The Duke of Beoran waited with his hand spread over his inflated chest. Finally, he raised that hand.

"I do not intend to be flippant. The matter is serious. If our king gives his word, is he not to be held to that oath? If he vows a thing, is he free simply to discard it? I think we know what the answer must be.

"I say His Majesty undertook *just* this risk when he begged his loan from this Council. Would we have granted it to him if we had known that we would never see it back? Are we all so wealthy? I fear that His Majesty knew what he did. I fear that he understood that we could not afford so great a gift and so must be cajoled. That we must be given some hope of seeing our fortunes again, or we would not open our hands. In short, I think he'd have promised us a moon."

Durand stared up through the whispers. Lamoric's men were all round him now.

"Our king is not some roving gallant free to beguile his realm with false promises."

"Oh pride, pride, Beoran."

"Every plowman owes the service he's sworn to. Should not the king be held to the same high standard?" Beoran asked. "He has made his promise, and to his promise he must hold. Through guile he has pocketed our money, and now the time has come to repay it. And, if he has not the coin, then he must pay the forfeit." Now half the hall was roaring, baying like hounds. Half the hall was on its feet. "The forfeit he, himself, chose!"

Jeers and shouts resounded in the feasting hall, but Radomor sat on, grave as the dead. His Rooks took it all in, amused at the braying and howling around them.

"Enough!" pronounced Ragnal.

He was up, both hands braced against the high table. Even the storm seemed to heed him.

"While I am still king here, we will have silence or sweep this hall of rabble. The Heavens' protest is enough."

All around Durand, friends and strangers stood cowed.

"Now we see the king as the battling warlord, berating his Council and his lords before their vote."

But the hall did not remain silent, and soon murmurs stewed and lightning flashed.

Durand noticed that Ragnal's black-clad functionaries were still picking at their food.

"You have heard the arguments for and against," said Ragnal, "and now I call upon my priest-arbiter."

The stooped prelate stood, smoothing the brocade over his chest. An Eye the size of a gold plate bobbed there. Finally, he nodded that he was ready.

"Is this a matter for the Great Council?" Ragnal demanded.

"It is, Sire. The issue is between the sovereign and his Great Council. His is the debt, and theirs is the power to forgive it."

"And the Crown?"

"It is within the rights of a king to set his kingship aside, as evinced in living memory by the . . ." The man hesitated. "By the abdication of Carondas, King of cherished memory."

"Have we spoken to you of our Radomor?" squirmed the voices in Durand's skull.

"Then we will hold the vote," said Ragnal.

"There he was on the battlefield. Among the Heithan barrows. Struck down doing his king's bidding. Struck down by chance. His career was a star rising, Durand. Dashed in a moment."

The arbiter's beard waggled. "There are several systems. The black and white stones. The split wands. The—"

"Is the choice mine?"

The arbiter blinked up into his king's face.

"Not wounded, only, but dying, you see. This is how we found him. Not a limb could he move, nor a finger lift. Everything he had made was laid waste in the Heithan muck. All lost."

"The choice is yours, Majesty."

Ragnal's savage grin spread, flickering in the stormy night.

"It is in such moments that a man takes up his doom. What is the sacrifice of a few picked men? Who would miss them or guess where they went in a battle?"

Creation raged at the windows like a city on fire, like refugees screaming over the walls before an invader's wrath.

"Then it will be an open vote. We will ask and each will answer. This is no time or place for games."

"It is permitted, Majesty," the arbiter hedged, but Ragnal only nodded his grim satisfaction. His liegemen must deny him to his face.

"Then," the king said, "we will begin.

"My Duke of Garelyn, we will put our question first to you. Come forward."

The tall lord walked through a paroxysm of thunderclaps, but fought his way around the table to kneel before his lord.

"We have petitioned this, our Great Council, that our debt be lifted. You must answer us, 'yea' it should be as we desire or 'nay' it should not. How say you Garelyn?"

"Garelyn answers 'yea.'" Durand could scarcely hear him, even without the storm and the Rooks rustling in his brains. "The debt should be forgiven."

Ragnal nodded sternly.

"He is wise to call first upon his allies. Perhaps he will cow the weak-willed among his enemies. The Book of Moons *tells us that a slender reed cannot stand against the gale."*

"We thank you Garelyn and call upon Windhover to answer."

A short dark man—not the blond Prince of Windhover—stalked through the howls of the Heavens and dropped to his knee.

"What is this?" the spinning words gabbled. *Is Prince Eodan not a tall man and blond as his brother? Where is our poor king's brother, do you think? Why does he linger in Windhover at such a time?"*

Durand strained to watch the dais as the Rooks' whisperings rattled at his mind, round and round. The dark man handed up a scroll under a black clot of sealing wax. He saw it swung to Ragnal's arbiter. "I bear a writ under the prince's seal, Majesty, and have been sent to speak his will."

The arbiter gave his nod.

"We have petitioned this council that our debt be lifted," said Ragnal. "You must answer us, 'yea' or 'nay.' How says Windhover?"

"How this question rings with double meaning now."

"Windhover answers 'yea,' Majesty," said the messenger. "The debt should be forgiven."

"How relieved our king must be. To have been put in such a place by his brother? It is beyond imagining."

Ragnal only nodded, calling the next duke to stand before him. Lamoric's elder brother took his father's place. Lord Moryn knelt at the feet of his liege lord, pale and rigid with the effort. Hellebore and Highshields cast their lots—this time, with apologies, against the king.

The Rooks teased the widow Maud as she surprised the Council with her steadfastness, lowering herself before the king and casting the votes of Germander and Saerdana both for forgiveness. Durand breathed like a runner, thinking that this was real hope.

"And she had them all guessing, while they fawned and circled her," said the thronging whispers. *"Pride again, or vanity. Look at Hellebore there. The man makes faces as though someone has poked a lemon past his lips. Your king must be pleased. It has all gone as he would hope."*

Heremund, who'd been making the rounds in silence, touched Durand's shoulder, not saying a word. The touch went through Durand like a shock on a cold morning. A shattering pain shot through his skull.

Radomor sat as grim as ever. The Rooks were smug. The big Champion sat near the high table. The bloom of mildew over the walls had spread still further. In the space of a few breaths, the whole hall would be smothered over. They must get Deorwen from the castle.

But Duke Ludegar of Beoran was walking around the high table, a blade bobbing in fittings of black leather and bright steel.

The man knelt, and Ragnal spoke the formula.

"We have petitioned this council that our debt be lifted. You must answer us, 'yea' or 'nay.' How says Beoran?"

Durand tried to wring thoughts from his crowded mind, even as he felt blood slip from his nose. With the tide turned, now was the duke's chance to save face. Without Maud, the best he could hope for was a tie. They could not vote the king down.

Durand pawed a drop from his lip. The black smear—it was

not blood—glistened for an instant, then flew like dry soot. Another wet drop landed.

"Beoran answers 'nay,' Majesty, and says the debt should be paid."

Ragnal nodded slowly, his face all stiff slashes under his beard.

"Now it comes," said the whispers, each syllable creaking at the sutures of his skull. *"Now it comes."*

Heremund and Berchard were speaking to him. He felt the not-blood running from his chin. The storm outside was madness now, howling fit to tear the stones from the old headland. His friends' hands were on him.

"We thank you Beoran, and call upon Yrlac to answer."

Now, Duke Radomor took his feet, slowly. Grime streaked his face. Tattered armor hung from his twisted shoulders. He crossed the dais and, locking the dark lodestones of his eyes on Ragnal's face, lowered one knee to the stone, and twitched a broad mantle wide over the dais.

"What will he say—will he say—will he say?"

"We have petitioned that our debt be lifted," said the king. "How say you, my Duke of Yrlac?"

Candles lashed and shuddered as Radomor stared up, his face brimming with defiance. "Yrlac answers 'nay,' cousin," Radomor said. "A man should pay his debts." He stood then, face-to-face with Ragnal. Even with his twisted back, the Duke of Yrlac looked down on his king. Somewhere outside, a great mass of stones fell thundering into the sea.

"Now watch, friend. Watch."

Durand caught hold of his blade once more.

"What is the vote?"

But it was tied. Unless Radomor meant to cut the king down before them all, it was finished. Beoran and Yrlac had both voted against their king, knowing they didn't have the numbers to carry it. You could not vote a man down with a stalemate.

A confused murmur arose in Tern Gyre as realization dawned among those loyal to the king: They had won.

"I don't understand," said Heremund. "I don't understand." Then, "Gods, Durand, are you all right? What's the matter?" Radomor had not left the dais.

"Sit down, Duke Radomor," said Ragnal, "you have not won today."

Radomor's bald skull tilted, only a fraction.

"You have been a loyal man," continued the king. "Now you must see where Beoran has led you."

Radomor looked from Ragnal without turning. "Priest," he said, "what is the vote?"

The arbiter, surprised, glanced to the parchment where he had been recording the events. "There are fourteen votes cast: seven for forgiveness, seven against."

Radomor hardly moved, simply listening: the only solid thing in the storm.

"And is a petition granted by a tied vote such as this?"

"*Gods*," said Heremund; Durand did not understand.

"Does a motion pass when it does not prevail in the vote?" Radomor pressed.

The arbiter stammered. "It . . . it does not."

Durand felt the world falling from under him, but only Radomor's dark eyes moved—a spark.

"Then, you have *lost* your bid for clemency, I think. You have asked, but your Great Council has not agreed."

As the duke smiled—a stained row of pearls—a dark wind bowled through the feasting hall, snatching flame from candles, and causing the blaze in the hearth to cringe against the stones. Radomor's cloak opened like wings.

A man could see little but the wink of the duke's teeth. Durand could hardly watch for the crushing pain in his skull.

"Here, here we have it. Now it is come."

"I have defended you," Radomor said. "I have shed my blood, and thrown my life in the balance to save yours. And, all the while, you have tripped and blundered and raged and stumbled until our realm is strained to the point of breaking, cousin." No king could have foreseen the chain of petty rebellions and hard harvests Errest had weathered. "Now, you have risked the very crown of our realm on a fool's wager."

It was happening, despite all they had done to stop it. Every window screamed like the climax of torture. Under the floor, the rock itself groaned. Through the bone-breaking agony in his skull, Durand imagined the entire realm quaking. He saw the hag stir under the walls of High Ashes. He saw the monks of Cop Alder, walking their glyph of soil. He saw the black-thorn men and the mad folk in the wastelands.

"There will be no new last chances. The time has come, cousin," Radomor said and raised his hands for the crown.

Then, as though some monstrous thing had settled its wings over the headland, a vast silence fell over Creation. It bulged at Durand's ears.

Durand blinked through flashes of pain, gulping to keep air in his chest. He thought of lands torn from Creation by smaller things than this. He had walked the trails of Hesperand and seen the duke and his lady lost. Somehow, he must do something. He was halfway to his feet, groping for his blade when a chance glimpse of Deorwen reached through the confusion.

Without Deorwen, that Lost Duke of Hesperand would have had him.

He touched the Green Lady's veil. If Deorwen had not saved him, the bit of green would have been another knot on old Duke Eorcan's lance.

He remembered.

Into the silence, Durand roared "No!"

He held the green knot in his fist. The voices were still. Even Radomor himself looked.

A dappled light shimmered through the arrow loops: a light full of beech trees and late summer evenings. Already, he could smell it in the air: the candle wax scent of Bower Mead.

He heard footfalls on the stair.

"What?" growled Radomor. The Rooks stared like carved monsters.

"One vote," stumbled Durand. "One vote is not cast."

Every eye abandoned Durand for the stairway, where a light swelled, and the ghostly warriors of Bower Mead had already made their way to the top of the stair—a twin file of dead men, silver-pale and young. How long had they been marching? When had they set out? In their wake came the Lady of the Bower, alive and glowing as though moonlight touched her flesh. The Lost knights bore her upon a palanquin.

She looked to Durand. He saw the clouded expression of someone struggling to recall a dream.

"The Lady," Durand whispered. "The Lady of Hesperand. She has come."

She passed through the silent hall, borne above the fighting men. As Radomor and Ragnal and every member of the Great Council stared, her bearers mounted the dais to set the palanquin on the tile before the king and his enemy. Both men had the hunched look of animals caught between snapping and fleeing for the trees.

"King of Errest," she said, looking up to Ragnal.

"I am," said the king, warily.

"I am the Lady of Hesperand. I bear a writ under the duke's seal, Great King, and I will speak his will." She produced a parchment under a clot of dark wax.

Ragnal glanced to his arbiter, and the prelate took the parchment, nodding. Hesperand had always had a seat at the Great Council.

Durand held his knot of veil and spoke. "You must cast your vote, my lady. You must cast your vote."

"Ask your question, my king," said the Lady.

Ragnal slowly nodded.

"There is a debt owing," he said. "I have petitioned this council that it be forgiven. You must answer, 'yea' or 'nay,' madam. How says . . . Hesperand?"

"Hesperand answers 'yea,' Majesty," said the Lady. Her eyes met Durand's then, down the length of the feasting hall, but she hardly faltered. "The debt should be forgiven."

No one heard the verdict, then. Knights and lords from every corner of Errest leapt to their feet—outrage and triumph both ringing from the vaults. Durand felt a hard grin spread across his face. The whoresons hadn't expected this. Radomor lurched away from the king, clutching at his blade, but wise enough to see he could not live a heartbeat if he struck out with the Septarim and Bower knights all around. Beoran caught up with Radomor, still on the dais, catching hold of his arm, ducking like a peasant and babbling apologies or reassurance. Very nearly, Radomor swept the man's head from his shoulders. A good foot of steel had left its scabbard before the enraged duke mastered himself enough to let the sword go and storm from the hall. Rooks and Champion and green knights all followed after.

In the next few moments, fully a third of the room emptied into the courtyard.

Friends clapped each other on the shoulders in rough jubilation, but Durand left them to it. He crossed to the dais where the Bower knights had lifted the palanquin once more.

He approached like a sickroom visitor. The Lady looked at him, clouds of confusion—of suspicion—drifting in the world beyond her eyes. He had the green veil in his fist.

"Ladyship, you left this with me," he said.

The Lost woman's lips parted a coin's width. She reached out her hand to touch and then to take the stiff and twisted bit of linen from his fingers.

The Bower knights were already turning. Some looked at him, almost accusing. He could see the wounds that had felled them, dark mouths and sockets cold and empty now. Remorselessly, they shouldered their burden and turned toward the stair. Their care of this woman was more than half a jailor's concern for his prisoner. She had been their deaths.

He looked away before he could find Cerlac's face.

"Thank you," said the Bower Lady.

He risked a glance, and saw her eyes, first looking at him, and then through him. The knights had begun their pallbearer's march. Though he could easily have stretched out his hand, Durand could see that they were already gone, the old circle closing around them. But she had followed her token from Hesperand, and perhaps this one new thing could start the old wheel wobbling. He hoped it might.

30. Peace in Moonlight

Durand limped outside where the waning Blood Moon rode high and bright above Creation. He and Tern Gyre had both had a rough time. The round watchtower above the Broken Crown had fallen, dropping Coensar's postern door to the waves. The wall was open to the wind.

He saw serving men on the run nearby.

A corner tower of Biedin's keep looked like a half-felled tree, and, when they scrambled to brace it, Durand joined them. They set to work ramming timbers tight between the wall and the living stone, and soon Durand and the castle men had a dozen sturdy beams meant for the prince's ceilings propping the tower.

As they caught their breath—and listened for the beams to crack—Durand found Heremund tottering around the corner.

The little man stared. "Does anyone inside know they're falling into the sea?"

"I should have been a carpenter," said Durand.

Heremund shook his head. "Some of this will have stood since Willan's Lost Princes." The sea shimmered beyond the gulfs like beaten foil.

"Come Durand," said Heremund. "You'll be making these fellows antsy." He winked, and Durand followed Heremund into the battered courtyard.

"You'd been gone some time," Heremund said, giving Durand a close look.

"I'm fine. Couldn't stand that hall another hour."

"You and the king. He's packed up that train of his and started the march south already. Prince Biedin had his own chambers set aside."

"The vote was finished."

Again, the little man gave Durand a close look.

Durand only smiled. "Worry over someone else, Heremund."

"You looked half mad in there, Durand. I don't want to see you summoning up green ghosts again for a few days, eh?"

Durand glanced toward the castle gate and the bridge beyond where royal and rebel had fled. "I'm going to get a little more air."

Heremund nodded, and Durand crossed the high bridge back to the camp. Animals grazed among the flattened tents. He passed the place of Waer's long fall. The low hump of Agryn's unhallowed burial lay dark in the grass. He found his tent where it sprawled over the trunks inside.

He got to work untangling his belongings.

But a sharp sound stopped him: south, toward the mainland, and too near for the treasonous lords riding home. *Tock*. He heard the swing and rap of a staff's heel on cobbles, and he froze, listening.

But then there was laughter. People from the castle back on the bridge. Berchard and Ouen traipsed over the high span.

"We squeezed it out of old Heremund," said Berchard. "You can't hide from us. Ouen picked the man right up off the ground." There was a flash of gold teeth.

"I've wanted to do that," Durand said.

Smiling, Berchard peered south. "These kings are shifty beasts. After tonight, His Majesty will be wanting to give you ten castles in Beoran. We'll have to catch him."

Ouen slapped his shoulder. "You'll be rich as a Mankyr merchant. He's bound to have a strongbox or two left somewhere."

Ouen took Durand's arm. "Now, though, His Highness, Prince Biedin, he'd put up some fine Vuranna claret to serve his royal brother. Now it'll only go to waste."

Berchard took an arm as well. "You'll taste the warm Eye of Heaven and the fragrant breezes of the Inner Seas."

"Under my own power, I think," said Durand.

The two nodded, and, once they were sure Durand was following, let him free.

"Maybe we can get Agryn buried properly," Durand said.

"Aye," said Berchard. "Even a Patriarch wouldn't say that was anything but war."

Durand nodded and looked up from the turned earth to see Deorwen picked out against the castle gates by moonlight.

For an instant, she stood alone on the bridge. But Ouen and Berchard were already bowing to her, each with an eye on Durand as they did so. Coensar and Lamoric walked from the gates.

Coensar's eye glinted. Lamoric beamed, taking his wife by the shoulder. Her expression was unreadable: a mask donned in haste.

"Come," Lamoric said. And they were all walking in.

Under the gate, however, Durand glanced back. This time he heard the staff click, clear but distant, as if the Traveler were moving off.